CADY HAMMER

Chasing Fate

First published by Black Lily Press 2022

First edition

ISBN: 9781736886373

Editing by Beth Hale
Cover art by Milan Krstevski

This book was professionally typeset on Reedsy.
Find out more at reedsy.com

To Morgan. Thank you for reading all of my books, twice, three times, every word. This series wouldn't be what it is without you.

Author's Note

Here we are, my friends, at the end of the story. We've been on quite a journey. When I started working on this series in 2018, I had no idea that it was going to be the one that I finally hit publish on. I was writing for myself and hanging onto an inkling of a dream that someday, I would be able to bring my stories to the world. Since publishing Chasing Fae in August 2020, my little dream has exploded and become so much bigger than me. I have loved interacting with the fans of my books over the years, and I can't wait to expand my readership now that this trilogy is complete. This book is a whirlwind; there is so much happening with so many subplots that have been introduced over the course of the series to tie up. I hope you will love how I've chosen to end this. Chasing Fate was a difficult conclusion to write, but an incredibly satisfying one. I hope you'll feel the same. Happy reading.

Chapter One

"It's time to take back the realm."

I have to admit, I said this with very little plan of how to pull it off. Which I suppose is somewhat par for the course.

Turning away from the chaos outside and heading inside is a strategic choice. I need a minute to think while no one is looking at my face. Everyone is behind me: political and military leaders from the Houses of the Sun and War, the House of the Evening's army, and the entire prophecy group. They're expecting me to have a plan: to know where to start and to set up a new alliance without any hiccups. But frankly, I'm overwhelmed, and it's obvious.

When the House of War's army rode through town, I couldn't believe what I was seeing. Our encounter with them certainly didn't go smoothly the first time, and their capital city was left in shambles. Their military strength may be enough to turn the tide of the war. I'm hoping Lord Gideon isn't as stubborn as his father and is willing to work with me without too much confrontation.

But Aiden showing up? In no way was I ready for that. I always knew he would come back; I mean, he had to. We need him for the prophecy. But we left things in such an awkward place. What had been building between us over the last several months came to a screeching halt. Or, at least, I thought it had. Just now, he kissed me like he was coming home to a loving partner. And I worry it's going to kill him to find out I'm no longer at his beck and call.

And Faolan… By the Lady, Faolan. We had just gotten somewhere with our… friendship? Relationship? Something? I don't know what to call it. He kissed me too. Or… did I kiss him? Either way, we definitely kissed. And there was something so different about it. He makes me feel… different? Stronger, maybe. I don't know how to describe it. And he certainly didn't walk out the door when it suited him. He was here for the hard work, and he's been nothing but trustworthy since he joined us. But he makes me feel so confused. What does he want from me? How real is all of this? He usually makes it very clear what he wants, but now I can't completely read him.

But *none of this matters right now* because there are hundreds upon hundreds of Fae outside that require my attention.

When I reach the Great Hall, I turn around to find that the prophecy members have followed me inside. Luna smiles at me reassuringly. Her general optimistic demeanor does somewhat calm the thoughts in my head. I admire that about her; she brings levity to any situation she's in, and it's enough to make me focus just that little bit better. *Though it wouldn't surprise me if she was reading my mind right now and knew that I needed someone to smile here.*

The group waits restlessly for me to tell them what to do next. Cary's tapping of her foot against the tile floor is like a hammer on my brain. I have to say something just to get her to stop. I take a deep breath. "Alright, here's what I want to see happen. Faolan, can you take Gideon to get the armies integrated and move them down to the barracks?"

The two men give each other a prolonged sideways glance. It's as if they are sizing each other up. Faolan finally nods to me. "I'll get it done."

"I would rather speak to you directly first, High Lady," Gideon counters. "I don't like to get settled before I've handled business."

"Well, there's a lot going on here that I need to handle first," I reply. "And my House's arrival is a top priority."

"I will speak to you as soon as I can, Lord Gideon," I reiterate. It makes me a little uneasy how insistent he is on being first. "Faolan, please show Gideon to the barracks." Once he has steered the Lord of War out of the building, I turn to the others. "Luna, Cary, I need you to be greeting all of the high ranking military officials. There's absolutely no way I'm going to be able to greet and take care of each one individually. You can knock out a good greeting, I assume?"

"That's a little below my pay grade," Cary snarks.

"Just do it," I say firmly, rolling my eyes. Luna links arms with her, much to Cary's horror, and drags her toward the door. "Aira, Kiara, I need you on hospitality duty. Can you arrange with the attendants how we're going to accommodate all these people? Also, I need someone to get a supply list of what the Houses of War and Sun have brought. Can you get someone on that?"

"Definitely," Aira says.

"Happy to help," Kiara echoes. The women move to their tasks right away.

Then I'm simply left with Aiden. "Aiden." I try to keep my voice even like I'm talking to any other official. "Aiden, I'd like you to go get settled as well. You know your way around the palace. You should be able to rest up just fine before we have a formal War Council meeting."

Aiden seems taken aback by my official tone. "Grace, I was hoping to speak to you in private. There's a lot to talk about."

"There's much more to do right now. I don't have time to talk to you."

"Make time," Aiden says simply. "Make time."

"I will not. I don't care what your feelings on the subject are."

Aiden grabs my arm suddenly and pulls me out of the front hall and into the throne room. I wrench it away as soon as I can as he shuts the door behind us. If he's going to force this conversation now, we might as well do it here. The silence between us is deafening. I avoid Aiden's eyes as I take my seat on my father's throne. My throne. When I finally look up at him, his blue eyes search mine. I hope they're not revealing too many answers.

"You look comfortable on that throne," Aiden finally says. "You look right."

"I don't feel it," I reply simply.

"I'm sorry about your father," Aiden tries to start.

"You did hear then." Part of me isn't surprised. News of a High Lord's death must have spread everywhere quickly. "You didn't reach out."

"Grace, I know I should have contacted you, but everything in the House of the Sun got so crazy. I really need to tell you about things; can we—"

"I am not interested in hearing anything you have to say until after I get a status report on what pertains directly to the war. I need to call an emergency meeting of the War Council within the hour to discuss what to do now that reinforcements have arrived. And I still need to speak to Gideon. You and I can have a discussion after the meeting. I'll set aside the time. For now, here is what you need to know. All of the prophecy members have been found. I will point them out to you later. We took back some key territory in the House of the Earth, but we have a long way to go."

"Yes, I heard about that. It was relatively easy to hear about which territories were saved and which fell from my position at home."

"Good, then you're up to speed for now."

Aiden looks at me with a sad smile. "All formalities then? Aren't you even a little happy to see me?"

My heart tightens. It's hard to hold him at arm's length without feeling some tinge of sadness inside of me. After everything we have been through, part of me feels like I should cut him some slack. "Aiden." I rise to my feet and walk over carefully, though I do stay at arm's length. "I am glad that you've come back. We could use you here."

"Could you use me here?"

"Isn't that what I just said?"

"No… you specifically. Can *you* use me here?"

Staring at him blankly, I barely have time to consider the question before the throne room door swings open and Gideon and Faolan step inside.

Faolan immediately locks eyes with me. They narrow as they take in Aiden's insistent face and my anxious one. "Did I interrupt something?" he asks.

"Yes," Aiden forces out.

"No," I say at the same time. When Aiden turns to me in shock, I wave my hand in dismissal. "Aiden was just leaving." The betrayal in Aiden's eyes is obvious, and I can't help but feel triumphant. *Now you know how it feels.* He bows his head to me as he exits the room.

Faolan smirks broadly after the Lord of the Sun as he exits. "High Lady Grace, Lord Gideon," he presents to me.

"Thank you, Faolan. I can take it from here." Faolan gives me a little salute before sauntering out the door. Brushing off myself and my mixed emotions, I turn to Gideon. "Thank you for waiting. We were all very excited to see you and your army arrive. Your presence here should have a monumental impact on the war. If you don't mind me asking, what convinced you to join us?"

"My brother was convinced that you led the demons right to us. But my father knew better. He thought you fought valiantly for having little training and to defend a homeland that wasn't your own. He's skeptical of the prophecy, but he thinks you likely aren't lying about it."

"And you?" I ask. "What do you think about the prophecy?"

"I don't dabble in divination arts. But a prophecy is a prophecy. If I can help fix the House of Darkness problem and provide safety and security to my House once again, then I'll go wherever I need to go. I may not understand it, but I'm sure as hell not going to ignore it."

"I can understand that. The whole prophecy thing is still a little crazy to me."

Gideon nods. "Let's get down to it then. I've got three thousand men with me with another three on the way as soon as the repairs to the capital are made. I've been able to secure four thousand swords, two hundred and fifty rounds of blasting potion, and—"

"Wait, wait, wait," I call out quickly and shake my head. "This is information the War Council needs to hear. I want this to be shared with the group."

"Why? You make the ultimate call."

"Not exactly. We do things as a group around here. Decisions are made by the majority."

"Why? Why in the world would you involve a dozen people when one would do?"

"As far as I'm aware, the War Council has always operated that way. That's why it exists." I furrow my eyebrows in confusion.

"I thought you would be different, that's all." Gideon's eyes tell me that that's not quite all. "We'll have to see if your way of leading is best."

"And if you find it lacking?" I ask.

Gideon doesn't answer, only quirks up a lip. "I will see you at the Council meeting, Lady Grace." With a bow of his head, he slips out the door. And I am left with a growing pit in my stomach as I'm faced with the prospects of the House of War on my doorstep.

Chapter Two

As soon as I regain my composure, I send for several attendants to scatter around the palace and notify the War Council members that an emergency meeting will be starting within the half hour. I don't want to waste any time in getting an inventory of the information and resources that we have and figuring out where to go from here. I make my way to the conference room without delay, and within the hour, the room starts to fill with people. I don't say much to anyone outside of a quick greeting. I need all of my focus to come up with some sort of opening statement that will kick this whole thing off and inspire confidence.

It's not working very well.

When Aira arrives, she makes a beeline for me. Her eyes hold mild concern. That does not help my mood at all. She approaches my seat and leans down to my ear. "My mother needs to speak to you in the hall."

Immediately, I'm nervous. *What could she possibly want right now, before the meeting? Hopefully, she's got some advice for me.* "Thank you, Aira." I get up from my seat and step outside to find the High Lady Morgana waiting for me. To my surprise, she's wearing an outer coat and carries a small satchel in her hands. I haven't seen a single High Lady carry a bag unless they were headed somewhere in their carriage. How could she be leaving right now?

"High Lady?" I ask.

She smiles at me. "High Lady Grace. I apologize for pulling you away from the conference, but I wanted to say goodbye."

"Goodbye?" My voice comes out louder and more terrified than I mean it to be. "Where are you going?"

"I'm returning to the House of Wind. I'm leaving Aira to continue to serve on the War Council. Her voice will be enough to carry us all."

"Why now?"

"There is an influx of refugees from the House of Peace making their way to my House. There's already a major refugee crisis in the House of the Wind, and I have just received a missive from my second in command. My people are fighting over resources with the newcomers, and I need to go home and deal with it. They need their High Lady now."

I take a deep breath and bow my head. "I understand. Thank you for your service thus far. You have been a major ally for me." People trust High Lady Morgana. She is smart, a good listener, and level-headed when it comes to taking on new ideas that may not have always sounded well thought out on the surface. Her presence will sorely be missed here.

The High Lady's smile grows softer, and she places both of her hands on my shoulders. "I believe that with the arrival of the House of the Sun and the House of War, you have enough allies now to make moves without people looking to me for an overarching view. You set the tone. It's difficult to be a High Lady, even more so in wartime. Don't lose faith."

I bow to her respectfully, but she stops me. Instead, she shakes my hand firmly. "Never bow to a High Lord or Lady again. You are one of us." With that, she leaves the hall, and I turn back to the conference hall.

Time to face the music.

When I reenter the room, all of the nobles have taken their seats at the table. I realize that for the first time since I sent all of the High Lords home, we have a full roster. All twelve seats are filled, five on each side with Gideon sitting opposite me at the foot of the table. There's something powerful about that, and it gives me hope for what's to come.

When everyone looks to me, I stand up. "Thank you for being here today," I decide to start. "I want to start off with a small piece of news. High Lady Morgana has just told me that she needs to return to the House of Wind immediately to take care of the current refugee crisis. She leaves Aira to continue in her seat to represent their House. She will not be joining us again."

There's a light hum of murmurs around the room. No one seems irritated by the news, only nervous. "We are on our own now. No supervision. No older generational voice to chime in. From here on out, we win or lose on our own merit. We either save the realm, or we condemn it to burn."

Ooh... that was good. That's what I'm looking for.

I indicate Aiden with my head. "I would like to welcome Lord Aiden back to the Council. He has returned with a portion of the House of the Sun army." A quiet smattering of applause makes its way around the table. Faolan's claps seem to be both the slowest and the loudest. I then nod to Gideon across the way. "And I would like to welcome Lord Gideon from the House of War to the table. Thank you for coming to our aid. The Realm is grateful for you." There's another round of applause, but it's noticeably strained. Obviously, there's tension around the House of War's presence here.

That's going to have to be addressed.

"Let me be clear, Lord Gideon," I address him directly. "You have the full support of me, the House of the Evening, and this War Council. If you need anything at all, don't hesitate to ask. I'd like to hear from you first, then Aiden about what and who you have brought with you so that we can take inventory. You have the floor."

Gideon chooses not to stand, instead leaning forward in his chair. He doesn't waste any time cutting straight to the point. "The House of War is available to provide six thousand men at this time to the war effort. Three thousand are with me, and another three will be here as soon as repairs to the capital city are complete. The rest of the standing army will remain at the House of War to protect our borders unless I call upon them. To aid in those efforts, in addition to the items needed to keep my army supplied, I have brought an additional four thousand swords, two hundred and fifty rounds of blasting potion, eight hundred horses, and a dozen wagons filled with additional crops from our farms to aid in feeding our people and yours. The rest of my army will be bringing additional supplies, which I will catalog once it arrives."

Taking a look around the table, I see that many of the nobles are deeply impressed. I am as well. This is the biggest addition of assistance that we have had since Faolan brought all of his black market contacts into the fold. "This is good, Gideon. Really good," I say. "Your men and resources should turn the tide for us." He nods to me in acknowledgement. "Aiden, can you talk about what you managed to glean from the House of the Sun?"

Aiden chooses to stand. "I don't have exact numbers like Gideon because we had to put this together very quickly in the middle of the night. But I was able to bring over about half of the House of the Sun army under the authority of Commander Jarvis Tompkins. Most of us have horses. We managed to bring three or four carts of weaponry, not nearly enough for your army, Grace, but one round of arms for ours and a little extra. I also managed to swipe one cart's worth of gold from the House's treasury. That should put a dent in the building of the resources needed to house and feed the additional men Gideon and I have brought on."

"Why not take action?" Faolan suddenly interjects.

Aiden is caught off guard. "What do you mean?"

"You were there in the midst of the lion's den. The two largest threats were nowhere in sight, and you didn't even take action besides convincing some hundreds of soldiers to not kill their own kind? Why not take action? Why didn't you raze the place on your way out? Burn the farmland, burn the weapons houses, burn something."

"I'm not going to raze my own House!" Aiden responds incredulously. "I can't think of a single person here who would have done that."

"So you're still not quite sure where your loyalties lie, are you?" Faolan jabs in again.

"Enough," I immediately intervene. "Thank you, Lord Aiden, for your contributions." Aiden, disgruntled, sits back down. Faolan smirks triumphantly, but his face falters at my harsh stare. "Alright," I continue. "That's what we have to work with in addition to our own resources. I want to talk about where we go from here. Who has thoughts?"

"I think we should strike now while the iron is hot," Faolan speaks immediately. "The House of Darkness doesn't know that we've thrown in with you lot. The longer we wait, the more likely they are to find out."

"What kind of a plan is that?" Aiden snarks.

"My intel says the news has not spread yet. There is a very narrow window of time, a few days maybe, if we're lucky. If you want to keep the element of surprise, we need to find a place to make a stand or take back some ground and start planning now. Today."

"I disagree." Aiden leans forward with both elbows on the table. Faolan stares at him coolly. "We've got three weary armies who have not had a chance to work together yet. Just establishing the chain of command is going to take some time. The soldiers need time to regroup before getting on task."

"My men need no time," Gideon says plainly.

"Well, mine do."

"Then we do an attack without you," Faolan responds.

"There's no reason to hit with the strength of only two when—"

"It makes perfect sense if they're not ready," Faolan interrupts. "We're not going to bring soldiers who aren't ready, but we're not going to stop just so we can fight."

"Faolan's right," Lord Jason from the House of the Day chimes in. "And Gideon. We need to move forward."

"I never thought I'd see the day where you admitted Faolan was right, Jace." Aiden laughs softly.

"Is it really that radical of a thought?" Faolan raises an eyebrow.

"Not what I'm saying, man."

"What are you saying then?"

I get to my feet fast and hold hands out to silence both of them. "Hey. None of that. We're not here to fight; we're here to make decisions. I see merit in both arguments. But I'm going to have to side with Aiden on this one."

"What?" Faolan is genuinely shocked. I would feel bad, but I'm in strategy mode. I can't be playing favorites, no matter what else is at stake.

"We have two options. One, we can attack now with an exhausted army with no additional training, no time to merge, no time to regain strength. Or we can wait three weeks. Let the House of Darkness and their spies figure out how large we are now. They'll fortify. But we'll be at full strength and will be able to overcome it. I don't want to go in half-assed just to keep the element of surprise. During that period of time, we choose a target and establish a chain of command that everyone can live with. Then we move forward with planning and launching our attack."

I turn to Faolan. "Do you think we can afford that long?"

"If my people focus on counterintelligence, then maybe. I don't know. But I'm willing to try."

"Gideon?"

"I'm not sure either, but it should be doable," the answer comes.

"All in favor?" It takes a few moments, but eventually everyone's hands go up. "Good. Then that's settled." As I look around the table, I feel confident that we'll manage to come to more compromises in the future. Even despite Faolan and Aiden's little spat. Hopefully it will stay that way.

Chapter Three

As the Council disperses, I wave Aiden over to me. "We need to finish our conversation," I tell him. "Can you stay after?"

"Absolutely," he replies, taking the seat beside me opposite of where Faolan was sitting. While the others leave, I notice Faolan stop at the doorway and turn back slightly to look over his shoulder at me. He tips his head just enough to non-verbally ask if I want him to stay. I imperceptibly shake my head, and after a moment of hesitation, he leaves.

I sit back down at the table and look up at Aiden. "Alright, I need to know what happened in the House of the Sun. I want the details. I didn't know what needed to be shared with the group or if you just wanted to share it with me, so I didn't ask at the meeting. What would you prefer?"

"I'd like to tell you. You can sort through it if you wish, and I'll tell the others at the next meeting."

"Understood. Go ahead."

Aiden leans in, both arms on the table. "When I arrived in town, my first thought was to contact my military commander who trained me. I knew if I could convince him to help me persuade a large majority of the military to move over to the good fight, we had a decent shot. I knew he was stationed at a base just outside of the capital city limits. I made my way there under cover of darkness, but I was discovered by a group of my father's men. They brought me to him."

"How did you manage to get out?" I ask.

"When I met with my father, he was upset that I had bailed on the family and the House without warning. But I was able to convince him that I had been chasing love by running away to you, and I eventually realized that what I was doing was silly and I decided to return home. It took some effort, but eventually he bought it. That's why I was gone for so long. I had to play the part of the dutiful son returned home. Most of my movements were being tracked."

"Most?"

Aiden smiles lightly. "Yes, there were a few moments where I was able to duck my guards. My shapeshifting magic came in handy for that."

"I've never seen you use it."

"It's pretty difficult to do. I can hold my shape for up to twelve hours, but I don't have all of my faculties. I can retain a few of my core memories, my drive and main goal and all that, but everything else is taken over by my shifted form. But strong enough shifting magic can hold off sensing magic for a short time."

"What is your shifted form?"

Aiden smiles. "A stag. It's good for blending into the surrounding environment."

"Well, what did you do when you were able to get away?"

"Through the grapevine, I discovered that many of my friends had been reassigned to the palace. In my moments of freedom, I met with them briefly and gave them the rundown on what had been going on outside of these walls throughout the war."

"Did they believe you?"

"Eventually. You have to remember, we were all trained not to question orders. To protect our House at all costs. That's hard to unlearn, even when you find that your superiors are doing the wrong thing."

"So you did convince them?" I clarify.

"Yeah." He nods. "And they informed me that our former trainer, the commander, would be visiting the palace soon to give my father an update on local skirmishes."

I raise an eyebrow. "I'm sorry, local skirmishes?"

"There are people in the House of the Sun who aren't happy with who my father has allied himself with, and it's causing friction. There have been lots of small protests and a few large ones. The castle is almost always dealing with a bunch of people at the gate. My father had to completely stop his personal dealings with the little people in town and send his advisors instead for his own safety."

"That could be useful to us," I point out. "We could convert them to our side."

"I know. We'll have to brainstorm on that later. Do you want to hear the rest of the story?" I motion for him to continue. "My fellow soldiers were able to manipulate the commander's schedule and distract his usual attendants long enough for me to have a brief meeting with him in the secret library office." I almost smile at the memory. "I showed him how deep my father was into this and how long it had been. We were being taken over by other Houses' interests, and we were not safe from being absorbed. I convinced him that duty to the House of the Sun no longer meant duty to my father. I could be the family representative instead. Between the two of us, we coordinated plans to persuade more soldiers to defect under his and my leadership. It took several more weeks, but like I said, we left with over half of the House of the Sun's army."

"That's great. It's going to be a huge help. Thank you for doing what you managed to do." I stand up. "Is there anything else?"

Aiden chuckles. "Isn't there?"

"I'm sorry, I'm not sure what you mean."

"Maybe how you found the remaining prophecy members?"

"Oh!" I laugh. "Of course. To be honest, the story is kind of quick when you sum it up. We discovered that Kiara had an abnormal amount of magic similar to the rest of ours. Faolan and I gathered some intel along with my tutor, Talon, before planning and executing a rescue mission. Obviously, that was successful. It was several weeks later before Cary realized that we hadn't considered the Twelfth House, the House of War. We sent word and traveled there where Luna was able to divine that Gideon was the final prophecy member. I ended up telling the High Lord about the prophecy to try and convince him to aid."

"Wow." Aiden whistles. "Did that work?"

I laugh shortly. "Absolutely not. He threw us out actually. But then we helped them in a demon attack and—"

"A demon attack? What do you mean by a demon attack?"

"You don't know? Your father never mentioned it?"

"No. Since when are demons involved?"

"Since the House of Peace rescue. High Lord Carron somehow managed to spring demons from the Lower Realm. I don't know why they're working with him; I don't know what he offered them. But there's demons involved, so… we gotta deal with that."

Aiden sighs and runs both hands through his hair. "Well… that's not ideal."

"No, it's not. But we'll figure it out. We always do." I make my way toward the door.

"Grace," Aiden calls. "Where are you going?"

"Um… downstairs?"

"We're not finished, are we?"

"I thought we were."

"We need to talk about the future of the War Council. We've got a full table now."

"Yeah, so?"

"Look, with all of these new voices at the table, you're going to need a strong partner at your side to sort through the chaos. I want to be that man for you, Grace. Let me step back in again."

"That's not gonna happen, Aiden."

"Why not?"

"Because you left, Aiden. I have already built a rapport with this team. We have a strong bond; we work well together. You and Gideon are technically new to the version of the group. You need to integrate into us. We'll absorb you fine, but you have to adjust too."

"But your right hand needs to be someone who can get the job done, Grace. Someone who knows you like the back of their hand."

"You don't know me like you think you do, Aiden," I say firmly. "You've been gone for months. You remember an older version of me. It's not the same thing."

"I can learn. I can fill that position."

The frustration from all of his irritating countering has built up in me so much that I just snap, "Faolan already fills that position just fine."

Aiden's face shifts immediately from pleading to furious. "What do you mean Faolan fills that position?"

"Faolan has been my second in command since the day after you left. Did you really think that you walked out and I would just hold a spot open for you? Faolan has connections that have been invaluable to the war effort, he knows when to speak up and when to back off, and *he* has been here the entire time," I list with vigor.

"I can't believe you've been working with Faolan like that! He's the son of High Lord Carron!"

"And you're your father's son. If we want to talk about whose side everyone is on—"

"It's not the same thing, Grace." Aiden shakes his head. "You know that it's different."

"How? How is it different?"

"He tried to kill us!"

"Then he saved us," I counter quickly. "And since you've been gone, he has more than redeemed himself in the eyes of everyone here. You are still living months in the past. The world has moved on. I have moved on."

"Moved on? Are you with him? I swear by the Lady, Grace, if he has—"

"This is not about you," I respond quickly, trying to circumvent the question he didn't quite finish asking. "By the Lady, Aiden, not everything settles around your return. You coming back changed a lot, but it did not change the partnerships we established while you were gone. This isn't about you versus Faolan. This is about me needing time to analyze what is happening and how you factor into patterns that already exist. Don't get it confused."

"Grace…"

"Stop saying my name like you are expecting me to melt as soon as you find the right tone to say it in." I sigh at him. "I was very clear with you when you left that—"

"Don't say it, Grace," Aiden interrupts me. "I don't even want to hear it. Do not tell me that it is too late to win you over. Not after everything we have been through. We traipsed across realms, the two of us, in search of answers about your brother. I know you felt things about me."

"Of course I did. But that's not even remotely the—"

"Then don't say there's not a chance. There's always a chance, Grace. Don't shut me down just yet."

An argument rises in my throat, but it dies just as quickly. I don't have the energy to tell him it's never going to happen when he looks at me with those pleading eyes. And for what it's worth, I am happy that he's back. But he introduces some old feelings in my chest that confuse me. And I need to speak to Faolan about it as soon as possible. Without saying a word, I shake my head once at Aiden and quickly exit the room. If words won't work, maybe actions will.

Chapter Four

I look for Faolan for hours after leaving Aiden, but he's nowhere to be found. I checked everywhere: his room, the training room, the arena, the grounds. I even went down into the town and snuck around, searching for him in the harder-to-find places. But there's no sign of him. I consider leaving a message for him to meet me when he resurfaces, but I'm too nervous to leave it out in the open for someone else to read. No, better to wait until I can ask him in person.

The following morning, still with no sign of him, I resign myself to meeting with Aiden again without Faolan's input. I honestly would have liked some insight into how I should approach this next conversation. But it looks like this one is on me. It takes me a while to decide where I should have the conversation. The library is private, but it feels too intimate. A garden walk would be good too, but it's a similar problem. Finally, I send a servant to tell Aiden to meet me in the throne room. It's way too formal for the situation, but it strikes the balance between public and private.

When he joins me, he sits in a chair across from me that I had pulled from storage. He gives me a half-smile that tugs on the right corner of his lips. "How did you sleep?" I ask awkwardly.

"Fine," he replies. "I've been set up in my old room. It feels nice to fall asleep and not have to watch my back all the time."

"Were you doing that a lot in the palace?"

"It felt like it. I still didn't trust that I wasn't going to wake up one day to find that my father had invited High Lord Carron into our midst."

"I can understand that. I still don't sleep fully." When Aiden nods, I sit forward on my throne. "Should we cut to the chase? Can you give me an idea of how large these protests were at the House of the Sun? How many people would you say would be interested in joining us?"

"See, I don't think I can quantify it like that. First of all, I don't have a good count of how many people were at the protests. None of us did. From what my father could gather, there were maybe hundreds, a couple thousand at most. The guards tried to wrangle them, keep them from overrunning the streets. Sometimes they succeeded. But most of the time, it was too much to control with just the palace guards. Occasionally, our troops had to be brought out for crowd control. The optics of it were not good for my father."

"Well, a few hundred on the low end is still a good amount to work with. Do you think they could be persuaded to join our cause?"

"Honestly, I don't know. It's definitely possible. But we have a lot of House pride. Even though they're pissed off at the High Lord, it doesn't necessarily mean it will translate into fighting against their homeland. I mean, I had to persuade the military it was okay to follow moral values by combining it with a legal line of succession loophole bullshit. A conversation needs to be started. At least to feel out where people stand. But I wouldn't know who the leaders were, let alone where to find them."

"We need to send envoys," I decide. "A couple of messengers sent to a central location who can start feeling out whether or not they would be willing to fight alongside us when the time comes."

"Where would we send them? What's the central location when you don't know the leadership, if there is leadership, or where they might meet?"

"The taverns. Since I've been here, all of the best information and the shadiest deals can be found there."

Aiden smiles. "You have a point there. Who should we send?"

"I don't think we need to send anyone, actually." I wave my hand in front of the throne room door as the housekeeper walks by. "Jeanine!"

She stops and pokes her head in. "Yes, High Lady?"

"Can you send for Faolan, please? See if you can find him? I need to speak to him immediately. Tell him it's urgent regarding the war effort."

"Yes, High Lady." She disappears down the hall.

"Faolan?" Aiden asks incredulously. "Why do we need Faolan?"

"Because there are already black market contacts stationed in the House of the Sun. They're well integrated. If we can get a message to them, they can take it from there."

"I don't want to involve—"

"You were looking for me, Grace?" Aiden is promptly interrupted by Faolan's arrival. My heart clenches lightly at seeing him again. He saunters in the room, making a beeline for me. He only stops when he finally notices Aiden sitting across from me. "Lord Aiden."

"Faolan."

The man in question turns to me again. "What did you need, Grace?"

"We need you to get a message to your contacts in the House of the Sun. I need them to go to all of the local taverns and keep an eye out for protestors, those who hate that the House of the Sun is in this war and want them out at any price. Identify the leaders and ease them into the conversation about what happens if we come to liberate them."

Faolan nods. "I can make it happen."

"Good."

"Is there anything else you need?"

"Yes... if you could stay, I need to talk to you in private." I look over to Aiden who looks absolutely appalled that I would dismiss him. Part of me gets a little rush of pride from that. *Yeah, that's right. Our business is done. I don't have to keep talking if I don't want to.* "Aiden, I think we've about covered it. Would you step out?"

His eyes trained on me, he slowly rises from his chair. "Are you serious?"

"Yes. My second and I need to have a private conversation."

Looking wounded, Aiden turns silently and leaves the room.

"We'll talk later!" I call after him. I don't know why; I guess maybe I'm throwing him a bone.

Faolan whistles. "Wow… you have no idea what you're doing, do you?"

"Oh, hush," I scold him. He laughs quietly. "I'm doing the best I can. I could have used some help trying to address the situation. I looked for you last night, but you were nowhere to be found."

"Sorry about that. You could have left me a message, you know."

"Didn't want to risk it being found."

He raises an eyebrow. "What were you going to say in said message?"

"I needed to ask you what you thought of all of this."

"With what?"

"Aiden's return!"

"Ah." He sighs. "That."

"Yes, that."

"Well, I think that he eventually had to come back if the prophecy was going to work out. I think the timing is good. The influx of new soldiers should be helpful. But I don't like how much he wants to jump directly back into the politics like he was here the whole time. His ideas shouldn't automatically get more merit."

"I won't let that happen."

"Good."

"But that's not really what I meant."

"What did you mean then?" His eyes lock onto mine and hold my gaze. If I didn't know his magic types, I'd say that he was trying to hypnotize me. But no… that's just me getting lost.

I shake myself out of it and look down. "How you feel… emotionally… about Aiden being back."

Faolan doesn't respond right away. It takes so long that I almost look back up to check that he's still there. But he finally says, "If we hadn't needed him for the prophecy… I would have laid him out in the courtyard for everyone to see, for kissing you like that."

My head flies up in shock. *Did I hear that right?* Unfortunately, I look up just in time to see him practically fly out the door.

You're just going to leave me with that?

Seriously?!

Chapter Five

The next few days are about establishing the chain of command with all of these voices in play. I call Aiden, Gideon, and all of our top commanders into a room to discuss strategic styles. There is quite a bit of back and forth. Which pretty much always happens when you put a bunch of leaders in the room and try to decide who gets to be the primary voice. I thought it would be obvious that as the head of the prophecy group and the leader of the War Council, I would be taking on the commander-in-chief position. But Gideon was fighting hard to take over the military aspect. He threw out every piece of knowledge he had that I didn't, every experience that he had been through and I hadn't. On one hand, he's not exactly wrong. I don't have the same experiences. But I've been in charge of this for so long that everyone looks to me. Turning it over to Gideon now would be a terrible idea, no matter the experience.

Eventually, the other commanders are able to convince him that I must remain in charge across all divisions for administrative and morale purposes. But when the military does their own strategizing among themselves, the House of War's top general will be the primary military contact, along with Gideon as a parallel leader. After that, the House of Evening and the House of the Sun fragment will take command in sequence. Gideon begrudgingly agrees to this, though I think that may have been to keep things moving. While there's still a little tension, I feel much more comfortable going forward with this plan in place.

At the end of the second week, Gideon's remaining forces arrive from the House of War. I am surprised they were able to repair the capital so quickly and find their way here. Gideon assures me that they work incredibly efficiently and only need the week to recover. I'm a little skeptical. On one hand, the scale that Gideon promised is exactly what was delivered. We have enough supplies to sustain us militarily for a period of time. But what I don't know is whether or not they left their own House behind in good enough shape. We need them and their supplies. But I don't want that to come at the expense of their people.

And at the end of the day, will it be enough to combat the demons and their magic? Either way, it is interesting that I find myself outnumbered in my own House.

A few days before the end of our self-imposed three week timeline, the War Council gathers in the throne room to discuss next steps. I have our attendants set up thrones in a circle similar to the impromptu meeting we had when Faolan and Cary joined us. There is a lot less tension in the room than the first meeting. With foundational elements in play and the couple day reprieve, I think it's given people time to adjust to new and old allies.

To my surprise, Faolan enters the room last with a guest in a hooded cloak. "Faolan?" I ask as I sit up on my throne. "Who is your guest?"

He offers me one of his business smirks. It's a little off-putting, given that I usually get one of his softer, more teasing smirks. It reminds me a lot of his sleaziness when I met him in the House of Darkness. "I have just received information about the House of Darkness's recent movements," he says. "I've brought the messenger so you can hear it from him directly."

"Alright, proceed." The messenger removes his hood, and to my absolute shock, Finn's head pops out. Finn, that smug Fae man who nearly got me killed when I first arrived in the Upper Realm. I jump to my feet. Aiden follows quickly behind, recognizing him. "Finn?" I shout.

His eyes widen to a comical degree. "You're High Lady Grace?"

"Yes, Finn, I am." I turn to Faolan quickly. "You have about three seconds to tell me why that man is in my palace."

Faolan shoots me a confused look. "Grace, I have no idea what you're talking about. Is there a problem with Finn?"

"He tried to have me killed when I first arrived in the Upper Realm! He sold me out to some soldiers in the mines. If Aiden hadn't rescued me, I would have been found and probably killed."

Faolan turns slowly to stare Finn down. It gives me great pleasure to see Finn cower under his eyes. "You didn't tell me that."

"Boss, I had no idea who that girl was. At the time, you were still with the High Lord; I thought I was doing what you would have wanted."

"I sent clear instructions to stay out of the dealings at the mines. I didn't want my people tangled up with it. Are you telling me you directly disobeyed an order?" There's a steady vibration of power starting to radiate around Faolan, and I feel a little bad for Finn. I've seen what Faolan can do to people who cross him.

"Faolan," I interrupt. The man turns to me, and I watch the fire in his eyes quickly die when he looks into my eyes. My heart flutters lightly as I realize I still have a lot of power over him. Maybe there's hope for us yet. "Does Finn have information that will be valuable to us?"

"Tell them," he growls at Finn who launches into his speech.

"High Lord Carron is ramping up for something big. More demons are migrating from the Lower Realm to the House of Day and the House of Peace. I have personally seen at least eighteen new beings.

And something's wrong with the High Lord."

"Wrong?" Gideon jumps on the detail. "Is he injured or ill?"

"No," Finn says. "The opposite, actually. Multiple sources indicate that he's actually accumulated more power."

"More?" Aira interjects. "How could he possibly accumulate more?"

"Aren't we born with a certain amount of power that we can't exceed?" Aiden asks.

Faolan chuckles harshly. "Seriously? You believe that bullshit?"

"Excuse me?" Aiden starts to rise to his feet.

"The bullshit that the power we're born with is all the power we're allowed to have in our lives. Think about it, we use all kinds of potions to augment our power. The more knowledgeable of us use blood magic to tap into more. If we can increase our power or access to our power with something as simple as that, is it really that unbelievable?"

"Come on, Faolan," Aiden rolls his eyes. "That's not even close to the same thing."

"Have there been any other reactions that could stem from the increased power levels?" Gideon interrupts.

"Increased mood swings, changes in voice character and tone, and increased brutality," Finn answers.

"Wait, wait, what do you mean by increased brutality?" Tristan interjects. "That could be literally anything knowing who we're dealing with."

"My father has been known for punishing at will. But not usually immediate execution," Faolan details.

"How do we know that this isn't just your father escalating?" Gideon asks.

"I know my father, and my intel has been good so far. It's your responsibility to figure out what to do with it."

As the conversation dissolves into smaller groups discussing back and forth how we need to assess this information, one of my guards appears with an unknown man. "High Lord Gideon, a messenger from the House of War," he announces. Gideon seems to recognize him and gets up to speak to him. I keep an eye on the two of them, particularly Gideon's facial expressions. He does not look happy. Something is worrying him, and I hope he'll bring it to the group.

"Grace." Gideon steps back into the circle quickly, turning heads. "We have a problem."

"What kind of problem?" I rise to my feet and walk over to meet him in the middle of the room.

"The High Lord of the House of the Peace tried to escape confinement this morning."

"Tried?" Faolan clarifies.

"Yes. He was caught almost instantly. The problem is that High Lord Carron is no longer playing around when it comes to prisoners. An execution order has been pushed through."

The room erupts into frantic conversation. Nothing like this has ever been done. An execution for a sitting High Lord? Not only is that punishment only ever used in cases of high treason, but to use it without a strong enough reason is high treason within itself. But it's wartime, and the rules have clearly changed.

"We have to go," I declare. "We have to go save him. Our target needs to be the House of Peace." Looking around the room, the other nobles are agreeing with me with nods and vocal affirmation. "Let's take a vote." One by one, hands go up in favor of liberating the House of Peace prior to the execution.

We found our first attack point.

Chapter Six

Once the House of Peace is chosen, it's like a whirlwind of activity is set off. Over the next several days, the Council engages in meeting after meeting structuring how this attack is going to go. There are so many factors in play. We need reliable transportation in and out of the realm and a way to enter with at least a partial element of surprise, which is going to be reasonably difficult given the size of our invasion. We also need an escape route in case things go horribly wrong. We have to figure out which armies are going and how many regiments and distribute weapons accordingly. And every decision, I have to sign off on. Luckily, the nobles work together to take as much off my plate as they can, coming to me for the important stuff and figuring out the rest themselves.

For peace of mind, I send my stepfamily off to Lady Elise's summer home. Neil takes offense to being rushed off to a safe place rather than staying in the thick of things. Honestly, I think he thought I would allow him to stay and run the House of the Evening just because the one time I needed him to come through after our father's death, he came through. But I can't trust him or his mother to stay out of noble business. My father isn't around to shield me anymore. I send Talon with them to act as a bodyguard for a period of time. I know he'll inform me if there's anything nefarious going on.

By now, we have to assume that the House of Darkness has gathered enough intel to know that the House of War is on our side. Although they haven't indicated any retaliatory attack against the House of War, there's no doubt in my mind that something will be coming at some point. Nevertheless, some subterfuge tactics are underway to make sure that the enemy doesn't obtain the exact location of our attack. Faolan coordinates his spies and those from our new ally to flood the enemy with false communication, indicating an attack landing on the House of the Earth. It must have worked at least a little bit because soldiers started being relocated to the House of the Earth from other held territories.

I arrange for Aiden to reach out to Master Xavier, who had managed to seek asylum in the House of War just before the House of Peace fell many months ago. He was one of the few that the High Lord accepted into the House's borders due to his renowned intellect. The House of War must have found some use for him. We need more information on how to fight demons, and who better to ask than the foremost scholar himself?

Just a couple of days before the planned battle, a new carriage rolls into town, heavily guarded by members of the House of War. When I hear the news, I rush downstairs. Aiden and Faolan follow closely on my heels. The doors fly open, and I move quickly to greet our guest as Master Xavier steps out of the vehicle. He looks much older than the last time I saw him back at the House of Peace library. He's more weary, and he walks with a cane. Aiden immediately offers him his arm to steady him while Faolan grabs his bags and confers with the guards who brought him.

"Master Xavier." I bow to him. "It is an honor to welcome you to the House of the Evening."

"High Lady Grace." He dips his head in acknowledgement. "I must admit, it is very strange calling you that after having met you in very different circumstances."

"Then please, call me Grace. I want you to feel comfortable."

"You are very kind, Miss Grace. Did the two of you ever reach the Lower Realm?" he says to me and Aiden.

"Yes, Master," Aiden replies. "We did, and it was quite a time."

The older man chuckles. "We have a lot to catch up on then," he says. The three of us and Faolan enter the palace and walk directly to the throne room where a circle of chairs have been set up for us to talk. Master Xavier eases himself into a chair, and the rest of us take our seats around him.

"Master Xavier, how was your journey here?" Aiden asks as he takes a seat next to him.

"Long," he answers. "But it couldn't be helped, and the men who accompanied me kept me in good spirits."

"I am glad to hear it, sir." I smile lightly. Then, I let my face shift back to something more serious. "Have you been brought up to speed on why we sent for you?"

"Aiden's letter summed it up pretty well." Master Xavier sighs. "And rumors abound in all parts of the Realm."

"Do you think they have truth to them, sir?" Faolan asks point-blank.

Master Xavier nods slowly. "I imagine you're referring to the ones about your father, High Lord Carron?" Faolan doesn't nod, but the older gentleman understands nonetheless. "Yes, I do believe there is truth to them. The bond between your father and the demons he decided to partner with is unusually strong. It requires more study. But first, I believe you need to understand the demonic types that you're going to be dealing with. It's crucial that you know the differences so that you can know what to do to combat them."

"Tell us everything you can," I encourage him.

The man lays back in his chair. "Demon magic increases in strength based on age. Demons are born with one level of power, and there are stages of growth where their magic grows exponentially until the end of their lifespan. Assuming they survive that long. Early on, their minds are ravaged by magic, and they can't even begin to control their power. As they grow older, they develop a greater control of their powers and of magical foundations themselves. They gain the ability to think and comprehend slowly, and that makes them even more dangerous."

The three of us nobles sit forward, hanging on to his every word as he continues. "The first stage of power are the Youthful Demons, from birth until about a century old. Those demons are reckless and wild, happily charging into anything with the intent to play. They have the ability to use their raw power, but are not able to form full spells, like what we would consider formalized magic. They care nothing for their own safety and play without thought to consequence, often resulting in the death of each other. They are unable to communicate with others at all."

"How do they survive?"

"By instinct alone. Many of them die in the earliest stage in the Lower Realm. Those that manage to survive become Elder Demons. Elders can take caution in their actions and communicate, albeit with extremely crude methods. These are most likely what you have been dealing with here. Aiden mentioned that one spoke to you, Grace, at one point. Because it could communicate a bit more thoroughly, it is likely on the older end of the spectrum where the demons are at least verbose, if still primarily emotional. Their magic patterns and organization and/or manipulation fits the description. But there may be one other type pulling the strings. Though you better hope they are not."

"What type?" Aiden asks.

"The Ancient Demons. They are over five thousand years old and have full comprehension of their actions. A flick of their finger can destroy the strongest of Fae. However, they don't usually see a point in attacking foes that are obviously weaker than they are. It doesn't quite fit the profile. But they have been known to control Youthful Demons with very little effort and do have some influence over the thoughts of Elder Demons. They are very prideful beings. There are rarely more than two in existence at any given time."

"Is that all?" Faolan snarks with a hint of worry in his voice.

"Technically, no. Final stage could be Demi Demons, though those are just a theory. Demonologists have worked on the hypothesis for years; those demons are believed to have mastered every form of magic in existence. But that's irrelevant because they would be so powerful, a being of pure magic with no physical body. They would be confined to the Lower Realm."

"No, we are most likely dealing with Elders and maybe an Ancient if you're unlucky."

"How do we stop them?" I ask.

"It's better to put a lot of power into one concentrated hit than to fire off a bunch of spells with less power in each," Master Xavier says. "Blasting spells work the best, so any Fae with disintegration magic should be confronting the demons. Fire magic works next best. And to be clear, this information is to give you a chance. None of this is a guarantee, no matter which stage of demon you are facing."

I nod absentmindedly as I ponder the information. It seems like everywhere I turn, I keep getting told these plans have "a chance" of succeeding, but only if everything goes perfectly. That's not really much to build a military strategy off of. "Thank you, Master Xavier. We will relay this information to our soldiers. If you would make yourself available periodically to answer questions, it would be greatly appreciated."

"I will do so. Though, I would like to rest first."

"Absolutely." I quickly get to my feet and shake the man's hand.

"Aiden will escort you to your room. Faolan, can you get his bags?"

Aiden takes his mentor's arm once more and exits the room. Faolan shoots a quick nod to me before following them with the suitcases. I take a moment to breathe, rubbing my hands tiredly over my face, before venturing off to fill in Gideon and the generals.

Chapter Seven

On the day before we move out to reach the House of Peace, I carve out a portion of my afternoon to escape the chaos of the palace and do some training in the arena on the palace grounds. Talon had to pull me aside and remind me that I needed to keep practicing my magic if I ever wanted to improve. Which is easy for him to say, he doesn't have to run a House and coordinate a war effort. But I agree with his point, so here I am.

Of course, I didn't want anyone to know that I was down here so that people could bother me, so I train against one of the magical dummies instead. I focus on my attack magic, the types that are going to be the most useful in the battle ahead. My elemental magic is progressing nicely. I'm able to generate a large amount of heat and flame and sustain it for longer periods of time. And my wind magic is growing every day, albeit with a little less control. Practicing disintegration magic requires the most effort overall. Each hit to the dummy has to be perfectly aimed, and each explosion depletes my magic just that little bit more. Luckily, the dummy is designed to regenerate using a special form of animation magic.

I also practice my force fields. It's somewhat hard to practice them without the pace of a battle. The dummy throws spells at me, but they come in a sort of regimented pattern. You can sense them before they're going to happen. I can hold my shields for longer and longer now, though the strength seems to fluctuate the longer I hold on. I worry about my defense and being able to defend others. I'm thinking maybe I should get a sparring partner to practice that bit.

"Grace," I hear a voice call from behind me. I cringe inwardly. *Not now...* I turn around to find Gideon midway down the stadium stairs, watching me train. This is the first time that I have seen him wearing something other than formal wear. I can clearly see the well-developed muscles through his short-sleeved shirt, and he's wearing dark brown pants tucked into a pair of leather boots. I have never seen him so casual. He could almost pass for one of the mortal guys I used to train with. He's carrying a couple of swords on his back. "Are you training down here?"

"Yes," I call back, "but I don't mind if you join me."

"I prefer to train alone."

"You don't like seeing what kind of competition that you have?" I tease lightly.

He looks down at me intensely. "You think you're some kind of competition for me?"

I shrug and turn back to my mechanical opponent. "I don't particularly care if I am or not. We're on the same side."

"But we are not at the same level," he presses.

I roll my eyes. "Of course we aren't on the same level. You've had, what, a decade and a half more years of training than I have? Of course, your skills are going to be more perfected. But what you should know is that I've been working extremely hard since I found out I was half-Fae, and my magic is extremely well developed for someone who has trained for only several months. So if you want to train, you can join me. If you don't, find somewhere else."

Gideon grunts, but he eventually makes his way down the stairs and into the arena. "Is there another one of those dummies?" he asks gruffly.

"In the tunnel over there. There's one or two more. But you don't have to fight an object. We could fight."

"Do you know what kind of realm-wide incident I would cause by fighting you?"

I resist the urge to roll my eyes again. "I imagine people would understand sparring over an actual fight between the two of us. Besides, as long as you don't kill me, we should be fine, right?"

He shrugs. "I guess."

"Then that's settled then." With a brush of my hand and a soft breeze, I send the dummy sliding toward the tunnel. "Wait... what kind of magic do you have?"

Gideon's upper lip quirks up into a partial smirk. All of a sudden, my body starts feeling heavier. It almost feels like a weight on my shoulders that slowly increases until I bend to its will. And sure enough, my body is slowly forced down to the ground. I land on my knees roughly before the pressure lets up. With a soft grunt, I get to my feet. "Gravity manipulation?"

"Yes," he answers. "No one else in my family has it."

"Interesting," I say as I dust the dirt off of my pants. "What else?"

"Nothing nearly as interesting. Most of it is physical magic rather than, say, elemental. I can absorb magical energy so it doesn't affect me as much. Combined with durability magic, I have a higher resistance to injury, which is helpful. Reflex amplification, strength, speed, and weapons amplification magic... that pretty much wraps it up."

"Then do your strengths lie then in a more physical battle? Less magical?"

"Not necessarily. I'm quick, and I'm good with a sword. Magic can only do so much. Especially for Fae that rely on it too much. Too many don't learn physical methods of fighting as well as magical. It puts them at a distinct disadvantage."

"I agree with that."

"You would, wouldn't you?" Gideon looks at me out of the corner of his eye. "I heard that at the Winter Solstice, you held your own against the other Fae heirs."

I laugh shortly. "You could say that. But I don't think all of them were in it to kill me."

"Perhaps." He then faces me fully. "Are you going to show me what you can do?"

I raise an eyebrow. "You're interested?"

"Yes. I've heard things about your power."

"From who?"

"People. I want to see if the stories are true."

With a soft wry chuckle, I acquiesce. With a wave of my hand, I summon a flame and let it glow in my hand before expanding it into a wide wall that I throw in front of me. Gideon watches off to the side. Kneeling to the ground on one knee, I blow gently and send a wild breeze ricocheting across the field. It swirls up the dirt and creates intricate shapes around the arena. I set it all on fire before blasting it to smithereens with one well placed blow. Finally, I let my wings unfurl and take a lap around the arena, enjoying the coolness of the air on my skin.

When I land back in front of Gideon, he looks at me with a somewhat disinterested look. "That's it?"

I roll my eyes. "No, that's not it. It's a taste. I have like half a dozen other powers, glamour, weapons amplification, force field generation. I didn't realize you wanted to see *every* power that I have."

"You're telling me you have almost a dozen separate powers?"

"Over a dozen, yes."

Gideon shakes his head. "Some Fae have all the luck. You think you're going to be able to handle yourself in a battle with so many different powers?"

"Yeah, I've been doing fine so far."

He tilts his head skeptically. "Alright."

"I'm sorry, first you have a problem with the way I lead, and now you have a problem with my magic? Is there anything about me you can tolerate?"

"Your cause."

I laugh shortly. "Uh-huh, great, I'm glad the cause of trying not to die in the eradication of half the realm is a good enough cause for you."

"I would just do things differently is all."

"That's not all, and you know it." I glare at him.

"You're right." He glares right back at me. "It's not. I think you should be turning leadership over to me."

I laugh out loud. "To you? You just got here. We have a dynamic going on. I'm the leader of the prophecy group, the head of the War Council—"

"Isn't it ridiculous that the head of the War Council isn't a member of the House of War? That a non-war leader is leading the Council?"

"I believe that was the House of War's decision. Just because you're the war lord doesn't mean you get to show up whenever the hell you want and demand to be in charge. Your House chose not to be involved until the last minute, you don't get to lead. It's that simple."

"I understand there are previous precedents that were voted upon, but you do not have the experience to save these people. You don't have the trust of the army as a commander and leader, and you do not fit. I was born and raised to lead an army. I was born for this. It is time to put your pride aside and let someone who *can* save everyone lead."

With an incredulous look, I step forward and get up in his face. "You know, we're going to have a lot of trouble if you keep disrespecting me."

"Disrespecting you? How have I disrespected you? My words are perfectly polite."

"Your words may be polite, but your intent is not. I see your experience, but the House of War isn't as trusted as you somehow believe. Your house has hidden away for hundreds of years, only helping yourselves until the entire realm was at stake. Do you think people see you as anything other than selfish? I will listen to your advice, and I will implement the pieces that I deem necessary. I truly believe you know what you're doing better than most of us. But you can't do it alone, not without the trust of the people. You have a lot of power and a lot of men that we need, but you need us too. You're a member of the prophecy whether you like it or not. Your fate is intertwined with ours. And so is your House's. Deal with it."

We stare at each other for a while, never breaking eye contact. Neither of us wants to be the first to look away. As I participate in this crazy standoff, all I can think is that we have a long way to go if we are ever going to make this work together. Eventually, I decide to back off, scoffing. "Go. Do your training alone like you want. I have no need to fight you today." Without waiting for a response, I whip around and storm back up the arena stairs.

Chapter Eight

Gideon, to his credit, doesn't give me any more leadership trouble after our conversation. And that's a good thing because it's finally time to storm the House of Peace. The first thing we have to do is establish our way in. Faolan's and my original way in when we rescued Kiara has got to be blocked off by now, or at the very least heavily guarded. The forest approach with the singular gate worked really well for that operation, and I look to find something similar. With the help of Gideon, we find a route that takes us through the House of War, down the Bhean Ocean, cutting east up the Calypso River, and invading via the inlet off of the Saeph River. On last intel, the House of Darkness doesn't have a strong navy, and if we can avoid the demons, we might be able to sneak across to the forest on the other side of the river. If we can do that, we can attack the House of Peace from the south side, take them by surprise.

We move out from the House of the Evening and cross the mountains to reach the House of War. They grant us fair accommodations and load us up with another round of supplies and a few more soldiers on a few of their ships. We sail under the cover of darkness south along the ocean before hanging a right to the Calypso River. The navy then lets us off near the southern forest for us to march the last stretch.

We make camp and sleep during the daytime so that we can make the major moves at nightfall. I don't know how much more of the element of surprise we have on our side, but we haven't been confronted yet. I want to ride that out as long as possible. It would be a lot easier to sail down the river and head into the city center. Make a big spectacle of everything. No, it's better we do this as stealthily and magic-free as possible.

We finally make our way to our attack point as the sun begins to barely peek over the horizon. As I look around at our group, the tiniest of glows brushes across my fellow prophecy members' faces, who have joined me for this attack. The soft orange casts a shadow across Faolan's chin that makes him look older and more stoic. A line of light sits across Gideon's eyes like a mask, making him look like an assassin preparing for the task ahead. Aiden and Kiara are also both illuminated as they take stock of our troops and supplies. I feel very privileged to have them by my side.

As dawn finally rises, we creep closer to Craine. Through the forest, we move with precision. Everyone has to keep maximum concentration. A dropped sword or a wry spell will give us away. The entire mission will fail. I can't stop the pounding in my chest. Every breath of mine is tense, and I don't know where my next step is until I make it. Leading the charge is much more difficult than I thought. If anything goes wrong before we get there, it's all on me. Part of me wonders if I should have left Gideon in charge. But this doesn't really feel like something that I could delegate.

Finally, we come upon the city. Only a few guards are stationed on the south side. They aren't expecting an attack through the woods on this angle. Our intel was right. My shoulders slump in relief. I slow us down several dozen feet away from the city's walls. I look to my people. I can't say a word without blowing our cover, but I communicate with basic hand signals. *Watch each other's backs. Remember the plan. Stick together. Fight until the very end with everything you have.* I glance at my friends. They're nodding to me, receiving my message, ready to go.

I give the signal.

There's a breath of silence.

And suddenly, we charge.

The guards on the top of the wall barely have time to react before we are upon them. Those who can fly soar over the top of the redoubt and take out the Fae they find there. Others rush at the wall, and disintegration magic in a few key places makes quick work of the stones. The wall crumbles to our feet as we dodge the falling rocks and rush into the city. The fliers stay behind to clean up the guards who manage to stay fighting after the wall knocks them down. Those with earth magic rush forward and fling the stones out of the way of our path.

The world becomes loud.

The House of Darkness is upon us now. Soldiers barrel toward us from all directions, and the moment we engage, the city explodes into bright lights and brilliant sound. I direct our soldiers into battle and then slip back to the middle of the pack. My general insisted that if I was going to be on the battlefield, I needed to be surrounded and protected. There are a few Fae captains assigned to protect me as I move around to attack.

So much of my magic is being used at once. I've never had so many powers working together at once. I throw fire spell after fire spell, combatting water and earth magic from the enemy. A fury of wind swirls around me, knocking other bodies and their spells aside. I draw in power from the magic around using conversion magic, and it is intoxicating, siphoning a little piece off of everyone else's spells. Each magic tastes different on my tongue, under my hands. Where magic won't do, I keep my sword swinging and hacking at those who try to get a piece of me.

I can barely see Aiden and Faolan from my position near the middle of the pack. From what I can tell, Faolan and his men are focusing on the demons, concentrating large amounts of magic to drain their energy. They work as a team, swarming on demons and isolating them from each other as best they can. It's not a perfect strategy, but it's working well enough. Gideon and Faolan came up with the plan together. Based on their research, it seemed clear that keeping the demons from working as a pack would minimize damage and potentially make them defeatable. Aiden leads his regiments toward the palace, attempting to clear the way to free the noble family trapped inside. Meanwhile, Kiara flits from zone to zone, acting as an on-site medic. Her healing magic patches up soldiers enough to keep going, or at least to get to safety to do more extensive medical work.

And Gideon? Gideon is a man-made hurricane. You can barely see his movements as he tears his way through the middle of a regiment single-handedly. His speed and reflex amplification magic puts him at an amazing advantage, and with the ability to manipulate gravity, most of the blows don't even touch him. What does touch him causes some damage, but he's absorbing the energy from every spell to make his own attacks stronger. His blade slices through the enemy with ease. All of the House of War soldiers have been trained so well. I really think we may have a shot here.

The enemy has come out in full force now and is giving us a run for our money. We engage passionately, each fighting for our lives and our livelihoods. Every breath needs another spell; every movement initiates another defensive maneuver with a weapon. It feels like so much has happened in the short time we have been in the city. And our actions are not without consequences. As the enemy falls, so do we. I try to block out the screams of my soldiers as their lives are ended by a well-placed blast or an intense burn. But they rip through my soul. The only thing that keeps me going without throwing up is the desire to keep it from happening to anyone else.

"Don't stop!" I shout at the top of my lungs. "Give 'em hell!" I push some psionic magic into my words like I do with my violin music.

Those around me hear me and take up the call. "For the Lady!" echoes throughout our ranks. With a loud cheer, our group of soldiers begins to push forward against the Fae in front of us. I jump into the group to aid. Packed in beside each other and pushing with bodies and magic, I feel a sense of solidarity with these Fae. We fight forward hard, inching step by step. Spells are flying all around us. Soldiers fall to my left and right, but I try not to pay attention and put up my shields whenever I see something. Some aren't paying as close attention though. The soldier in front of me panics and deflects the spell into me, grazing my arm. There is a sharp, thin line of pain before my blood stains the dirt.

We manage to get them back to the Saeph River line. I look to Faolan across the field and frantically shoot a telepathic message his way to send another signal. When it lands so loudly in his brain that he takes a step backward to recover, he turns to look at me before thrusting his arm into the sky and shooting up a bolt of red light. Shielding myself for the moment to look up, I watch it soar for the sky. I pray to the Lady that the signal is picked up. Then I get back to fighting, throwing blasting spells here and fire there, shielding every so often.

Suddenly, I hear shouts from the enemy lines. I look up to see dozens of ships steering toward us from across the river. The House of War's navy stands tall and proud as they race toward us. It is about then that the House of Darkness's army realizes that we have reinforcements, and they are blocking their means of escape. The fear is palpable. Those that can fly take off. Others try to fight, while the rest turn tail and run.

"Let's go!" I shout, forcing more magic into the yell. "Don't let them escape!" At my command, the regiment around me cheers and takes off in different directions, chasing down errant soldiers or continuing to push forward and force a squeeze between us and the soldiers coming down the river. As the ships from the House of War come within firing range, cannons begin to fire off. By boat and by air, Fae soldiers begin to pour off of the ships to come to our aid. I take to the air myself to get a better look at the whole scene. Our troops overwhelm them from all sides. We take the upper hand by force, slashing through dozens and dozens of enemy soldiers. Within minutes, the House of the Darkness's army has crumbled, either dead or captured with a very small few escaping out the front gates of the city. While the demons do not flee, we now can focus all of our attention on bringing them down.

My heart finally clenches as I realize… *we won.*

Chapter Nine

As the remnants of the House of Darkness's army in this region flees the city, a few regiments take off after them to see how many captures they could make. When the area is completely clear of enemy presence, there's still so much activity happening around me. Healers are frantically attending to those needing emergency care, headed by Kiara. The major commanders and generals are making their way to each other and working out a plan of how to figure out losses. There's quite a bit of ringing in my ears as the adrenaline slowly winds down.

The absence of spells flying left and right and buildings collapsing around us is stark. The people who managed to stay in their houses during the fight haven't emerged. It breaks my heart to imagine people huddled in the corners, trying to decide whether or not it's safe enough to come out yet. As soon as I get things settled here, I need to send some people around to make sure that they know it's safe. I wouldn't come out until someone came to get me if I was in that position.

Faolan flies over, careening toward the ground to meet me in the middle of the street, calling my name. When he reaches me, however, he takes my arms lightly in a gesture that doesn't match his previous pace. He looks me over frantically, scanning me for injuries. "Are you alright?" he asks.

I nod. "Yeah, I'm alright. Are you?"

"No injuries here."

"Good, good." I run my hands slowly up his arms. "We did it."

"Hell yeah, we did." Faolan grins at me. "It's a good start."

"Grace!" Aiden runs up behind Faolan. "Are you okay?" He freezes, and his eyes narrow at Faolan's arms on mine.

Before I have a chance to respond, Faolan slides his arms away from mine slowly. His eyes reveal nothing about how he is feeling. Steeling myself, I answer, "I'm fine. What do you know about the others?"

"The nobles are fine. We've lost a lot of soldiers. I don't have an inventory for you right now, but I can get one."

"I will be getting her one." Faolan glares at Aiden before running off to speak to one of the generals a little ways down the road.

"I could have done that," Aiden says crossly as he watches Faolan leave.

I don't see a single building that is completely intact. Everything has damage, from a little to a lot. Half the town has fully caved in. All around, I watch soldiers help each other to their feet or collect dead brothers to carry back to the palace. I am nearly stopped in my tracks as I think of Leo and Aiden and whether or not his brothers in arms carried him out of the mine where he died. Others help the injured, soldiers and citizens, to someplace safe where they can tend to their wounds. Healers have moved in and are tending to people in the street. The scene saddens me so much that I have to force myself to keep moving forward. Many of my people rise when I pass them. I wave them off. I know it's tradition to rise for a commander, but I don't want to interrupt any of the vital work happening here.

When we reach the palace, Kiara rushes up from a side street to meet me. Before she can speak, I launch a question at her. "The High Lord and his family? Are they alright? Have you heard anything?"

"I just got here. I heard Gideon is releasing them now. They should be up here any moment."

"Good, thank you." Kiara can't stop herself from dancing from foot to foot. She's anxious to see her family. I walk over and lay a hand on her arm. "Hey, they're going to be fine."

"I know," she says absentmindedly. "I need to do something to distract myself from waiting." Before I can say something, she darts over to help someone heal an injured man.

Within a few minutes, Gideon and his men bring up the noble family. High Lord Gabriel looks weary and much older than the last time I saw him, but unharmed. His long hair, now turned gray, hangs in his face, and he has to keep brushing it out of his eyes. The High Lady holds her two other daughters close to her sides, practically pinning them to her as she steps forward into the light. She still seems to be in disbelief that she is outside.

A loud cry comes from behind me, and I whip around to see where it came from. Kiara stands at the edge of the courtyard with her hand covering her mouth. "Papa!" she cries out. She takes off across the courtyard and leaps into her father's arms. For the first time, I see a High Lord abandon noble appearances and embrace his child with force and genuine emotion. He sobs as he holds his child close. The High Lady moves to the other side and squeezes them both in an embrace. The two sisters, both in noticeable tears join the hug from the outside. I watch wistfully. I wish my father would have looked at me like that when he found out he had a child. I wish I myself could let my guard down long enough to display that kind of emotion without a thought to what anyone else would think. The family looks so happy to be together again. Who knows what they must have gone through over the last few months.

When they finally break apart, the High Lord makes his way over to me. "Thank you, High Lady Grace," he says sincerely, grasping my hands. "Thank you for rescuing us."

"It was my honor, High Lord Gabriel. It was hard-fought, but we managed it. Your daughter is an amazing healer. She was an integral part of winning this battle. Have you met Lords Aiden and Gideon?"

"I believe I have had the privilege once or twice," the High Lord answers as he reaches out to shake the hands of each man in turn. "Except perhaps for Lord Gideon."

"I was a young boy when you last saw me, High Lord," Gideon tells him as he shakes his hand.

"Well, I am grateful to have such a young man present today to liberate us. The House of Peace will not forget your efforts."

"Thank you, High Lord."

"No, thank you." High Lord Gabriel looks to all of us. "Thank you all." He pulls his family aside to reunite in private, and I respect his need to do so. There should be plenty of time to talk about what he knows later.

Gideon then walks up to me. "We've secured the perimeter. Three more House of Darkness soldiers have been caught, and we'll be taking them to the palace dungeon for holding. I don't know if you want to do questioning here or if you want them transported."

"What would you suggest?"

"I would say let's question them here. Who knows what could happen in transport?"

"Would you take care of that, Gideon?"

"My men are on it." He bows his head to me before quickly moving back over to his men to discuss the interrogation.

"Grace!" Faolan's voice catches my ear before I can think of what to do next.

I spin around to greet him. "By the Lady, that was fast. How did you get an inventory that fast?"

"I have contacts," he states simply. "When I send out a call, they get it done."

"What did you find out?"

"I had people cover about two-thirds of the town, so this is not complete. But it's close, and I'm sending some of my people to the last third to get the rest of the information. There's an estimated eight hundred soldiers dead. About half of them are on our side, half theirs. There's also another five or six dozen citizen deaths."

"Citizen deaths?"

"Yes," Faolan answers solemnly. "Most of them are adults."

"Most?" I'm almost afraid to ask.

"A few teenagers. No young children dead at this time."

I gulp and nod. "Thank you. What else can you tell me?"

"We've counted about forty buildings completely demolished, another two dozen damaged in some significant way. Parts of the city held up fairly well, given the scale of the attack. But it's going to take a lot of time and manpower to build it back up."

I reach over and squeeze Faolan's arm. "Thank you. Let me know when you get the final count, please."

"Will do."

I squeeze my hands into fists back and forth by my sides. "I... I want to keep you here. I wish you could just stand here for a minute."

"I can if you need me to."

"I have to speak to the High Lord."

"Do you need backup?"

"I'm alright."

"Then I'll go take care of things, alright?" He reaches over and squeezes my hand once before jogging off.

I make my way over to the celebrating family. "High Lord Gabriel, I apologize but I need to speak to you briefly." The man nods and separates reluctantly from his family, allowing me to pull him aside. "I thought you might want to know the state of your city and your people."

He nods quickly. "Yes."

"There are five to six dozen of your citizens dead, and there's several hundred of our allied soldiers. I don't have the specific numbers from your military, but I should have it within the hour."

He closes his eyes and breathes quietly. "Too many."

"Yes. There is moderate property damage, but most of the city remains intact. There's a lot to be built back."

"We'll manage."

"The High Lord of the House of War has offered a significant amount of aid to you if they are allowed to set up in the city limits for a period of time until the war ends to hold a better position for you and them. Gideon is drafting a document that I am hoping you will be open to sign."

"How did you manage to convince the House of War to join us?"

I chuckle awkwardly. "It's complicated, High Lord."

"Say no more. I know how difficult it can be to sort these things out. I won't ask too many questions."

"Thank you, High Lord. If you don't mind me asking, is there anything you can tell me about the House of Darkness and their occupation? Any details could be important."

"I'm sorry, High Lady Grace. I have very little to share. I was kept in my own dungeon and only saw people when they brought me food. I barely heard any news except for a couple small conversations my guards were having. I was sorry to hear about your father from their lips. He was a good friend of mine and a respectable High Lord. I am deeply sorry for your loss."

"Thank you, High Lord." I bow my head lightly to him as I try to stamp down my sadness at the memory of my father. "Please get back to your family. We will speak again soon."

"Absolutely. Thank you." He leaves my side to greet his family again. I turn my back to the happy reunion and look out over the smoky remnants of the city. As happy as I am that we won, the victory is only the beginning. There is so much more to do to bring this back to a functional House who can aid us in the war effort. I walk away from the view and head into the palace to get started.

Chapter Ten

After a few days in the House of the Peace, the bulk of us return home to the House of the Evening. We are greeted with joyous cheering and music around every street corner. This is the first major victory for our side, and the excitement is palpable. Spirits are high all around. A few members of the Council suggest having a small celebration with the people in the town, but I disagree. This is only the beginning, and there's so much further to go. If I spend all my time planning parties for the victories we do win, I won't have time to plan more victories.

Our healers quickly transport the wounded soldiers upstairs to the hospital wing, and the recovery process for them begins. The remaining soldiers reorganize under their commanders and continue their training. The War Council meets briefly the following afternoon to discuss next steps. We ultimately decide to capitalize on our momentum and prepare for another journey in a few days' time. This time, the Houses of Moon, Wind, and Evening will move to take more land in the House of the Earth from the House of Fire. I volunteer to lead this expedition myself, and Faolan quickly agrees to go with me. I'm surprised by this, but grateful. Maybe he's decided not to hide from me anymore after the battle. I instruct Aiden and Gideon to stay behind and maintain the status quo at home. There is some significant grumbling about this from both parties, but eventually, they concede.

A couple nights later, after a long day, I am so ready to have a moment to myself in my own room. As soon as the door is closed, I don't even bother to take anything off. Instead, I make a beeline for my bed and flop face first on the covers. A long groan escapes my mouth. It feels so nice to be able to do that without someone staring at you like you're crazy. Having to be 'on' at all times is exhausting.

A knock on the door interrupts my relaxation. With a frustrated sigh, I push myself up. Stalking over to the entryway, I grumble, "Don't you people know the meaning of—" When I fling open the door, I am stopped dead in my tracks by Faolan's dark eyes. "Oh! I… Faolan."

He raises his eyebrows slightly. "Expecting someone else this time of night?"

I blush and shake my head rapidly. "No. No one comes to my room unless they need something. Thought you were someone coming to have another discussion."

"Not particularly, no. I have no desire to debate, though I guess I could if you want." He smirks lightly at me.

"No!" I shout, eyes wide. "Not at all." A harsh laugh escapes me. "No more of that today, please." I lean against the door frame with my head down at the thought of having to argue more. Faolan chuckles at me, and I can't help but smile. When I look up again, he is watching me somewhat expectantly. Feeling awkward, I bite my lip. "Um… would you like to come in?" Faolan nods and slips into the room behind me, allowing me to close the door once again. I keep my body turned away from him at first as I try to figure out what he might be here for. I am painfully aware that this is the second time Faolan has been in my room and the first time I have been alone with him since our kiss, before chaos ensued and Aiden and Gideon arrived.

"It's been a while," I settle on saying before moving to sit on the edge of my bed. "Since we've been able to talk." When I look at him, all I can think about is his lips on mine that night up against the column. I have to turn away.

"It has," Faolan replies. "A few interesting things have happened."

I chuckle dryly. "You can say that again." I sigh and shake my head. "I'm sorry… about what Aiden did when he showed up." I can't bring myself to say the word 'kiss'. "I should have said that before. He shouldn't have done that. We ended… things. When he left. And he shouldn't have tried to supersede your position as my right hand. I told him off for it."

"He seems to disagree that things ended."

"I have tried to make it clear that they did."

"So you ended things without him knowing?"

"Absolutely not," I say immediately. I absolutely do not, under any circumstances, want Faolan to think I kissed him while with someone else. "When he told me he was headed to the House of the Sun, I told him in no uncertain terms that if he left, don't expect me to be waiting for him when he returned."

"Seems they weren't uncertain enough."

"He didn't listen before; I'm not surprised that he didn't listen now. It's complicated."

"Then will you explain it to me?" Faolan leans against my dresser and watches me pointedly. As much as he's giving me small smirks and playful smiles, I can see the steel behind his gaze. Aiden's arrival at the precise moment that he did was clearly not well received.

"I wish I could. The one time we've spoken one on one since he returned, Aiden seems to believe that I hadn't replaced him at the right hand position. Or there was an interim person rather than a permanent placement. He was not happy when I told him I wasn't getting rid of you."

"I'm glad you didn't drop me on a dime," Faolan concedes, "but I am the now-deposed heir to the House of Darkness. The trust isn't there. And he's a charismatic and large public fixture. There will be repercussions."

"I don't care," I say fiercely. "You've done enough to prove yourself these last few months. Anyone who thinks otherwise can go through me."

"And what examples would you give people to prove it?"

"Plenty." I begin to list them off on my fingers. "You were integral to rescuing Kiara, you trained me in more finessed magic, your connections brought us information, resources, tools. Your men aided us in the House of the Earth. You're an essential part of this team."

"Yes, but I can be essential when I'm not your advisor under those ideas. You must convince others I should stay your second, not me."

"Come on," I exclaim. "No one has questioned you yet. Not even with Aiden's behavior at the Council meeting. Unless you've heard something." I raise an eyebrow.

Faolan chuckles, but his eyes fall. "Of course they question, Grace."

"Who is questioning you?" I jump to my feet. "Who dares to now after everything we've been through?"

"All of them question. They may not say it, but they do."

In a rush of frustration, I growl and send one of my pillows flying across the room toward the door. "You don't deserve it," I snap.

"Neither did that pillow."

When he says it so simply, I can't help but burst out laughing. I laugh so much that I double over on the bed and giggle quite a bit longer than I should. Meanwhile, Faolan smiles at my antics and sits down on the edge of the bed next to me. I turn over to him, still chuckling. "I'm sorry. I haven't laughed like that in forever."

"Then I'm glad you did," he says plainly. I watch him carefully, studying the lines of his face and neck. He raises an eyebrow back. "Yes?"

With a deep breath, I press forward. "We never talked about… the night we got back from the House of War." Again, I can't seem to define what happened. *How hard is it to just say 'kiss'?*

"Was there something to warrant discussion?"

I blush furiously and turn away. That's not the answer I was looking for. "No. I guess not."

"You seem to be unsure."

I get up and move over to the dresser, opening a drawer and ruffling through my pajamas just to have something to do to distract myself from how I feel. If he doesn't think there's anything to discuss, then maybe it didn't mean as much to him as I thought. Maybe I've been reading the situation all wrong. "It's nothing," I say quickly. "You said there's nothing, so there's nothing." My heart pounds in my chest.

Faolan chuckles in an irritating way. "Didn't think it was nothing."

I turn around to look at him. "You didn't?"

"Just said it didn't warrant discussion."

"But… what does that mean?"

"Do we need to discuss what it means?" Faolan gets up from the bed and stalks closer to me.

I gulp. "Maybe…" I lean toward him slightly myself. "Do you want to…" My body takes a step forward. I mean to finish my sentence with 'continue the discussion', but the way he's looking at me makes me lose my train of thought.

Faolan smirks softly at me. "I do." In a breath, he kisses me suddenly, sliding an arm around my hips. Caught off guard, I melt into the kiss, slipping my fingers into his hair smoothly. He pulls me tighter into his chest as he deepens the kiss. All I can do is hold on tight. After what feels like hours, I pull back to catch my breath, looking up into his amber eyes. Faolan smiles as he runs his fingers through my hair.

"Does this answer your question?" His chest rumbles as he speaks.

"Yes," I breathe back lightly against his lips before he catches mine again. My eyes slide closed as his kiss consumes me. For a moment, I forget about everything else happening outside of my bedroom. For a moment, it all just *slips away*. This time last year, I never would have imagined that anyone could make me feel like that. Faolan's kisses are so much more demanding than Aiden's; yet, they're warm and safe.

That man may very well burn the world down to get to me. And I might let him.

Suddenly, there's another knock at the door. I fly back from Faolan. If I wasn't so worried about being caught with him in my room, I may have enjoyed the fact that his usual polished appearance was a bit wild and disheveled.

"Who is it now?" he asks, running a hand through his hair.

"I have no idea!" I frantically respond as I try to fix my hair and my clothes. "You have to hide."

He laughs. "Hide? Why?"

"Please." I look up at him with urging eyes. When he finally nods, I run around to the doorway and just open it enough to see who's outside. My shoulders slump in relief when I find one of my maids. "Hello?"

"You requested an extra blanket, High Lady?" She offers me a medium white blanket. I inwardly groan. I can't believe I forgot; I sent for one early this morning when the temperature dropped last night. This must have been the first available opportunity to bring one, what with all the people here.

"Yes." I open the door a tiny bit forward. "Yes. Thank you."

"Have a good night, High Lady." The maid bows her head to me before leaving. I quickly shut the door and toss the blanket on the bed as I whip around the corner toward my closet.

"Faolan?"

"I'm here," the response comes quickly. Faolan steps forward from the shadows cast against my walls, his magic fading as he comes into focus. I can't help but let out the sigh of relief that escapes my lips. He smiles when he hears it and moves to embrace me again. I allow him to for a moment before I lean back, holding his arms.

"Hi."

He grins. "Hello."

I lean back into his chest for a moment. "I really should be getting to sleep."

"Of course." Before I can blink, he sweeps me off of my feet and carries me toward my bed. I laugh as he lightly tosses me on top of the covers and climbs in after me. When he pulls me into his arms, I give him a tight squeeze. When he leans down to kiss me, I let him because I just can't help myself. Everything about this feels so right, it scares me. So when his hands move from my hair down my arms to my hips, I press my hand lightly to his chest and gently separate myself. He doesn't move to pull me back, instead allowing me to take some space and shifting his hands back to my arms.

"Are you alright? Am I going too fast?"

"Yes."

"I'm sorry." He looks at me with remorse. "I didn't mean to."

"I just… I don't want to move fast with you. I still don't know where my head's at, and there's a war going on outside. It's not fair to try for something without a full understanding of what I want or need. If I let you stay…"

He smiles gently. "I understand." He lets go of me completely now, and the loss of warmth is so pronounced that I nearly throw caution to the wind and ask him to stay. He seems to know my thoughts and gently kisses my forehead. "I'll go if you'd like."

"I don't like," I find myself saying, "but I should."

"At least let me see you off to sleep."

"You seem to do that a lot."

"What can I say? I like to make sure you're safe." His eyes are filled with warmth as he heads into the bathroom. "Get changed, and get into bed. Call me when you're ready." I chuckle softly at his antics, but quickly comply with his request. I slip into something and climb back into bed, throwing the covers back.

"You can come back in now," I call with a little teasing exasperation in my voice.

Faolan smirks as he comes around the corner and leans on the door frame. He smiles at me. "Look at you."

"What are you looking at?" I laugh. "I'm all buried under blankets."

"You still look beautiful." He walks over to me and sits on the edge of the bed.

"Uh-huh." I chuckle. "Get out of here."

"Not without a goodnight kiss." He leans down and kisses me deeply again with one hand running through my hair. He leaves me breathless before pulling away and letting my head fall back to the pillow.

"Goodnight, Grace," he says as he moves to the balcony door.

"The front door's that way," I answer, raising an eyebrow.

"This is quicker." When he opens the door, a cool breeze slides through and sends a shiver through me. I burrow down further in my covers and peek over the top as Faolan smiles at me. "See you tomorrow, princess." With a playful smirk, he slips outside and closes the door behind him. I hear a few careful footsteps and a swishing of wings as he presumably disappears from my balcony.

Chapter Eleven

The next time I see Faolan alone is a few days later while we are leading a march toward the House of the Earth. It's been a couple of months at this point since we took Willowdale back from the House of Fire, and rebuilding efforts there have been going strong. Faolan left several of his black market contacts there to oversee the process, including Mahlin. He's the one we're supposed to be coordinating with once we're on the ground there.

Talon joins us at the last minute as well. Bodyguarding for my stepfamily didn't go as well as I had hoped. They're much too contemptuous for him, particularly my stepmother. I ended up having to put some of my personal guards there instead and to bring Talon back to the palace. He hasn't been involved in a battle yet as I have been pushing him to work with the other mages in the lab to generate as many magical potions as we could with our current resources. Personally, I think he's better suited to working there. He churns out more magic than the rest of them, and he's pretty much been the de facto leader. But he wanted to come out here to this one, and after an hour of hearing him list all of the possible reasons that he could be a benefit to the team, I finally relented. I did tell Faolan to have some of his guys keep an eye on him. He's a good fighter, but I worry about him. It's much more difficult out in the field than it is in a controlled environment.

The march to Willowdale is a steady endeavor. We move through covered areas whenever we can, but there's always the worry there will be an attack in close quarters. Several of our soldiers are assigned to keep an eye out for anything suspicious, and a few of Faolan's contacts clear the way area by area as we move ahead. It's a good thing that Faolan had the foresight to send them ahead because at least three ambushes of small parties were thwarted by well-placed blasts. Intel usually gets out one way or another that one of the sides is moving, but it does concern me. I'm afraid we may be in for a big fight come our arrival.

We reach Willowdale by the following afternoon when the golden sun sits high above us. It casts a perky radiance over the bustle of the tiny town. The destruction brought about by the battle has been about half rebuilt. I'm impressed. Under the supervision of one of my regiments in conjunction with the black market underground, we managed to funnel supplies into the region to rebuild their infrastructure and establish our own outpost. Their old dull mud brick buildings have been replaced by sturdier, more vibrant structures reminiscent of the more prosperous farm towns in the House of the Earth. Everything has been fortified by magic, and I am hoping that the buildings will hold better this time if there is another major battle here. Honestly, the air feels hopeful, like we're getting a glimpse at what it would look like to build back the realm.

But I can't help but feel worried.

Once I drop off our troops at the reconstructed tavern where our army reunites, I join Faolan near the town gates with Mahlin. "High Lady." Mahlin indicates my presence with a gruff nod of his head.

I dip my head coolly in response. "Mahlin."

Faolan laughs. "I forgot you two have history. Come on, Grace. He helped us take back this town, right?"

"He also refused to carry my message to the Middle Realm and probably would have tried to take me out if you hadn't shown up that day in the House of Darkness."

"Please, I didn't touch you." Mahlin laughs. "I wouldn't have killed you without my boss's permission."

"Great. That makes me feel so much better."

"You have to admit, he follows orders very well," Faolan counters. "Take a look at how well he's managed this place."

"How both our people managed this place," I correct lightly. "But you have done a decent job, Mahlin. Do you have a report for me?"

"Yes, High Lady. Willowdale is about seventy percent reconstructed. There's been three crews switching off, working around the clock to get things back to an original yet improved state. Those who did not want to stay have been evacuated to the House of the Wind and to the House of the Evening and successfully integrated as refugees. Those who chose to stay have done their part to hold down the fort. There have been three attacks to date. Two smaller attacks took out two newly constructed barracks, which we rebuilt. We successfully held them off and apprehended several enemy combatants."

"I'm aware of those attacks," I confirm. "You sent prisoners to us. My generals interrogated them. But what about the third?"

"Last week? Why wasn't I informed of this?"

"Faolan was."

"Faolan." I snap my head to glare at him.

He puts his hands up. "I handled it. You were busy."

"I'm never too busy for this."

"I'm just doing what a right hand is supposed to do. Handle it. I handled it, and now you're getting the report."

I resist the urge to roll my eyes. But if I think about it a little longer, I feel a little warmth in my chest. He handled it. Without me. A task I didn't have to do… without asking for my input. How perfect. "Fine," I say shortly, trying to keep up at least some air of indignation. "Next time, however, I would like a report."

"Understood," Faolan replies softly with a smile.

I turn back to Mahlin. "What happened?"

"Intel came in about a full-blown offensive by two House of Fire regiments, a couple hundred soldiers, headed toward Willowdale. It was too late to send people out to meet them away from the town or call for help. We had maybe a half day before they arrived. So instead, we prepared for battle. We gathered up everyone in the town who was able and ready to fight, and we took up defensive positions. Luckily, we had just spent the last two weeks developing a supply of potions, based on your Court's recommendations. We used most of it during the attack."

"What were the results?" I ask softly.

"Could have been a lot worse," Mahlin admits, rubbing the back of his neck. "We were on the ropes for a while. Ultimately, there were sixty casualties on our side. But we took out enough of them to send them packing. We held the town."

I let out a rush of breath with my eyes tightly closed. "Alright," I finally answer as my eyes open abruptly. "Alright, thank you." You've done a lot of fantastic work here. Thank you for your service."

To my surprise, Mahlin laughs. Faolan does too. "Please don't thank me for my service," Mahlin says. "You make me feel all formal and... *ugh*." He cringes. "Just... don't."

An incredulous laugh slips from my lips. "Alright, if you say so." I offer my hand for Mahlin to shake, and he grasps it firmly for a brief moment.

"Can we talk intel?" Faolan asks as our hands fall back to our sides. "Do you have any indication of which town we should focus our efforts toward?"

"Pumpkin Hollow."

Um.

"I'm sorry, what?" I ask incredulously.

"That's a fucking terrible name," Faolan says matter-of-factly.

"Yeah, I said the same thing." Mahlin laughs. "But apparently, the founder's last name was Pumpkin. Ray Pumpkin. Either way, regardless of the stupid name, it's the third largest village in the House of the Earth. The House of Fire has been holding it ever since the initial invasion. They have a bunch of troops and a ton of supplies holed up there, and they're due to get reinforcements in a few days. If we can strike before those reinforcements arrive, I think we'll be in a good position to liberate the entire House."

"What do you think we should be utilizing for the attack?" Faolan asks.

"All soldiers who are ready and able out on the battlefield. A few should be kept in reserve in case the entire mission fails so that someone can get back to the House of the Evening to report. In fact, we should send somebody to update them now. Maybe Luna can foresee if there's any major issues. Take fifty percent of the potion supply out to the battlefield. Keep some potions back to heal those who return. We'll put you two near the back, protect you when all else fails. Neither of you should be at the front of this one."

"I don't like sending my soldiers into battle without me in the thick of things," I argue.

"Trust me, you'll be in the thick of things. This army fights well and hard. There will be no shortage of carnage for you to engage in, High Lady. But in the back, we can keep you and Faolan here from being immediate targets. Even a few moments' delay could be the difference. Do you think you can manage that?"

"Fine." I wave dismissively. "We'll manage."

Mahlin nods in agreement. "I'll make the arrangements." He bows his head to both of us before heading toward the tavern to take charge.

Faolan offers me his hand. "Come with me, my dear," he says quietly.

"Your army awaits you."

Chapter Twelve

The afternoon is spent pouring over supply reports, battle plans, and going over what needs to be done to bolster the town in the future. I head to sleep that night with a clean to-do list but a muddled head. It's not the best state to be in before a battle, but it's the best I can do. I don't know how my father managed to do all of this. Hell, I don't know how High Lord Carron manages to keep it all straight. Surely something has to give at some point. We can't all just keep going until we drop. What would the realm do then?

When the morning comes, I wake up and quickly move to prepare for battle. Faolan, Talon, and I can't stay here long. The enemy may be aware of a move being made, but it isn't clear whether they know two major players are here. If they find out we've stepped out here to help in a smaller area, they will likely send reinforcements to come take us out here. Faolan's confident that a couple days won't cause any harm. A few days here, a few days there, then rest up in the heavily fortified House of the Evening. I trust his judgment. But I wish I knew more about what the hell I was doing.

When I make my way downstairs, I am confronted by Mahlin and Faolan. Their grim faces almost make me turn around and head back upstairs. "Oh, come on," I groan. "Seriously? Can't one damn thing go according to plan?" I resist the urge to slam my fist into the wall. "What happened?"

"Well," Faolan drawls. "The good news is their reinforcements haven't arrived. We're still dealing with the exact same number we previously estimated."

"Well, that's good, right?" I answer.

"Except, we have recently obtained intel on one of the members who will be leading the defense if we strike today," Mahlin counters. "Ariel Elizabeth Halden."

"The House of Fire daughter?"

"Yes. She's sixteen, and her father's put her out here to hold down the fort in the House of the Earth."

"She's sixteen?" *What kind of father puts their young daughter in charge of an army in the middle of a war that he caused?*

"Don't underestimate her for her age," Faolan cautions. "She's a fierce warrior. She'll do whatever she needs to do to get her way. My father looked into a betrothal between the two of us for a while." I feel a rush of anger at the thought of that. "Her being on the battlefield today poses an interesting dilemma for us. None of the soldiers here are prepared for her level of power."

"What does that mean for us?"

"It means you and I have to engage with her."

"So no hanging back?"

"Oh no, you'll still start there," Mahlin clarifies. "We'll be on the lookout for Ariel, and as soon as she's identified, we'll direct you two to her. If you can keep her pre-occupied while we take the bulk of the town, we may have a fighting chance."

"Okay. When do we head out?" I ask.

"In the next twenty minutes. Can you handle it?"

I cock my head slightly and chuckle. "Yeah."

"Good. Let's gear up."

* * *

Once we reach Pumpkin Hollow, I'm on the lookout to take stock of the army we're about to encounter. Any small details that I can identify right away may aid us in our pursuit. Two men on the lookout tower. A couple dozen scattered in various positions on several of the roofs throughout the outside of the town. I'll admit, it's a smart use of defensive space when one has no major defensive walls. A quick glance tells me that there's a Fae soldier stationed at every alleyway in and out of the town, and it's enough that it will block us from entering swiftly. On top of that, a group of soldiers are circling the town, doing rounds to check on every entrance and all current defenses.

"I say we go up and over the roofs," I mumble to Faolan.

"Won't they be expecting that?" he whispers back. "The defenses are too uneven. Manning every alleyway, but way fewer on the roofs? No, they've got something big up there. Mostly like a magical item or additional forces crouching behind the eaves. We need to go in on the ground."

"Those alleyways are tight."

"We're not going through those. At least not as narrow as they are." He subtly indicates to me the corners of some of the buildings. Once again, it becomes clear that Mahlin and his team have placed charges at the corners. We're gonna blow our way through.

"Have the buildings been cleared?" I ask, concerned. I'm not in the market to blow up family homes.

"Don't worry, these buildings are entirely military barracks. The risk to innocents is minimal."

I hesitate for a moment. I don't know if it's the best idea in the world. But if Faolan thinks it's worth it, then I trust him. "Alright. When do we go?"

The corner of Faolan's lip quirks up. "At your signal, my lady."

I look around to find everyone is watching me. Despite being a secondary planner for the majority of this offensive, they're still waiting for me to make the final choice. To attack or not to attack. It feels so heavy, being the one who ultimately decides whether or not a mission can move forward. Despite my anxiety, I look around and raise my hand. With that, Mahlin snaps his fingers, and his fire magic lights the charges. The sound of the fuses cause the soldiers defending the town to look around. But they have no time to react before the village erupts.

Our group charges as brick, stone, and roof thatch come cascading down like tiny avalanches, leaving destruction in its wake. The House of Fire's soldiers jump to attention and rush to meet us. Magic meets magic in a fiery blaze. The primary spell type is, in fact, fire, given the nature of the army we are fighting. Luckily, this is a place where I really shine. I pull out every ounce of power that I have. The ground burns like hellfire under me. I send waves of flame out in every direction. I use my conversion magic to feed off of other fire spells and fuel my own. Faolan adds his own augmentation magic to strengthen my attacks. While he doesn't have the magic to shield me, he does a pretty solid job of blocking attacks that I miss with his amplified reflexes. Anyone that I can't take out with my fire magic, I use my sword. Many of these soldiers aren't as skilled in hand-to-hand combat as other armies, and they fall quickly when confronted with it.

Mahlin drives his soldiers forward with vigor. They attack with no reservations. The small group that he corrals throws the nastiest of spells, those meant not only to kill, but to maim. There's an abnormal amount of crazed screams coming from over that direction. I try not to think about where that comes from. Mahlin himself fights furiously, a swirling mass of dark magic and gusts of wind. He's a solid leader; I can see why Faolan chose him as a right hand.

I don't like this battle. I don't like any of them, but particularly not this kind. There is so much fire. The smell of burnt flesh lingers in my nose, and I'm terrified that I'll never be able to get it out. Every breath I take, I inhale smoke. I feel like it may permanently take out my lungs. The soldiers around me seem to feel the same way. Even the enemy I am fighting seems done with it all and just trying to get through everyone so they can stop. People are being lazy with their swordplay, swinging wildly and hacking away at any inch of skin they can find. The injury count from this is going to be very high, no matter what way it goes.

"Grace," Faolan's voice suddenly hisses in my brain through telepathy. "Ariel has arrived. I can't get to her from where I am. I need you to take care of it."

I turn around to find the powerful woman striding onto the battlefield with a massive spear. She looks so much younger than she really is. She almost looks like she's playing dress-up in this oversized armor that she has on. But her blue eyes reveal her dark intentions, and when she locks eyes with me, they sparkle menacingly. I charge at her.

She meets me swiftly with fire in one hand and her spear in the other. I throw up my shield and send a blast of fire her way. She dodges with ease and sends spirals of flame after me. They're almost impossible to avoid. They keep chasing after me with each move. It takes all of my concentration to keep my shield up to keep them from slicing into me while also sending more magic her way. I try using some wind to ruffle her, but she refuses to be deterred.

Her fire magic is certainly stronger than mine. It takes all of my resistance to keep myself from being singed too badly. The heat coming off of her fire is so much hotter than anything I have ever felt come close to my skin. However, her swordplay could use a lot of work. In that way, I am able to keep her on her toes. In my head, Faolan reminds me that we are here to keep her distracted, keep her away from helping the rest of her army. She has so much to prove here, and beating me would do the trick.

All I have to do is keep distracting her. Every second is a second that she isn't focusing on her army. A second that my people can take hers down.

And it works. While she tries to take me down, Mahlin and his soldiers take out the majority of the House of Fire's soldiers in a rapid sweep. It comes at a heavy cost. The bodies litter the street and pile high along the sides of buildings. Eventually, Ariel realizes she is outnumbered. I take advantage of her momentary distraction and send a lash of flame her way. It cuts across her cheek and leaves a bright red bleeding line. Her mouth gapes in horror at being struck directly. She turns tail and takes to the sky, fleeing with the remnants of the troops she was meant to lead. When I'm certain that I'm clear of people trying to kill me, I fall to my knees, breathing heavily. That damned smell intensifies at every inhale. It's a decisive victory, and it may ultimately make all the difference here.

But by the Lady... the horror of it all.

We clear the streets as best we can and let the people know that they have been liberated. I personally aid my men in burying as many bodies as we can, our dead and theirs. I won't let anyone go without a proper burial. The troops make camp while the senior officers manage to commandeer a few rooms in a small inn that managed to survive the chaos. Faolan heads upstairs to collapse while I stay downstairs to manage the next stages: lists of repairs, accounting of the dead, getting communications back to the House of the Evening. He tries to get me to come upstairs with him, but I can't rest. Not until more is done. It is many hours before I head upstairs to sleep.

I wake up in the middle of the night at the cawing of a crow outside my window. The sound startles me enough that as soon as I open my eyes, I am sitting up. It takes a few minutes for me to realize how tragic that is. In the Middle Realm, home in Lisden, I would never have given the bird a second thought. Before Leo died, I wouldn't even have woken up. Now I worry; now that I'm up, I may never get back to sleep. I have a hard time sleeping now with the war going on. My mind races too much.

I try to listen to the sounds outside of my window, hoping that I'll hear something calming to help me sleep again. There's minimal cawing, breezes that I have to strain my ears to figure out if they are natural or magical, rustling of leaves. There are chirping crickets all vying to see who is the loudest. It all builds up in my ears, in my chest. It's driving me crazy. I need to sleep. I need to turn my brain off.

In a rush of emotion, I climb out of bed and slip outside of the room and into the hallway. Counting the doors as I pass by, I pray to the Lady that I've found the right one. I knock quietly, but firmly on the fifth door from mine. The few second wait is agonizing. As I move to knock again, the door opens inward, and a shirtless Faolan stands in the doorway. He blinks away tiredness before he registers that it's me standing there.

"Grace?" he says in a hushed low voice. "Are you alright?"

"Can't sleep," I say quickly and gruffly. "I want you to put me under."

"I'm sorry, you want what?"

"I want you to put me under. Do that darkness thing that you do that puts me to sleep. I can't... there's too many sounds," I finish lamely. Fortunately, Faolan only nods like he understands what I'm trying to say.

"Come on in." He holds the door open and steps aside against the wall.

I look at him quickly. "You want me to... come in?"

"You can't put someone to sleep with the darkness without supervision. It's just not a good practice. You do that to enemies, not people you care about. You can come in if you want to sleep."

With a hesitant breath, I summon my courage and walk into the room quickly. I make a beeline for the bed. The covers have been tossed onto the end of the bed haphazardly in his attempt to get to the door. I climb into bed without looking at him and straighten the covers over me. When I finally look up at him, he's looking at me with a tiny smile on his face. "What?" I ask awkwardly.

"Nothing." His smile turns into a light smirk. "Just not how I pictured the next time you ending up in my bed."

I blush furiously and pull the covers higher, turning onto my side to face the window. "Just do it. I'm tired." My words may be blunt, but inside, I'm dying for him to join me. I need the comfort more than the magic. Faolan chuckles deeply, and I feel him climbing into bed beside me. His bare chest is incredibly warm against my back as he comes over to rest against me. "Are you ready?"

"Yes," I repeat softly.

"Then sleep." His breath whispers in my ear as he reaches around to lightly run two fingers down from my forehead over my eyelids. The darkness creeps in as he gently touches me, and I sink down into a deep sleep.

Chapter Thirteen

Once Faolan and I have secured the situation in the House of the Earth, we return to the House of the Evening with a smaller portion of our troops. Most of the soldiers we took stay behind to hold position and help out the liberated people. When we arrive back at the palace, I decide to get the prophecy members together and finally have a closed door meeting about what to do next. I slip messages under people's doors to get them to come to the library late the following night. Now that the War Council is aware of the prophecy, I don't exactly have to be sneaking around like this. But I want to keep these meetings free from political interference if I can.

When the group assembles, I actually have to pull extra chairs and an extra table up to fit all of us around. It's strange now that all of the members of the prophecy are here. It almost feels like we should be able to dust our hands off, go find High Lord Carron, and end this thing. But finding everybody was only half of the problem at hand. Now we need to figure out what the heck we're supposed to do.

When everyone has sat down around the table, I go ahead and speak. "Alright, as you can tell, we're finally a complete group with the addition of Gideon and the return of Aiden. I would like to briefly go over what we know, who fulfills which roles, and then get down to analyzing what our role may be in this war. Is everyone cool with that?"

"I haven't even heard the whole thing yet," Gideon states firmly. "Actually, I haven't heard any of it yet. I staked my life and my men's life on this. I'd like to hear it."

"Fine, we'll do a recap. Luna, do you want to do the honors?"

With a bright beam, she folds her hands on the table and launches into the prophecy. "The Lady has foretold to us the Coven of Eight; That shall overturn impending war; To shift the balance of an impossible fate; Even an uneven score. The Bringer of Light burns the longest and the brightest, for his sacrifice for the greater good shall not be the lightest. The Soothsayer shall bring clarity to that which is blurry; But a sharp word of warning, as her words cannot be hurried. The Potioner will craft her potions like her spells. Intensely pure, combating those who rebel. The Deliverer shall bring more than sheer strength and power; he will bring in the last known ally to usher in the final hour."

Gideon studies her carefully as she continues. "The lost child shall be the Spinner, the strongest of the women's breed. Spinner of tales and spinner of winds, only she can commence the final deed. The Witch and the Conjurer, knights of the red; upon darkness and shadow will they always tread. But in the light, what the others won't expect: The Witch is to serve, the Conjurer to protect. The Enchantress shall unite the mages, and rewrite every inch of the realm's history pages. With untapped power that spans both mortal and Fae, she is the only one who will call night to an endless day. The Coven of Eight must protect the many, from mortal and magic, both and any. With a bond that's stronger than the fabric of magic, to override the destined to be powerful and tragic."

When she finishes her dramatic reading, Gideon leans back in his chair. "Well, that's a lot to deal with."

"Yeah, that's about where we've been at for the last several months." Cary sighs.

"And you haven't been able to get any more clarity?"

"No," Luna says. "I've been trying to channel the psychic energies and such, but there's nothing more that I'm getting. I think we're supposed to break it down and figure it out ourselves."

"Do you know who everyone is now?" Aiden asks.

"Yeah, we do. I'm the Enchantress, the leader of this little group. Faolan and Cary are the Conjurer and Witch, respectively. Aira is the Spinner. Gideon," I indicate him, "you are the Deliverer. Potioner is Kiara, Luna is the Soothsayer, obviously; and Aiden is the Bringer of Light."

"Wow." Aiden whistles. "Y'all figured out a lot while I was gone."

"So you know who everyone is," Gideon interrupts. "When do we start actually playing our roles?"

"I think your part has played out, Gideon, actually," Aira speaks up. "The prophecy mentions that the Deliverer brings the last ally that ushers in the final hour. Your arrival in the House of the Evening with your House was the catalyst that has set the prophecy into motion."

"You might be right, Aira," I agree. "I didn't think of it like that. But the prophecy is officially in play now."

"It's been centuries since a prophecy was heard," Kiara argues back. "The last time a prophecy was read, none of us were a twinkle in our ancestors' eyes. We don't really know anything."

"Which is why we try to figure it out," Aiden reassures her.

"How are you fine with all of this responsibility?" she asks him. "It scares the hell out of me. The prophecy tells you that you have to make a sacrifice for the greater good, a heavy one. Don't you think about what that might be and whether or not you're willing to?"

"Of course I do," Aiden answers quietly. It makes me uncomfortable, the way he looks at me as he answers. It's like his eyes won't leave mine. "But I'm prepared for it. Whatever needs to happen to make the realm and the people that I care about safe, that's what I'm gonna do.

And I've already done it, haven't I? I had to turn my back completely on my family, my House. My father and brother, if they survive the war, will most likely never speak to me again. Especially not after the stunt I pulled, stealing their soldiers. My House may never accept me as a titled Lord again. It's a complete lifestyle change. I miss my family dearly. But I couldn't condone what they were doing. No matter how much I love them."

"I don't even understand why you're nervous, Kiara." Cary scoffs. "Your line is about brewing potions. You've got those skills down pat; you don't need to worry about it."

"But what am I brewing potions for? Are they for healing or destroying? I don't… I just don't like when I don't know what I'm supposed to be doing." When Kiara finishes speaking, Aira rubs her back and talks to her in a low voice in her ear.

I try to draw attention away from them. "Luna, as the Soothsayer, you're keeping track of the prophecy, and you're supposed to bring… some sort of clarity at some point?"

"Maybe," she says. "We can hope so."

"And then Faolan and Cary," I continue, "you two are clearly meant to play major roles, I believe on the battlefront? Cary, as the Witch, there's some sort of role that you are meant to directly serve."

"I don't agree with that line at all," Cary interrupts me. "I wasn't built to serve. And that's not what a witch does! A witch is a badass bitch who doesn't give a shit who her magic takes out."

"Okay, we'll revisit that. Faolan, there's likely a protective role you are taking on. I'm not sure for who or what yet. Do you have ideas?"

"Yes." Faolan's eyes bear into mine. It is very purposeful, and there's no way others in the room don't notice.

"Okay…" I draw the word out. "Do you want to share?"

"The Conjurer, to me, is supposed to have a particular set of magical skills, specifically strong spell work, that are supposed to protect the assets of the group that pull this all together. My responsibilities change around depending on who's involved in a particular battle or incident. But when it boils down to it, Grace, I think the Conjurer's role is to protect those who push the prophecy forward. And usually, that's you."

"Why her?" Aiden interjects, staring him down.

"Simple. I'm sure all of you can agree that Grace is the person that ties us together. Not only does she lead us as the Enchantress of the prophecy, but every single one of us was brought into this fold by her. She found all of us, one way or another. She may have had help for a couple, but she was the one who convinced each of us. Whether or not you agree with me about my role, you have to agree that Grace has taken each of us off the path we were headed and brought us here to serve the realm in a way that none of us ever expected. And I, for one, am grateful for that." Faolan tilts his head and looks at me pointedly.

"I agree," Aira breaks the silence. "He's right. None of us end up here without the right pieces falling into place."

"That is how prophecies work," Gideon snarks lightly, but nods at me in begrudging approval.

"I couldn't ask for a better leader," Aiden says as he stares at me deeply, trying to one-up Faolan.

"That's debatable," Cary counters, but smiles. "But she's decent."

"Thank you all." I sigh. "I will try to be worthy of those words. I think that's all I have planned for today. There are a lot of things to do outside of this room tomorrow, and it's late. You all need sleep. Thank you for joining me tonight." With murmured good nights and quiet conversations, we exit the library and head to bed.

Chapter Fourteen

I could have slept for four days if I had been allowed to. Between the back-to-back battles and all the planning involved, I desperately need to just lie in bed and do nothing. Even twenty-four hours would be enough for me. Unfortunately, a loud knock wakes me from a dead sleep. *Someone had better be dying.* I stumble over to the door and fling it open to find the housekeeper. "Jeanine?" I ask groggily.

"I am so sorry to disturb you, High Lady. But someone needed to let you know. There's a party happening downstairs."

"A party?" I must have misheard her. *Why would anyone be throwing a party now? And how would they be throwing a party?*

"With the most recent victories, the nobles' spirits are high. They've thrown something together for themselves and the soldiers. Your staff was not involved, not until it had grown to a size requiring attendants. And as soon as I was made aware, I came to you."

I sigh and rub my eyes. "Thank you, Jeanine. I'll… I'll be down in a minute." Cursing my fellow heirs' existence, I throw on a nice blouse and pants and make my way downstairs. When I reach the ballroom, I'm taken aback. Jeanine wasn't wrong. There are people everywhere. Nobles are opening up bottles of champagne, and some of our highest generals and commanders are drinking and mingling among them, engaging in regular conversation. I walk into the room where Lord Tristan of the House of Water greets me with two glasses in hand. He offers one to me. "There you are, High Lady! Come join the festivities!"

"Am I missing something?" I ask with a soft laugh as I take the glass from him. "Did I plan something and forget to show up?"

"Not at all. Lord Jason snuck into your wine cellar and brought up some of this stuff, and we thought it might be appropriate to celebrate a little. Hope you don't mind."

"I'm sorry; he snuck into where?"

"Jason!" he calls over to the man in question. "Apologize to the High Lady!"

Jason pops up next to Tristan out of nowhere. "Sorry, Grace, the opportunity was just too good to pass up." He raises his glass to me. "Here's to your recent victories and many, many more under your leadership." I am pleasantly surprised to see that Jason gets much more jovial when intoxicated.

I chuckle at the ridiculousness of it all, but clink my glass to his and take a sip. I look around and quietly admire the scenery. The pale walls with the tiny gold flecks sparkle in the bright sunlight streaming in through the floor to ceiling windows. Blue curtains hang down in front of every architectural archway, both on this floor and on the second level where they hang from the ceiling. There's a smattering of light conversation happening around the room and some laid-back antics between the heirs. I love it. It's kind of strange to see these young adults act like teenagers again, but it makes sense. We all had to grow up really fast, some more than others. I wish I could capture this moment and break it out when my spirits are low again. I feel myself smiling brighter and brighter.

Somewhere toward the back of the room, music begins to play. The melodies of a flute, a fast fiddle, and a good bass echoes around the space. I follow it to the wall where I find a few soldiers entertaining the crowd. A few people begin to dance. The fiddle player spots me and moves to me, offering me the instrument. I shake my head quickly, not wanting to interrupt the playing. But Luna comes up behind me and pushes me forward. "Grace, you have to play for us!"

"Yes!" Aira echoes. "You have to play."

"Come on, Grace," I hear Aiden's voice somewhere toward the front of the room near the doors. "We want to hear you play."

The prophecy members in the room begin chanting my name while those who address me more formally clap along. I have to take the violin just to get them to stop. I quickly launch into a complementary melody to the other players. I can't help but lace it with a little psionic magic to heighten the happiness of those around me. Cheers ring out, and more people get into dancing. It's nothing like the formal dancing that you see at Solstice gatherings and the like. There's something so relaxed and free about it. I grin and play faster, picking up the tempo. The others follow suit, and together we create something beautiful to fill up the space.

When the song finishes, the people applaud loudly. I flush at the random cheers from my friends on the Council. Quickly passing off the violin to its owner, I duck down and push my way through the crowd toward the front of the room again. Aiden waits for me by the door. "Beautiful as always," he says, his eyes pointedly staring into mine. When I raise my eyebrow, he merely smiles. "The playing, of course."

"Uh-huh." I roll my eyes. "Don't push it."

As Aiden laughs, Faolan enters the room from a side door. When I turn to look at him. He waves me over with an insistent air. I nod to Aiden in a goodbye and quickly make my way over to him. "Faolan, I was hoping to find you again."

"Something's wrong." Faolan leans over and speaks to me in a rushed, quiet tone. "Something's not right, Grace."

"What is it?" I immediately set my drink down and move us into an out of the way corner.

"I'm not getting information out of my contacts in the House of Darkness regions. The influx of tips has slowed way down. I think my father's trying to cut them off there. The one thing that I did manage to get out is that my father is planning something big. We need to get prepared immediately."

"Immediately? Can't we celebrate for a bit first?"

"I don't—"

Boom

A quiet, but ominous noise through the glass catches my attention. The ground under my feet shakes ever so slightly. "Faolan…" I say cautiously as I look around the building.

Boom

"Faolan?"

"Grace, I don't—"

When the first blow hits the palace wall, the world speeds up. The windows shatter inward toward the celebration, and half of the ceiling falls off in patches. A few more blasting spells send everyone scattering to find cover. Someone screams to run. Everyone in the great hall files out through the doors or through holes in the walls that have broken apart. I lose Faolan as we are forced to dodge falling debris.

I run outside the doors and am immediately drawn to the sky.

We are under attack by the House of Darkness. And by the Lady, it is terrifying.

Dozens and dozens of demons swoop down from the sky and descend on the town down below us. The screams of the people echo toward the palace, and the fear in them grips my heart. A dozen winged Fae hover above me with blasting spells trained on the palace, causing as much damage as possible. Some of my soldiers have managed to take to the air and are attempting to stave them off.

But others still are pouring in, sending fireballs raining down around us.

Within an instant, I hit the air, wings shooting out of my back wildly as I zoom toward my town to help. I'm not as concerned about the palace itself, not more than my people, so I leave the others to handle it. Dodging enemies left and right, I shoot a desperate fire spell toward a Fae trying to break down a local home's roof. He tumbles off and lands in the street, motionless. I touch down on the opposite side of the road. The town is burning around me. There are a handful of soldiers who are defending the people valiantly, but the main armies haven't made it down here yet, preoccupied at the palace. Most of those trying to fend off the attackers are general citizens. Fathers, mothers, sons, daughters: absolutely everyone is out and trying to do something whether it's throwing spells or trying to get others to safety. I rush in to try and help.

And in the center of the chaos, striding down the middle of Main Street without a care in the world is High Lord Carron. He is a whirlwind in battle. He is a whirlwind of darkness and shadows. His magic moves like nothing I have ever seen. The darkness emanating from his hands snatch the light from everything. People stumble away blind and into the magic of others. Shadows grip around people's throats and seem to rip the life from them. It's dark magic, very… very dark magic. It never misses its target; it can only be deflected away. Fail to deflect, and you're down for the count. When I catch a glimpse of his eyes, I can see why there had been reports of increased magic. They glow with a vibrant white light from behind the eyeballs, while the iris color is jet black. Every once in a while, if you look closely enough, you can see magic pulsating underneath his skin. He almost shimmers. He locks eyes on me and breaks into a sudden toothy grin. You can practically see the glint of his teeth from here before I can breathe, his fingers twitch.

Suddenly, my arm is grabbed from behind, and I am flung against the side of a building as something black narrowly misses my head. When my eyes adjust, I see that it was one of the High Lord's deadly shadows. My head turns to the right as Faolan grips it carefully to make me look at him. "Are you okay?" he asks sternly.

I nod quickly. "I'm good. We should move." I make a move to take off running back toward the battle, but Faolan's arm traps me in place against the wall. "Faolan."

"Wait," he practically growls as he looks left and right as the chaos unfolds around us. Spells fly in front of us in a wide array of colors and sounds. All the while, High Lord Carron merely stalks closer and closer to our position. The world darkens around him with every step. Faolan sees an opening and steps out, leaving me against the wall and sending a nasty disintegration spell toward his father. The man dodges with ease and laughs loudly.

"Faolan!" High Lord Carron opens his arms wide as if preparing to greet his son with a hug. "I see you and Cary got a little lost on your way back home."

"Oh, you didn't notice?" Faolan sneers. "We didn't get lost. What reason could we possibly have to return home to you?"

"Oh, you poor boy. You really thought you could escape me? Come now, forget all of this nonsense and come home." The man's grin changes to something more sinister. "You won't get a better offer than the one I'm giving now."

"Let's see," Faolan replies. "Eternal darkness with a sociopath or not drowning in eternal darkness with the good guys. I think the choice is pretty clear, Dad."

"You never knew when to take your losses, son."

"Runs in the family."

Before I can blink, the two of them launch darkness spells at each other. I have to take a few steps to avoid being caught in the crossfire.

I begin to fire off my own fire spell at the High Lord, but someone suddenly grips by arm and yanks me backward out of the line of fire. I spin around to fight my attacker only to find Aiden. "Aiden? What the fuck are you doing?"

"Trying to pull you out of harm's way, you idiot. That man is a maniac, and I'm not going to let you take him on!"

"*Let me?* Faolan is out there by himself, and you can't stop me from going after him."

"Where the hell is your sense of self-preservation? Where did it go? I wasn't gone for that long, was I? And for him? What happened to you?"

"Shut up, Aiden, and get out of my Lady-damned way!" When I try to shove him out of the way, a sudden flash of white light blinds me. Aiden goes flying and hits a wall way behind us with a loud thud and drops to the ground. I can barely hear his pained groan. "Aiden!" I call out in worry. I start to run to him to try to help him up.

But suddenly, a loud blast goes off behind me, and I whip around to see Faolan's body go flying. My heart is ripped from my chest as it lands among the rubble of a building. There's a sickening crack when his head slams into a stone. I see his eyes roll back once before they slide closed. He doesn't move again. "Faolan!" I scream at the top of my lungs, turning all heads in the vicinity toward me, allies and enemies.

Something pulses out from me and ripples through the battle-ground, causing everyone to freeze at the raw sound and feeling. When I can't exhale anymore, I take a painful breath and spin toward his attacker.

To my horror, I see his own father watching his son's fallen body with what I can only describe as smug pride.

I see red, and without thinking, I charge toward the High Lord. Throwing a disintegration spell to his chest, my hands practically explode with flame as I aim a punch directly for his jaw. In a blink of an eye, he's behind me and gripping my hair tightly. He yanks my head back painfully. "You took him from me," he hisses in my ear.

"He ran to me," I spit back.

"And for that, I will make sure he dies." I wrench my body out of his grip and shove him away. He doesn't even stumble, smirking at me.

"If you touch him…" I breathe harshly.

"You'll what?" Carron interrupts. "You can't even protect yourself! How do you expect to keep anyone safe? No one is better than me now. There is no one more powerful than me."

"I beg to differ." With a thrust of my hands, I sink every ounce of strength I have left into a blasting spell. He deflects it with a flick of his hand and sends a shadow barrelling toward me. It lifts me up and yanks me forward. I struggle to stay on my feet as I fight not to yield to his magic. Not even my shields are enough to break the shadow's hold. Finally, I end up just under the High Lord's face.

Battle-weary, I look up into the High Lord's eyes, hoping to look unafraid. But it is impossible to keep my composure when I am face to face with the man up close. When he laughs darkly, I spit in his face. Instead of getting angrier, he only smiles. "It doesn't matter how much you play dress-up and pretend that you can lead. You will never be one of us. You're a pretty little mortal, but you don't have what it takes to be a queen."

I struggle in his grasp, but his hands only tighten around me. In my bones, I feel a rush of anger and fear that overtakes every crevice of my body. It boils up and up until it explodes from my mouth. I scream again, but this time, it's like my voice is completely separate from my body. When I cry out, it comes out in a much stronger, high-pitched wail. My magic reacts to the sound, and power explodes out of me very similarly to the incident at the duel of the heirs. Except this time, it uses many of my types all at once. Fire, wind, psionic, telekinesis, forcefield generation. It's raw power like the demons use, and it's terrifying.

The High Lord is blown away from me, throwing me to the ground. I barely keep my face from slamming into the dirt. I force myself to raise it, locking eyes with the man. For the first time since he invaded, I see a flash of fear on his face. But it's gone just as fast as it appeared. The High Lord tilts his head and chuckles lightly at me before raising his hand with a delicate air like he's about to address a crowd and he needs complete quiet. A slow trail of red and black smoke wisps out of his hand toward the sky. When it passes the rooftops of the buildings around us, a high-pitched ringing cries out. I am forced to cover my ears.

Then, to my shock, the entire population of demons circling overhead stops their attacks. A few stragglers exhibit just enough magic to knock those attacking them out of the sky. The demons group up and fly west away from the city. My eyes widen. "What?" I breathe quietly.

The High Lord seems to hear me and turns back to leer down at me. "I think I've made my point pretty clear, don't you?" Even with the arrogance in his voice, he wavers ever so slightly. With the words lingering in the air, he takes off into the air and follows the demons. All at once, his followers and soldiers follow behind, those who can fly carrying those who can't. It's a mass exodus.

I take to the sky suddenly, my body straining with aching muscles as I try to chase after the High Lord. But my magic is drained and with a few weak flaps, my wings give out. I barely make it a dozen feet up before tumbling back to the ground. Every inch of my body, inside and out, is in a deep-seated pain.

I couldn't protect them.

I couldn't protect any of them.

Chapter Fifteen

After the House of Darkness recedes from our House, it's like the aftermath of a tsunami. The damage is extensive. I don't even know where to look first. Buildings are crumbling down all around me. Complete houses lie broken in the street. People are running around me, narrowly missing stepping on my body. Many of them rush to dead loved ones lying in the street and wail at the sight. There's nowhere to turn, and it takes minutes before I'm able to safely roll away and get to my feet.

My first coherent thought is of Faolan. I whip around and fight through a group of rushing people to get to his prone body. I push away a large pile of debris furiously to uncover his frame. The man is practically unrecognizable under scrapes and a coating of thick dust. I pull him into my lap and try to brush the dust off of his face. "Faolan," I yell quietly as I try to rouse him. "Faolan, wake up. Faolan, please wake up. Come on, Faolan."

"Faolan!" A loud shout comes from behind me, and I whip around to find Cary racing toward me. When she reaches me, she practically yanks him out of my arms. "What the hell happened?"

"He took on the High Lord head-on," I answer frantically. "There's so much blood."

"What do you mean he took our father head-on?" Cary's arm lashes out and grabs me by the collar and yanks me toward her. "What did you see?!"

"Grace!" Gideon's voice shouts out over the top of the ringing in my ears. I turn my head to see him running toward me with two of his men at his side. "What the hell happened?"

"That's what I just asked," Cary snaps at him.

"Please, just get him to the hospital room," I plead to Gideon.

He doesn't hesitate in pulling Faolan from Cary and giving him to the soldiers. "Get him to the palace fast. Don't stop for anything." Before I can even blink, Cary is on her feet and chasing after them, after her brother. Gideon then pulls me to my feet. "Are you hurt?" I look down at myself, and I finally notice the blood all over me. I check my skin for injuries, but I'm not seeing anything that would produce that much blood. *Why is there so much blood?* "Grace." My head snaps back to Gideon, who is still expecting me to answer.

"Yes… I mean, no. I don't think so." I look around at the ruins and rubble around me. "Aiden… he's… he's hurt somewhere."

"Yeah, I found him. He's on his way back to the palace too. You need to get back there as well."

"No." I shake my head quickly, my ears still ringing. "I can't go back. The people… they need help."

"The armies will take care of what needs to be done here. You need to get back to the palace," he orders firmly.

"No… why would I—"

Gideon grips both of my shoulders firmly. "Grace. You need to listen to me. You do not look like a leader right now. You do not look like a leader right now, and within the hour, your people are going to want to see a leader. How you carry yourself, how you present yourself immediately after the attack will be the difference between whether or not your people will be able to push on from this. Do *not* fail your people now. Go get checked out. Go fix your face. Do whatever you have to do to get your shit together and get back out here to *lead*."

I want to be insulted, but I know that he's right. If I look anywhere remotely close to how I feel, I'm afraid I might be terrifying. And after a day like today, when everyone is going to need reassurance, I have to look strong. I nod quickly to him. "Is there a clear path to get back?"

"Take this back alleyway." Gideon gestures to a section of the street behind a couple of ruined buildings. "The path is mostly cleared."

"Thank you," I say sincerely before taking off down the alley. Gideon was right; there isn't too much debris, and no one is coming back here to find me when there's so much to see on the other side of this line of buildings. I want to run fast, but all I can manage is a half-spring, half-stumble toward the palace. Whenever I pass people, I try to act like nothing is wrong. The wind bites against my bruised and battered skin. Every step brings me closer to another form of destruction they wreaked on my House. But I don't stop moving forward even for a second until I reach the palace.

The courtyard is a sea of activity as soldiers flood out toward the town to give aid while the injured flow in where healers and servants are attending to them in a makeshift field hospital. The palace looks a mess. Entire sections have been blasted off, and others are crumbling. It looks like it's primarily special interest rooms like the gym and the music room, but it's devastating nonetheless. A few people try to stop me to talk, but I push past them without answering. I just know someone is going to pull me into something if I don't go see if Faolan and Aiden are alright.

My eyes immediately fall on Aiden in a bed nearest to the palace door. My chest floods with relief when I see him breathing and blinking groggily while holding his head. I rush over and touch his shoulder. "Aiden? By the Lady, Aiden."

"Hey," he groans. "You okay?"

"I should be asking you that, you moron," I hiss back at him. I whip around to the nurse. "Is he okay?"

"He was very lucky," she replies. "He's got a mild concussion, bruised ribs, and a sprained ankle. I've got some potions for him to take, and he needs plenty of rest."

"I need to get back out there and help," Aiden argues weakly.

"No, you need to stay here and rest," I counter. "That's an order."

"Fine," he groans.

I turn back to the nurse. "Is Faolan here?"

"No, he is not."

"What do you mean he's not? Gideon's men were supposed to bring him here."

"Well, he made it here, but his sister insisted he be taken to his own room to heal. She has some black market healers up there working on him."

The fury that rips through my body runs through me like a knife. *How dare Cary move him! What if it exacerbated his injuries?* I thank the nurse, squeeze Aiden's hand once, and then rush out of the room. As soon as I leave the hospital wing, I practically spring down the hallway toward Faolan's bedroom. I can't believe Cary would require him to be taken care of separately. I get that he has all of these cultivated specialists and I guess healers that he might want taking care of him more, but it was an emergency! I'm certain that the healers here could have handled his injuries just fine and faster than the people she had to call in from who knows where. *How did she even know who to contact and who would get here in a short amount of time?*

When I reach the room, I burst through the door to find a bustling group of healers and nurses running around. I have to fight my way through a sea of people to even get a glimpse of Faolan's bed. The sight of him horrifies me. His skin is abnormally pale, and his clothes are soaked through with blood. His hairline is stained with blood from an egregious head wound. Two healers attend to his physical injuries while another two have their hands glowing with some sort of orange healing magic. It's a color I haven't seen before, and I'm terrified it means that Faolan's injuries are extensive.

A blur of black hair hits me in the face as someone forcibly grabs my arms and tries to steer me back to the bedroom door. I fight against it hard before I realize it's Cary. "Cary! Stop, it's me!"

"You need to leave," she says firmly, still shoving me toward the door. My first instinct is to use magic to stop her. But I'm afraid if I throw a spell and it goes the wrong way, it could interfere with Faolan's care. I throw an elbow into Cary's gut, and her grunt of pain and slight loosening of her fingers give me just enough time to put some space in between us and get my hands up to fight her off again if necessary.

"I'm not going anywhere," I say firmly.

"Grace, you have no idea what is happening in here," she repeats. "You have to get out of here."

"The only reason that I don't know what is happening is because you pulled him from the hospital room and set him up in here to be healed by his black market contacts. You could have cost him valuable time!"

"He would have wanted to be healed by his own people. There are more factors involved than you realize."

"He would have told me."

"Don't flatter yourself," she sneers. "He doesn't tell you everything. He doesn't owe you all of his information. I told you to get out, now *get out.*"

"You're gonna have to throw me out." I look her directly in the eye. "You're gonna have to magically remove me from this room, and you better believe I will throw spells back. If you don't want to be knocked out of your brother's care, step back."

Cary's eyes flash with a deep fury, something I've never seen from her before. Her face changes multiple times before she finally settles on a stern resignation. "Fine. Just stay out of the way and keep your mouth shut." She storms away and returns to her brother's side, hitting me in the face with her hair once again. I tighten my jaw, but say nothing as I watch carefully from the other side of the bed.

The healers work together to flip him over onto his stomach. One rips the back of his shirt open. My eyes widen as I see not only fresh lines of blood across his back, but old scars as well. There are jagged lines, deep healed-over cuts, and thin white scratches that span the entire length of his back. I've never seen him with his shirt off before. I try not to let my jaw drop, but I can't help but let out a tiny gasp. Cary's head snaps back to me violently. She shoots me a warning glare. "Keep your mouth shut," she hisses. I swallow any further sounds and watch as the healers get to work on his marred skin. They heal lines piece by piece. Many of them are cut deep and take a lot of energy and concentration.

It's almost a half hour before they finish their task. Once completed, Cary thanks them quietly and shoos them away. Because of this, we become the only ones in the room. She sits on the edge of the bed and watches her brother silently. To be honest, I feel a little out of place. Behind the anger, Cary looks anxious for the first time. I don't want to make any sudden moves or say anything to startle her. Everyone deserves a moment to be vulnerable when they need to be.

"You had no right to be here," she finally says to me, unwilling to look up.

"Cary—"

"I didn't want to fight over his body. I would have thrown you out of the Lady-damned window, but you were willing to fight me just as hard. But you had absolutely no right to be here. This is not your place. He is not your family."

"I'm sorry," I reply sincerely.

She doesn't acknowledge my apology at all. We stand in silence for several minutes. I'm unsure whether I should stay or go. "I know you saw them," she says to me finally. "The scars."

"Yes," I answer cautiously. "I saw them."

"Are you going to ask me?"

"I'm not sure if I should."

She chuckles shortly. "Now you want to stop pushing?"

"I'm not sure I should be prying into this without… without his input."

"It's too late," she says. "He is very careful that no one sees those marks. Now that you've seen them, you have to be brought into the fold."

"I won't say anything that would—"

"It doesn't matter anymore," she repeats herself. "For the few people that have seen them, we have always formed an oath of silence. Faolan insists upon it. The healers are all under its compulsion. You're going to need to hear this so that when he wakes up, you can be brought into the fold."

"An oath?"

"Yes. One that kills if you ever try to reveal even a fraction of the secret."

"But what about you?"

"I'm family. We're as close as it gets. I didn't need to swear an oath. Now are you willing to swear when he wakes up, or do I have to find a way to kill you after the war is over?"

I gulp once, but nod. "Consider it done. Tell me what happened."

Cary sighs and holds one of Faolan's hands. She is silent a long time before speaking. "Our father is not a good man. He's never really been one. As twins, it was up to him to decide which child would be the heir. We were both trained, but Faolan… our father really wanted

Faolan to succeed. He spent more time with him than me by a long shot. Gave him special insights into the court, extra magic training, and personal coaching whenever possible." She breathes out harshly once. "But he was hard on him. Any sign of failure was met with force."

"Physical… or magical?" I ask carefully.

"Both," she answers bluntly. "Hands, canes, staffs, magical blows, whatever he could reach, really. The bastard delighted in pain. He wanted to break Faolan so he could remold him into another version of himself, one who could carry out the dream of realm domination. But Faolan wanted more for himself. He was always dark, but… he could never go fully dark. No matter how hard our father tried."

I look down at Faolan's unconscious face. A tiny bit of color has just started to return to his skin. He looks so young laying in that bed. "I can't believe I never noticed."

"Don't beat yourself up. No one notices unless he wants them to. Which he usually doesn't."

I sigh and reach down to run my hand through his soft hair. It has obviously been washed recently because it's still slightly damp to the touch. It pains me to think of how much blood they must have had to wash out of it. "I should have noticed," I repeat quietly.

"Look, don't think I don't see or hear about what's going on between you two," Cary says sternly.

"I don't know what you're talking about."

"Yes, you do. He may not have told me about anything directly, but I see the way he looks at you." Cary chuckles dryly. "My brother is not an easy man to love. But I have never seen him fall for somebody the way he's fallen for you. You can't lead him on."

"I'm not leading him on."

"Not yet. But you haven't committed yet either. Everyone knows Aiden's still trying to get you back."

"I told him no."

"You're right. You have. But you haven't been clear about Faolan either. What, are you just waiting for it all to magically work out? There's not an easy fix for your problem. But there's no reason you can't figure out which of these men you want to love."

"You don't understand… We're in the middle of a war here, I can't just—"

"I understand just fine," she interrupts. "But it's not fair to wait until the war is over to make up your mind. And if you hurt him unnecessarily because you're confused, I'm gonna take you out. Do you understand *that*?"

When Cary looks into my eyes with her piercing gaze, I understand a lot more than I'm able to tell her. So instead, I let my hand slip from Faolan's head. "Will you have someone come get me the second he's awake?"

"I will do that. After I speak to him." Her glare is a challenge to my authority. But I don't have the heart to argue with her. Not with what I know now. "Fine. Just have someone call for me. Please."

"Okay," she responds before turning her full attention back to her comatose sibling. She doesn't look up again, even when I leave the room. As I leave, a thousand feelings are running through my head. Everything feels disjointed. Love, fear, hatred of the High Lord who damaged his son so much, anxiety, sadness, and some of deep, deep despair at having almost lost Faolan that I can't even begin to put into words. I pray to the Lady over and over under my breath as I make my way back downstairs that he stays alive… and that he wakes up soon.

Chapter Sixteen

I give myself only a few moments after leaving Faolan's room to pull myself together. Regardless of how I feel inside, I have to face my people. I send one of my House of the Evening regiments down to the town to let everyone know that I will be returning there immediately to speak to the people and assess the state of things. Then I get in the bath to wash the stench of battle off of me.

It isn't lost on me that I'm washing off Aiden and Faolan's blood from my body. It isn't lost on me that I'm erasing any trace that I was traumatized today watching the people of my House fight and fall. It feels so wrong. I should be wearing those battle scars just as well as everyone else is out there. Making myself look perfect and untouched just feels… by the Lady, I can't pretend like nothing has happened to me. To the people that I care about.

When I came here to find answers about Leo, I never expected that I would end up in this position. I've already seen too much death and destruction in my life. Leo's death was just the catalyst. I thought I would never recover from it. He was my world. I didn't have a lot of friends; I didn't go to a formal school. It was always just me and him taking on life together. When he was gone, what was there left for me? My mother's mind broke. I know she loved me, but she wasn't in a position to give me what I needed. I met my father, but he died too in a war no one asked for. Now the bodies around me are dropping left and right, and there's nothing I can do about it.

My mind is numb when I climb out of the bath and stand in front of the mirror, letting the water roll off of me. I should be grabbing a towel, but I can barely move. I'm not really looking at anything. It's almost like I'm trying to see straight through the glass, past where my eyes can actually see the reflection. One side of my brain tries to coax me to step away, go get dressed, and make my way downstairs. *My people are waiting for me. I can't let them down.* But the other side? It's not even there. I'm not even here.

I don't know what ultimately dragged me out of the bathroom. Maybe it was because I was getting really cold standing there. Maybe it's because I knew that the longer I stayed here, the less likely it was that I would ever leave the room. But more likely, it's because my body eventually went into autopilot and started moving without instruction. I slip on a navy blue dress, the official mourning color of the House of the Evening, and finally exit the room.

When I reach the Great Hall, I ignore the many, many voices asking me questions, asking me what I'm going to do, asking me for my input, begging for help. My eyes lock on Gideon talking to some of his soldiers recovering in the courtyard hospital. Feet moving of their own accord, I make a beeline for him. When he spots me coming, he immediately pulls away from his men and walks to me. "High Lady Grace?"

"Take me to town," I say simply.

"I'll call for a driver," he replies.

"No." I shake my head violently. "You. Take me to town."

Gideon must have seen something concerning in my face because he doesn't hesitate to summon two of his own horses and lead me to them. I climb onto one of them and take the reins. Without another word, the two of us begin walking toward town.

About halfway there, I regain feeling in my hands. *Thank the Lady. I was starting to get worried about that.* I start running my thumbs lightly over the leather reins in my hands. Gideon sees me move and speaks to me. "Grace?"

"Yes?'

"Do you know what you're going to say?"

"Not yet." I lower my head and stare down at the back of the horse's head for a moment.

Gideon clears his throat. "That's okay. It'll come to you. Most of the time, you have to be in the middle of it to know what you want to say. Do you want some advice?"

"Whatever you have."

"Focus on the future. Speak on the horrible tragedy that has just occurred, but then focus on how the House will be rebuilt and triumph again."

The laugh that comes out of my mouth is bitter. "The future? That's the best you've got?"

Gideon doesn't react to my vitriol. "Yes. That's what you need."

"How am I supposed to talk about the future when there are bodies lying in the street? How am I supposed to talk about how *hopeful* I am that we can rebuild when I don't even know if we'll survive the week?"

His horse neighs as his rider whips him around to block me and my horse from moving any further forward. "You beat down every ounce of worry and regret that you feel in your soul right now and you find the deepest darkest part of you that wants to make the whole world burn to the ground for what it has done to you. You take it, and you yank it out of your chest, put it on your face, and you make sure your people see you as the powerful leader that is going to make sure those motherfuckers regret every last death they caused."

The intensity of his eyes shakes me from my stupor once and for all. That's not a man trying to give advice simply to help out another leader. That's a man who's seen some shit and is watching it play out again in real time. I gulp. "Is that what you did? When the demons invaded your House?"

Lowering his head, Gideon pulls his horse out of the way and continues on toward town. "Yes. It's what my father did. And my brother. And me, when it was my turn."

"All of you spoke to the townspeople?"

"Yes. We were sent to every sector of the city. We made our rounds, we paid our respects, and we spoke. The speeches weren't all the same, but they meant the same thing." He takes a breath. "I know, Grace, what it is like to watch everything that you stand for, everything that you are responsible for, suddenly burst into flames. Even if you had no way to stop it, you feel responsible. I feel responsible for not knowing that the House of Darkness was going to invade our land. I feel responsible for not fighting hard to prevent more death. It is what it is. You have to pack it up in a box and shelve it for another time, a time where there aren't people depending on you not breaking."

I hesitate before asking my next question. "Did you want to break?"

Gideon grants me a slight smile. "We all do, for one reason or another. But we don't. Sometimes even for the same reasons."

In that moment, everything I know about Gideon comes together. He hasn't been gruff and grim because he's got a particular problem with the way that I run things. He wants to take over because he feels like it's the best way to properly serve his people. He may not see me as strong, but that's not completely my fault. Or his, for that matter. He's looking for someone like himself to advocate for his people, and I just don't fit the bill. Do I agree? Maybe not. But do I understand? Yeah.

When we finally reach the town, we head right for the central square where people have gathered to find information about the condition of their homes and their loved ones in various neighborhoods around the city. When they see us coming, the noise and the franticness dies down considerably. A hushed silence falls over the crowd as we move through. All around me, I see the forlorn face of my people. There's fear, apprehension, confusion, pain. But underneath that, there's anger. Not in seeing me, but in seeing the destruction around us. I let that anger fuel me and give me strength as I dismount.

I reach a hand up to Gideon. "Thank you."

He raises an eyebrow in light confusion, but takes my hand to shake it. "What for?"

"For being the leader we needed today."

He doesn't say anything, but I know what I said got to him. He grips my hand a little tighter and shakes it once more firmly before letting go. I then turn to my people and walk to the center of them. I can sense everyone holding their breath, hanging on to the promise of what my words might be.

I have to do this right.

"We were attacked today," I start. "We were caught completely unaware through no fault of our own. Our intel was snatched from us by High Lord Carron, and he succeeded in making sure that we had no knowledge of an attack within our borders. They came in, hands blazing, and they won. Today… the enemy won." I gulp and blink away the emotion welling up in the corner of my eyes. "I want to take a moment of silence for the people we lost today."

The air grows stiller for a moment as the square seems to collectively stop shuffling, stop whispering. In those few seconds, I think of my father. I think of my brother. I wonder if they would be proud of me for what I'm trying to do here. I wonder if they would believe that I had the strength to carry us forward.

"Thank you," I say roughly. "Today… we lost the battle. But I swear by the Lady that this is not our last stand. We will repair. We will build back. We will regain our footing and then we will strike back with the might of five armies. The one thing that the House of Darkness and its allies cannot take from the House of the Evening is our spirit. Our thirst for life. Our desire to create something beautiful and put it out into the world for others to enjoy. No matter how hard they try, they can never strip us of that. There will be music in the streets again, and we will rejoice in victory once more."

I don't get a chance to say much more because the crowd takes my words to heart and begins to cheer. They chant my title and my name and pull me into their ranks, shaking my hand and kissing my hands as they kneel to me. I don't know if I did any of the fallen justice. But when I look to Gideon for reassurance, he bows his head to me in respect.

We will build back.

We will recover.

But High Lord Carron?

I'm coming for you, motherfucker.

Chapter Seventeen

Unfortunately, in understanding the scale of the destruction during the House of Darkness's attack, I learn that other places in the House of the Evening had been hit. Although none of them fell, the damage is extensive. I am informed that the safe house where my stepfamily is staying had been compromised. No one was injured, but the structural damage to the building is going to need extensive repairs. The general assigned to guarding them at the time speaks to me directly and advises me to bring them to the palace if I want to keep them the safest. That's how I end up standing in the Great Hall waiting for the former High Lady and my stepsiblings to return.

Is this what I want to be doing when there's so much work to be done and I don't trust two out of three of my guests to behave? No. Do I know I have to anyway? Begrudgingly, yes.

When the doors swing open, I straighten my shoulders and look into the eyes of the former High Lord's wife, Elise. She doesn't look much different from when she left with her children. She has the same steely eyes, haughty gaze, and straightened spine that made her such a visually powerful and stringent woman while in power. Although her attendants bow their heads to me as a sign of respect, she refuses to. Not that I'm surprised. We'll see if she tries to act as High Lady again while she's here.

Analise seems subdued, but she curtsies to me with a tiny smile.

I offer open arms to her, and she steps into them carefully. I ruffle her hair lightly as I hug her. By the Lady, I hate that she has had to deal with all of this at her age. Between her father's death, leaving her home, and then returning to it under dire circumstances, there's no way she's getting out of this without some sort of trauma. I get down to her level and make a silly face. She laughs and gives me a larger smile. I make a mental note to keep an eye out for her and her mental well-being. By contrast, Neil seems to have a bit of nervous energy. He doesn't bow to me, which is a normal interaction for him, but there's this tiny dip of his head that could indicate he's trying to show deference. His fingers twitch against his sides as he tries to look anywhere but me. *Strange.*

"Welcome back," I say warmly. As warmly as I can manage anyway.

"Thanks," Analise answers first.

"Darling," her mother addresses her, "why don't you run along to your bedroom and get your things arranged? I'll send the attendants up after you." The little girl complies, kissing her mother on the cheek and running upstairs. I watch her go before turning back to Lady Elise. She finally speaks to me, "So nice of you to bring us back to our own palace after we had been traumatized."

I should have anticipated this. "You know exactly why you left. You know that was the safest place for you. Look what happened here. It could have been so much worse for you. No one was anticipating an attack within the borders. No one had intel on it, not even the best of the best."

"The best of the best being the black market?" She leers at me like she's caught me in some sort of trap.

I simply smile back. "And the House of War's spies."

"Ah yes," she replies. "The people who notoriously have stayed alone for centuries didn't manage to help."

"They have been a major asset to our alliances and have aided in securing multiple victories for us. Haven't you been paying attention, Lady Elise? Things are moving quickly around here."

She straightens her shoulders. "I trust you'll stay out of our way."

"On the contrary, ma'am, I trust that *you* will stay out of *my* way." I level her with a stern gaze. She's the first to look away.

"Neil, come."

"Neil," I call to him as he and his mother turn to exit to their quarters. He stops and looks over his shoulder. "I would like to speak to you briefly."

He narrows his eyes in confusion, but breaks away and makes his way over to me. I lead him into the throne room and close the door behind us. "What do you want?" he forces out.

And now we're back to attitude. "Well, hello to you too," I mumble. "Isn't there any part of you that's happy to be back?"

"Come on. You only brought us back because it's not safe there anymore. You practically said so yourself."

"I wasn't going to ban you from the palace forever."

"But you could, couldn't you? If you wanted to. Because you're the High Lady now."

"I would never do that to you or your sister."

"Sure." Neil rolls his eyes.

"By the Lady, I'm trying to ask you to help out around here, you fucking asshole. I was trying to get you involved!"

Neil looks taken aback. "What did you want to speak to me about?" he asks me warily.

"I wanted to ask you if you would consider taking on a role in the war effort," I propose matter-of-factly.

"Really?" I have caught him by surprise. His stoic face has broken into something that more resembles abject confusion.

"Yes," I continue quietly. "I could use your help managing some of the day-to-day tasks. After the attack, there is more to do than ever.

You have the knowledge of this House and its people, as well as the interrelations of the other Houses that I only have bits and pieces of. I would like you to work on my behalf locally on the ground, welcoming lesser diplomats as they come through, assisting in coordinating the military efforts, and working with local officials in the towns and cities whenever necessary."

"Do you trust me to get the job done?" he asks bluntly.

I consider my words carefully before answering, "I trust that you will do what is best for your family and this House. That means that I trust that you won't do anything major to sabotage my efforts to bring the Upper Realm together and manage this House. If you were to do so, I promise you that it wouldn't end well for you."

He nods sharply. "I understand. You can count on me."

I raise an eyebrow. "May I ask why the change of pace?"

"I don't know what you mean."

"A few months ago, you hated my guts. Hell, up until a few minutes ago even. Now you're ready to play nice. What changed?"

"The attack. We've never had a breach within our walls, not for hundreds of years. This is an unprecedented situation. My family was shaken. I was shaken. If you need help making sure that never happens again and the people who instigated it are punished severely, I'll do whatever you say. Half-mortal or not."

"Good," I say bluntly. "Then get ready because I need you to get to work right away."

"Consider it done."

Nodding once, I wave a hand toward the steps. "Get yourself together and head to the barracks. Tell Gideon I sent you. He'll get you briefed."

"Will do." Neil takes off up the stairs in a jog.

Just as I'm rubbing my face with my hands in relief, an attendant taps me on the shoulder. "High Lady Grace?"

Resisting the urge to groan, I turn around. "Yes?"

"You requested for someone to tell you when Lord Faolan regains consciousness? He's awake now."

My heart surges forward in my chest. "Thank you," I mumble offhandedly as I race upstairs toward Faolan.

Chapter Eighteen

I can't even begin to describe the sheer relief that washed over me when I see Faolan sitting semi-propped up in bed. His eyes are hazy with exhaustion, and his lips seem permanently fixed in a pained grimace. His torso is completely wrapped with white bandages that disappear past where the blankets cover his waist. When he turns to look at me, he offers me a slight smile. "Is there something on my face?" His voice is hoarse, but full of mischievousness. I laugh tearily and rush over to his side to hug him tightly. He squeezes back lightly before wincing. I immediately step back. "Come on, Grace, don't carry on. I'm gonna be fine."

"You have no idea how it looked… how it sounded when you hit the wall."

"Grace, I'm fine. Look at me. I'll be back to normal in no time."

"Can I do something for you? Can I get you anything?"

"Grace." Faolan sighs in a bit of irritation. "You're gonna sit down, and you're going to stop worrying. Or Cary's gonna come in here and throw you out for stressing me out."

"Am I stressing you out?"

"No, doll. But she's gonna think so."

"Fair enough." I sit down next to him and squeeze his hand.

"How bad is the damage to the town?"

"You don't need to be worried about that right now."

"How bad is the damage?" he insists.

"It's pretty bad," I admit. "The demons focused a lot more on property damage than they did on taking out human life. But a lot of our citizens are dead. Mostly people who got caught up in the wrong place and the right time in a building that was invaded, or those that chose to fight. We still haven't found everybody in the list. Morale is gone. They just… took everything." I feel myself starting to tear up. "They came into my House and took… everything. They broke everything. I don't know how they got in, and then they just… he just left…"

"Alright, alright," Faolan says as he sits up, gripping my hand tighter. "We're gonna find a way to get back at him. You understand that, right? He doesn't survive this war, no matter what it takes."

Looking deep into his determined eyes, I nod with him. "No. He doesn't survive the war."

Faolan squeezes again before letting his hand in mine fall to the bed. The way it falls, it seems as though all of his strength has left him. I take some time now to slowly go over his injuries again. Many of his fresh ones, particularly the most severe, have healed really well for it having only been a few days. I imagine Cary instructed them to use blood magic. His older scars, though, remain. It fills me with such anger to see him in such pain. It gives me more when I see him trying to hide it from me. Every movement he makes is careful. He watches me every time he shifts to make sure I'm not looking when he winces or has a sharper intake of breath. Though truly, I have no idea why.

"You don't have to hide your pain, you know," I say quietly.

He chuckles, but looks sideways toward the door. "It's a habit, darling."

"I…" I debate whether or not to tell him what I know. On one hand, he could feel embarrassed or hurt and kick me out. I'm not ready to leave him right now. But on the other hand, I don't want to lie to him about what I know. He's always been honest with me about everything that matters. It wasn't Cary's secret to tell, but he should know that someone else knows. "Cary told me."

Faolan looks confused, but it doesn't take long for his jaw to tighten and his eyes to narrow. "Told you what?"

"About… your history. With your father."

Faolan swears loudly. "That conniving little—"

"Wait!" I quickly interrupt. "I know you're pissed at her, and you have every right to be, but I forced my way in and was pushing her about your care. I was worried that you had been sequestered away in here and that you weren't getting the medical care that you needed. I won't say anything to anyone. I promise." I talk so quickly, trying to assuage him, trying to calm him down before he reacts any more.

"You should never have known."

"I know. But I pushed her. She didn't take you to the hospital wing, and I didn't understand why. She tried to kick me out of the room. But I wouldn't leave. I threatened her. It's my fault."

Faolan is silent for a long time, staring down at the blankets. I wait, frozen, for his reaction. I don't want to make any sudden movements. I can practically see the wheels spinning in his head, and he is analyzing very carefully how to respond. I don't want to say anything until he does. Finally, he asks me quietly, "Did you say you threatened Cary?"

"I did."

To my surprise, he laughs lightly. "You threatened Cary. By the Lady, I wish I had been awake to see that."

"I could do it again if it would make you happy." That comment earns me an outright laugh.

But all too quickly, Faolan's smile fades away to a much more stoic face. "Darling, you have no idea what I have had to endure. It's not something I want others to see."

"I understand," I reply quickly. "But I'm asking you not to hide it from me."

"I don't like showing pain."

"Neither do I."

"It's not the same."

"Why?"

"Some people are not meant to reveal how broken their bones are."

"I don't believe that. I don't believe that at all."

"I'm not going to answer your questions, Grace."

It strikes me as odd that he keeps telling me that. I haven't questioned him at all so far. In fact, I've been resisting the urge to ask for some small detail. "I haven't asked any. And even if I did, you don't have to answer my questions, Faolan. Unless you want to."

I watch his throat bulge slightly as he gulps harshly. He looks uncomfortable. "Alright then," he says quietly. There's a long silence as Faolan slowly lets go of my hand. I wring my hands in my lap for a while before I realize that I need to busy myself with something.

"Can I get you a glass of water?" I blurt out. I move to get off the bed, but Faolan stops me.

"Grace..." he says, dragging out the end of my name. He sighs quietly. "Ask. Please."

I sit back down closer to him, taking his hand again. This time, he doesn't pull away. "Tell me what you want to... about your father."

"No, Grace, you have to ask me," he repeats firmly. "I can't... not without a question."

"When did your father start hurting you?" The question comes out of my mouth before I even have a chance to think it through.

Faolan stares at me for a while. His eyes are blank like he's looking past me, somewhere far, far into the past. "My earliest memory of my father is him spanking me violently. I was four years old. I was supposed to be home for dinner, but I wanted to run around outside on the castle grounds. I remember it being abnormally rough, and my ass was black and blue. My mother held me for a while afterwards, once he had stormed out. She said 'That's just how Daddy shows he's worried about you.'" He lets out a short laugh. "I don't think I believed her even then."

"That's awful," I respond quietly.

"It just got worse. You have to understand, it's all about negotiations with my father. Negotiate for attention, negotiate for favor, for information regarding the House. I was certainly his first pick for heir between Cary and I, but that doesn't mean that he was just going to hand me the title without many trials."

"What did he have you do?"

"On the surface, every task seemed like a normal activity for a potential heir to the throne to undergo. I was educated well in magic, diplomacy, and politics. I learned swordplay and archery under the hands of my father's guardsmen. But after every lesson, there would be a test. First, my tutors' test. Then my father's. Failing either of those would result in a beating. Every time. I learned very quickly not to make mistakes."

"Are all of your scars from those beatings?"

"Not all of them. But most of them. There aren't scars from every beating. He was usually very careful. Most magic can heal your basic punches and slaps. But there were a few times where he liked to use more… technical methods."

My heart is pounding in my chest. "What do you mean by that?" I ask. When Faolan closes his eyes painfully, I feel like I've made a terrible mistake. "Faolan, please, you don't have to—"

"One of the last ones," Faolan interrupts me. "One of the last beatings I had at sixteen. My father used magic that time. He immobilized me and then used his magic to generate intense heat in tiny balls of light. He burned me. In the tiniest of sections over and over again. Then the whip. He made sure no one was allowed to heal me. I spent three months hidden away from the public so that I could heal slowly on my own. At that point, I had just started building the black market. My recovery would have been longer if I hadn't had access to a few potions intermittently when Mahlin could get to the castle. I was in no shape to meet him in town, you see."

I never felt them start, but suddenly, I find tears pouring out of my eyes. I had no idea. On the surface, there's not a single person here outside of Cary who would have known. Every move that he has made since I have known him has been calculated, but suddenly, I see everything in a different light. The construction of the image is so careful. And now he's letting me into it.

What do I say? What must I say?

"Faolan, I…" I move in to try to hug him.

He stops me abruptly with both hands, gripping my shoulders with more strength than I have seen him display since I arrived in the room. "Do not feel sorry for me. Do not give me your pity right now, Grace. I don't want it. Just promise me that you will keep my secrets as I have kept yours."

I quickly cover both of his hands with mine. "Yes. No one will hear anything from me."

"I'm serious, Grace. I will do everything I have to in order to keep the world from knowing that part of my life. Or giving my father the satisfaction of knowing it got to me. Everything." He looks at me pointedly, and a wary feeling grows in my stomach. I wonder what everything means, though I am pretty sure that I know.

"I would want you to. To do whatever you have to," I clarify, "if I said anything. I'm willing to swear the blood oath. I want to."

Faolan has that far-away look in his eyes again, and I feel that I've said enough now. I slowly remove myself from his grasp and get to my feet. Faolan slowly slides one hand over mine again, holding it gently this time. "Look at me, Grace."

I look over and meet his gaze. His eyes are a little softer now. "Do not mistake my anger over you finding out to be anger at you. You… have nothing to fear from me."

"Nothing?"

"Nothing. I'd sooner die than lay a hand on you. Even if you betrayed me."

"I wouldn't."

"No." He smiles softly. "I don't suppose you would."

Leaning over the bed, I kiss his head once before heading toward the door, the echoes of what Faolan shared with me turning over and over in my head.

Chapter Nineteen

As I'm walking around the palace, I continue to mull things over. I can't believe he's been dealing with all of this for the majority of his life. Thank the Lady he built a network of people over his teenage years that could help him escape even a little bit from his father's influence. Thank the Lady Cary was able to relieve him from even a fraction of it. But she couldn't stop his father from doing all the rest of it, nor was it her responsibility to. The little fraction of emotion that I saw from her makes it seem like she feels responsible, though. I need to pay more attention to how she acts and talks around Faolan. I think he and she are a lot more like Leo and I were than I may have previously assumed.

I want to kill High Lord Carron more now than I did before. I don't think I've ever held this type of rage in my body before. First, he tried to have me killed in the duel of the heirs. Then, he started a war, took my father from me, tried to assassinate me, and invaded my House. And now… now I find out that he spent his entire children's lives trying to break their spirits. Faolan's spirits. My hands are vibrating with magical energy.

When I turn the corner, lost in my thoughts, I suddenly crash into a body. "Ow!"

"I am so sorry!" I immediately reply. I look up to find Aiden looking back at me, rubbing a sore spot on his forehead. "Aiden."

"Hey, stranger," he replies. "I've been looking for you. Didn't expect to run directly into you. Ow."

"Are you alright?"

"I'm fine. Just aggravating my injuries here."

I swear under my breath. "Let me see." I bat his hand away and hold his head in my hands. I feel around the front and back of his head for sore places. There's still some tenderness, but he's not bruised or bleeding. When I take a step back, there's a peculiar expression on Aiden's face. "Are you okay? Did I hurt you?"

"No… no. It's not that."

I chuckle. "Then what is it?"

"You haven't voluntarily touched me in ages."

Immediately, my mood shifts. "I see…" I trail off. *Is he always thinking about the relationship? Isn't he ever thinking about maybe trying to be friends?* "Well, what were you looking for me for?"

"You never came to see me in the field hospital."

"Yes, I did. Immediately after the battle, I came to see you."

"You were there for like two seconds. You were so worried about Faolan, I barely got a chance to speak to you."

"Oh, I'm sorry, do I need your permission to go check on my right hand, who by the way, was significantly more injured than you?"

"Of course not! But you didn't come back!"

I take a deep breath. Arguing with Aiden over semantics isn't helping my temper. I need to calm down before I do something I regret. "I apologize that I did not come back to visit you. Are you feeling better?"

Aiden seems satisfied with my answer. "My injuries are fine. Everything's healed up pretty well. A little soreness, but nothing I can't handle. I was hoping for a status report on what's happening in the House. I tried to get a hold of some of the nobles, but everyone's pretty much holed themselves up in their rooms."

I nod. "I think everyone's in mourning right now. I want to give them one more day before figuring out what our response is going to be."

"What is the response going to be?"

I shrug. "We have to talk over the rebuilding process. We need to get the word out to our ally Houses that we are down, but not out. We need to pick the next place to take a stand. I want to bring morale up for everyone. We can't let this defeat sit with us too long. And finally, we need to figure out what happened with intel and how to reestablish it."

Aiden scoffs. "Well, we know exactly what happened with intel, don't we?"

I furrow my eyebrows "What do you mean?"

"The twins. Obviously."

"No... absolutely not."

"It has to be one of them. Or both of them."

"No, it does not! Why would they help their father after all this time? Why would they help him while they are here and can be taken to task for it?"

"Because they have the perfect alibi! Why else would they stay and not immediately return with their father? They're staying here and gathering more information to send to him. There's no way Faolan conveniently lost contact with the black market the minute before this attack began. No way."

My ears are aching with the sound of my heart pounding in them. I bite my tongue as hard as I can, tasting blood, before finally replying, "Faolan and Cary have been working just as hard as the rest of us during this war. They have provided more aid and more insight than many of the folks on the Council. And both of them fought with every ounce of power at that battle. And they suffered."

Aiden chuckles. "Like he's really suffering up there. I bet after you leave, the two of them laugh about how they're pulling one over on all of us."

My control snaps.

I lunge at Aiden, slamming up back against the stone wall. His breath rushes out at once as I press my entire body into his stomach and chest, laying my arm over his throat. His eyes grow wide as I push down on his airway. "What the fuck?" he breathes.

"Faolan was upstairs for days in a coma!" I scream at him. "I saw him when the healers were doing their Lady-damned best to revive him after he lost so much blood, he was drowning in it. He just woke up, and there's no telling what state he will be in when he recovers. His sister has been up there for days protecting his prone body and barely keeping herself together. Could you do it, Aiden? Could you sit next to your brother's unconscious body, unsure of if he'll ever wake up again, and not move? How would you feel if someone broke his body to pieces?"

Aiden doesn't respond to me, and his eyes don't grow any smaller. I don't care. I don't stop yelling in his face. "Do you think his father injured him for an act? You think you could have woken him up? You think he was faking it? I should have let you try and watch Cary destroy you, you arrogant piece of shit. Maybe it's you! Maybe it's you who stopped the black market intel from reaching us in time. Maybe you let something slip to your father on your trip and he told High Lord Carron. Maybe it's all your fault."

"Grace," Aiden chokes out.

"How does it feel?" I hiss. "How does it feel to be accused of treason after everything you've done? How does it feel, Aiden?"

We stay frozen in this position, my arm still blocking off part of his airway. He breathes in short, shallow breaths. I've never seen him look so scared in his life, and that leaves the tiniest crack in my rage for regret to rush in. I immediately scramble backward. Aiden falls off the wall and bends over, coughing. Now it's my breathing that's coming out short.

What the hell did I just do?

"Grace…"

"You make sure no one is accusing him."

"Grace, the talk is already happening. I'm sorry I said that." Although shaky, his voice tries to calm me. "I'm sorry I accused him of it. I'm sorry. He's your right hand. You picked him. If you trust him, so do I."

Hands shaking, I wave my hands at him. "You make sure. You make sure…" Without waiting for a response, I flee the hall.

What the ever-loving hell did I just do?

Chapter Twenty

I don't have any time to think about what went down in the hallway between Aiden and I. I don't really have any time to think about the rage that I displayed. Concerning? Probably. Relevant? Not at the moment. I'll visit it again when I have time. If I have to. And maybe this outburst will keep Aiden from bothering me, at least for a little while. Buy me some time. All I need is a little more time.

While Faolan has not fully recovered yet, I have no choice but to keep moving forward with the war effort. It has been nearly three days since the attack, and I have to call a Council meeting. I told Faolan not to get out of bed, but he insisted on being present for this. Cary couldn't stop him either. Since he was planning on heading down to the conference room by himself, Cary and I begrudgingly help him downstairs. He won't sit in a chair and be moved, so the two of us each take an arm and move carefully through the halls and down the stairs. All in all, it takes us almost forty-five minutes to get ourselves to the meeting.

When I step into the room, I take stock of how everyone appears. Aiden looks to be in much better shape than the last time I saw him. His arm is mostly healed up, and the scratches and scrapes seem to be in decent shape. The long line above his left eyebrow, though, cuts deep into his face. It gives him a rugged appearance, making him seem much older. Lord Jason's leg is in a tight binding, having been broken in two places when a section of a palace wall collapsed on him during our escape. Lady Alena and Aurora both look bruised up as well, though they seem to be wearing quite a bit of powder to keep up appearances.

Cary and I help Faolan to his seat. Aiden stares at him as he lowers himself down. Faolan catches him and asks, "What are you looking at?"

"Just wondering how you are," he says cooly.

"I'm managing," Faolan replies shortly. "And your arm?"

"Managed," Aiden snarks back lightly.

"Good."

"Good."

The two of them stare at each other warily. I can't tell if they're regarding each other with begrudging respect or if they are biding their time to start something. I breathe out quickly. "Right." I quickly move to the head of the table. "Alright, everybody, we've got a lot to cover, so we need to get started. The attack on the House of the Evening was a devastating one, and I want a full report on what we know so far. How was the House of Darkness able to breach our defenses?"

"Sheer overwhelming force," Gideon responds immediately. "They brought a shit ton of demons to the front gates, and it was too much for my regiments and yours. The defenses fell quickly with almost total casualty. Three or four of my men survived, but all but one is in a coma."

"I want to speak with the man who survived as soon as this meeting is over," I tell him.

"I can arrange that."

"Good. I want to address next where our intel failed and how we plan on rebuilding those connections."

"I can speak to this," Faolan replies, leaning forward gingerly in his seat. "I was able to get some more information about that day."

"Why are you here?" Jason interrupts him.

"Why are any of us here?" he replies quickly. "There's a war going on, genius."

"No, why are you and your sister still here? The plan worked. You got what you wanted. We all know why the intel failed. There was never any to begin with. You helped your father get in!"

"Lord Jason, that may just be the stupidest thing you have ever said. And you've got a great track record."

Jason jumps to his feet, but shockingly, Aiden grips his arm and yanks him back. "Stop. Faolan has been a loyal member of the team for months now. His contacts have always provided solid information before. I may not have been here the whole time, but it's clear to me that without that information, we wouldn't be nearly as fortunate as we are right now. So cool it. I want to hear what he has to say." When he finishes talking, Aiden raises his eyes to me. He gives me a brief nod of solidarity. I grant him the first real smile that I have since he came home. I can tell that it shocks him.

Faolan looks shocked too by being defended by Aiden, but he eventually regains his voice. "My father found out that there are spies of ours within the borders of the House of Darkness. He couldn't prove who the specific people were, but he did know that he was being watched. He issued a lockdown order. Every single citizen there is being watched heavily. All communications, all movements. You even look at a guard the wrong way, and they're taking you in for questioning. And the House of Darkness interrogation methods are not pretty. I have received one message from within their borders yesterday that gave me this information, and it's not likely I'll receive more anytime soon. I have reached out, and the connections in the House of Fire, House of the Sun, and their held territories are still intact for now."

I sigh. "Thank you for the update, Faolan. Any objections to his intel?" I glare around the table, and no one responds. "Good. Moving on. We're looking at approximately sixty percent of the city having been destroyed. I don't have the final casualty numbers; people are still being pulled from the debris, alive. But at last count, there were over three hundred and fifty men, women… and children dead."

Around the room, there are multiple hushed sounds of pain and sorrow. "There are children who died?" Alena asks tearily.

I struggle to answer properly. "Yes. There are about fifteen."

"Oh, by the Lady," she breathes once before sobbing into her hands. It's hard for me to watch. I try to look anywhere else.

"Rebuilding efforts have already begun," I continue carefully. "We hope to have the main structures back in place in the next few weeks. Half of the team focuses on the structures needed to maintain positive defense for the city and the realm, like the front gates and the barracks. The other half focuses on family homes. As soon as the defenses are repaired, everyone there will focus on getting our families back to their lands while the smaller team completes the palace. We are lucky that it was not much, much worse." I take a small breath. "Unfortunately, we can't wait for these things to be complete before thinking about what comes next."

"I can't even imagine thinking about what comes next," Aira says. "Where would we even go from here?"

"We can't let the House of Darkness and their attack stop our progress," I declare. "We have to keep going, and we have to choose our next target. We need to liberate more territory. But we need to do it quickly and effectively before they have a chance to strike again."

"House of Water," Tristan shoots off right away.

"Of course you'd say that." Jason rolls his eyes. "It's your own land."

"The House of Water has been down and out *forever*," Tristan draws out. "It fell even before the House of Peace! It's been long enough. We need to go in and liberate them."

"Under that logic, the House of the Day should be next," Jason argues. "We were conquered directly after the House of the Earth."

"The House of the Day is across the Realm! We would have to cross so much territory to get there. So many places where we could be attacked."

"What about the House of Light?" Alena interjects. "Our home is important too."

Aurora adds, "And we have an avenue to reach our House, through the House of Peace that we just liberated. House of Light makes sense."

I listen to the conversation as it goes around the table as various people argue for different locations. Not everyone argues for their own House. Jason comes around to Tristan's point of view on the House of Water once he explains that bringing the navy back under the alliance's command would be incredibly beneficial. Aiden sides with both of them. Conversely, Faolan and Cary lean more toward the House of Light, citing the proximity to the House of Peace and the ability to move people quickly to supplement our main troops. After listening for a while, I hold up my hands to stop the debate. "Okay, let's take a minute. I think there's merit to two arguments here. The House of Water did fall shortly after the House of the Earth, and the addition of their navy to our forces would be incredibly impactful. On the other hand, we already have a running start at the House of Light through the House of Peace."

"Do you have an opinion, High Lady?" Aiden asks me in a surprisingly formal manner.

After a moment, I nod slowly. "I do. Faolan, Gideon." I indicate the two men at the table. "Do you think we have enough military force available for a two-war front?"

Gideon raises an eyebrow. "I'm sorry, are you suggesting that you want to take on the liberation of both the House of Water and the

House of Light simultaneously?"

"Do you think we have enough military force available?" I repeat myself, leveling my eyes at him.

"I mean… give me a second to calculate," he answers, shaking his head.

I look at Faolan who has the most curious smile on his face. "Faolan?"

"I am not positive how many people I could contribute to both locations, but I imagine I could get a modest group together for at least one. Supplies will be trickier, but should be more evenly spread between the two fronts. It's a ballsy move, but after we crunch some numbers, I think we may have a shot."

"I would need to call in more troops from the House of War. It would be a tough sell to my father," Gideon chimes in.

"But?" I raise my eyebrow.

Gideon shakes his head, but gives a grim smile. "But I could do it if the Council believes that it is the best call."

"Then what does the Council think?" I ask. "Let's put it to a vote."

After a quiet roundtable vote, the plan is confirmed. Gideon quickly leaves to make arrangements with his generals. We make another plan to meet to discuss more details the following day. When the meeting disperses, the group begins to rise from the table and head off in their separate directions. As Faolan rises, he stumbles and grips the table for support. I walk over to him quickly. "Hey, are you okay?" I ask.

"I'm fine," he grumbles to me. "Don't make a scene." He takes a couple of steps away from the table, but swings a hand back to grip the chair almost immediately after.

"Don't be stubborn then." I walk up to him and put his arm around my shoulders. "Let me help you back to your room, at least."

"Fine," Faolan grumbles. He leans against me though without

protest. *Guess he's a lot more tired than he's letting on.* We exit the conference room together. I catch Aiden giving me a side-eye glance. I ignore it. If he's going to get irritated about me doing a good deed, he can take his ass somewhere else. Turning down one of the hallways, we walk steadily toward the staircase.

Before we can reach the entryway, however, my stepmother descends to our hallway. When she sees me, she raises her head a little higher and strides on with a bit more purpose in her step. I imagine she doesn't want me to think she's being lazy now that she's in the palace. Not that I really care what she does as long as she stays out of my way. I'm intent on ignoring her presence whenever I can.

But Faolan tenses up next to me when he sees Elise. He stops me by stepping one of his legs in front of mine. I nearly trip over it. "Ow! What was that for?"

"What is she doing here?" he growls.

"Elise? There was an issue with the safe house when the House of Darkness attacked. It was safer to bring the stepfamily here. Is there something wrong?"

Before I get an answer though, Elise reaches us and attempts to pass. Faolan suddenly throws out a hand and grips her arm tightly. My eyes widen. I've never seen him manhandle someone in a position of authority. "Lord Faolan! What do you think you're doing?" she shouts shrilly. "Unhand me at once!"

"You're lucky all I'm doing is grabbing your arm, Elise," he says dangerously. "I suggest you pack your things and get out of this castle before I decide you deserve something more."

"Faolan, what are you doing?" I begin tugging on him, trying to pull him away from my stepmother. Her eyes are growing more and more frantic as she struggles under his tight grip.

"Do you want to tell her," he hisses, "or should I?"

"I don't know what you're talking about!" she shouts. "Let go of me!"

"You know *exactly* what I'm talking about!" Faolan finally snaps as he throws her arm aside. He turns to me with furious eyes. "Grace, I don't want you alone with her under any circumstances. She hired an assassin to try to kill you."

Chapter Twenty-One

I have to admit, my first thought upon hearing Faolan's confession is *which assassin?* Then I realize how sad it is that I have undergone multiple assassination attempts already at my age. But honestly, it doesn't matter which assassination attempt he was referring to; it only matters that Elise doesn't look shocked at the accusation. She looks guilty. Her first reaction wasn't to immediately proclaim her innocence. Instead, her eyes shift sideways and she scoffs. "You don't know what you're talking about," she says with a hint of a tremble in her usually steady voice. "I really must be getting on my way."

My eyes narrow. "No," I declare simply while gripping her other arm. "No, we're gonna talk." With Faolan on one arm and Elise struggling to get out of my other, I pull them both into a nearby guest room. I close the door behind us and stand between it and Elise, blocking her escape. Faolan stumbles lightly along the wall into a nearby chair.

"I don't know what you think you are doing, Lady Grace, but—"

"That's High Lady Grace, Lady Elise," I correct firmly. "And I think you and I have a lot to talk about." I look at Faolan. "Care to explain what you know?"

"My father and I were on a diplomatic mission to the House of Fire right before the Spring Solstice. He was laying the groundwork for the House of Fire attack on the House of the Earth. While the

High Lords were engaged in business, I went about making my own connections with people on site to strengthen the black market. That's when I caught wind of an assassination request issued for you, Grace. A rather well thought out plot with a man pretending to be one of the House of the Evening's personal guards sneaking in at night and murdering you while you were in transit. The most interesting piece of information regarding that plot was that it came from the top of the House of the Evening food chain. And seeing as your father adored you, there's only one person it could be."

"You," I breathe quietly as I stare at Elise. For the first time since I arrived, I see genuine fear in her eyes. She doesn't know what I'll do to her now that I've found out. And I can see why as the intense resentment rises up in my chest. I see her in a new light now. She's not just irritating and judgmental, she's lethal. She tried to kill me. I knew she wanted me dead, but I thought that was just to get me out of the way for her precious son to become High Lord. I didn't think she would actually try to make it happen.

"Now at the time, we were enemies, so I didn't think much of it," Faolan continues, watching me carefully like he's afraid I'm going to blame him for not informing me. Of course, it's not ideal, but we've come a long way from that. "But seeing her back in the palace reminded me. You don't want her anywhere near you, Grace. She was willing to take you out to put her kid on the throne."

"It was his throne to begin with," Elise blurts out.

I can't help but chuckle. "I knew you hated me, hated my existence. Didn't think you'd try to kill me though. My mistake."

"I told you a long time ago that you do not belong here. Everyone in the Realm agrees with me."

"Not anymore." I smile at her brightly. "I'm leading the House of the Evening against the Darkness alliance. We're making progress. The people look to me now."

"They look to you because they have to!" my stepmother shouts at me. "If we weren't under attack, they would hate you as much as I do. Just because you're a decent military strategist does not mean you are a good ruler. Or the *right* ruler."

"Regardless of what you or anyone else thinks about me, the whole reason that I am installed in this position in the first place is that the law states that the first-born heir gets to rule the House. The heirship is *mine*."

"Hence the assassin, dear." Elise laughs harshly. "No need to rewrite Fae law when your death would solve the line of succession perfectly."

"So you freely admit that you hired a man to kill me."

"Yes, I admit it. You were never supposed to be here. You should never have come here. Lowly mortal thinking she could just waltz in and take over everything that I built!"

"*You* built? What the hell have you built?"

"I ensured a future for me and my family!" Elise shouts and moves closer to me, getting up in my face. Faolan starts to get up to come to my aid, but I wave him off with a hand. He looks at me with concern, but stands down. "You have no idea what I have sacrificed to get here," Elise hisses at me.

"What did you sacrifice?"

"I came from a middle-class family with no hope of upward mobility. I had a high education, but no connections to get where I wanted to go. My magic was powerful, but not enough to catch the eye of someone who could take me to the top. When the High Lord's son came of age, I entered myself into the contest for the future heir's bride. I did everything I could to knock the others out of the competition. I sabotaged, I spread rumors, I stole, I fought my way to the top until the High Lord finally chose me to be his son's bride."

"So you never loved my father?" I snap. "Is that what you're telling me? He was a means to an end for you?"

Elise slaps me across the face in a quick motion. I stumble backward, and Faolan tries to force himself to his feet to pull her back. She pushes him back and screams at me, "*How dare you! How dare you* tell me I didn't love him! We grew up together. He was one of my dearest friends. We wanted to be together. He knew exactly what I needed, and he allowed me to flourish. His death ripped me apart, so don't you dare… don't you dare tell me I did not love him. I let him bring you into this palace."

"You didn't let him do anything. You fought it every step of the way." I breathe heavily.

"What was I supposed to do? My son, my Neil, who had been brought up to rise to the heirship and rule over the House someday, was passed over for some half-breed who never should have been born. My boy, my son, suddenly saw his options disappear. I wasn't going to let my son live a life in the shadows. So I hired someone to take you out of the equation. But it didn't work. You had been trained just enough to ward him off, and the other guards came too damn fast. You should have died that day, and none of us would be in this mess!"

While she shouts at me, I feel an odd sense of despair well up inside of me. There's nothing I can ever do to sway this woman. And what if she's right about the people of the House of the Evening? What if they are only loyal during the war, the whole 'any captain in a storm' situation? The truth is I don't know what they will think of me when the realm is quiet again.

I have to think of what to do with her. I can't let this go unanswered, especially with such a blatant admission of guilt. I don't feel comfortable being anywhere near her knowing that she tried to have me killed. At the same time, the House doesn't need any more turmoil. Kicking out my father's wife, the former High Lady, putting her on trial: it would almost certainly lower morale. I can't have that after such a huge blow dealt by the House of Darkness.

"Grace." Faolan interrupts my thoughts. I look up to find him standing between the former High Lady and me. "She's admitted to treason. What do you want to do?"

After a few minutes of thought, I shake my head. "Let her go."

"What?" Faolan and Elise both say simultaneously before glaring at each other.

"Let her go." I walk around Faolan to face Elise myself. "Me letting you go doesn't mean you're not going to pay for what you did. From now on, your access to this palace will be restricted. You will be confined to your room and your children's rooms. When you leave to go anywhere, you will be escorted by two armed guards of my choosing." She starts to smile haughtily, but I shut that down fast. "Don't think you can get away with corrupting them; I'll be assigning some of Faolan's men." Her face immediately falls. "You will not be making any more movements in this castle without me knowing about it. Your every move will be tracked. Your correspondence will be read. When this war is over, then we will discuss what happens to you next."

"You can't possibly think you have the authority to do this," she scolds.

I only smile. "You can't possibly think that as High Lady, I don't." Striding over to the door, I hold it open for her. "Go get whatever it is you were looking for a moment ago because it will be your last time walking on your own for a while." With an uncomfortable grimace, she strides out the door, albeit with a little less spring in her step.

I shut the door tightly and lean back against the wall, rubbing my hands over my face. "By the Lady," I mumble.

"What was that? Why is she not in the dungeon right now?" Faolan snaps. "You do realize she tried to kill you, right? Every moment that she is in this palace, you are in danger."

"I'm in danger whether I'm in this palace or outside of it, Faolan. At this point, it's just a fact of life. At least here, I can keep her under my nose."

"But—"

"But nothing, Faolan. After the attack, we can't afford to lose morale now."

He sighs. "I know that. I just don't like it."

"I'll be fine. We'll make it through."

"Well, I'll be keeping a closer eye on you."

I chuckle. "Uh-huh. Good luck with that. Let's get you upstairs." Faolan groans as he throws an arm over my shoulders again, and we continue making our way to the hospital room.

Chapter Twenty-Two

Sorting out the details of the two-pronged attack runs smoothly, for the most part. Hoping to spread the expertise around a bit, Faolan offers to take himself, Cary, and Gideon to the House of Light while I take a group to the House of Water. Aiden quickly volunteers to join me there, and I accept. I don't know if that's opening myself up to something with him, but it's a risk I need to take. Particularly after the confrontation in the hallway. I'm afraid he'll tell somebody.

I don't know how I feel about Faolan not being by my side for this one. We haven't really fought in completely separate locations before. After his most recent major injury, I just don't know if I want to be that far away from him. What if his father shows up again? He can't go round two with him so soon after the first time. *Come on, Grace. He can handle himself. Cary and Gideon are both going with him. The three of them together are a mighty force to be reckoned with.*

All of these thoughts weigh heavy on my mind a couple weeks later as I run upstairs to search for Faolan. I need to check on him before he leaves. Maybe I can persuade him to stay home or even come to the House of Water instead. I don't think he'd actually take my advice, but it's worth a try anyway. When I reach his bedroom, I knock on the door. It swings open at the touch of my knuckles. I step inside and shut it behind me. "Faolan?"

"He's not here." Cary startles me as she comes around the corner from his closet. "I was looking for him too."

"Oh. You haven't found him?"

"I assume he's getting his affairs in order for the trip to the House of Light."

"That's what I wanted to talk to him about."

"Oh really?" Cary sits on the edge of the bed and watches me coolly. "What were you planning on saying?"

"Hoping to convince him not to put the strain on himself."

Cary chuckles. "Yeah, good luck with that. He's doing a lot better. He's moving around like he used to. His mind is sharp. He's even been out practicing his battle spells in the arena."

"He has? I didn't know that."

"You've been busy," she replies simply. "But no, he's doing much better. Do you think I would allow him to go if he wasn't?"

"You have a point there. So I'm supposed to trust your judgment and not bother him?"

"It would be nice if you did."

I nod slowly to myself. She has a point. Before I really knew what their relationship was like, I would have been skeptical. But she's more than proven that she will take him out of the equation in a heartbeat if she thought it was the best choice for him. "Alright then. You protect him out there, okay? You watch his back."

"I always do."

"Good." I turn to leave the room.

"Can I talk to you about the prophecy?"

Surprised, I spin around to look at her. "Absolutely. What is it?"

"I'm highly uncomfortable with my supposed position in the prophecy. And I want to know: how set in stone is it all?"

"Set in stone?"

"Yeah, are the words ironclad? Do we have any say at all about our role? The wording makes me uncomfortable, and I'm wondering if it has to… be that wording if you know what I mean."

"I'm sorry, this really isn't something I know a lot about. Your question is more Luna's department."

"I don't want to talk to Luna. I want to talk to you. You were there at the initial reading of the prophecy. You have to know something."

"I'm afraid the prophecy is as it is. There really isn't a way to change it." Cary doesn't respond, but her jaw tightens. "What's bothering you about it?"

Cary punches her fists down into Faolan's mattress. "I don't like the part about serving. The whole 'The Witch is to serve' bit. It rubs me the wrong way."

"Why? It seems like it should be one of the easier roles to fulfill."

"Because I don't do subservience."

"Subservience? That's not…"

"I have never heard of service in any other form than submitting yourself to someone else's will or for someone else's benefit," Cary interrupts. "And I'm not good at putting other people first."

"I don't see what this has to do with—"

"I don't want to screw it up!" she shouts at me. "I don't want to do something wrong that's going to screw it up for everyone. I'm not… nice. I don't serve. I go off by myself, and I just… exist. Maybe I lead. I've led here before. Serve? What if I screw it up?"

"Hey, hey, take a second," I try to calm her down. Her entire body is wound up so tight, it honestly seems like she may snap at any moment. I never thought about Cary as being so worried before. I thought she was one of those girls who didn't give a damn about what anyone thought of her. But she's in front of me completely coming apart at the seams over… not wanting to disappoint anyone. Over something we have minimal control over. Coupled with her reaction to Faolan's injuries, I'm starting to see her heart.

"First of all, you can't singlehandedly screw up the prophecy," I answer her. "The outcome may not be certain, but the elements are all set in stone. One way or another, your piece will come to pass. You can't screw up something that you were built to do. It's just not possible." I push both of my hands into my hair and grip onto my scalp. "Trust me, I've been running from this. I've been trying. It's not working. So trust me, you cannot fail, at least not at fulfilling your role."

"Okay…" she responds slowly.

"Secondly, from what I understand, you haven't had the opportunities in your House to serve the people of the House of Darkness like Faolan did. They weren't offered to you. Maybe service isn't about some great act of good. Maybe it's about finally getting a chance to serve your House, your people, your homeland and give them somebody to look to. All they've got right now is your father. Maybe you can be something for them. Maybe when you fight, you show people that the House of Darkness isn't all evil. Bad, yes. Badass, yes. But not evil."

Cary seems to contemplate my words. "So you think it's going to be fine?"

I laugh lightly. "As fine as any of this is going to be."

Her head tilts slightly to the side as she stares at me. Soon enough, a real smile spreads across her face. "You know, you're not as bad as I thought. At least you've got a brain."

"Ha ha, very funny. Are you good?"

"I'm good."

"Good. Can we go look for Faolan?"

"Absolutely." Cary jumps off the bed, and the two of us exit the room to search for Faolan.

Chapter Twenty-Three

It takes four weeks total for us to build back enough of our manpower and firepower to even consider taking on a two-front war. I don't think I slept more than five hours a day the entire time. The first task was to build back our people. I set every available healer, potioner, and plant mage on replenishing our potion supply. It takes a while as every potion pretty much gets used up the second it's created to heal the wounded. One benefit to magic is that healing injuries doesn't take as long as the mortal way. But many of them require extensive spell work and multiple days of treatment. I stopped in everyday to check on my soldiers' progress. The healers told me my visits meant something to the people, so I made sure never to forget it.

The rebuilding process for Silvervale is happening slowly. We've made little progress since we decided on the two-front plan as much of the building team has been focusing on repairing and constructing ships. I diverted the smaller team working on the palace to continue repairing residential and commercial areas. This is yet another project that I have to oversee. I try to pass by the bulk of the work every other day to show my face. Unfortunately, they won't let me get my hands dirty as much as I want to. It's not proper for a High Lady to help rebuild the town, apparently.

Several days before I was supposed to leave for battle, I had an unexpected visit from Neil. He's been a decent help so far with the work I had assigned to him. He had completed several excursions to some of the outer towns that needed assistance after the invasion. When he came to me, he looked haunted by what he had seen there. He begged me to let him join in the next military expedition. "I can't stand by and do nothing," he pleaded. Against my better judgment, I gave in and gave him full permission to join whichever group he wanted. He chose mine.

All too soon, Aiden, Neil, and I board the head naval ship to travel to the House of Water. Being stuck on another boat with Aiden for an extended period of time with no way to escape interaction doesn't exactly sound like a holiday right now. I know I promised myself that I would at least give him a chance, but I thought maybe I'd have had a little time to talk to him before we left to prepare him and myself. With all my responsibilities and the emergencies and the necessities, it just never happened. I don't know if I can handle him right now. But the House of Water needs our help, and if it has to be Aiden, then it has to be Aiden. The rest of the nobles see us off at the House of the Evening's main dock. At the last minute, yet again, Talon runs up after us. I almost protest seeing as we haven't even discussed it yet, but I welcome a distraction who could engage with Aiden and Neil on my behalf.

The generals pass off the Captain's Quarters to me. The larger room has a slightly higher ceiling, and I don't feel the swaying as much from here. It's a decent place to hide out in. As we make the journey toward our destination, I stay in my room as much as possible. I only let the soldiers who are trying to coordinate battle plans in as visitors. I keep Aiden shut out, though he knocks multiple times. Eventually, he must have been able to tell I wasn't ready to talk as the knocks stopped coming.

Unlike the previous battles, there's no need to conceal our approach. We need full light to execute this mission, and when we come upon the House of Water, there will be nowhere to hide regardless out on the open ocean. At sunrise, I move up topside to prepare for an impending attack. Aiden is already waiting for me. He stares at me for a moment before turning toward the ocean. *Good. No need for words yet.*

As we move the ship through the final turn, we come upon the House of Water. None of my travels through my time in the Upper Realm ever took me this direction, so I've never seen it before. The coast is beautiful, the way the pure white sand meets the ocean. The coastal town is made up of all kinds of white stone architecture with interesting curved shapes that match the shapes of the landscape. I see the winding cobblestone roads that move through the buildings, merging together in some sort of square. A tall white castle with rust colored towers sits upon a rocky hill, flying the House of Fire's flag, souring the whole view a bit. I'd like to see the House of Water's flag back up on the parapet.

"Get ready," Aiden finally says to me as he meets me up by the railing. "The House of Fire is going to see us approaching very soon. And there's likely to…."

A sudden boom echoes from across the water. A cannon.

"Attack," Aiden finishes. "Get into the air."

Without hesitation, the two of us take to the sky. Within seconds, a cannonball hits the side of the ship. It rips through the first several layers of building material, but keeps from knocking out the main core. Unfortunately, once one hits, a slew of others follow. Several of the soldiers on board use animation magic to try to suspend them in the air before they destroy the ship. Aiden and I wait only moments before we spot more winged Fae like us speeding toward us.

"Soldiers!" I shout. "To the skies!"

One after another, the troops who can launch themselves into the sky. Across the water, the enemy's soldiers do the same. We are quite the sight, winged war machines colliding into one another. When we meet, there's no time to take a breath as magic starts flying past us. Although most battles are like this on the ground, somehow I feel more precarious in the air. It's harder to dodge the spells with these big wings on my back. I'm inhibited by them even though I feel as light as a cloud. Using my shields is more important than ever.

Aiden seems to arrive at the same conclusion because he soon takes a position at my back, pressing our wings to each other. By fighting back to back, we can assure each other's wings are protected from these two sides. We both fight with fire to start in an attempt to match up with the House of Fire's soldiers. Then I switch off to manipulating the wind to knock the winged Fae from the sky. Several tumble down toward the sea and crash into the ocean. Others fall far, but manage to catch themselves over the ship where the unwinged, led by Neil, fight like all hell to preserve our fleet. All around, cannons go off with booming blasts that seem to shake the air itself.

Aiden's and my shields overlap and act as one as we fly closer together. The closeness feels familiar like when we fought against the heirs all those months ago. I can tell he's feeling it too because he keeps leaning back just enough to keep bumping against my skin. It's a small reminder that we're both alive and we're both still fighting. I appreciate the check-in, more than I think I'll be able to say.

We continue to fight for our lives when horrific shouts come from below us on our ship. With one quick look over our shoulders at each other, we spiral down to the boat. As soon as my feet plant down, I immediately have to duck to avoid two spinning swords aimed directly at my head. It takes several moments to realize that they're being continuously wielded by a man almost twice my size with clear Weapons Amplification magic.

That's about the time that I notice that the ship's deck is littered in limbs and fallen soldiers. My eyes land on Talon, missing an arm, who lies over by the stairs to the lower decks. His eyes are glassy, but his chest still moves up and down.

I see red.

Thrusting my hands into the air, I catch the next round of swords that the giant man throws, gripping the handles tightly. *He thinks he knows weapons magic? I'll show you weapons magic.* I lunge at him and attack with quick jabbing motions. He takes two swords and meets me with the same amount of ire. We circle each other in a delicate dance, jabbing forward and parrying back. I slash at every inch of skin I can find. I'm so pissed, I don't even remember to keep my full shield up. But I appear to be fully protected regardless, and I realize that Aiden is maintaining the protection while at Talon's side. It gives me a boost of confidence, and I stab the intruder directly in the chest, bringing him to the deck.

A loud cheer erupts from my soldiers who are still with me. I breathe heavily as I look up to watch the enemy turning tail and fleeing back to the House of Water to regroup. My soldiers return to me from the places that they have been scattered. As the shock sets in and our medics quickly get to healing people on the deck, I look around at the carnage on my own ship. We've won here, but at what cost?

Chapter Twenty-Four

Immediately following the battle, our ships encircle the House of Water, intent on beginning a siege. By blocking off their supply lines, we should be able to starve the military out and decrease their available weaponry. No one goes in, no one goes out without our say-so. Not until the House of Fire yields to us. I hope it won't take too long to break them because the people of the House of Water will suffer from this as well. Our intel is unclear at the moment as to whether or not the House of Fire plans to wait us out or attack. Either way, we will be ready.

The injured men, including Talon, are whisked down to the ship's sick bay. Many of them need extensive magical care to prevent further damage to their body after losing limbs. Emergency surgeries go on all night. First thing in the morning, I rush down to see Talon. After yesterday's battle, I need to know if he's going to make a full recovery. He looks so tired, lying in that bed. The healers have worked tirelessly, and the stump where his arm used to be looks clean and healthy. At the very least, he shouldn't be in any danger of infection. "Talon," I greet him quietly.

"High Lady," he replies in a hoarse voice.

"Hey, none of that. You know I prefer to be called Grace."

"Didn't really seem right to be informal when the High Lady comes to my wounded self's bedside."

"You're a good man, Talon." I take his hand and squeeze it once. "I am so sorry that—"

"Grace," Talon interrupts me, shaking his head grimly. "Please don't."

"You don't like pity either?"

"Either?"

"All of the men in this realm seem to hate anyone fussing over them, even when they're severely injured."

Talon laughs and coughs with the jarring force to his lungs. "I'm sorry to say, Grace, but I think that's a common trait in all the realms."

"Seriously, though." I bring my tone back down to a serious one. "How are you coping?"

His face falls, and I feel terrible that I'm the one to have brought him down to that. He looks over at his lack of a right arm. "I'm alright. I'm left-handed, so I will still be able to write. Everything else... well, I'll have to relearn."

"I'm..." I stop myself before I can apologize again. "I'm sure that you will be able to. You have been a great teacher, and I'm sure you were a fast learner in school."

He smiles lightly at that. "Yes... yes, I was."

"Then you'll be back on your feet in no time." I reach over and squeeze his shoulder. "Hold on, alright? Have someone send for me if you need anything at all."

"I should be fine. Someone's bringing my books."

"Good, good." I notice Talon's face getting more and more tired as he continues sitting up to talk to me. I don't want to put him out for too long, so I say my goodbyes and make my way up to the top deck.

Despite the war-torn House on the opposite side of the boat, on this side there is nothing but smooth, calm waters. The soldiers up on deck are keeping an eye out for another attack, but there have been no signs so far. I climb out and find my way to an open section of the rail to watch the waves move. After a few days on board, the nausea is gone, and I can stand for longer periods of time without having to lie down.

I take a deep breath of the salty air and let my shoulders relax for just a moment. There are just so few moments to relax in this realm. But you have to take the little time that you have when you have it and just… try to breathe.

"Grace?" Aiden comes up behind me slowly. Immediately, I feel my shoulders start tensing up again. *So much for a break.*

Without looking over my shoulder, I answer, "What do you need, Aiden?"

"Nothing in particular. I was just seeing if you were alright."

"I'm fine."

To my chagrin, he moves beside me and leans on his elbows against the rail. I avoid his eyes. "Yesterday was pretty chaotic, yeah?" he says.

I resist the urge to roll my eyes. "It was a battle, Aiden. Of course it was chaotic."

"I know that." He quickly stumbles over his words. "That's not what I meant."

"What did you mean then?"

"Come on, Grace…" Aiden's voice gets tentatively frustrated. "When are you going to talk to me like you used to?"

"I don't know what you're talking about," I answer as I turn my head completely to look in a different direction over the water.

"Yes, you do. When are you gonna talk to me like you care? Like I'm someone you trust? Ever since I got back, you've been treating me like a stranger. Some Fae soldier you don't even know. It's hurtful. I'm sick of it."

"Do you think it's been easy for me?" I look at him. "To keep you at arm's length?"

"So you have been pushing me away."

"Of course I have. What else am I supposed to do? Of course I haven't forgotten what it was like to be on an expedition that was just the two of us. When it was you and I against the world, and everything was way less complicated. Even when it was stressful, it wasn't that complicated! But then you abandoned me."

"I did not abandon you."

"Yes, you did." I sigh and shake my head in frustration. "You can convince yourself that you were doing it for the right reasons or that you were always intending on coming back to me. But I told you I needed you to stay, and you couldn't. You didn't. So yes, Aiden. Everything is different now. I feel differently about you. And I can't define that for you in the middle of a war. It's impossible."

"Can you at least try? I'm trying to give you time here, but we're stuck on a boat together. Again. Don't you think it's a little poetic?"

"Poetic?" I laugh. "No. I think it's twisted, actually. Put me in a place where I'm only semi-comfortable and have me deal with a man I'm only semi-comfortable with."

"Are you serious?" Aiden almost sounds hurt. "You're only partially comfortable with me? I wasn't gone for that long."

"But you *were* gone for that long. In the time you were gone, we found two more prophecy members, infiltrated the House of Peace for a rescue mission, were attacked on our Founder's Day. I was almost assassinated again by the way." Aiden tries to interrupt me after that statement to apologize, but I don't let him. "My father died, we took back House of the Earth territory, and then we ran to the House of War for aid and nearly died *again* in a demon led attack. So forgive me if I've formed other opinions about who I am comfortable with and who I am not based on the many, many emotional, life-threatening experiences that I went through while you were away."

"Grace, if I could take it all back, I would. But I brought you aid, I brought you men and supplies and—"

"So what, you brought some men. You weren't there for me. That's what it boils down to. You were there for the war effort and your duty to your House, but not me. I'm allowed to be mad about that."

"But I came back!"

"You get points for being back. You don't get to start where you left off."

"Grace," Aiden pleads. "Why can't—"

"I kissed Faolan," I blurt out.

Dead silence.

Well, that shut him up. I should have done that ages ago.

"You did what?" Aiden growls.

I stare at him haughtily. "I kissed Faolan."

"Why the hell would you do that?"

"Because I wanted to!"

"You wanted to kiss Faolan?"

"Yes! Yes, I did. Because he was there for me. He stepped up after you left. He stood by me as my second-in-command and led with me. He protected me from countless enemies. He carried me back to the palace when I couldn't move after a significant amount of my magic was drained from me. He makes me feel… good."

"I don't want to hear this." Aiden throws up his hands and starts to pull away from the rail.

I grab onto his hand and force him back to the rail. "No. You are going to listen. I want to be your friend. I want to be your companion. You can't keep coming to me expecting me to love you."

"Do you love him?" Aiden asks urgently. "Do you love him?"

"I don't know. But I like him."

"You loved me though."

"I thought I did. I thought what we had was love. I felt something for you that I had never felt for anyone else before. But Faolan came along, and I feel something different."

"You loved me though…"

"Aiden."

"I had no idea all of this was going to crumble down," he says desperately. "I didn't think that this one choice was going to change everything. Grace, I had to go home. My family was headed off the rails, and I needed to save them. I needed to save my House from crumbling when this is all over. Please, you have to understand what that's like."

I lay my hand on Aiden's arm, surprising him. "I understand more than you know. I left home to find answers for my mother and I. I thought maybe if I could bring reasons back to her, she could finally find some peace and we could be a family again. But it was stupid when I did it, and it's stupid that you're doing it. She was never going to be the same again. And neither are your father and your brother. This doesn't end well for them. I'm sorry. But there's nothing you can do about that."

"I know," he whispers. "I know. But I had to try."

"I don't begrudge you the opportunity to try. I wasn't upset that you felt the need to go. I was upset because you left without discussing it with me. You left without any kind of plan, and you didn't communicate with me at all once you were there."

"You didn't back me up that day. You sided with Faolan over me."

"By the Lady, are you still on about that?" I laugh out loud at the ridiculousness of the entire conversation. "His idea was better than anything you had brought up. Get over it."

"I can't!" he shouts. "Not when I keep picturing you with him."

"This conversation is over," I say, heading toward the stairs.

To my surprise, Aiden grabs my arm. "Like hell it is."

"Aiden!" I shout at him. My anger must show on my face because he steps back away from me in a heartbeat, releasing my arm.

"Grace, I…"

"Do not speak to me for the next day unless we are under attack, do you understand me?"

"Yes," he says, resigned. "I understand."

"Good." Without saying another word, I storm back downstairs. As much as I hate being below deck, I cannot get away from him fast enough. The more he pushes, the more I feel trapped. Trapped between two men, two fighting styles, two completely different ways of life. And the more questions he asks, the more I feel forced to choose. I'm not ready to share any more of myself with Aiden right now. I'm just not ready.

Chapter Twenty-Five

A few hours later, when I'm convinced that Aiden must have left the upper deck by now, I slowly creep back upstairs. I really don't want to spend my entire time on this boat avoiding people or making commands or fighting in an actual battle. Can't a girl just get some sunlight without having a war offensive going on at the same time? Unfortunately, once I arrive on the deck, I see Neil across the way, having his own reflective moment. *By the Lady. First one irritating Fae male and now another one. Maybe he won't see me.*

I am not that lucky, of course, as he turns around almost immediately to find me standing by the stairway. But he chooses not to engage, to my surprise. He simply turns back to the view across the water. I move to the railing on the opposite end of the ship and stare back at the House of Water in the distance. From here, it doesn't seem like it's completely overrun by evil people. The sand-colored buildings stand out against the brilliant blue backdrop of the ocean and sky. The rust-colored towers have these huge balconies that stretch out toward the view of the horizon. I wonder what it looks like from the top. Once we liberate the House, I would love to tour the area further. I haven't been to the beach since the Middle Realm.

By the Lady, that seems like it was so long ago.

"How's the view in that direction?" Neil's voice interrupts my thoughts. I have to look over my shoulder to figure out whether he was speaking to me. But there's no one else at the railing, and Neil is looking directly at me.

"It's fine," I answer cautiously.

"Are you looking out for attackers?"

"No, just wanting a nice view."

"The view's less stressful over here."

"I didn't want to interrupt."

"You're not. Join me."

This is an odd change of pace. Cautiously, I make my way over to the railing where Neil is standing. He makes room for me, and the two of us lean over the side, arms propping us up. He's not wrong. The view is much, much better over here. No sign of the war in sight. I feel like I should say something to him, give him the same politeness he gave me. "Thank you for coming on this mission with us," I offer quietly. "Having you along has been good for morale. Everyone here knows you and respects you."

"You're welcome. Glad to be here."

"Really?"

"Yeah." Neil sighs. "To be completely honest, I needed to get out of the castle."

"Have your accommodations been less than satisfying?"

"Ha. No. It's my castle, too, you know. No, the accommodations are fine. I am just tired of sitting and waiting around for things to happen."

"Oh." I sigh. "I know that feeling."

"At least you're out there in the field doing what needs to be done. Leading."

"Yeah... sorry about that."

"Oh, now you're apologizing for being in charge? When we're in the middle of a freaking war?"

"Would you prefer that, or would you prefer me to tell you that I would never give it back?"

For a moment, I think that statement was a little harsh, but then Neil laughs. "To be honest, if I was in your shoes now, I probably would try to give it back. I was trained for situations like these, but you never know how intense it's going to be until the whole event begins."

"At least you had training. I'm going off of a handful of diplomatic and military books and my gut."

"Yeah, but you've got allies. The whole Council is behind you. I still can't believe you did that."

"Did what?"

"Threw all of the old guys out."

I laugh. "I didn't throw them out."

"Oh please, you absolutely did. From what I heard through the gossip network at the palace, you told them what's what and insisted that their children come down to work with you instead. And they did."

"It turned out much better that way. Ideas are sharper, more creative. I think we've been moving in a good direction despite the more recent setbacks."

"Yeah." Neil sighs. "The House of Darkness attack was intense."

"What was it like for you?" I ask. "We never really…"

"Sat down and talked about it? No, that's not our style, is it?" Neil's lips quirk up slightly before falling. "It was brutal. Half the safe house got taken down in one fireball hit. We lost a few of our guards. Thank the Lady we were on the opposite side of the house when the attack began. We were trying to flee toward safety, but it was unclear where safety would be. We ended up taking shelter in the basement of one of my mother's old neighbors' homes until the chaos stopped. Analise was so scared." Neil shakes his head. "I did my best to shield her from all of this but… she's gonna grow up traumatized."

"We'll fix it all for her," I tell him. "I promise."

"I don't know if that's something you can promise."

"Maybe not. But I'm gonna try."

Neil nods to me and looks out over the water for a few moments. He then turns back to me. "So… what were you and my mother fighting about the other day?"

"I'm sorry?"

"The day you called the War Council after the attack. She went downstairs to get something and came back in an awful state. I've only ever seen her that bad when she interacts with you."

"Oh, so it's my fault?" I snap.

"I never said that. I just want to know what bothered her so much."

I stay very quiet. I'm not exactly sure whether or not I should tell him. We've been having such a decent conversation so far, and I'm worried that this will cause a big fight. I'm so tired of grand emotional arguments right now.

"Come on, Grace. Whatever you want to tell me, just go ahead and say it. I promise I won't blow up."

I sigh quietly and look over the railing. "Your mother tried to kill me."

Neil bursts out laughing. "You can't be serious."

I gulp. This already isn't going well. "I am."

Neil stops laughing and shakes his head in irritation. "Grace, you can't possibly expect me to believe that my mother hired an assassin to kill you."

"You can ask Faolan. He was at the House of Fire when word spread around about the top of the House of the Evening requesting an assassin to take me out on the way to the Spring Solstice. Your mother even admitted it to my face when the two of us pulled her aside."

"You think I'm going to trust Faolan's word over my mother's?"

"I don't care if you believe me. But you needed to know."

The two of us look out silently over the water for a while as Neil processes the information I have just given him. I don't expect him to get it all right away. After all, he does want my place on the throne. But he's been reasonable enough since we got on the boat. Hopefully, he'll come around eventually.

"What did she say... allegedly? About why she wanted you dead."

"She wasn't looking for the realm to rewrite the laws about heirship. If I was dead, you were back on the throne, nice and easy. She would do anything for you."

Neil sighs. "Yeah... she would. But would she really go that far?"

I chuckle lightly. "You would need to talk to her about that. I don't know if she'll tell you. But there's a chance."

"I'll have to, then." He taps his fingers on the railing lightly in thought. "If you're right... she should have never gone that far. I don't like you, but I don't want you dead."

"Do you think you did once?" I ask quietly. "When I first came here?"

Neil shakes his head. "I don't think so. I got really, really mad. And I wished you had never existed. But I didn't want someone to actively kill you. Just make you go away."

"That's understandable."

"Yeah... to be completely honest," he says as he turns to me, "you're not a half-bad leader."

I raise an eyebrow. "Really?"

Neil laughs lightly. "Yeah. Your strategic decisions are pretty decent for someone with zero political training."

I laugh back. "That's true."

"Are you just winging it?"

"Pretty much."

The two of us smile at each other as we dissolve into chuckles. "Well," Neil says. "If you ever need some practical advice, you know you can ask me anytime."

"You'll actually help?"

"Yeah, I'll help you."

"Well… thank you for that."

"You're welcome."

I think in silence for a moment. "How were you trained? I mean, how long did it take you to master your magic?"

"I had to work pretty hard at it. I didn't take to magic right away. I had way more time than you, of course, but I had to break down each category of magic into sets of spells and build up my skill level from there."

"I never would have guessed that about you."

"I never wanted you to. No offense, but I absolutely hate how you took to magic so quickly. There you were, striding in from the Middle Realm with no perception about your heritage and your powers, but there you were, holding your own against me in that fight we had. You were throwing spells in a few weeks that took me multiple months to master. You're just…" Neil makes several grasping motions with his hand like he wants to reach out and wrap his hands around my throat. "So infuriating."

I don't know whether or not I'm supposed to chuckle or say something. The conversation dies down a bit after that. We take a few minutes to contemplate the view again. But I can't seem to ignore this nagging feeling deep in my chest to ask Neil something personal. It's never clear exactly what may make us brutal enemies again, but I can't resist asking, "When did our father know that you were ready to take on the heirship? I mean, I know it's tradition and blood and everything, but… when did he tell you that you were ready?"

Neil stands very still. At first, I wonder if he even heard me. But eventually, he speaks slowly and evenly. "It was a couple of weeks before you arrived. My mother had been feeling ill on and off for the last month or so, and my father thought that the Solstice events would be too much for her and she would end up worse off. He asked me if I would be willing to stay home and keep an eye on her while overseeing the House of the Evening in his absence. This honor is usually left to my father's second as I would usually attend these events. It was my very first time ever being asked to do this, and it was a true sign that my father trusted the House in my hands."

"Wow… yeah, I really screwed things up for you then, didn't I?"

"Yes."

All of this has given me a lot to think about. Our father really did trust him. If I hadn't been added to the picture, Neil would have gone on to rule admirably. It only takes me moments to realize that Neil, despite all of our issues, is in fact the next best person to lead the House. Faolan is my right hand for the war, but I need someone who can keep the House going if I'm gone. "Neil," I say quickly. "Go home."

"Excuse me?" He turns to me in shock. "I tell you the truth, and you send me away?"

"No, no, no," I correct quickly, grabbing both of Neil's shoulders before he can storm off. "I need you to go home because if I am hurt here, you have to be the leader."

Neil blinks in surprise. "What?"

"You are my heir. You are the heir to the House of the Evening, and you can't be here. You have to survive. If all else fails, you have to survive. Our father put you in charge for a reason. I will do the same. I'll get all the papers in order, and you'll have them before you leave."

Neil's disbelief is so apparent on his face, it almost makes me smile. After a few moments, he snaps out of his daze and nods to me. "Alright. I'll leave on the next supply run."

"Someone will take you in the morning."

"Okay then." Neil pats my shoulder once before rushing below deck to gather his belongings. I turn back to the sea, praying to the Lady that I have made the right decision. I do not know whether or not I will survive this war, but I can at least feel a little bit better that the people of the House of the Evening will have a fighting chance.

Chapter Twenty-Six

I send Neil off with the transport ship that comes to resupply us in the middle of the night. I'm surprised I didn't think of sending him home earlier. Just as it didn't make sense for us to put all of the War Council members in one location, it doesn't make sense to put both heirs to the House of the Evening in one place either. I mean, practically, I suppose Neil's sister could be regent with Lady Elise supervising, but frankly, I would come back from the dead just to prevent the former High Lady from sitting on the primary throne. No, better that Neil go home.

Our fleet engages with the House of Fire in several smaller skirmishes over the next several days. I am somewhat surprised they haven't made a concentrated offensive attack yet. We manage to keep them at bay for quite a while, sending their limited army acting as navy back to the House of Water with their tails between their legs. Thanks to our black market intel, we arrived here just as the House of Fire was about to refuel and resupply. We stopped their transports in their tracks and took the supplies for ourselves. Who knows what kind of impact that will have down the line.

But our luck wouldn't last forever.

On the seventh morning of the siege, Aiden and I come up to the top deck to complete an inspection of our weaponry. It's important to keep a running list of everything that we have, what works, and what needs repair. The more complete the list, the quicker we can get the things we need from our supply runs. This is the first time I've seen Aiden since our fight, and it's clear that he's feeling uncomfortable around me. He barely acknowledges my presence. Although this is what I asked for, it does feel kind of unsettling.

Before we can really get to work, however, we are interrupted.

"Incoming!" our captain shouts.

Aiden and I whip around. "Oh boy," Aiden breathes.

Barreling toward us is an entire fleet of the House of Water's ships being commanded by the House of Fire. There must be at least a dozen ships. On board, hundreds of soldiers roar as they race toward us at breakneck speed. This is the attack we have been waiting for. Some quick calculations based on our intel tell me that this is the vast majority of the House of Fire's military stationed here. I'm sure they left a few soldiers behind to keep guard, but this is meant to overwhelm us. They're trying to break the siege by sheer force. If we don't move our asses now, they may very well succeed.

"I need everyone on deck now!" I shout to the captain who amplifies his voice to repeat the same. The Fae soldiers from below deck rush upstairs and join us up top. They man their battle stations and prepare for confrontation. A few grab the ropes to steer us directly toward the group of ships. Our two sides are now sailing toward each other at top speed, gearing up for a head-on collision. Although I know we'll end up going alongside each other at some point, it doesn't seem like anyone is going to back down first.

"Load the cannons!" Aiden calls out. Despite all the magic between both sides, physical weaponry still plays a part. I rush to help my men load the cannons. The faster we can fire these things off, the more damage we can do before they reach us. Maybe we'll even sink a ship or two. I light the weapon myself with a snap of my fingers and quickly cover my ears as it fires off. One by one, all of our cannons go off.

I watch with bated breath as each collides with one of the moving ships. A few are hit in just the right place and begin to fill with water. Enemy soldiers rush to repair the damage. Water mages work to siphon the water from where it is pouring in and send it toward us. Unfortunately, we have not damaged enough to make much of a difference. We're going to have to engage. That's about the time I remember they have cannons too, and a dozen cannonballs are headed for our ship. "Brace for impact!" I shout. "Those who can fly, get ready!"

The first two cannonballs collide with the side of the ship, and the boat rocks. Another skates along the side and creates a long tear along the side of the wood. The soldiers on that side of the ship move to make repairs. A few other cannonballs land around us in the ocean, sending large plumes of water into the sky. I take to the air and motion for some of my men to follow me. Those who can join me do, including Aiden, and we rush to meet those below us. The House of Fire soldiers who can fly take off with a shout, rushing toward us. Where we meet, the battle truly begins.

Fighting in the air is a completely different experience from fighting on the ground or on the ship. There's no stability beneath our feet, so I'm relying entirely on my wings and my magical concentration to keep myself from falling out of the sky. It's an extra element that I have to factor into the fight. As I slash and cast, I try to shift my position as much as possible. Everything is unpredictable up here. And you have to take into account what's coming up from the sea, as one of the House of Fire's soldiers learned the hard way as a cannonball took out his wing and sent him spiraling toward the water.

The battle devolves quickly. We have them outnumbered, but they've gathered all of their resources together for one big push. Many of them have all their energy, and we're battle weary from the last several days. I narrowly avoid getting my wings cut off by an unruly young man with a thirst for blood. Aiden saves me by surrounding me with a quick force field and taking him out with a fireball.

"Grace!" Aiden calls to me. I fly over to him, dodging projectiles. He yanks me away from a cannonball as it barely misses my wings. "We gotta do something."

"What do you think I'm trying to do here? Do you want to make a suggestion?"

"Have you ever done a joint spell?"

"A joint spell? No. I mean, I've done some overlapping stuff in the heat of battle, but not like a formal joint spell. Why?"

"We need to merge our fire magic."

"I have no idea how to do that."

"It's pretty simple. We need to will our magic together. Which means you have to trust me and let my magic intertwine with yours and be guided by two minds."

"What does that feel like? How do we know if we're getting it right? Can it do any damage?"

"I don't know. I haven't done it before. I really only studied the theory."

"You want to try merging magic based on theoretical knowledge and a prayer to the Lady?"

"We can do this." Aiden grips my hands firmly and squeezes them. "Do you trust me?"

I don't have much time to respond, let alone think about what he's asking me. In this specific situation, absolutely. With a battle going on, I trust him to merge our magic together to the best of his abilities without crushing mine. He's very focused when it comes to these types of things. If we work together, we should be able to create the perfect balance of power and control. And that is intimate, isn't it? I have no idea if that's something that is considered intimate in this world, but it just feels that way to me. And I'm not sure if I want to do something like this with him. Especially given our history, given the way he walked out without so much as a discussion.

But we really don't have much of a choice, do we?

"Alright," I finally answer. "Tell me what you need me to do."

"Focus on the ship, and don't get startled, no matter what you see or hear." He lets go of my right hand, but holds on tight to the left. "We need to move as one mind and one body. Follow my lead."

The two of us fly down over the main enemy ship, soaring together until we reach the mast. Moving together has caused us to be a pretty big target for the people below to hit, and they're taking advantage of it. Both of us put our shields up as we are completely pummeled with magic and debris. Although everything bounces off, I feel every impact rattle through my consciousness. It makes it more difficult to hold my control, and now I have to try to funnel that control into a major spell.

Aiden spins to face me, taking both of my hands. At his signal, we both tap into our fire magic. I feel Aiden's magic move through my arm and meet with my magic. His feels so different from mine. It's warm, almost too warm, and it heats my body as it moves underneath my skin. I imagine he's feeling mine right now, flowing into him. "Now," he hisses in my ear.

Both of us tilt our heads back, our limbs naturally spreading outward with the force of the magic moving through both of us. From our bodies, sparks of fire magic tumble down toward the ship. When they reach halfway, the sparks split apart into two, four, eight tinier sparks. Those sparks suddenly explode into flame, raining down droplets of flame onto the ship and those surrounding it. The more we hold on, the more sparks that fall. Our hands vibrate together violently with the sheer force of our magic together. I struggle to hold on.

The ships beneath us catch on fire, and the flames spread quickly. Water mages rush to try to repair the damage, but the flames are too strong. Fire mages try to control the spread, but even they are struggling. Our armies take full advantage of this and launch another attack with renewed strength. Aiden and I move on to attacking other ships with the same technique. Each time, our strength falters a little more. The sparks eventually grow smaller and smaller until we are no longer able to summon the spell.

But it seems to have been enough. The head ship finally sinks, having been completely overrun. Others are falling to more cannonball attacks. Dozens and dozens of House of Fire soldiers are in the water. No one is able to escape as our remaining ships move around to pick them up as our prisoners. By the end of it, we've killed or detained every single soldier we could catch. A few escape in a makeshift raft, but they sail away from the House of Water. They're abandoning it.

The House of Water is ours.

Aiden and I let go of each other's hands, but quickly meet in an embrace. *We did it.* As I laugh and settle against his chest, I think about how nice it is to actually celebrate with him like old times. Maybe there's hope for us yet.

Chapter Twenty-Seven

Finally being on the ground in the House of Water is a great relief. The smell of the salt air just feels slightly different on the ground. When we de-boat, I leave the dock and head toward the shoreline first. There are so many things that need to get done, but I need to center myself with my feet in the sand. I take off my shoes and run down barefoot onto the beach. A few people try to call after me, but I hear Aiden wave them off and tell them to let me go. A tiny bit of heat spreads through my chest when I think about how easily he remembers the little things about me.

The sand underneath my toes feels warm and fills in all the tiny crevices of both my feet and my soul. The panic that seems to be a constant these days recedes just a little bit, and I feel my body relax. *This is what I'm looking for.* I wind my way down to the water and let the waves wash over my toes. The cold ocean sends shivers from my feet all the way up my legs, but it's worth every second. Closing my eyes, I put my arms out wide and tilt my head up toward the sun. I take a deep breath in and absorb as much salt air as I can in sixty seconds. *One minute. Just one minute of peace.*

"High Lady Grace!" an unfamiliar voice calls out to me. I turn around to find High Lord Triton of the House of Water rushing toward me down the beach. He has been held here for months with his family once they took the House. He retains a regal air about him, even without his crown on his head, but he wears a rugged beard and his clothes appear disheveled. Once he reaches me, he clasps my hands firmly. "High Lady Grace, thank you on behalf of the entire House for liberating us," he says. "We owe you a life debt."

"It was a joint effort, High Lord," I reply as I squeeze his hands. "Your son did much of the convincing to get us here when we did. He's a good leader."

"I have always thought so."

"Thank you for holding on the way you did. Are you and your family alright?"

"We're okay. No one was injured. The House of Fire guards were relatively tame here. We weren't a hot zone for military activity."

"Good." I pat the High Lord on the shoulder and begin walking up the beach to retrieve my shoes. "You should attend to your people, give them the news. I will survey the damage with the rest of my team." The High Lord thanks me profusely as we separate.

After putting back on my shoes, I disperse Aiden and my generals to go assess the damage. I myself walk toward the town past the palace. The castle itself is in decent shape. We managed not to send any of our spells and cannonballs this way, and it doesn't appear that the House of Fire did much damage. The grounds are a little worse for wear, having not been tended to for months, but all of that is fixable. I walk down a small alleyway with half a dozen merchant shops. Despite being occupied, it appears that these sellers attempted to keep things running smoothly. Inside, there are all kinds of beautiful, fine objects that I haven't seen in a long time. Not things like the jewelry and silks of the palace. More little things. Tiny chandeliers made of sea glass. Little seashells adorning keepsake boxes. Conch shells for sale so that children can hear the sea from anywhere.

It's a little portrait of what life here should be.

I reach the first square to find a criss-cross of canals that divides the remaining streets and alleyways in this town into a grid. Along each line, there is an array of homes, shops, and businesses. Scattered among them are little carts and stands that I assume use to hold their own goods and wares for sale. My eyes widen. It's an incredible marketplace. But it's going to take ages to find my way across each little waterway and find out where the hell it all leads to. It could take days just to go over this one town for someone not familiar with the area.

"Grace." I look to my left to find Aiden calling to me from a small dock in the canal line. I walk over to him.

"Do you need something?" I ask.

"No," he says. "But I would like to know if you would like to see the House of Water. You've never been here before. I could show you some of the places that I know."

"I do, but I've got to assess the damage."

Aiden carefully places a hand on my back. "There's no better way to do that than by water." He steps aside to reveal a small, two-person canoe. "Let me take you around the canals. We can assess as we go."

I hesitate at first. This is another crossroads. To do something alone with Aiden or to continue to stand apart. It's something I don't necessarily want to go into lightly. But he looks so hopeful, and I do need to see the town. So instead of answering, I simply nod once and climb into the canoe. Grinning, he jumps in after me and starts to paddle us down the first channel.

Ultimately, he wasn't wrong. I do prefer seeing the House of Water through the canal line. The little waterways go for miles, and they split apart into various channels all throughout the town. I can imagine that in its heyday, the marketplace must be overwhelming with sights, sounds, and smells as people pass through it. Now though, it is quite quiet. There isn't much damage, which is good, but it does seem like it's missing a certain spirit.

Other places, however, there has been extensive damage. There are entire neighborhoods that have been decimated. I notice that not all of them, however, were in the line of fire on any of the battles that I had a hand in putting together. At first, I think maybe my army destroyed them by a stray cannon or major spell effort. But when I find evidence of darker magic, I realize that demonic magic had a hand here. My heart aches when I think about all the people who must have suffered for however long before we were able to put ourselves together to liberate them.

I should have done more sooner. I just should have done more.

"Hey," Aiden says softly, interrupting my thoughts. "We couldn't have gotten here any quicker."

"How did you know that's what I was thinking?"

He smiles. "Your brow furrows in a specific way every time you start feeling guilty. I learned to recognize it after a while."

"Of course I feel guilty. I feel like we could have gotten here earlier."

"At the expense of whom? Who were we going to tell that we couldn't get to them? Someone was going to suffer either way, Grace. We've done everything we can."

"Have we?"

"Not quite yet," he concedes. "We'll reallocate troops and resources, help them to start to rebuild like we have for everyone else. And you, Talon, and I will head home."

"That's all we can do."

"That's all we can do," Aiden repeats. "Until the war is over."

"Yeah… let's get on that, shall we?"

"We shall," Aiden says quietly as we continue our way through the canal system.

Chapter Twenty-Eight

We spend a few days in the House of Water re-establishing the control of the noble family and gathering an inventory of what is needed to start repairing the infrastructure. High Lord Triton hosts us with as much generosity as one can give in a broken state, sending us off with a modest dinner celebration. Aiden, Talon, and I then return home with the majority of the soldiers we went with.

It is still very difficult for Talon to move around. He's trying to get used to maneuvering things without both of his limbs. Potions mixing has become more fraught for him, as has research without the use of one of his hands to turn the pages. But he's determined to get it right one way or another. He requests that I leave him to his own devices, and so I do.

Instead, I get up to speed on what has been going on in the House of Light. Faolan and Cary's group return a few days after ours as the House of the Light liberation took a little bit longer than the House of Water. I can't even begin to describe the relief I felt when I saw the three of them, intact, leading our army back home. Faolan and I don't embrace in front of everyone, but our arms do brush against each other intently as I and the War Council greet the group. Their siege met much firmer resistance with more weapons and more soldiers to fight. But ultimately, they were able to liberate the House of Light's capital. More soldiers stayed behind to help work their way through the border towns.

Everyone seems fairly satisfied with how things went. While we're coming down from the high of sharing stories around the conference table and a few small laughs, Gideon stands up. "I have information to share." Without waiting for someone to acknowledge him, he presses on. "My spies have picked up new buzz in the ranks of the House of Fire coming directly from the top. The entire strategy of the House of Darkness alliance is about to shift."

"What's their plan?" Aira asks.

"The new plan is to hold the territories that they have now and subdue the Middle Realm instead. They believe they can't push farther without running into our armies. By taking the Middle Realm, they can have all the territory they want with little resistance. The mortals won't have any way to stop them, particularly with demon involvement."

My jaw drops. "Are you serious?" I ask. My heart has just about stopped. It has been hard enough trying to keep the House of Darkness from devouring the realm with magic. Mortals wouldn't just have any way to stop them; it would be an absolute bloodbath.

"Yes," Gideon answers. "I wouldn't joke about something like that."

I wave him off. "That's not what I meant. We have to—"

"Well, that fixes our military problem somewhat, doesn't it?" Jason offers from across the table.

I narrow my eyes. "What do you mean?"

"Gives us time to regroup. Hold our positions. Rebuild, maybe even heal a bit. I think it's a blessing in disguise."

"A blessing in disguise?" I leap to my feet, the indignation rising in my chest

"It kind of is, Grace," Tristan adds sheepishly. "They're taking their eyes off of us."

"And putting them on defenseless people!" I shout.

"But not our people," Jason argues.

"I can't believe I'm hearing this." I barely resist the urge to throw my hands up in disgust. I'm barely holding onto my control in general not to beat his ass.

"Grace, I know that you have a soft spot for the Middle Realm," Aurora starts to soothe.

"It's my home."

"It was your home," Tristan corrects. "You live here now."

"There are innocent people there!"

"There are innocent people here too!" Jason gets to his feet too, leaning on the table. "Soldiers that we don't need to send to a foreign realm to protect people that aren't theirs to protect."

"So you're perfectly content sending your merchants, your officials, your armed guards to the Middle Realm to keep order and to keep your political and economic agenda secure, but when the Middle Realm might need your support to stop everyone from dying, you turn a blind eye!" I have never been angrier in my entire life than I am right now. I thought that watching my brother's life thrown callously away for the House of Darkness's evil purposes would be the worst. But the supposed "good team" is willing to throw away innocent lives for what? A break? If they could, my eyes would be glowing red.

"Don't put it like that," Aurora whines. "It's not about that. We need a break; we need time to recover."

"And if the rest of us had allowed your Houses to fall without help because we needed a break, that would have been okay with you?" I argue back.

"Of course not! But that's different."

"What makes it so different? What makes it so different?"

"Grace, drop it," Jason scolds. "We've decided."

"Who? Who has decided? I don't remember calling a vote."

"We're not calling a damned vote!" he shouts. "I'm telling you flat out none of my soldiers or my resources will go to aiding the Middle Realm."

"Maybe I'll withdraw aid to your Lady-damned House then!" I snap. "No food, no materials, no resources, I'll pull all of my soldiers out of your House right now, and you can pick up the pieces by yourself!"

"Are you threatening me?"

"What gave it away? I'm sorry, I'll be clearer next time."

"Grace." Faolan speaks in a low voice next to me. It's a warning, a warning that I'm going too far.

But I don't really care.

"If any of us, any of our Houses had left each other behind, left them to fall to the House of Darkness and the demons, they would have been condemned. You know they would have. The mortals are not beneath us. I have led you all with everything I have, and I am half-mortal. You don't see me as being beneath you, do you?"

The uncomfortable silence from the non-prophecy members is deafening, and it pierces my soul.

"Are you serious?" I ask incredulously, my voice taking on a higher pitch.

"Grace, why are you even asking that?" Tristan says. "You're Fae now; you're a High Lady. No one thinks you're—"

"Then why did no one answer?"

"Because it's a dumb question," Jason says angrily. "Of course we're not going to say you're beneath us, but you have to know that we have to ignore your heritage in order to work with you. Focus on the Fae sides. It makes it easier."

"There are no sides! I am mortal. I am Fae. My personality doesn't change between the two!"

"But you're not really mortal anymore," Alena says gently. "You're practically a full Fae."

"But I'm not," I emphasize with a big rush of breath. "I'm not."

When I look at the other nobles' faces, I can see that I'm not getting through to them at all. They literally cannot see that I am both. Have I become so Fae that I have lost every action that makes me mortal? What does make me mortal vs. Fae? "I want to put this to a vote," I finally say wearily. "But you go on record with your vote. No paper. Words only."

"Fine," Jason says. "I vote no aid."

"No aid from me," Tristan repeats.

"No aid," the two House of Light sisters say together.

As I go around the table, I feel betrayed when Cary and Gideon both vote no to sending aid to the Middle Realm. I can't believe they wouldn't side with me. I never thought they would discriminate against mortals knowing that I am one. There has to be another explanation. But what other explanation could there be? I thought we were coming to some sort of understanding, Gideon and I and Cary and I. At the end of the vote, the tally is six nays, six ayes. We have to have a majority to send that amount of aid; I can't pull a tiebreaker vote without causing more chaos around the table.

Gritting my teeth, I force out my words. "The vote is six to six. We have a tie. No aid will be sent at this time." I throw myself to my feet and storm out of the room. "Meeting adjourned." I think I hear Faolan or Aiden call my name, maybe both. But I don't stop for anyone, running through the hallway and fleeing outside before I explode.

Chapter Twenty-Nine

I have never felt more anger than I do right now.

And it's completely my fault.

You might think that sounds ridiculous, but it's true. I lost myself. I don't really know how or when it happened, but somewhere between the time I entered the Upper Realm looking for answers about Leo and becoming a Fae heir, I lost my mortal self. I was always a Fae, but I didn't know that. For the first nineteen years of my life, I was a mortal and only a mortal. I survived so much operating under this premise. I built a life under this premise. And then suddenly, I become Fae, a noble Fae, and just forget everything I've been taught. When was the last time I thought of my mother or my uncle back home? What about David? Does he even think about me anymore?

How did I get here? How did I wind up fighting in one realm for another realm I used to live in, but don't seem to truly believe in anymore? Am I just homeless? Do I belong anywhere at this point? Too Fae to be mortal, and too mortal to be truly Fae. What option is left to me? Other than to lead a House I have no business leading other than blood. Maybe Neil was right all along. Perhaps I never should have claimed the throne as readily as I had. What had I been thinking?

The anger building inside of me needs a release. I need to get it out of me, or I'm going to end up hurting myself in my rage against the world. In my blind running, I have found myself in the arena where I do most of my training. I press my hand into the ground and light it ablaze. My flames create intricate designs in lines and swirls throughout the arena and climb high toward the sky. I push it to go farther, higher, until the whole place is on fire.

It isn't enough.

It just isn't enough.

"Grace." Talon's voice startles me from behind. I whip around to face him, nearly tumbling into my own magic. He grabs my arm quickly before I can fall and pulls me away as the flames slowly die down. "Grace, what are you doing?"

"You…" I breathe heavily. "You don't know what happened in there."

"In where?"

"The conference room! You don't know what they said about my… my people."

"The House of the Evening?"

"No!" I snap so abruptly, he takes a step back. "The Middle Realm. They're letting it burn."

"Grace, what is going on?"

"They're letting it burn," I repeat, quieter this time.

Talon finally seems to recognize that I am in no mood to discuss things. "What do you need right now?" he asks. "What can I do?"

"I need to fight," I answer immediately.

"You want to spar?" I nod vigorously. "Alright. Get in the ring."

I feel a pang of worry. "Talon, you're not in any shape to—"

"I need to get back into training," he interrupts. "There's no reason I can't fight. I will be able to wield my magic just as well with one arm as with two. Are you scared that I'll kick your ass?"

My eyes narrow. Talon isn't usually this blunt with me. But hey, it's fueling my anger, so I'm inclined to give in to his request. I move to face him. His expression is grim, teeth gritted and jaw tightened.

"Get it out of your system," he says. I let him throw the first attack. Then I let loose.

I fight like all hell against Talon. I don't know if I'm even seeing him as a friend or solely as a combatant in the way of my emotional suffering. I throw blast after blast at him, countering his spells with ease and slipping past his defenses. My flames are brighter than they have ever been, and I am able to push them further and more complexly than I have in a while.

He doesn't back down no matter what I'm hitting him with. Instead, he engages me with just enough power to be frustrating. His spells poke me, prod me, needle at my patience until my fury comes out in full force. It's the same story all over again. Words meant to hurt me, spells meant to annoy me, people trying to push my buttons. My emotions bubble up in my chest, and I let out a blood-curdling scream. With that scream, I release my control over my magic in a huge burst of power. Instead of a specific spell, it's just a magic pulse with some real weight. Talon is thrown backward onto the ground with a hard thud.

I hold my hands up in shock. *That did not sound good.* "Talon?" He doesn't answer. "Talon, are you alright?" I rush over to him.

He looks up at me with wild eyes and gasps, drawing air into his lungs for the first time since he hit the ground. He then lets out a series of coughs. I quickly help him to a seated position. When he regains his breath, he turns to me solemnly. "Grace, we have a problem."

"I'm really sorry, I didn't mean to use so much."

"That's the problem. I should have anticipated this, honestly, given your intensity of power. Your emotions have always had a huge influence on your power. Especially with your propensity for psionic magic. Some of your best spells have been when you intertwined the two together. The problem is now that your emotions have become so grand, so volatile that your magic has adapted itself to match. Now that can be incredible, but Grace, it may also be lethal."

"Isn't that a good thing? Don't I need to be lethal for this war?"

"There's a difference, Grace. When you're intentionally trying to be lethal, your magic moves outward toward your target. When you're not trying though, your magic can also move inward on yourself. If you don't get that in check, you could kill yourself the same way you would kill another."

"How is that possible?"

"It's an unfortunate side effect for those with empathetic magic. You have to calm down and focus your energy. Do you understand what I'm telling you?"

I nod slowly. "Yeah, I understand. But what do you expect me to do? I can't just… bottle it all inside."

"I know that. You're going to have to let it out. Talk to somebody or play your violin or something. But you have got to be careful, or you're going to end up hurting someone accidentally."

"Do you really think it's that bad?"

"Look at where I am now." He gestures to his prone state on the ground. I offer him my hand and pull him to his feet. "Be careful, Grace. I'm worried for you."

I sigh quietly. "I'm worried for me too."

Chapter Thirty

I try to do what Talon asked of me over the next few days. To me, this means limiting my interaction with the people who have irritated me. Which at this point is literally everyone. I can't think of a single person who is actually helping me right now, physically or mentally. Sometimes, you're just done. I ask the servants in the castle to bring my meals to my bedroom door and leave them there without seeing me. I have to put up shields around both my interior door and my balcony door to keep Aiden and Faolan from coming in. Aiden tries several times, but he eventually gets bored of trying. Faolan, however, doesn't stop trying. It actually takes a lot of my energy to keep thwarting his attempts. Some would maybe consider it romantic that he doesn't want to leave me alone when I'm hurting.

Well, I find it irritating.

I finally come downstairs on the fourth day, mostly because we are due for another War Council meeting. As I make my way downstairs, to my slight dismay, Faolan comes out of the front hall. "Grace," he says in surprise as he walks toward me. "You're out of your room."

"Yes, for now."

"Are you feeling better?"

"I don't know. I didn't get a lot of uninterrupted break time since you didn't leave me alone."

Faolan shrugs. "Maybe if you had let me in, I could have helped."

"Maybe I wasn't in the mood for help."

"Maybe that's exactly why you needed help."

I sigh quietly. "Can we agree to disagree on that?"

Faolan offers a conceding nod. "Of course." The longer he looks at me, the more his lips slowly turn into a soft smile. As frustrated as I am, I like the way he looks when he does that. Because he only does it for me.

"Alright," I finally say.

"What have I missed? What do we need to take care of today?"

"Lord Faolan." We both turn our heads to see a messenger standing at the front door, having just been let in by my guards. "There is a message for you from the Middle Realm."

My heart clenches tightly in my chest. Faolan brushes my arm lightly and waves the messenger to the side. They speak in low voices, and Faolan keeps his back to me so I can't read his face. I hate him for that. He's only delaying the inevitable. I pray to the Lady that it's not bad news, but I know it's just got to be. No one comes to this palace with good news anymore.

Faolan walks over to me slowly as the messenger walks away. The look in his eyes puts me on edge immediately. He's approaching me cautiously like he knows that what he's about to say is going to drive me off the edge. "Uh-uh," I shake my head. "I know that look. Whatever you want to say, I don't want to hear it."

"You need to hear this, Grace," he says quietly.

"No," I repeat. "I don't want to hear it." Faolan doesn't say another word, only looks into my eyes and waits for me to give in. I hate that he thinks that he can just look at me and I'll decide to do the right thing. Well, maybe I don't want to hear what he has to say. Maybe I don't want to hear the bad news. But his grim demeanor is insistent, and eventually, I feel the need to give in. "Fine. Say it."

Faolan looks off to the side before looking back at me. "Do you want it straight?"

"Yes," I answer incredulously. *What other way would I want it?*

He sighs. "Earlier this morning, the House of Darkness invaded the Middle Realm." My breath catches in my throat. "Fort Faol in the west was an easy target once the House of Darkness breached the mountains. The mortals never saw it coming."

"How many dead?" I manage to choke out.

"There was… a lot of damage to the city. Magic broke down walls with a wave of a hand. There were a lot of fire mages that cast spells to raze the city."

"How many dead, Faolan?"

"The city was breached within a matter of minutes, and—"

"Faolan!" I shout. He flinches lightly. That's the first time I've ever seen him flinch. I never want to make him do that again. I force myself to even out my tone. "Tell me how many are dead."

"Preliminary reports are fourteen thousand."

"Fourteen thousand?"

"Fourteen thousand… dead upon arrival. The number in the remainder of the battle is still unclear."

I stumble backward in shock. Fourteen thousand was nearly half the city lost just upon arrival of the Fae army. With no numbers coming in about how far the devastation had spread, that can only mean that it was catastrophic. My fingers twitch as sparks rise to the tips. I warned them. I warned them all that this exact thing would happen. And they didn't listen. Now look at what they've done.

"Grace?"

I hear Faolan's voice in my ears, but my brain refuses to respond to it. My hands pulsate with the fury running through my veins. It's both hot and cold at the same time, and it trails from my hands down through every part of my body. How could they let High Lord Carron destroy everything in my realm without consequences? What if my family moved? What if David was in the city? What if they're all dead too?

I will rip their heads off.

"Call the Council," I force out through gritted teeth.

"Grace..."

"Call the Council!" I bellow. I see a flash of something in Faolan's eyes, an emotion I haven't seen from him before, and he dashes off upstairs to gather the members together. *I just told myself not to do that again. Stupid, stupid girl. You'll be lucky if he even talks to you again.*

Overcome with self-pity, I storm off in a huff. This whole tragedy never needed to happen. The Council's inaction literally cost thousands of lives. I should have overridden them. Rules be damned. I should have just said screw it and sent all of my army there to help them. Somebody should have helped them, and it definitely should have been me. I head straight down the back stairs, winding all the way down to the training room. I can't even see physical objects around me at this point, my vision has narrowed so much with pure rage. The only thing that solidifies for me is the training dummy in the middle of the room.

I don't even remember casting the first spell. But suddenly, everything is exploding around me. Anything that is glass shatters instantaneously, and the swords on the back wall rack fall to the ground. The dummy in this room is much more powerful than the one in the arena. But it doesn't matter. It tries to fight back, but my body is lashing out at everything. Most of my spells don't even land directly on it. Instead, various fireballs scorch the walls, I break sections of the floor with blasting spells, and the sheer power of everything leaves a few cracks in the floorboards. Finally, I send the dummy flying across the room with such speed that the whole thing shatters into dozens and dozens of pieces against the training room wall. Breathing heavily, I take stock of the room. *I've broken so much.*

By the Lady. It's gonna cost a fortune just to restock the room, let alone put it back together.

"Well, you've made a right mess of things, haven't you?" Faolan's voice creeps up on my ears. I'm already done with its presence.

"Get out if you don't want to get stabbed," I snap.

"And if I am in the mood to get stabbed?" he says, stepping from the now doorless entryway into the room.

"I'm not joking around today, Faolan. Get out."

"Well, you asked me to summon the War Council. They're waiting upstairs for you."

"They can wait until I'm damn well ready. Now *get out.*"

"Now, let me tell you why I'm not going to do that. You keep avoiding me."

"I'm not avoiding you; I'm trying to win a war."

"See, I get that. And it does help that you're avoiding Aiden too, so I know I haven't lost to anyone yet. But if you don't talk to me, pretty soon I'm gonna think that everything that's been going on between us has been a fluke." I don't answer him, clenching my teeth tightly together. He slides up behind me, his breath tickling the back of my neck. "Now I don't think it was a fluke. So do you want to talk to me or continue to destroy an already destroyed room?"

I let out a sigh. "Fine. I guess we can talk." I turn around to face him. *Damn those eyes to hell.* "What do you want to talk about?"

"How about start with what turned you into a raging lunatic?"

"You know the answer to that question."

"I know what I think it is. I want to hear it from you."

"The Middle Realm. Part of my home destroyed. Ignorant Fae who would rather sit up in their palaces, even in the midst of their own war, and let every mortal die before they'll listen to reason and have basic empathy."

"You still consider the Middle Realm home?"

I groan. "Please, I don't want to talk about this."

"Hey, I'm not here to judge. I don't exactly consider the House of Darkness my home either. You and I are wanderers. We make a home with people, not in a place."

"I want to hurt them," I admit in a whisper. "I want to hurt them for what they took."

"What who took?"

"The people upstairs. They could have helped. They could have helped him, and they didn't. We could have sent an army, we could have even sent a few regiments. Anything would have been better than nothing. And now, whenever I see any of them, I want to… mmm." I ball my hands into fists. "I want to make them suffer."

Faolan walks up to me and grips my wrist. "Hurt me."

I blink in confusion. "What?"

"Hurt me."

"I won't! What are you talking about?"

"Spar with me. Get it out of your system because you have to go up there and make nice with them anyway to get what you need for both of your realms. Take it out on me."

I blink. *What an offer. Talon did say I need to find a release for my power…* I shake off my internal thoughts.

"I can't just… I can't do that."

"Do you think it would help? To fight all out, to take out all that magical rage on someone who's not going to implode the second you touch them?"

Faolan's pushing too many buttons for me. He's handed me this golden opportunity to fight with someone who has enough power to break me the way that I could him, but whom I trust not to completely rip me to shreds. My hands itch with sparks of magic. He grins when he looks down at my hands. "Come on," he teases. "Your body is telling you what you need. Let it happen."

"Fine," I finally concede. "But I need to be able to not hold back."

"Well, I won't be either. So I expect nothing less from you." Suddenly, he grips my hand and spins me across the room. I fly to a starting position just as he fires a blasting spell at the ground under my feet. I jump to avoid it, but another one immediately follows and shakes the ground under me, sending me down to it. I look up at Faolan to cut me some slack, but he only smirks at me. "I quite like you on your back."

Bastard.

I leap to my feet and throw a spear of flame at him. His reflex amplification magic allows him to dodge effortlessly and aim another blast. My wind swirls around the both of us as we alternate blows. All the while, he telepathically whispers in my ear, needling me with pet names and tiny teasing comments about the way I look, the way I fight. *You look beautiful when you're pissed. Is that the best you can do, darling? Use your head, dear, where was that spell headed?* When I yank him toward me with a breeze, he laughs and kisses the back of my neck before vanishing from my grasp once more.

The way we move around the room is an intricate magical dance. Our spells seem to interact with each other like we always have: strong, teasing, playing together like they were meant to collide. Faolan's magic is so much stronger than Talon's. I feel like I'm competing against an equal even though everyone's pretty certain I have more raw power. He's got more training and refinement than I do, and it shows in the preciseness of his spells. Each one lands exactly where he wants them to go.

My breath is suddenly snatched from my lungs as Faolan sneaks a spell by my feet that knocks me flat on my back. He laughs as I hit the ground. "You're still not quite quick enough," he teases. I quirk my lip before wrapping a breeze around his ankles and yanking him down. Caught off guard, he tumbles to the ground beside me.

"Now who's slow?" I quip. He chuckles at my response. Instead of getting up, he tilts his head to look at me, his body inching just slightly closer to mine. Our fingers lightly touch each other as he shifts his hand. We're not fully holding hands, but it feels intimate anyway. I'm not quite sure what to say, so I stay silent and watch his eyes carefully. I love the way the amber swirls in them. "Thank you," I finally decide on saying. "For this."

"Do you feel any better?"

"A little bit."

"That's all I was going for." All too soon, he pushes himself to his feet and offers me his hand. He pulls me up. "Now your head can be clear to focus on what's going on upstairs. Do you feel up for the challenge?"

"I'll try," I reply quietly.

He nods at me and leads me to the door, still holding onto one of my hands. "Let me know if you need anything, alright?" And deep down, underneath all the pain, I feel like I might do just that.

Chapter Thirty-One

Faolan leaves me just outside the conference room doors to let the War Council know that I am coming. Which is probably a good idea. Those who cross me should always be warned to give them a chance to back down. When he signals to me, I open the door and stride through. Every single noble looks extremely wary of me. It's clear that Faolan gave them the information he received from the Middle Realm well before I arrived. Everyone knows they fucked up, and now they're going to pay. I'm furious, and there's not a single person who is safe from my rage right now. When each of them takes their seats, Faolan closes the doors behind us. He sits at the foot of the table this time, directly across from me. His eyes level directly at mine. *Take a breath, Grace.* I hear his voice in my mind telepathically. *We still need some of these people, you know.*

I really... *really* hate when he's right.

"Several of you," I begin stoically, "believed that the Middle Realm was not worth protecting. That there was nothing there for us to be holding onto. Because of this, there was an attack, and thousands of lives were lost. We still don't have the final death toll. The city was burned to the ground. Faolan, I'd like you to detail the report that you received."

Faolan nods and leans forward to put his hands on the table. "The House of Darkness and the demon army invaded Fort Faol on the western border early yesterday morning. The mortals were completely unprepared for such an attack. Not that it would have made much of a difference. Without magic or magical resources, they stood no chance. It took less than ten minutes for the city to fall. Fourteen thousand people were dead on arrival, and the final count is likely total and a half. Grace is correct about the city being burned to the ground. Everything but the camp they have established there is gone. I do not know the intent behind it, but my sources say the demons got a bit carried away."

Hearing the full report crushes me. The numbers shocked me at first, so much so that it sent me into a blind rage. But now hearing the whole story, I'm pissed off and wide awake. I look around the table to see what kind of reaction the others are having. Gideon's face looks grave. Alena and Aurora look physically disturbed by the details. They may be easy enough to sway. Jason, though, has absolutely no change in his face. He looks like he could simply be listening to someone telling him what's for dinner.

"Forgive me for interrupting you, Faolan," Jason interjects. "But I'm not sure why we are sitting here discussing this matter when it's clearly been resolved."

"Resolved? There was an attack," I answer incredulously. "Sure, the attack has been resolved. But now we have to decide how to respond."

"No," Jason says as he stands up. "No, we don't. I will not be sitting here to continue to have this conversation. There will be no response."

"You will sit down!" I shout and jump to my feet.

Jason gets up in my face. "No… No, I will not. You continue to bring up the Middle Realm and rehash this point over and over again, and you are starting to really piss me off."

"Oh honey, you haven't seen me angry yet."

Jason laughs. "I don't particularly care what it looks like when you get angry. The second you attack me, I pull every single soldier of mine, and we go back to the House of the Day regardless of what you want or need."

"And I pull all of my aid from your House, cut off trade permanently, and watch your House crumble."

"Let's take a step back," Aiden interjects. "There's no need for this to become hostile."

"Become hostile? She made it hostile," Jason replies. "So focused on her precious Middle Realm that she can't even see that she is mismanaging her House."

"Mismanaging my House? I seem to remember that this House has protected you and supplied you for months at this point without asking for anything in return!"

"Except to join forces and fight in a war against one of our own!"

"You would have let the realm fall?"

"No!" he shouts. "But I certainly would have done better than you at managing it. You make steps, High Lady Grace. You make steps and you make mistakes, but your heart really isn't all the way into it. Everyone knows you've been sleeping with the enemy."

"Excuse me?" Faolan's voice is dangerously low as he walks over toward the House of the Day nobleman.

"Everyone can see the doe-eyed stares and the secret meetings in every goddamn place in the castle. Even when you're not together, the way he talks about you, it's so obvious."

My hands ball into fists. Too many people at the table are looking down awkwardly and avoiding eye contact or responding. Aiden, Cary, and Faolan are the only ones who are staring at Jason like they want to rip his head off. "I have not been sleeping with *anyone* in this room. And even if I was, it would be none of your damn business. On top of that, Faolan is not the enemy."

"Once House of Darkness, always House of Darkness. He and Cary may have agreed to help us for now, and don't get me wrong, they've been perfectly helpful. But you have not known them as long as I have. They will cut us down as soon as it is in their best interest. They don't have to rejoin their father to do that." Jason leans into my face again. "And I'm starting to think that you're just like them. The difference is your threats are empty. The second you pull anything shady with me or any of us, I will make it my sole life's mission to see you thrown out of this realm on your ass. Fae law may dictate that you are ruler of the House of the Evening, but Fae laws can be rewritten." He turns away and begins moving toward the door. "I refuse to vote on this issue, and based on Fae law, there can be no vote."

"Lord Jason," Faolan spits out harshly.

"I will not be forced into supporting a realm that I do not wish to."

"They won't be stopping with Fort Faol," I find myself pleading. "They will continue on until they've taken everything."

"And until that problem directly affects the House of the Day, I will not listen any further." Without another word, Jason pushes open the conference room door and storms out. The table is once again silent.

Sinking back down into my chair, I close my eyes. "Is there any way around the traditional Council rules?" I ask quietly.

"No," Lord Tristan replies. "There isn't. There are loopholes for things like illness or death, but a stark refusal like that means that nothing can be done."

"Nothing?"

"Nothing," Aiden echoes.

"Fine." I sigh. "Council dismissed."

"Grace…" Aiden tries to speak again.

"Council dismissed," I speak over him. "Everybody get out." It takes several moments for anyone to start moving, but once they do, the room empties quickly. Although a few people try to speak to me, I keep my eyes shut and don't move a single muscle until the room is clear. When everything is quiet once again, I let myself open my eyes and look around at the empty room. It mocks me in its starkness. I rise slowly and carefully from my chair and walk out of the room in quick certain steps, my heels clicking against the tile floor.

Chapter Thirty-Two

The Council meeting leaves me seeing red. They have the audacity to deny the Middle Realm aid a second time after a devastating attack? I wonder how they'll like it when I pull my aid to their Houses. I am trying to take a moment to calm down and think about this rationally, but the worse half of me wants to go to my commanders right now and tell them to pull every last House of the Evening resource out of everywhere that isn't us. They want to be selfish and stingy? Oh, I'll show them selfish and stingy. They can rebuild on their own. They can see how long it will take them to build up enough resources to get their people back on track.

But I can't stoop that low. Their citizens didn't do anything. I wouldn't dare revoke aid for something like that. My heart twists in knots when I think about how the only real betrayal the Council has committed is to my former homeland and not to the House of the Evening. It's crushing how I recognize the distinction.

I find myself in the throne room, pacing back and forth in front of the noble paintings. Across the back wall, there are portraits of the last several generations of Faelie rulers. Their piercing eyes seem to bear right into my soul. They judge me. Even my father's portrait with his stern face asks me how the hell I couldn't hack it. *I taught you better than this. You should be doing better than this.*

Or maybe that's my own voice in my head.

"Grace?" I resist the urge to groan as Neil's voice enters the room. "May I speak to you for a moment?"

"Respectfully, Neil, now is really not a good time."

"I understand. I simply wanted to thank you for sorting out the heirship situation. It feels good to be back holding some semblance of power again."

"Well, I'm glad. You deserve the position. There's no one else better to take my place if I die."

"I heard what happened at the War Council meeting."

I chuckle dryly and turn around to face him. "I'm sure the whole palace has heard by now."

"I'm sorry that the negotiations didn't go your way."

"Are you? Would you have voted to send aid to the Middle Realm?"

"Do I have to answer that question? I really need to talk to you, and the second I give you an honest, thought-out answer to that question, I don't think you're going to want to talk to me anymore."

So he wouldn't send aid either. Bastard.

I take a very slow deep breath to calm myself. "What did you want to speak to me about?"

"I confronted my mother about what you and I talked about on the ship."

I raise an eyebrow. Now that, I was not expecting. "Really?"

"Yes. When you sent me home, I really couldn't stop thinking about our conversation. I know I told you that I thought you were ridiculous, but something about it was still rubbing me the wrong way. It took me a few days, but I finally asked her about it when we were alone."

"And how did that go?"

"Well, I started by telling her the decision you had made about naming me heir. She was very excited, but also very surprised. She wondered how I had convinced you."

"What did you tell her?"

"I said you had made the call on your own. I thought you deserved a little credit."

"Well, thank you for that. What did she say when you asked her about the assassination attempt?"

"I didn't exactly flat out ask her. She actually volunteered a comment about it."

"About my assassination attempt?"

"No, about attempts in general. She got this really weird look on her face and brought up the need for me to be careful of attempts on my life. She said anything can happen in this political climate and that I needed to be vigilant."

I sigh and make my way over to sit on my throne. "So you didn't ask her anything."

"No. But I believe you all the same."

"Really?" This, I am surprised by.

"It didn't sit right with me, the way she brought it up. It was a red flag. So I took action and did some digging of my own."

"What did you find?"

"Honestly, not much."

My heart sinks. I can't afford to lose another ally in this House. Even a relatively neutral one. "I see," I reply. *But then again, he said he believed me. What's that all about?*

"I did find one connection though."

"You did?" My spirits lift ever so slightly.

"My mom's favorite bodyguard took a little vacation to the House of Fire right before the war. That man hasn't taken a vacation in like twelve years, and he doesn't go anywhere without my mother's say-so. I can't prove that anything went down there or who he talked to, but I know a rat when I see one."

"So you believe me?"

"Yes. I believe you."

I slump backward into the throne in relief. "I can't even begin to describe how good it is to have you believe me."

"I am sorry about what she did. And what I did. I should have believed you back on the boat. I didn't want to. You and I may never fully get along, but I didn't want you dead. And throughout all of this, you have never lied to me. You've yelled at me, you've said stuff that I didn't like, but you never lied."

"What are you going to do about it?"

Neil shakes his head. "Nothing for now. I'm going to keep an eye on her and her movements. I believe that since you made me heir, your life will be safe from an inside job for now."

"Good." I slowly get to my feet. "I should get up. Try to move forward."

Neil approaches me and offers me his hand to shake. "For what it's worth, I am sorry about your homeland."

I shake his hand firmly. "Thank you." When I let go, I can't help but ask one more question. "Do you have any advice for me?"

Neil pauses for a moment before looking up at me. "If I was speaking to you strictly about the House of the Evening, I would tell you to let it go and move on quickly so that you can get back to business."

My shoulders fall. "Of course."

"But if I was speaking to you as a leader," he continues to my surprise, "I would tell you to find a new avenue. Make it impossible for them to say no to you. Make it matter to them and their Houses. I don't pretend to know how you would do that... but if anyone could, I imagine it's you."

I grant him a smile. "Thank you."

"Best of luck to you."

"And to you as well."

We part ways, me out the door on the left and him to the right. In another world, we probably would have been good friends. I am partial to brothers after all. But we've both said too much and come too far to be anything more than tentative allies. At the end of the day, me naming him as heir was enough for him, and him believing me about his mother is enough for me. We'll never be friends, but at least I don't have to worry about him killing me anymore. Who knows, he might even save me from the final kill strike someday.

Well... maybe not that far.

Chapter Thirty-Three

As soon as I make it up the stairs, I find Aiden standing in front of my bedroom door, knocking wildly. "Grace! Grace, open up!"

"Can't open up when I'm not inside," I call down the hallway.

Aiden jumps back when he hears my voice and turns to look at me. "By the Lady, Grace. I've been pounding on your door for, like, ten minutes."

"Well, I'm sorry."

"Where have you been? You left the War Council meeting so quickly."

I scoff as I open my bedroom door. "Why do you think?"

"I'm sorry."

"Yeah, everyone seems to be saying that a lot. But sorry doesn't exactly help here."

"I understand that," Aiden says as he steps inside behind me and shuts the door. I make a beeline for my bed and sit on the end of it, leaning back on my hands. "But you can't deny that it will be nice for us to regroup, solidify the positions we have in the Realm, maybe even rebuild a little."

"I wish everyone would shut up about that," I spit out harshly. "I don't need to hear the same thing twelve hundred times."

"But it's not wrong to say it."

"No, Aiden. No, it's not wrong to say it. I'm sure for everyone in the alliance it's fucking amazing."

"And your House"

"I'm sorry?"

"Your House. The House of the Evening. You know, the House you run?" Aiden looks at me, confused. I look down and turn a light shade of red. "Grace," he says with slight exasperation in his voice. He comes over to me to kneel in front of me. "What's going on with you? You've been acting really off since the Middle Realm news."

I chuckle. "Are you really asking me this question?"

"It's more than just surface level stuff. It's not just because it's the Middle Realm. You're pissed at everyone. Even me and Faolan."

"Don't tell me who I'm mad at."

"Hell yeah, I will. Talk to me, Grace. What's going on?"

"I'm tired of everyone telling me how great this is for me as a leader! I'm not just a leader of a House here. I come from the Middle Realm; I'm a child of two realms."

"But you're not. Not really."

"By the Lady, Aiden, are you really gonna be anti-mortal too? After everything we've been through."

Aiden laughs harshly and gets off his knees, shaking his head. "Grace." He walks a ways into the entryway before turning around and moving back to me quickly. "This isn't about mortal vs. Fae. It's about you being the leader of a noble House. It doesn't matter where you come from. You're a High Lady. You are contractually obligated to put your House first in every single endeavor regardless of your personal feelings."

"But I'm not just a High Lady!" I leap to my feet and push my hands into my hair to grip it tight. "I'm so, so tired of people dismissing my mortal heritage. I really, really don't give a shit that everyone would love to just forget where I come from and speak to me like I've been here my entire life and of course I know what to do."

"No one looks at you like that."

"Everyone does. You heard the Council just a few days ago. Half of them prefer to forget my mortal side because it's easier. I don't care if I'm a Fae leader. I'm a mortal too. I come from humble roots. I didn't grow up in all this opulence. I didn't get trained in magic. I didn't get to learn half of what the rest of you know. What I do have over the rest of you is that I know what it's like to live in darkness and poverty and the bad times. I know what the people are suffering from. I lived it. None of you have."

"Then you should know even more clearly exactly why most of the Council doesn't want to go to bat for the Middle Realm," Aiden argues.

"I'm betraying them!" I shout. Aiden falls silent. "I'm betraying my realm the longer we wait!"

"Which realm, Grace?" Aiden asks quietly. "Which realm is yours?"

My frustration falters. My words stop just before they escape, and my breath trembles. I'm terrified to answer this question. I'm terrified that I may have to choose ultimately, and I'm terrified that I won't be able to. This is it, the crux of the entire issue, and he's just taken a knife to my skin and exposed it to the air. And once I stopped speaking, I became bare.

And he sees it.

"That's it, isn't it?" he says. "You haven't decided."

"Aiden…"

"No," he interrupts me. "Don't try to hide it. It's too late. You haven't decided which realm your allegiance lies with."

"I'm here, aren't I?"

"But it wasn't entirely your choice. You were brought here. You may have come at the request of your father, but it wasn't a full choice. You were caught between a rock and a hard place, and you stepped into the heirship. Then you became High Lady when your father died, and you didn't choose that either. And with that, you became the head of the War Council. That wasn't your choice. And the prophecy? You haven't had a single major choice for yourself in ages. Probably before all this, with Leo and your search. You've been called to action. You didn't go looking for. It came to you. And now you don't know what you want. And you're floundering."

There's rushing in my ears. Every word he says is like another tiny cut of his knife, carving away at my body until he reaches my heart. And he's fucking right. I can't remember the last time I said this is where I want to be. This is what I want to be doing. What does that mean for me? I never truly gave up the mortal piece of me, and the Fae part hasn't taken over me entirely even though I thought it had by now.

"What am I?" I thought I said it in my head, but judging by Aiden's face, I spoke aloud. "Am I Fae or mortal or both?"

"I can't answer that for you."

"Can I lead when the war is over, Aiden? Will the people continue to accept me when times are good and I'm keeping them from dying? Do they only accept me because we're winning? What happens if…" I trail off. I can't bring myself to say the rest of that sentence: what happens if I start losing?

"I don't know, Grace. I don't know the House of the Evening like you do or Neil does. You could talk to him about it."

I shake my head. "I don't think we could get into that."

"I do know two things for certain. One, you have done everything you can up until this point to protect us all. You have given everything you have to this war effort, and as much as you complain in private and sometimes in public, you haven't walked away."

My shoulders relax. He's right there. No matter how conflicted I feel in my soul, I never walked away.

"But two, if you push for aid to the Middle Realm, if you try to send an army in… the allies will never accept you."

Everything comes to a screeching halt.

"What?" I ask.

"They can't accept you if you cause them to lose lives of their House's people for a cause they don't believe in. You will be a pariah forever, regardless of the outcome of the war. You will be an outcast. You will never be seen as more than the mortal who took over a House by pure chance."

"That's not how it happened."

"You know that. I know that. But it doesn't change what people will see when they look at you."

I blink slowly, my shoulders slowly hunching in on themselves. I reach back behind me and stumble back into a seated position on the bed. My mind is racing. How can I just give up on the Middle Realm? What about my family there? Are they safe? If I don't step in, who will? But if I do step in, will I damn myself and my House to political exile forever?

Aiden shuffles forward briefly before stepping back. "I'm sorry to have said all that."

"I'm… I'm sorry I yelled," I reply absentmindedly.

Sensing he's not going to be getting much more from me, he takes another several steps back. "I'll leave you to think. Let me know if you want to talk." He opens the bedroom door and exits the room. When the door clicks shut, it echoes loudly in my head as I am left alone with the gravity of my thoughts.

Who am I?

What am I?

Chapter Thirty-Four

Aiden's words linger with me for a long time. I hate how much I am aware that he is right. My feelings about my identity really can't have any bearing on the type of political decisions that I make, no matter how conflicted I am. I may not have had all the choices that I would have liked, but I'm in charge of a House. I have to put their interests first. Despite how much it makes me want to throw up, I have to push down my emotions about the Middle Realm attack and move forward. If it's better for my people that we don't engage and take some time to heal, then that's what we're going to do.

That decision doesn't stop me from spending the next couple of days in bed, though.

When I do finally come out of the haze of self-pity, I receive an urgent message via my housekeeper from Aira, asking me to come to the library as soon as I can. I drag myself out of bed and get dressed before rushing down to meet her. The sight I am greeted with can only be described as a book explosion. Kiara sits in the center of a circle of tables that she's pulled together to effectively trap herself within it. She looks like she hasn't slept in days. Her hair sticks out in all directions. She flips pages of the book at the table she's facing frantically and takes notes before sliding her chair over to another table and flipping through that book.

Aira steps over to me from the shelves. "Grace! Thank the Lady you're here. You've gotta help me. Well, her. But also me. She's driving me crazy."

"Slow down, slow down," I say. "What's going on?"

"Kiara. She's been hunkered down here for days. She's only come out for the last couple of War Council meetings. I can barely convince her to eat or sleep."

"What is she doing?"

"Researching potions! She's still trying to figure out which potion the prophecy may require her to make. She's hyper-fixated on it, and I can't snap her out of it. You have to talk to her."

"What makes you think I can fix her?"

"I heard you talked to Cary and helped her figure out her role in the prophecy. I thought you could try again with Kiara."

"I can give it a shot." I follow behind Aira to where Kiara is working. "Hey Kiara," I greet her cautiously, unsure of whether or not she will react. As expected, she acts like she doesn't hear me. She's so deep in the moment, I doubt she even knows there are other people in the room. "Kiara." No response. "Kiara!"

When I raise my voice, she jumps in her chair and whips around to face me. "Grace. Hey. Aira? What are you guys doing here?"

"Aira said you needed some help," I reply.

"Oh, no. I don't want to trouble anybody. I've got it under control," Kiara speaks quickly. She's got that dismissive tone in her voice that I use when I don't want to talk to anybody or to let anybody know what I'm up to.

"It's no trouble, Kiara," I answer. "We're all in this together. What are you trying to figure out?"

"Grace, I don't need help."

"Please?"

At my plea, she completely breaks down, throwing the book in her hand across the room. It lands page side down with a loud crinkle.

"I can't figure this freaking thing out! I've gone over every potion book and encyclopedia I can find. Nothing, nothing jumps out to me. There are no ingredients that seem extraordinary enough to meet the challenge of a mystical final battle. Nothing seems incredible enough for me to brew. There's half a dozen special potions I could make that would aid in strengthening magic, but I have no idea what I would make. And what works for one person's magic is not going to work on another's magic. It's driving me crazy!"

Aira and I stand there stunned for a moment. I've never seen Kiara go off like that before. She's usually so calm and quiet. Aira starts laughing. "Finally!" she exclaims. "Why didn't you just say that before?"

Kiara flushes. "I'm under a lot of stress, okay? It's easier to just… block it all out."

I chuckle and pull up a chair across the table from her. "Don't I know it. Alright, I'm gonna tell you the same thing I told Cary. Whatever choice you make, it's already been fated. It's already the right choice. If you trust your instincts, you can't go wrong."

Kiara groans. "But I have no instincts! Every decision I try to make, I agonize over. I can't make a choice to save my life."

"But you did," I insist. "You communicated with me telepathically from your town in the House of Peace. You escaped with me. That took guts. You could have stayed there."

"I guess you're right. I did do that."

"Come on… take a look at the books again. Tell me the first thing that comes to your mind. What's the potion that's going to give us the best chance to succeed here? You said you're worried about picking something that's going to work for everyone's magic. Is there some sort of individualized potion you can make?"

Kiara thinks for a moment and flips a couple pages in the book in her hands. Then her eyes grow wide and she practically leaps from her chair to grab an encyclopedia of rare brews from the opposite side of the circle. She slams it down in front of me and thumbs through the book's edge until she finds a page sticking out. Whipping the cover over to that page, she celebrates. "Yes!"

"What is it?" Aira asks, leaning over to see over Kiara's shoulder.

"Blood magic."

"Blood magic?" Aira and I ask at the same time.

Kiara's face lights up. "Yes. Haven't you heard of it?"

"Yes…" I answer. "I've seen Faolan use one before. Aren't they incredibly complicated to make?"

"They're crazy to try to make!" Aira cries. "You have to be a crazy person to try to make them. It takes years and years of training to be able to put one together."

"I studied under one of the best potioners that I know," Kiara responds. "We never made one, but he taught me all the basic principles behind personalized potions. It's gonna take a lot of research and time in the lab, but I can put it together. I'm gonna need access to the lab, Grace. And I'm gonna need blood samples from everyone and a list of magic and—"

"Slow down!" I laugh and grip Kiara's shoulders. "You can have anything you need."

"Aira, I need your help. Can you help me bring these to the lab?"

"I'm on it!" Aira immediately begins gathering books. Kiara sits on the table, swings her legs around, and practically leaps off of the table. She heads into the stacks to search for more books.

I chuckle and get up from my seat, slowly backing out of the library. I think they've got it covered for now.

Chapter Thirty-Five

Kiara takes to her potion work right away. She still doesn't come out for meals and sleep very often, but at least she seems much happier about it. Every once in a while, she'll send a message to me about needing a certain set of books or a group of potion ingredients. I send someone to give her everything she needs. I'm happy to see that at least one element of the prophecy is moving along nicely. Who knows how long it's going to take to come to fruition. But it's a start nonetheless.

A few days later, I run into Faolan in the hallway on my way back from a meeting with my generals. In fact, I crash straight into him. The papers in my arms go flying everywhere. "Oh! Ugh," I groan as I get on my hands and knees to pick them up. "I'm sorry."

"No need," Faolan says as he joins me on the ground. "I haven't seen you in ages."

"I'm sorry. I feel like I've been running around since the last time I was alone with you. There are so many people to speak to, and just because we're regrouping doesn't mean that the war isn't still going on."

He smiles softly. "I understand, Grace. You don't need to explain it to me. I've been absent too. A lot of trips in and out of the palace to meet with my contacts."

"You've been out of the palace? How many times? How come you didn't tell me? Or did you tell me and I didn't notice?"

"Grace." Faolan grips my shoulders tightly. "Relax. Breathe. I didn't tell you because they were only short excursions into the city or the nearby towns. I haven't been outside the House of the Evening, I promise." He lightly pushes my hair behind my ear. "It hasn't been that long."

I sigh in relief and look down. "I'm so exhausted."

"How would you like to get away for a little while?"

"I really can't leave the palace. There are concerns from my men about future attacks or assassination attempts. I've essentially been asked to stay in the palace as much as possible."

Faolan smiles. "Who said we have to leave the palace?"

* * *

After stashing my papers in my room, Faolan leads me through a confusing series of doors and hallways, parts of the palace that I haven't fully explored before. He eventually opens a door on the top floor of the castle to reveal a staircase that continues upwards. "Where are you taking me?" I ask. "There aren't any towers on this side of the palace. And this is the top floor."

"A little place I found while exploring when I first got here. It was my secret, and now it can be yours too." He offers me his hand, which I take willingly. He pulls me up the stairs, opens the door on the other end, and we step out into the sunlight. I find myself on the palace roof, a flat shingled surface that the two of us are able to walk across with decorative iron spikes around the edge. I let go of Faolan's hands lightly and walk over to the edge to find the most spectacular view of my House. I can see the entire mountainside from here and the river on the opposite side of the city. In the sunlight, everything sparkles.

If I narrow my eyes, I can see little dots walking through the streets. My people.

"It's beautiful up here," I breathe.

"I'm glad you like it. I come up here when I need to think. I've always enjoyed being high above the crowd, observing things."

"Really?" I trail my hands over the spikes. "I used to do that too."

"Oh?"

I turn back to look at him. "Yes. There was a rooftop in Lisden on top of an old hotel. It used to be a rooftop patio where all the best parties happened. But when the city grew poorer, the hotel couldn't afford to stay open, and nothing ended up taking its place. But I liked to go up there and forget my troubles for a bit. It was nice to lay in the sun and be warm for a while."

"Well, this seems like as good a place as any, don't you think?" He offers me the roof with his hand.

I chuckle. "Sure. I wish I had a…"

"Blanket?" he suggests as he pulls one out from in between the roof tiles and the ceiling.

"Where is that from?"

"I stashed inside this little opening ages ago. It's nice to have up here." With a flick of his wrists, he spreads the blanket out for both of us and lays down on the right side. I join him on the left. With another motion of his hand, Faolan conjures a shadow to shield our eyes so that we can look up at the sky without blinding ourselves. We lie together basking in the warmth.

"What's your favorite high place?" I ask Faolan as I absentmindedly trace over the fabric of the blanket.

"There are too many to count. There are skyscrapers in the House of Darkness that I'm partial to. There are palaces, of course."

"This isn't the first palace roof that you've been on?"

Faolan laughs. "No, of course not. But it is the one with the prettiest view." He turns on his side to look at me and winks.

I roll my eyes, but give him a smile. "You're ridiculous."

"No, dear. Just honest."

I study him carefully. "Do you have any idea where you might want to go after all of this?"

"What do you mean?"

"I mean… when the war is over and the dust settles. Where might you go?"

"I don't know," he answers. "I've never really thought about it. If my father is gone or imprisoned, I suppose that makes me the next heir to the House of Darkness. If the Council will allow it."

"I'm sure I can make that happen."

"I doubt even you will be able to get a unanimous vote on that."

"I will if I have to."

"Are you suggesting blackmailing Council members, Grace?" Faolan's jaw drops in mock surprise. "Maybe you have a little darkness in you after all."

I give him a little shove. "Maybe I won't help you then."

Faolan laughs. "What about you? What do you want to do?"

"I don't know either."

"You'll be the conquering hero of every story told for the next hundred years. You'll have quite the street cred."

"I'm sure I will. But… if I'm being perfectly honest, I think I would just like to be ordinary again. Even for a little while. Take some time off when the war is over."

"Well, I certainly hope you get to do that."

"Thank you."

"Of course."

The two of us stay on the roof for hours, idly chatting about whatever comes to our minds and soaking in the morning sun. I tell him stories about my childhood, running around with Leo and terrorizing our little neighborhood. He tells me about his travels running the Black Market, sharing small details of Houses that I've never been to and never would have guessed in a hundred years. If there was ever a man to know where the hidden treasures are, it would be Faolan. He shows me how to make little figures out of light and darkness, and I create tiny elemental ornaments of wind and fire. We have a little contest, seeing how long his figures can toss around the spheres before I burst them into dust. I can't stop laughing as he struggles to keep my fireball from exploding. The way he smiles knowingly at me when I laugh thrills me.

This feels right.

This just feels... right.

Chapter Thirty-Six

After my meeting with Faolan, I feel reenergized. It's so nice to escape from it all temporarily, particularly in a place where I can look down on the world and let it pass by without me. And Faolan, he doesn't force me to think about anything that I'm not ready to think about. We take it slow and we talk about whatever comes to mind. It was really, really nice to be able to get to know him a little better. He doesn't tell many stories. I feel honored that he allows me to see behind the tough exterior.

With my spirits high, I decide to go for a walk outside of the palace. I may not be able to leave the grounds right now without an escort for the House's fear of additional attacks and/or assassination attempts, but I can at least make my way around the gardens and the training areas. In another life, at another time, I would probably even enjoy the palace gardens. It's one of the most colorful places in the House of the Evening. Every pathway is lined with beautiful flowers of all shapes and sizes and topiary sculptures that reach toward the sky. There are fountains that mark where each path intersects, impressive structures carved from marble and precious stones. It's something to distract me, to keep me in high spirits until I have to come back down to earth.

When I reach the arena area, I hear the sounds of magic being practiced. There are light thuds as spells hit the training dummy or the dirt. I peer over the top to see who is training to find Aiden. I watch as he sends flames in a wide circle to take out a set of targets. When he brings his hands together, he raises up a section of the ground with his earth magic, sand on top of dirt on top of rock. He changes the angle and drives the makeshift post straight into the target's heart. I have to admit, I love watching the raw power that many of the prophecy members exude.

Aiden looks over his shoulder and finds me watching him. "Hey!" he shouts up at me.

"Hello!" I call back. "You're doing great."

He laughs. "Why don't you come down here and get a closer look?"

I think on it for a moment and decide to offer him a bit of grace since I'm in such a good mood. I rush down the stairs until I get to the bottom of the arena. The familiar feeling of packed sand under my toes centers me as I walk over to him. "What brings you to the arena?"

"Well, everyone else seems to have been taking their turns here. I thought it was probably time I get in a little practice myself."

"Do you want a sparring partner?"

Aiden raises an eyebrow. "Really? You're willing to get in the ring with me?"

"Why not? I'm avoiding my other responsibilities at the moment, so you would be a welcome distraction."

Aiden chuckles and rolls his eyes. "Alright. What's the game?"

"Whoever can knock the other off their feet the fastest wins."

"Physically or magically?"

"Which one do you need more practice with?"

"You remember the last time I fought you with a sword?"

"Oh, you want to take it all the way back to that? If you remember correctly, I gave you a rough fight."

"Magic it is."

I wave him forward. "Take your position then."

With a small smirk, Aiden backs away and faces me with both hands at the ready. I bring my hands up as well and smile back. A good fight always lights a fire under me. Speaking of… I start us off, sending a wave of fire toward Aiden. He blocks it with one of his shields before sending a concentrated fireball at me. I duck, and the game begins.

We move against each other in a delicate dance, stepping forward and backward as the spells cause it. He sends me spinning across the arena as I try to avoid the ground that he is exploding under me. He's quick. He anticipates my movements as I'm making them. His sourcing magic makes it impossible for me to surprise him. But that doesn't mean I'm not holding my own. My fire magic is stronger than Aiden's, and each time our magic comes into conflict with each other, my flames push his back a little more each time. I send strong gusts of wind his way, pushing his feet back. His force fields do quite a bit to block it, but even he is forced to take a few steps back.

To try to trip him up, I use my telekinesis powers to move one of the test dummies to his back, hoping to knock him over. But he forces the earth up behind him to block its advance. "Nice try, Grace," Aiden teases. "But you're not going to pull one over on me that easily."

"It's a pretty even fight here," I reply, breathing heavily. "Wanna make it more interesting?"

"How so?"

"Fist fight? No magic allowed."

"Lovely."

Aiden charges at me, but I'm ready for him. I swing my arm up to catch his and catch him right in the stomach. In his outrush of breath, I push him over intent on slamming him to the ground. To my surprise though, Aiden has the strength to flip me up and over his shoulder. I hit the ground hard, sending the air out of my lungs as he rolls over and pins me to the ground. "Gotcha," he says.

I cough hard for a couple of seconds and then laugh. "Ow."

Aiden laughs. "Sorry about that."

"It's fine," I reply. "You win."

"You're getting pretty good at controlling your magic."

"Thanks. You're not so bad yourself." Aiden laughs again, and I shake my head lightly at the silliness of it all. It's about then that I notice that Aiden's arms are still pinning me down. "Are you planning on letting me up?"

"Oh yeah, of course." Despite his reply, Aiden doesn't make any move to let me up from my position on the ground. His hands lighten their grip on my wrists, but they don't let go. He has the strangest look in his eyes when he looks at me. I don't know what he's thinking.

"Aiden?" I ask.

Suddenly, his lips are on mine.

I'm in a complete state of shock. Aiden's lips feel warm, too warm against mine as he kisses me. I immediately kick upwards, hitting his thigh and forcing him up. I roll out from underneath him and scramble to my feet. He looks at me so confused. "Grace? What's wrong?"

"What… what's wrong? What's wrong? You kissed me!"

"I thought it was a good time!"

"Why in the world would you think that was a good time to kiss me?"

"Things were going so well. You looked so happy and you were talking to me and laughing with me, I just… I just went for it. I'm sorry."

"Sorry! You're sorry? What makes you think I want you to kiss me? We've been over this a million times, Aiden."

"But things have been better! You and I got along just fine in the House of Water toward the end, you let me into your room only a few days ago to talk, and now we're sparring. It's just like the old days,

CHAPTER THIRTY-SIX

Grace."

"It is not just like the old days, Aiden. I told you we're finished!"

"And I refuse to believe that! You know what we had!"

"*Had*, Aiden. Had!"

"You are the love of my life, Grace. I have spent years looking for someone who could even come close to matching what I'm looking for. I made a mistake going home. I chose duty over love. I won't do the same thing again. Please, all I want is one more chance. Give me a chance to prove to you that this is real to me."

It's heartbreaking to watch him plead with me. There's the tiniest part of me that is still in love with him. There's so much history between us. He was my first true introduction to the Upper Realm. He saved me from the soldiers, he followed me on my journey, he saved my life more than once. And I saved his in the duel of the heirs. He was my first. That's not something that you ever really forget. I loved him for so long. But the hurt that I feel for the way he left cuts too deep. And the way he came back, expecting to be forgiven quickly, pushing for me to be with him like nothing has changed? I can't excuse that.

Everything has changed. I'm not the same girl he left behind.

"Get out," I say quietly.

"What?"

"Get out. I don't want to see you. Go back to the palace."

"Grace..."

"I said *get out.*"

Aiden watches me as he slowly picks himself up off the ground. He's searching for a hint of sympathy in my eyes, some part of me that wants to ask him to stay. But it's not there. He sighs quietly and heads up the stairs to leave the arena. I don't take my eyes off of his back until he's gone, and then I collapse to the ground.

Chapter Thirty-Seven

The weight of what just happened forces me to the ground, laying flat in the middle of the arena. I stare up at the sky and the sun, hoping it will blind me and put me out of my misery. *Why does this have to be so complicated? Why can't we just cut straight to the case and fight the big evil so that we can all just... stop? Or at least send all the people back home. Maybe then I could finally have some time to think.*

"Hey!" A loud female voice shouts from the top of the arena. I look up to find a furious Cary storming down the stairs toward me.

"Whatever you've come to yell at me about, I'm not in the mood," I groan at her as I push myself to a standing position.

"I saw you, you stupid woman," she sneers at me. "I saw you and Aiden. I saw you kiss."

"I'm guessing you missed the part where he kissed me against my wishes?"

"Oh, I saw the whole confrontation. Specifically how you didn't fling him across the goddamn arena for what he tried to do to you!"

"Cary." I hold my hands up to try to assuage her anger. "I don't throw my friends."

She scoffs. "Some friend. Friends know how to take no for an answer." She jabs her finger into my chest. "I don't think you're telling the whole truth. Did you tell him about Faolan?"

"Yes! I did."

"Did you tell him you kissed?"

"Yes!"

"Did you tell him you're in love with him?" When I don't answer her, she growls. "That's it, isn't it? You haven't told Aiden there's no hope yet."

"I shouldn't have to."

"No! You shouldn't. But you've been playing both sides for a while now. Too scared to tell Aiden the truth, too bone-headed to tell my brother how you feel. You just keep putting off the inevitable, and you are hurting people unnecessarily."

"We are in the middle of a Lady-damned war, Cary! Not everything can be about matters of the heart."

"Oh, stop using that as your excuse!" Cary shoves me backward. I tumble to the ground in surprise. "How long are you going to pretend that this is just about the war? This is about your indecision. This is about your inability to say no. It's about your need to drag both of these men along so they'll do your bidding."

"My bidding?"

"Both of those men are prepared to die for you. You do realize that, right? And one of them is my brother, so you're going to have to do a hell of a lot better than that to convince me that you're not just toying with other's lives at will."

"I don't toy with anyone," I spit back at her as I stand back up. "And I didn't choose this."

"No. But you've enabled it."

"I'm not the enemy here, Cary."

"Then stop acting like it. If you hurt him, Grace, I swear to the Lady I will hunt you down."

"You know Faolan will never let you get near me."

"What he doesn't know won't hurt him."

"And what are you going to tell him about this little encounter?" I ask.

"Don't worry, High Lady. I'm not going to tell him now. Not until I know what the hell you're up to."

"Not going to tell me what?" The two of us whip around to find Faolan coming down the stairs. My breath catches in my chest. *Damn.*

"It's nothing, Faolan," Cary says through gritted teeth. "Grace and I were just having a little chat."

"Uh-uh." Faolan shakes his head at her. "I know that face. You don't just have 'little chats' with anyone. What happened?" Neither Cary nor I answer the question. His eyes narrow. "What happened?"

"Aiden kissed me," I blurt out. Cary groans as soon as I admit it. Faolan freezes. "What?"

"We sparred, and we were having just a regular fight and he beat me, and I asked him to let me up, but suddenly he kissed me! I pushed him off of me right afterwards, but he—"

I don't get to finish my sentence because suddenly, Faolan takes off like a shot up the stairs and out of the arena. Cary and I immediately take off after him. Faolan storms directly into the palace. Unfortunately, Aiden is coming down the front stairs, still looking as despondent as he did earlier. When he sees us running toward him, he starts to speak. I never find out what that is because Faolan draws back his hand and punches him directly in the face. There's a hard crunching sound before Aiden falls back and slides down the stairs, taking Faolan down with him. The two tumble down several steps to the ground. Cary immediately rips Faolan off of Aiden before he can land another punch. I stand frozen in the entryway.

"What the hell, man?" Aiden shouts as he tries to stop the bleeding of his nose. "What the hell did I do to you?"

"Keep… your hands off of her," Faolan forces out through his teeth. "You keep your hands off of her. If you touch her again without her permission, I'll rip you limb from limb."

CHAPTER THIRTY-SEVEN

"Faolan," I manage to breathe.

The man looks at me, and the amber in his eyes softens just the slightest bit. "If he does it again," he says gruffly. "You tell me." With that, he pushes Cary off of him and storms outside. She rushes after him, but I stay frozen to my spot. I can't seem to force my feet to move. Someone helps Aiden off the ground and moves him in the direction of the healer's office.

What the hell just happened?

I feel like everything that I have been trying to keep in a delicate balance is spiraling out of control around me. Cary was right, I have been trying to spare everyone's feelings while I've been working through my own issues. And look where that's got me. Faolan's angry, Aiden's hurt, and Cary might kill me if the assassins don't finish the job first. Maybe staying away from everybody is best for me right now. No sense in causing any more damage.

Chapter Thirty-Eight

To avoid the Fae men, I decide to stick to the potion lab with Kiara and Aira. I watch Kiara day in and day out experimenting with different ingredient combinations to match everyone's magical blood type. Apparently some people's blood magic potions are turning out to be much more difficult than others. Especially mine. Because my magic signature is so complex with all of my magic types, it's not a combination that has been particularly cataloged. So she is having to try a ton of different ingredients and brews in hopes of finding a potion that will be stable enough. I suggested that she seek out Talon for his expertise. He agrees to help eagerly. Researching seems to put him back in good spirits.

During one of their brewing sessions, progress seems to finally be coming along. I sit with my arm outstretched as they swab various substances on my arm to see how they react. It's a little bit slimy and cold, but this is still much better than dealing with my emotional problems outside this room. I absentmindedly stare at the door while they work. I must have zoned out because I jump out of my seat when the door suddenly flies open. Kiara has to scramble to catch potion vials before they fall over and break. Neil of all people rushes in.

"Hey Neil, what's going on?" I ask.

"I need you to come with me right now," he replies with an urgent look in his eyes.

"I'm in the middle of something for the war effort. Can it wait?"

"No, it can't. There's a massive brawl that's broken out in the town center between the townspeople and the most recent influx of refugees. I don't know the details, but we have to go right now."

My eyes widen, and I immediately grab the cloth on the table and wipe off my arm. "I've got to go," I toss out as a quick explanation to my friends and rush after Neil outside. As we run through the palace, my mind is racing. I have no idea what could be happening out there right now. What could have caused something like this? Has the House of Darkness infiltrated again? Or the House of Fire? Is someone pulling the strings of the people? What in the world would have made them snap like this?

Neil summons a couple of horses from the stables, and the two of us gallop off toward the town in the distance. "Why aren't we taking the carriages?" I shout at him.

"No time!" he calls back. "We need to stop this before it gets out of hand!"

"How? Are we supposed to get in the middle of it?"

"I have no idea, Grace. But our presence will hopefully be enough to help stop it."

Once we reach the town, we can barely get in. It's a horrifying sight. The market streets are clogged with people in an all-out fist fight. Bodies are packed tightly together as the sounds of punches, kicks, and cries ring out in the square. The tables where rations are usually passed out to the people have been knocked over. Food and supplies are scattered all across the ground, and those who aren't caught in the crowd are scrambling to collect them and run off. Others who have broken away charge for them. Similarly to when the House of Darkness attacked, there is magic flying left and right. This time however, it's the people against themselves.

Our horses are too scared to try to navigate the chaos, so Neil and I immediately jump off. "What are we gonna do?" I ask.

"I don't know. What do you want to do? You're the High Lady."

I sigh harshly. "Right." Thinking fast, I send out a strong pulse of empathetic magic through the crowd. It causes a few of them to freeze where they stand and turn around to see where the magic is coming from. "You have empathetic magic, don't you?" I ask Neil.

"Yes. It's a House of the Evening trait."

"Good. Use it."

Working together, the two of us send multiple powerful pulses of magic through the crowd. I don't know which emotions Neil is using, but I am pushing a desperate need for the people to stop and look around to see what they are doing to each other. Desperation, despair… it's powerful stuff. Eventually, the crowd turns into an emotional wreck, looking around at each other in panicked confusion. Once the fighting has stopped, I rush up to the broken tables to speak to my people in charge of the distribution.

"What happened?" I ask the nearest guard.

"It was chaos. Today, the supply transport that came in had way less grain than usual. We couldn't give out the rations like we originally planned, so we had to cut things down significantly."

"How much?"

"By nearly a third."

I wince. "That's not good."

"No. It's been bad here recently."

"Why haven't I heard about this?"

"Because up until today, it was primarily items that were already in low supply. Certain fabrics, fruit, sweets. Certain kinds of meats. But today, when the main staples were cut so dramatically, people started to get frustrated. Someone saw a refugee from the House of Light try to take a little extra for her and her husband. He tried to take it out of her hands, but her husband came in and punched him. That was the last thing I saw clearly before suddenly everyone was fighting. People were getting trampled, being pulled away. It was unlike anything I've ever seen before."

"Why was the supply transport so depleted?"

"Well, the extra supply we were getting to help supplement our House comes from the Middle Realm. I don't know anything specific, but I do know that suddenly, wherever we were getting it from stopped trading with us."

I draw in a sharp breath. The consequences of not dealing with the House of Darkness and the Middle Realm. It's finally caught up with us. I just knew that eventually, not doing anything to stop it would come to affect all of us. And I was fucking right. My mind races. This could be the thing that finally convinces the War Council it's time to act.

"What do you want us to do, High Lady?" the guard asks me.

I immediately motion for Neil to come over to join me. He rushes over from where he was helping a group of people back to their feet. "Neil, I need you to work with these guards to take stock of what supplies are salvageable. Then I need you to call down every available healer that we have at the palace. I am going back to the palace to see what supplies we can spare from our stores to help the people. I'll be back with reinforcements."

"Alright. Hurry back," he replies, patting me once on the back.

I race off to my horse, swinging myself onto her and racing back to the palace. As I ride down the path, I think about how close we are coming to breaking apart. Me, my friends, my House. Something needs to change, or we're going to destroy ourselves before the enemy does.

Chapter Thirty-Nine

I call the War Council in for an emergency meeting immediately the next morning. This resource issue needs to be resolved quickly or the people are going to tear each other apart. As the nobles file in, I notice that all of them look incredibly wary of me. It occurs to me that this is the first time many of them have seen me since Lord Jason and I got into that verbal smackdown. I wonder if they think I'm going to lose my temper again. I'll do my best not to.

But I make no promises.

"Okay," I begin. "So many of you heard or were witness to the brawl that broke out in the town center yesterday. It is clear that we have a major problem with the flow of resources into the House of the Evening. The supply chain has slowed to a barely manageable level, and with the influx of refugees into town plus all of the armies centered in one place, we have finally reached a boiling point."

"I've never seen anything like what I saw yesterday," Tristan says quietly. "People willing to use their magic against their neighbors without fear of repercussions. Over grain and salt, no less."

"Wars have been started over less," Faolan replies gravely.

"The first thing that I can think of to start alleviating the problem immediately is the slowing of aid to the Houses that have been liberated," I declare.

"Absolutely not!" Kiara cries out.

"No way," the twins from the House of Light echo.

"There's got to be another way," Jason insists. "Cutting that aid now would be disastrous for our Houses. Our farms are barely back up and running. Some will take months to be in good enough repair. We can't be without food and supplies that long."

"Well, the House of the Evening can't go much longer with this much strain," I reply quickly. "Look, like it or not, I and my House have been supporting almost all of you and your Houses for months at this point. We have sacrificed plenty during wartime to make sure that everyone stayed fed and reasonably stocked. I sent soldiers, carpenters, architects, stonemasons, agricultural liaisons, merchants, money, crops, weapons to every House that we have liberated. The Treasury is nearly depleted. Our supplies are tapped out. We cannot afford any longer to support everyone."

"What triggered this sudden implosion?" Jason asks. "We were doing okay before. People grumbled about having to take rations, but no one complained. Everyone knew that this was what needed to be done so that everyone could make it through the war. But what changed to cause people to start fighting each other in the streets?"

"I did some digging," I chime in. Everyone turns to look at me as I slide several inventories around the table. "Turns out that Fort Faol has a decent sized salt mine. It is responsible for around thirty percent of the House of the Evening's salt supply. Additionally, Fort Faol was responsible for fifteen percent of the House's supplementary grain stock. When the city fell, there was nothing there to replace it." I relish in the room's shocked silence. "So, by not putting our best foot forward into the Middle Realm, we are now in dire straits."

"High Lady Grace, there was no way we could have known that—" Jason attempts to speak.

"Yes, there was," I snap and quickly jump to my feet, leaning in close to him. He shrinks back, and I relish in it. "You could have listened to me the first time. You could have listened to me when I told you that we had a responsibility to the people that the Fae tied to their fate a long time ago. You could have—"

"Understood that when the Middle Realm falls, we fall," Faolan interrupts me. I turn to stare at him, glowering. He ignores me. "The resources that we get from the Middle Realm are invaluable to the functioning of our society, particularly salt and supplementary grain. They've taken at least one city. Decimated it. It won't be long before they take the others, and those resources will cease to exist for our Realm. Whether you like it or not, we have a financial responsibility to protect them. If you don't believe in the moral responsibility," he quickly adds after seeing my face.

"What are you proposing?" Tristan asks.

Faolan keeps his eyes toward me as he speaks. "I am proposing that we send a small delegation to the Middle Realm… to Lisden." My anger recedes just a little bit. *A chance to go home. Maybe he won't be mad at me forever.* "We should send a small amount of aid: some weapons, food, basic supplies. Not enough to deplete our stores, but enough to show that we do care what happens to them and keep relations open. I will prep my black market mortals on the ground to shore up defenses in Lisden and spread that information to other towns and cities."

"How many of us need to go?"

"I will be going," I declare.

"You're our leader. You can't just leave," Jason says.

"The people of Lisden know me. I am their best chance. Neil will be in charge of the House of the Evening while I'm gone, and I will appoint someone to take care of the War Council duties. It won't be disruptive to our plans."

"I would also want to take Aiden, Aira, and Luna," Faolan adds. "Their Houses have had the most dealings with the Middle Realm, and their presence should be enough." The named people react differently to being called. Aiden seems surprised that Faolan suggested he join us, but he seems to come to terms with the idea very quickly. After all, he did come there briefly. Luna is excited to travel, practically bouncing on the edge of her seat at the opportunity. Aira, however, looks nervous as hell. She looks like she wants to turn it down.

"Do you all agree with the proposition?" I ask. "Will you go?"

"Absolutely," Aiden replies.

"Of course," Luna echoes.

Aira takes longer to answer. She avoids my gaze. "Aira?" I ask again, a little more gently.

"I'm in," she finally says.

"Good." I then return to my steely eyed face to address the rest of the Council.

"I want a unanimous vote here," I enunciate. "I expect a unanimous vote."

My dark eyes must be enough to whip them into shape because I get what I want.

Finally.

I'm going home.

Chapter Forty

As we plan for our trip to the Middle Realm, I have to figure out who I am placing in charge of the War Council in my absence. Many of the obvious people that I would consider putting in charge, my most trusted, are coming with me. For a while, I contemplated placing Gideon in charge. He's certainly qualified to do so. But I realized that it was highly possible that he would take over and likely not cede control back to me when I returned. He also won't simply maintain the status quo or act solely in emergencies. No, he's an action-seeker. Plus I am still pissed at him about his vote against the Middle Realm aid. Cary should have been an option too. But she also voted against the aid, and she's still pissed at me about Aiden. My explanation didn't do much to calm her down. Ultimately, I put Tristan in charge. He may have voted against the aid in the beginning, but he was definitely the easiest to sway with emotional arguments. He's not the weakest among the group, but not the strongest either. Gideon and Cary should be able to steer him in a good direction.

My group leaves as swiftly as we can, making our way to the House of War via the ocean route. They welcome our delegation with open arms. Well, about as open as the House of War can be: they allow us to stay in an inn near the dock with their protection before we depart in the morning. One calm cargo ship ride later, we arrive at Bay Point on the Middle Realm coast. I thank the Lady that it was a smoother trip than the last time I had to make the journey with Aiden. From there, I book a train to Lisden.

Entering the city makes me feel both excited and nervous. I can't believe I'm back here again. It looks the same as when I left it. The smells of the grocery stores and the smog from the factories are the same, the sounds of people making their way to and from work. But I have no idea what's going to happen next. The last time I was here, I brought in a Fae lord and fought and lost a friend of mine. That was before, before I learned anything about who I was. I never even visited my family.

I try not to allow myself any time to linger. Not until the work is done. I promptly lead the small group of us directly from the train station to the governor's office. The brick building sits in the middle of the city surrounded by a small park. When we walk inside, I am surprised that we are able to make it as far as the main chamber before running into any security. Unfortunately, the same cannot be said for when we reach the governor's front office. The guards, the secretary, and those working at nearby desks seem to recognize us as Fae instantly as the whole room goes silent. I feel stares upon me as I approach the secretary at her desk.

"I am Grace Andrea Richardson Faelie, the High Lady of the House of the Evening," I say, opting for a softer polite voice rather than a commanding one. "And I need to speak to the governor immediately."

The mortal security surrounding the office lock ranks, staring me down. I don't know what they believe they are accomplishing by this. I mean them no harm, nor do I mean the governor any harm. I'm trying to do this the polite way by asking and waiting to be received. Storming in isn't going to look good, particularly with what the House of Darkness has done to the realm so far. But I will be speaking to him, one way or another.

The secretary looks at me with disdain. "You need an appointment to speak with the Governor. Your status in your Realm does not give you any privilege here. Not anymore."

"It is urgent. It's regarding the recent attacks."

"By your kind."

"Those Fae are not my kind. I am not one of them."

"And yet you are."

"Ma'am, we do not mean any harm," Faolan speaks from behind my shoulder.

"I will speak to them," a new male voice joins the conversation. I look up to find the governor of Lisden standing in the doorway to his office. He's a tall, stately gentleman with grayish hair and pale eyes. He holds my gaze with intensity, a frown crossing his lips. "I want to hear what they have to say."

"Thank you, Governor," I answer quickly. The others echo my words. We follow behind him into his office. The guards stand watch as the doors close, two on the inside and the rest on the outside. The governor takes a seat at his desk while the rest of us remain standing.

"I'm not sure I have spoken to you before, High Lady," the governor says to me. "I was under the impression that the head of the House of the Evening was an older man."

The question shakes me, but I keep my head held high. "That would be my late father, sir. I have taken his place."

"I see." The governor noticeably does not offer condolences. "What do you wish to discuss with me, High Lady?"

"We need to speak with you about the attack in the West."

"Yes… the attack. The attack your people levied on mortal land."

"Not my people," I quickly counter. "A sector of the Upper Realm has gone rogue and has and has begun trying to take land and resources that are not theirs to take."

"That is inconsistent with our reports."

"What have you been hearing?" Faolan asks.

"We were informed that the Fae grow tired of their trade dealings with us, and they have chosen to show their disdain by capturing one of our cities. Intel says you plan to take every single one until you have subjugated this realm fully."

"Your intel is incorrect."

"Is it? Because now you're here. There hasn't been a formal noble Fae visit in decades. You always send an underling to do your bidding."

"I wish you would stop using the word 'you'," I say cooly. "I have not sent anyone. Not only have I not sent anyone, I have not been a Fae noble for very long."

"I do not trust you. You are Fae, and Fae cannot be trusted."

The strength of his conviction and the blank stare in his eyes remind me of myself. I looked exactly the way he did when those Fae soldiers brought news of my brother's death. So much hate and so little understanding. I can't explain the intensity of how I felt in those days, but if I could describe it, I would pinpoint it as the look staring back at me from the governor's face. It is unnerving to be on the other end of it.

"I am not only Fae," I reply quietly. I feel Faolan stiffen behind me as I admit the truth. "I am mortal too."

"You lie!" the governor shouts and gets to his feet, slamming his fists on his desk. I can't help but step back quickly at his unexpected explosion. I feel Faolan steady me from behind.

"I do not!" I shout back. "I was born mortal. I lived here in Lisden for nineteen years; I was born here. You can check your records. I was born Grace Andrea Richardson. My mother is Amelia Richardson; there is no father on the birth certificate. I am not a liar."

"Get them out of my office," he says to the guards. "I want them out!"

My friends close ranks around me, prepared to fight to hold our ground. I'm not prepared for this meeting to come to blows. This has gone so wrong already. I hold my hands up in surrender. "Alright! Alright! We'll walk out. We do not need to be thrown out. We will leave of our own volition."

The governor looks skeptical, but he waves his guards off. "I want you to leave my city right now."

"This is my city too. I will leave your office, but I will leave when I am good and ready to leave. I hope to speak to you again with better results shortly." With that, I lead my friends out of the office and toward the exit of the building.

Once we're outside, the panic starts to set in. "What are we gonna do now?" Aira hisses to me. "They won't even talk to us."

"I have no idea," I respond honestly. "But we're not gonna get anywhere arguing with everyone. We'll get a plan together and try again." I take a slow deep breath. "But there's somewhere I need to be first."

Chapter Forty-One

I stand in front of my uncle's apartment door with my hands in fists down by my sides. I know I can't stand here forever with the entire group behind me waiting for me to make a move. The silence is deafening as I try to get my body to move forward, to raise my hand and knock on the door. But even if I could get myself to that point, I have no idea what happens next. Does he even still live in this apartment? Is my mother with him? And if he is, what do I say? Where do I even begin to tell him where I've been all this time? And by the Lady, I look so different. What if he's scared of me or pissed at me like the others were?

"Grace?" Aiden interrupts my thoughts. Snapping out of my head, I quickly knock three times on the door. After a long pause, no one answers. Closing my eyes, I knock again. Once, twice, thr— The door flies open before I can complete the last knock. My uncle stands in the doorway with a kitchen towel in his hand. When he sees me, his fingers release almost immediately, and the towel falls to the floor. He stares at me intensely, not a muscle in his body moving. I stare back at him, unsure of what to say or what to do, just waiting for his reaction to know how I should respond.

Suddenly, he grabs my hand and pulls me in tightly, hugging me in a vice-like grip. His body shakes against mine, and I realize that he's sobbing into my hair. I wrap my arms around him tightly, and I feel tears in my own eyes. My uncle clutches me close like he's never going to let go. "Grace… you're alive," his broken voice sobs in my ear.

"I'm alive… I'm alive… I'm so sorry." The words tumble from my mouth in incoherent strings through my cries. I had no idea what it was going to feel like to return home after all this time and see my family. It's like the floor has been ripped from under me and I'm just free falling. I can't control it. It takes many minutes before we are able to let go of each other.

"Grace," my uncle says, his eyes suddenly focusing on the people behind me. "Who are they? What is going on? How did you…" His voice trails off.

I chuckle in spite of myself. "It's a really… really long story. Can we sit down? You're really gonna want to sit down for this."

The group of us move into my uncle's kitchen. My friends stand against the walls off to the side, giving me and my uncle a little space. The two of us sit down, and I launch into the tale. I start with the months after Leo's death where I prepared for the journey to the Upper Realm. I talk about how David helped me to get the supplies I needed and how difficult it was for me to have left him that note the night I left. I walked through the journey through the Upper Realm, picking up clues along the way. I explained Aiden and Faolan and as many of the other characters I met along the way and have brought with me.

When I tell him I am Fae, he stares at me a long time before answering. "When your mother told me about the weeks she spent with the man who turned out to be your father, I thought there was something mysterious about him. The way she talked about him, the way he looked, the way he moved, she was always in awe of him. And when you were born, you were a very different baby. You were always able to be soothed by music or humming or singing the way your brother never was." He brushes my hair behind my ear to look at it more closely. "And your ears… I can see it now."

"You're not upset with me?" I ask.

My uncle's eyes grow wide with surprise. "Upset? Why would I be upset with you for the way you were born?"

My breath rushes out like a rapid gust. I was very worried that my uncle would reject me for my heritage. I take both of his hands and squeeze them tightly. "Thank you."

"Of course. Now what brings you here?"

"I want to know about my mother. Is she alright?" My uncle tilts his head slightly, hesitating. I pick up on it immediately. "What's wrong?" I immediately demand. "What happened?" My heart seizes. "Is she dead?"

"No, no, she's not dead," he quickly reassures. "It's complicated."

"Is she well? Is she here? I have to see her."

"Grace…"

"Did she move away? Is she gone?" My brain is running through all of the possibilities. *I have to find her.*

"Who is making all of that racket?" My mother's voice meets my ears, and I immediately whip around to see her coming into the kitchen. Looking at her is like looking directly into the past. Nothing has changed. Her hair is tied back in her favorite style, and she's wearing that blue floral dress with her white apron that always meant she was getting ready to cook something amazing. I grin brightly and leap up from my seat.

"Mama." I rush forward to meet her, but my uncle's arm stops me quickly. I look at him in confusion.

"Grace?" My mother looks at me with haunted bewilderment. "Grace?"

"It's me, Mom. I'm home."

"Grace," my uncle speaks to me in a warning tone.

I don't get to hear what the rest of the warning is because suddenly, my mother shrieks at the top of her lungs. All of my friends and my uncle cover their ears. I am too in shock to move to do so myself. "Mom!" I try to shout over the noise. She barely hears me. I push past my uncle's arm and hug her tightly. "Mom, it's me!" She doesn't move at all in my embrace.

I pull back to look at her, and that's when I see her eyes. They stare so far away like they're looking at something in a completely different realm, maybe even past the Three Realms. I wave in front of them, and when they reconnect back with mine, she gasps and shoves me away from her. I tumble backward. Aiden catches me before I can hit the ground. As he steadies me, I stare back at her in horror. "You're not my daughter!" she screams. "You're not my daughter! Get out, Fae scum!"

"Mom," I whisper, heartbroken.

"You took my babies," she sobs brokenly. "Get out!"

Something inside me snaps, and I sprint out of the room to the front door. I spot my old violin on the wall, sitting as a tribute to my memory. It's the only thing that feels familiar to me in the room, possibly in the whole city. In a fit of passion, I wrench it off the wall and take it with me. The door slams against the wall as I fling it open and take off down the hallway. I hear Aiden and Faolan both shout after me, but I can't get my feet to stop. I fly down the hall, down the back stairway, and into the street.

My chest aches with heavy sobs. My own mother doesn't recognize me. I have come home to ruin. Everywhere I go, everywhere I leave, I leave nothing but ruin.

My feet do the thinking for me, taking me to the rooftop where I spent much of my more emotional times overlooking the city. But when I look out over the cityscape now, all I see is gray and misery. The clouds sit low, blocking most of the beauty from me. Looking down at the violin in my hand, all I can feel is the pain and utter torture of having my mom yell at me with such ire. The stupid instrument feels like a reminder of everything I lost by choosing to stay in the Upper Realm. By the Lady, do I regret it now. Maybe I could have saved her. No, I could have saved her. If I had just come home… maybe if I never would have left in the first place.

A rush of anger overwhelms me, and I turn away from the edge and throw the violin across the roof as hard as I can. It makes a horrifying musical choking sound as the neck and the bridge separate from the instrument. I thought I would feel sad watching it break, but I feel nothing. I look back over the roof at the city I left behind and… feel numb.

"Grace," a soft male voice beckons to me. When I turn around to the back stairs, Faolan stands there, watching me. I turn away from him quickly.

"Go away."

"Can't do that."

"I want to be alone."

"I don't think you do."

I laugh in irritation. "What do you know about it?"

"I know you," he says, walking over to me. I turn my back to him, trying to make it exceptionally clear that I do not want company. But I hear him move closer anyway and feel his breath on my neck. "You ran out of there pretty fast."

"You saw why."

"There was an explanation. Would you like to hear it?"

My heart lightens just a tiny bit when I hear that. Maybe it wasn't all on me. "I would like to."

"Can we sit down?" He motions over to the seats that are still here, even after all of this time. I nod carefully and move to join him. I look up at his face for the first time since he arrived to find a soft expression, one I rarely get to see. He keeps his mouth and eyes gentle, soft edges. I must look positively mad if he has chosen to bring his own demeanor all the way down to something like this. I start some deep breathing, hoping to bring myself down to that level.

"Please tell me," I say quietly.

He takes both of my hands. "Your uncle told us that your mother has been ill for quite some time. After you left, her mind started to deteriorate further in her grief. She believed that you had been taken by the Fae despite the note you left that you had left of your own accord. Your uncle took her in immediately, but she began to have these episodes where she was not cognizant of anything happening around her. Currently, there are very few times where she can tell the difference between fiction and reality."

My heart shatters further, if that's even possible. It isn't until Faolan reaches up to cup both of my cheeks in his hand that I even recognize that I'm crying. He wipes my tears away and pulls my entire body into his lap like I weigh nothing more than a rag doll. I don't have the strength to protest, instead sinking into his shoulder and weeping. *My poor mother. I left her all alone.* He whispers soft words into my hair, kissing the top of my head and running his hands soothingly over my back. I cry quietly, mostly in silent shakes of my body, until I can't physically get any more water out of my eyes.

When I pull back from him, Faolan runs both of his thumbs under my eyes. "Are you alright?"

"No," I answer almost immediately, my voice hoarse. "No."

He nods and looks around the roof. He gently sets me down off of his lap and stands up, crossing the roof. Pausing for a moment, he reaches down and picks up my broken violin. My heart aches when I see it. "Oh." I sigh aloud.

"Is this yours?" he asks quietly.

"Yes... I wasn't thinking. But... oh... my mother gave that to me." A fresh round of tears spills out of my eyes. "I shouldn't have thrown it."

"Hey, hey." Faolan rushes back to me. He wraps one arm around me. "We'll fix it, okay?"

"We will?"

"Yes. I know exactly who to send it to. I know a guy; he's the best in repairs like these. It'll be back to you, good as new. I promise."

I lean against him and choke out my thanks. He hushes me again and runs a hand through my hair. "How did you know where to find me?" I ask tearily.

"Aiden sent me," he says simply.

If I had more energy, I would be in awe of how Aiden knew that I would rather see Faolan in this moment than him and knew exactly where to send him. But I don't have it. So I merely hold my broken violin between my hands and Faolan's and allow myself to grieve my broken family one more time.

Chapter Forty-Two

I wish I could have stayed on the roof longer. Frankly, I wish I could just set up shop and live on that roof. It's quiet, it's above the crowd, pretty much no one knows it's even still there, and I bet I could start some little vegetable garden up here and I would never have to go down. I wonder if Faolan would allow the black market to deliver here. He probably would if I asked. But that's not a reasonable plan for the future. And there's a war beneath me that I have to deal with.

One thing I am grateful for is that again, Faolan doesn't push my grieving process. Similarly to when my father died, he sits with me and holds me until I'm ready to move. That's something that I really like about him. He takes my lead on things that matter to me and the things that I'm in charge of. Yet he also takes care of things that need to be done without adding more to my plate. When we stand up to leave the roof, I kiss his cheek softly in thanks. He offers me a light smile.

We wind our way down to the street where we run into Aiden, Luna, and Aira. By the looks of it, they've been waiting here for a while. Aira offers me a sympathetic smile. "Are you feeling alright?" she asks.

"Yeah," I answer. "I am. Thank you all for waiting."

"Of course," Aiden says, locking eyes with me. "Any time." I mouth my thanks again directly to him, and he nods imperceptibly in response. He gets the message.

"Alright, what's the plan?" Faolan asks.

"We gotta get out of here," I decide. "We need to find somewhere to stay for the night. I want to regroup and try the governor's office again. I was thinking we could go back to the House of the—"

Boom.

"What was that?" I ask carefully, tilting my head toward the sound. It sounds like it's coming from several blocks away, and it sounds suspiciously like an explosion.

Boom.

"Something's not right," Luna says cryptically.

Boom.

After the last boom, a high-pitched noise echoes from the same general region. It takes me a moment to recognize it as screaming. I immediately take off in that direction, the others sprinting behind me. I have no idea what I'm heading into, but I know that something has gone terribly, terribly wrong.

Suddenly, the street opens up in a place it should not open up to reveal a completely demolished set of city blocks. Skyscrapers have collapsed straight to the ground, and the cries of helplessly trapped mortals pierce the air. The very sky is on fire as demons descend down from the heavens to wreak havoc on the ground. Swarms of dark Fae pour in to add to the chaos, firing off spells left and right. In every place they hit, blood and debris spray. Any mortal in their path doesn't stand a chance.

"We have to help them!" I shriek, rushing into the frenzy without a single thought for myself.

"Grace!" Aiden and Faolan shout together.

I run headfirst into the collapsing city, screaming my head off as I send a disintegration spell directly at the head of an incoming Fae. His pained cry right before he loses his head is both sickening and thrilling at the same time. I unleash everything I've got, magic-wise. A strong tornado whips the debris around me into a frenzy, and I take out whoever I can with just sheer brute force of objects. In between, lines of fire jerk out from my body and light my enemies on fire.

I am in an uncontrollable magic spiral, and I revel in it.

In the outskirts of my mind, I hear the others trying to get to me. But I'm completely surrounded by Fae soldiers. I'm burning through them as quickly as I can, but there's only one of me and hundreds upon hundreds of them. Suddenly, both my arms are being gripped, and I fly backward out of the crowd. My brain snaps out of its magical trance, and I find Aiden and Faolan on either side, flying me away from the chaos and physically dragging me alongside.

"What the hell were you thinking?" Faolan snaps at me.

"We have to help them!" I shout back.

"You don't charge into a situation like that without backup! You know better than that." He throws his hands up. "Why surround yourself with good people if you aren't even going to listen to them?"

"Hey, calm down," Aiden insists. "She's not hurt. Are you?"

"No, of course I'm not," I reply. "I had everything under control."

"Okay, no, you didn't have it all under control," Faolan scolds.

"I was doing just fine."

"Maybe we all need to calm down and figure out what to do," Aiden tries to interject.

"You really think she's gonna listen?"

"She's doing her best!"

"Her best sucks!"

"Aiden, watch out!" I shout as another building collapses and half a wall comes tumbling toward his head. Faolan yanks me backward as Aiden throws his hands up, generating a quick force field. The wall shatters around it and falls off the top of the synthetic dome. He brings the shield down and laughs in shock.

"See, that wasn't so—" Aiden's words get caught off suddenly as a jet black spell slams hard into his back. The humor dies in his eyes. His body freezes completely before his limbs suddenly start to contort, causing him to tumble to the ground.

"Aiden!" I shriek. I look around wildly until I lock eyes with a darkly laughing troll demon. His body, covered in pustules, heaves as he yells in childlike delight.

I scream at the top of my lungs in pure adrenaline as I charge the demon. Before I can reach him to stab him, however, he evaporates like mist into thin air. In my blind rage, there is nowhere for my power to go. My body and my magic slam hard into the building in front of me, blowing what's left of it to pieces. That debris rains down around me on the still warring Fae, demons, and mortals. There's a rush of sharp pain to my body that settles deep inside and aches. But there's no time to linger on it. I spin back around to see Aiden writhing on the ground, grunting in pain. I sprint back to him, heart pounding in my chest.

Faolan gets there before me and pins him hard to the ground. "What the hell happened?" he barks at me.

"I don't know!" I shout back. "He got hit with a demon's spell. I don't know what kind."

Faolan looks over his shoulder at me. "We need to get out of here, Grace."

"But the battle's not over. We could still turn it around."

"Grace, look at me," Faolan pleads with me firmly as he struggles to keep hold of Aiden. "We cannot turn this around. We have to get out of here now. There's only five of us. We cannot win this battle alone. It is far better to retreat now while we still have a chance, regroup, and live to fight another day."

"But—"

"Grace, please!" Faolan snaps.

"Okay, okay! Where are the others?"

"Right here!" Aira shouts, dragging Luna along with her. Luna looks worse for wear. I have no idea what happened to her, but half of her face is dripping with blood.

"What happened to her?"

"I don't know!" Aira shouts in a panic. "Someone came up behind us, and Luna blocked it from me, but not her. How are we going to get out of here?"

"We're going to have to run," Faolan says, wrenching Aiden upright.

"With him like this?" I ask incredulously.

"I got it." Faolan waves a hand over his head, and similarly to when he put me to sleep those few times, Aiden knocks right on out. "We need to get horses. I don't know where we're gonna go."

"We'll head south," I answer quickly. "There's a small town not too far from here. We can lay low there."

"Good. Let's go." Faolan slings Aiden's arm over his shoulder and half carries, half-drags him away from the fighting. I look back over my shoulder at the carnage as the others begin to escape. I don't want to leave my city behind, but we're just not strong enough. My heart aches as I turn around and flee after my companions.

Chapter Forty-Three

The disorder and disarray swirling around my body right now has never felt more intense than it does right now. Not when I first discovered my magic, not when I kickstarted the retaliation of an unjustly instigated war, not even when Faolan kissed me for the first time. No, this is different. I feel violent and drained of all energy, all at the same time. My friends are pretty much all down for the count, and it's my responsibility to take control of the uncontrollable situation we have found ourselves in. It's my job to manage this.

The problem is… who's going to take control of me? Before I completely lose my mind.

My first responsibility is to get communication back to the Upper Realm. We're trying to lay low in Eroba, one of the southernmost towns. We could disappear here. Despite this, I have to get a message through somehow. Faolan is able to find one lone black market contact here who I pass off a single folded sheet of paper to in a food exchange. Maybe we don't need to be that cautious. No one has seemed to notice our presence so far. But I'm not taking any chances.

We have been hiding out in a hotel for days. We paid a bunch of money to reserve a wing for ourselves. Aiden has been severely injured. By what, I don't even know yet. He's been unconscious the majority of the time we have been here. Every time he wakes up for half a second, he starts going crazy. His magic lashes out and destroys anything in the room that it touches. But it's not quite his magic. It's the same color as his usual powers, but mixed with a grittier black magic. It's freaking me out. I had to stash Faolan on guard duty to essentially knock him out any time he comes to. He won't let me trade off with him.

There are no healers within miles of here, so we can't get a good gauge on what's wrong with him. Aira does her best to heal him, but it appears to only work on his physical wounds. Healing of the mind and of magic is such a precise art, she's afraid to do anything more. One wrong move and his entire personality is gone. Because demons were involved, Faolan suggests we reach out to a specialist in demonic magic. There's really only one we can trust. He's pretty far away, but I jot off a quick message to Master Xavier back in the Upper Realm and rush it off to the messenger. All we can do now is wait.

Luna and Aira keep to themselves while we're here. Aira makes sense to me. She's been nervous about being here the whole time. But Luna? Since the battle, she's been surprisingly absent. I haven't even had a chance to check on her. When I finally take a clear breath again, I pay her a visit. When I come to Luna's room, I knock lightly on the door. "Come in," she says in her usual happy voice. I sigh in relief. At least she's feeling better. Maybe I can ask her for a bit of her divination magic, figure out where we are supposed to go next, what I'm supposed to do next. Maybe she can tell me if Aiden is going to be okay. Luna has always been a stabilizing influence in this group, oddly enough. I can trust her with my concerns.

When I go inside her room, I find her peacefully sitting in the room's chair, feet resting on a small ottoman. Covered with a blanket, she holds an unopened book in her hands, slowly tracing her fingers over the cover. "Hey, Luna," I say. "Thank goodness you're feeling alright. I could really use your help. Everything just feels so crazy right now."

Luna raises her head slowly and looks at me. And that's when I see it.

Her eyes are cloudy. The beautiful blue eyes that stood out against her super pale skin are marred by a milkiness that can only mean one thing.

"No," I breathe.

"Grace." She says my name very calmly.

Meanwhile, I am spiraling out of control. I double over. "No, no, no, no, no. That's not possible. You weren't hurt. You didn't get hurt."

"Grace," Luna repeats. "It was a delayed-effect spell. Demonic magic is unpredictable. No one could have known until very recently. I called Aira as soon as my sight began to fade. She confirmed what I already knew."

"No, you didn't know. It can't be."

"I'm blind, Grace."

I pace the room back and forth in rapid lines. I fear that if I stop moving, I'm going to completely melt down. "No, no. You're... you're not."

"Grace, it's alright."

"Alright?" I stop dead in my tracks. "How can it be alright?"

"I'm not afraid of it. I knew going into this war that there was a chance I would be permanently injured, if not dead. I haven't lost any limbs. I can still move. I can still speak. My magic is still fully functional. It's going to take some getting used to. But I'll be okay. It's going to be fine."

"It's not. It's not going to be fine," I mutter out loud. "It's not."

"But it is."

"You're blind."

"Yes. And I'll manage."

"How are you so calm about this?" I practically shout at the poor woman.

"Because I feel that my being calm is integral to who I am and my role on this team. I'm fun and interesting and a little strange, but everyone needs that in this war. Everyone needs that person who can break the ice, break the tension, and make people forget that they are at war. What would you have me do? Yell at you? Scream and cry until I can't breathe anymore? No. That's not my style."

"But you are upset."

"Of course I am. I miss seeing." There is a barely detectable waver in her voice, and that breaks me even further. She is trying so hard not to show how much it is getting to her already. So I try not to acknowledge it. I make my feelings look like the same panic attack I was already having rather than a new one. "I will never see my family's faces again, even if I do survive," she continues. "But I will be strong, and I will soldier on, and I will make it home to hold them."

I open my mouth to protest more, but she holds up a hand to stop me. "Please don't say anything else," she says. "I love you, but I can't hear any more apologies right now. I need to sit with this by myself a little while longer before I'm ready to deal with it. Will you please go?"

I nod before I realize she can't see me. "Yes. Of course." Unsure of exactly how to say goodbye, I opt not to, sneaking out into the hallway and closing the door. Once I'm out there, however, it's like the wind is knocked out of me, and I sink to the ground outside of the room. Sitting on this dusty carpet, I drop my head into my hands and struggle to breathe.

A warm presence appears in front of me, and I don't even have to open my eyes to know who it is. "Do you have a beacon on me or something that lights up every time I'm in trouble?" I force out.

"Something like that," Faolan replies as he grips my arms. "Let's get you up."

"My ribs hurt. I don't want to get up."

"Did you check yourself out after the battle? Did Aira look at you?"

My silence is enough to send Faolan seething. "You are by far the most ridiculous woman I have ever met." He pulls me up and takes me back to my room. "Give me your key." I don't protest because his tone implies that being quiet is the best option right now. He unlocks the door and steers me to the bed. Setting me down on it, he goes into the bathroom to find the first aid kit. When he returns, cotton balls and rubbing alcohol are in his hands.

"Shirt up," he demands. I roll up the bottom of my shirt and pull it up just enough to reveal my ribs. At first glance… yeah, maybe I should have taken a look sooner. Nothing appears to be broken, which Faolan confirms by pressing against them. But they're sore as all get out. The bruising is pretty wicked, and there are some cuts that should have been cleaned ages ago.

"Oh… no," I sigh.

Faolan scoffs. "Oh no. Oh no, she says." Kneeling down in front of me, he presses the first soaked cotton ball to a cut. I wince hard, hissing through my teeth.

"Ow!"

"That's what you get for being an idiot." Despite his harsh words, he does start to move around the cuts much slower and more softly. His pinky keeps brushing against my skin, and the feeling is driving me mad. He bandages me up pretty cleanly before pulling my shirt down himself. All the while, he doesn't speak to me further. He is completely focused on his task.

When Faolan finishes putting away the first aid materials, he heads for the door. I reach out to stop him. "Wait. Where are you going?"

"Back to my post. Aiden could wake up at any time."

"You can't stay at all?" I hate how emotional I sound.

Faolan sighs. "I can't, Grace." He looks over his shoulder at me. "We keep ending up in these rooms together in the middle of everything. You still haven't given me a good answer. Or any answer for that matter."

"An answer?"

"You know what I'm talking about. I won't push because we're in the middle of the war. But don't torture me like this."

"Torture you?"

"Take care of yourself. Please. Stop putting yourself further in harm's way by ignoring your injuries. Physical or mental. It's infuriating." He sighs again, this time with a hint more aggression. "I wish I could just… take you out of here." He looks like he needs to say something more, but he grunts and opens my door, slipping out without another word.

Not going after him tonight may be one of the biggest mistakes I ever make. But my body on its own accord slumps to the bed, and I stare at the ceiling for several more hours before descending into a shaky sleep.

Chapter Forty-Four

To everyone's surprise, Aiden wakes up the following morning as his usual self. Well, as close as he could be to that with an unknown spell in his body. After forty-eight hours, he has only had a few smaller magical reactions, so Faolan clears him for visitors. When I go to talk to him, he is much more reserved than I have ever seen him be. He talks quietly and in short sentences. His brow furrows like he's still fighting something in his head. It makes me incredibly nervous, especially when he doesn't let me stay in the room very long.

Shortly after, we get word that our communication finally arrived in the Upper Realm. Given the details that we enclosed, the Council sent Master Xavier to us right away, escorted by black market contacts. Faolan arranged for us to meet at an out-of-the-way basement tavern location. It should be quiet enough and low-key to keep mortals from noticing what we are up to. Faolan and I support Aiden discreetly as the three of us make our way to the table where Master Xavier is sitting, hood sitting low over his head. I feel relieved that he made it. We need his help desperately. I take notice of all of the exit points and where our men were, just in case something goes down. It's difficult, hiding from both mortals and Fae simultaneously. I hope this is the only time we'll have to do it.

"High Lady Grace. Lord Faolan, Lord Aiden," Master Xavier greets us. "I was very troubled when I received your message. I got on the road as soon as I could."

"Thank you for meeting us down here," I say quietly. "Your expertise is sorely needed."

"You read the full details of the incident?" Aiden asks.

"Yes, I did read everything you wrote. Are there any additional details? Can you remember anything else about what spells you were hit with, colors, sounds, anything?"

"Everything I can remember was in the letter," I respond.

"And I don't remember much after the spell hit me," Aiden adds.

"What do you think has happened to him?" I ask, cutting right to the point. "We don't have much time to talk in private."

"I have my theories, but nothing incredibly concrete," Xavier replies.

"Just tell us what you've got," Aiden says, his voice crackling. "A theory is better than nothing."

Xavier sighs and crosses his hands on the table. "There is an ancient demonic magic regarding possession that has not physically been seen in my nor my grandparents' lifetimes. It is rumored that certain demons have the power not only to possess another Fae, but to merge fully with their soul and take over their body."

"A complete takeover?" I feel like I've been punched in the gut. I can't even begin to process what that might mean.

Xavier nods gravely. "Yes. It is so much more than a possession of the mind; it is a consuming. There will be nothing left of the host unless the demon chooses for portions to remain."

"How can you tell if a demon is beginning to take over a host?" Faolan asks.

"There will be physical indicators. First, the mind will begin to deteriorate slowly. A person may make more rash decisions than usual. There will be intense power increases. At first, it will seem like the mage is in control of the new power. But steadily, they will lose control of it. Spells will go awry; power will emanate in all directions.

If the power is truly too much, skin begins to peel and melt away. The demon and the host will share a face. Then finally, the soul is consumed, the demon will become the only face."

My lungs squeeze together tightly. If Aiden has in fact absorbed a demon's presence, that creature could still be inside of him. And if it's still inside of him, that means that he can still be possessed. If the process hasn't already begun. I look over at Aiden to see his reaction, and he's got a stone cold expression on his face. I can't quite tell if he's trying to formulate a plan or whether he's internally having a panic attack. My panic attack is about to become external at this rate if I don't slow down my thoughts or my breathing.

Faolan, however, looks like he's been struck by lightning. "My father," he whispers under his breath, staring at Master Xavier.

And suddenly, the final piece falls into place, and it all makes sense.

"No, no, no, no," I breathe. "It's not possible."

"You heard him." Faolan still looks like he's seen a ghost. "It's all the same signs. Every single last one of them."

"What are you two talking about?" Master Xavier asks.

"It's my father," Faolan says gravely. "You know, the High Lord who started the damn war? He has all of the signs you mentioned. All of them. And his power has only been increasing. Erratically. Every movement he makes… is… is…" Faolan trails off, his voice getting quieter and quieter. He is freaking me out. I have never seen him like this.

"Bringing the demons from the Lower Realm was an odd choice for a strategic move, even for the High Lord," Xavier muses. "I know for a fact that his magical training in such dark arts as Necromancy would have given him enough of a basic background in Demonology to know that that was a bad idea."

"You think he was possessed before trying to bring the other demons over?" I ask.

Xavier shakes his head. "No, I don't think it's that simple. A demon could not break out of the Lower Realm without assistance. The magic at the border is set up precisely to avoid those kinds of issues. But a Fae with enough power could create enough of an opening in the barrier to let a demon through to speak to." The man turns to Faolan. "Did your father ever spend time in the Middle Realm?"

"Not that I know of," Faolan replies. "But he did take several business trips supposedly down to the Upper-Middle Realm border many months ago. They were longer trips. There would have been plenty of time for him to make the trip and back. But I can't imagine he would have done it himself. My father hates mortals."

"He would have done it if he believed that reaching the Lower Realm would give him the power and the strength that he needed to conquer the land he wanted to conquer," Xavier counters.

"Perhaps," Faolan concedes quietly. His eyes stare at the door, vacant. Nobody could reach him where his mind is right now, even if they tried.

"This is really big news," Aiden says shortly. "And I don't want to detract from that at all. But can we get back to the main question on the table? Am I possessed?"

"It's not clear at the moment. But given your appearance and the way your magic has struggled since the battle, I would say that it is reasonably likely to assume so," Xavier says gravely.

"Then I'm going to die."

"You're not going to die," I quickly interject.

"It's very possible," Xavier says at the same time.

I whip around to face him. "There's got to be another way. A solution of some kind, a potion or a spell."

"I am unfamiliar with any such methods, High Lady Grace. And I am the foremost scholar on the subject."

In my desperation, an idea finally reveals itself. "Except for the

CHAPTER FORTY-FOUR

Half-Fae Coven."

"They're legend, my dear."

"No… they're not. Aiden and I met them in the Middle Realm."

"You met them?" Now Xavier is the one to look as if he's being haunted. The change in his eyes happened so fast, before I could even blink.

My eyes narrow. "Yes, we did. So you don't quite know everything about the Middle Realm." When Xavier's facial expression doesn't change at all, I start to get more wary. "You told us the Coven was legend. So you couldn't have known." By the third sentence with no shift, there's no denying that there is something that Master Xavier is not saying here. "You lied to us."

"Grace," Aiden chastises lightly.

"No, Aiden," Xavier corrects. "She's right. I did lie to you some time ago. I have met the Half-Fae Coven. Though they weren't the Coven then."

"They weren't?" I ask. *Well, now I'm confused.*

"That's a story for another time." Xavier waves off my question. "But they will not be able to tell you anything different from me, I can assure you."

I get to my feet. "If all you're going to do is tell me that the situation is hopeless, then I have nothing more to say to you. Master Xavier." I dip my head once in a mild show of respect before storming away from the table. Aiden tries to grab my arm, but I throw my shoulder forward and wrench out of it. Faolan says my name in that resigned, sighing way he does when I'm doing something I shouldn't. I ignore him. In fact, I don't think I properly heard anything until I was already out the door.

I don't care what anyone else says. We're going to the Lower Realm.

Chapter Forty-Five

Once I had ultimately made the decision to take the lot of us to the Lower Realm, there was no changing my mind. I don't care how we had to get there or what we had to leave behind in our wake: I was getting us to the Half-Fae Coven. Once Aiden had healed up enough from his physical injuries to make the journey, I booked tickets on the last train down to the southern border for the group. I went shopping and shrouded the group in mortal clothes. I included hats to cover everyone's ears. At this point, being Fae was a bad idea with the invaders being Fae as well.

I stayed silent the entire train journey down. Aira, Aiden, and Faolan all tried to approach me to start a conversation. About what, I'm not really sure. I keep my eyes trained out the window as the landscape flashes by us, and eventually, they all leave. To be honest, I don't really think I was trying to ignore them intentionally. I just didn't know if I wanted to talk. I knew they were coming to try to persuade me to change my mind, and any points that they had to bring up, I really didn't want to hear. I can't fix the Upper Realm. I can't save the Middle Realm. But I can at least save Aiden. I have to be able to save Aiden.

When the train finally stops, I lead us to the border. When we're all standing at the high rock wall, Faolan tries to caution me. "Are you sure you want to do this, Grace?" he asks me for the umpteenth time.

"*Yes,*" I snap with a slight hiss on the end of my words. "I am."

"Grace." Aiden's voice forces out my name harshly. I turn around to look at him in his haggard state. His chest heaves with every breath, and his skin looks even more mottled than before. It still looks like there's something under his skin trying to crawl out. I have to turn away before I am too horrified by the sight.

"What?" I ask a little softer, eyes to the ground.

"We don't need to go to the Lower Realm, Grace."

"Shut up, Aiden." My harsh words are somewhat betrayed by the slight waver in my voice. "If there's a chance the Half-Fae Coven can heal you, it's worth taking the chance."

With that, I storm off down the rock wall's face. There is not a single person in this realm, let alone in this group who could stop me from breaking into the demon realm if there's even one thing that the Coven can try. I don't even wait for the others. Once I find the opening that leads to the Lower Realm, I get down in the dirt on my hands and knees and crawl through. My fury and intense worry blocks out all the feelings of claustrophobia until I reach the other side.

To my immense surprise, I find the demon realm to be empty and barren, somehow more than it was before. Many of the trees that used to line the entire expanse of the land have been slashed or burned to the ground. Instead of a dense forest, I am now looking at a blank wasteland. At least half of the trees in total are now gone. What remains exists in clumps, tiny pockets that are still holding on to an old way of life. I keep scanning the landscape for signs of demon life, but I come up empty.

How many are already above? How many went with High Lord Carron? Is it already too late? Have we been overrun?

When the others join me, they look just as uneasy as I feel about the lack of demons in the demon realm. "Is this what it was like when you were here?" Aira whispers to me. "All dark and spooky and…. empty?"

"Not at all," I answer. "The forest was much larger, and there were demons around every corner. Constant danger. This is strange. I don't like it."

Aira doesn't like that answer very much and shrinks back to join Luna. I catch Faolan's eye next. He doesn't appear to be afraid. He's taking in the surroundings and analyzing as he goes along. But when he looks at me, I see something different. I see a subtle question behind his eyes, asking me if I'm really doing the right thing here, bringing us all to the Lower Realm. I don't have a good answer for him, so I ultimately turn away.

"Which way should we go?" Aira asks. "Where is the oasis?"

"The oasis can be anywhere. It travels around the Realm by the magic of the coven, trying to find a safe place from demons. Since most of the demons have gone, I'm hoping it's relatively nearby. But it could be days."

"Unless that's it," Faolan chimes in, pointing to our north. In the distance, I can just make out the outline of the magical haven. Because of the destruction of the forest, the oasis is clear, sitting just in front of us like it had been waiting here for us to arrive. For the first time in ages, my heart grows a little lighter.

I grin. "That's it. Let's go." I take off like a shot toward it. Faolan follows close behind while the others take a more leisurely jog. In hindsight, I probably should have thought more about Aiden's injuries and the pace that he was able to keep. But my mind was solely on getting him cured, and if it took an all-out sprint to make that happen faster, then that was what I was going to do.

"Grace!" Faolan interrupts my thoughts. "What are you going to say when we get there?"

"What do you mean?"

"I mean, are we just showing up and demanding help from an all-powerful Half-Fae Coven?"

"Yes!"

"And you think that's going to work."

"Hell yeah, it will," I say quieter, almost to myself, before running further ahead.

It takes several minutes for me and Faolan to reach the oasis and another ten or so before the rest of the group catches up. All of us are out of breath. Aiden looks a wreck, but I really don't have time to feel guilty about that. We enter the sacred place as a group, disheveled, but determined. Everything is almost exactly as I remember it: the water, the homes, the caves. I usher everyone to drink from the healing water. Part of me wishes naively that a simple drink will be enough to fix Aiden, but he experiences no change. The others, however, feel rejuvenated and breathe much more easily.

When I look around with a clear head, I find that all of the people within the barriers of this place are staring at us, shocked.

Oh. Right. People.

"Grace," Faolan says quietly to me. "You did not say anything about all the people."

I blush lightly. "Yeah… about that. There's actually a lot more half-Fae."

"All of them?"

"All of them."

"You've got to be kidding me."

"What is the meaning of this intrusion?" The Enchantress's voice booms out over the ground, magically amplified. When she sees me, however, the fury on her face dies quickly. "Grace?"

"Enchantress." I kneel to her as I did the last time I saw her. Upon seeing me do so, my other companions follow suit. When I raise my eyes again, I find the rest of the Half-Fae Coven stepping in behind her. All of them look concerned. The Enchantress motions for us to rise, and I stand with my crew. The way everyone is facing off against each other, it seems like it's a meeting of old and new magic. My coven and hers standing together in a silent show of strength. I wish the rest of the group was here so that she could see that I understood the prophecy. I had done my duty. Most of it anyway.

And now it's time to be repaid.

"You have grown, High Lady Grace," the Enchantress says with a brilliant smile. "You have almost fully stepped into your heritage now."

"It would have been much easier if you had told me." I chuckle.

"But I did tell you," she replies simply. "It just took you longer to understand. But now I have to ask, why are you here? Your task is not yet complete."

"Not yet, no. But I have put together the eight prophecy members that you detailed. These are a few of them." I gesture to the group behind me. Everyone seems to stand a little taller.

"I see. But that doesn't explain what you're doing here."

Suddenly, as if on cue, a gurgling noise comes from behind me. I turn around just to see Aiden's eyes roll into the back of his head as he tumbles to the ground, convulsing. Aira screams, and I dive to the ground beside him. Aiden's skin cracks slowly like glass, showing tiny fractures along his face and arms. From each crack, a soft black mist seems to be pouring from him. I grab him and pull him into my lap, trying to still him as he bucks wildly. One of his arms flies up and hits me directly in the face, and I tumble back and hit the ground. Faolan swears, and he and Aira immediately jump in to try to hold him back.

There's red pouring into the corner of my eyes.

I'm bleeding.

From above me, the Enchantress kneels by my side and calmly pours some of the oasis's water over me, healing the wound. The pain immediately clears. "Please tell me that you can do something about him," I beg.

The Enchantress waves over a few attendants. "Please take this young man to the healing chamber. We will be along to tend to him shortly." A handful of men and women rush in to take Aiden from Faolan and Aira. When he slumps over, the group just picks him up and carries him out of the cave. My heart aches as I watch him leave. Once he is out of the room, the Enchantress turns back to me. "What happened?"

"We were fighting in the Middle Realm in my hometown of Lisden; there was a big battle. There's a whole war going on up—"

"We're aware of the war, Grace. Explain the details."

"Oh." I shake my head quickly to straighten out my thoughts. "Well, there's been demon involvement the entire time. But this time was different. Aiden was hit directly in the chest with a strand of demonic magic that none of us had ever seen before. There's a professor who studies it, um, Master Xavier."

"Xavier's still alive?" an unfamiliar female voice asks. One of the coven members has spoken. The Soothsayer, I believe. Her eyes change from a more poised air to something much more vulnerable. I've never heard her speak before outside of the prophecy reading. "Um…" I don't know how to respond.

"What did Xavier say?" The Enchantress presses.

"He said that there was an ancient demon possession magic that Aiden may have been hit with. He said it may cause Aiden's body to be completely taken over by demonic magic."

The Enchantress makes a soft humming sound. She shakes her head. "Elder demon, most likely. Did Xavier not explain the particulars to you?"

I tighten my jaw. "He did. But I thought you could fix it."

"We can't fix this, Grace."

"But—"

"Grace. This is magic that is far outside even our purview. There is nothing that can be done. The magic to do so simply doesn't exist within the magic of a Fae. Even the most powerful ones couldn't undo it."

"Then do we need demon magic?" I ask demandingly. "Will demon magic undo it?"

"There are no demons that would help you undo it," she answers simply. "And none of our magic is strong enough to physically harness the power of a demon. I don't want to tell you that you have come here for nothing, but we cannot fix this."

"So there's absolutely nothing you can do?" My voice is getting hysterical now, much to my horror. I've never heard that tone come out of my mouth before.

"I never said that." The Enchantress moves closer to me. "What we can do is attempt to slow the effects. We can try to trap the demonic magic by an intricate series of spells. It will take time for the magic to break free, and it may buy you enough time to make arrangements."

"Make arrangements?"

"Complete the prophecy."

"You expect me to complete the prophecy while the man is dying?" I shout.

The Enchantress shows no sign of being phased by my anger. "Your job is to complete the prophecy. We will do our best to help you. Now, as before, you and your companions are permitted to stay with us until our task is complete. After that, however, you will have to leave."

My fervor has reached its peak now, and I scream full out at her. "You're just going to patch him up and send him back up to the war to die?"

The Enchantress smiles softly at me. "I must attend to your friend now, High Lady. I trust you'll find your accommodations to your satisfaction." She bows her head once to me before turning around and signaling to the Coven. The eight of them follow down the path where the people took Aiden. The other half-Fae around us stare at me carefully, waiting to see if I might explode.

I just might.

Chapter Forty-Six

There's a heaviness over the oasis tonight as I exit the main square. Grey clouds have rolled in above the oasis, and it has started to rain. The sky reflects my dismal and rapidly deteriorating mood. The Half-Fae women attending the Coven bring me to the same place that Aiden and I stayed at the last time we were here. It infuriates me. The attendants seem to recognize this and make themselves scarce shortly after dropping me off. Probably for the best.

The cave looks the exact same as it did when I first came to the Lower Realm, right down to the sheets on the beds. Light steam rolls off the bathing pool, as if beckoning to me to shed my worries and soak for a while. But all the comfort around me is only making me more frustrated. My magic struggles to stay dormant under the surface. To let off some anger, I throw my bag across the room, slamming it into the back wall. *Mmm... only slightly satisfying.* Growling under my breath, I send out a wave of flames, setting the bathing pool on fire temporarily. It should have burned out quickly with the water's presence, but it holds longer than I expected.

"Grace, don't," Faolan's voice states suddenly from behind me.

I whip around with a small shriek. "Faolan! By the Lady, stop sneaking up on me. I swear I'm getting you a bell."

"I just walked in. No sneaking involved." He raises an eyebrow at me. I just glare back. "Don't glare at me. You're the one trying to burn the camp down."

"I'm not trying to…" My voice trails off as I breathe heavily. "Burn it down."

"What are you doing then, Grace?"

Instead of answering the question, I walk over and collect my bag from its palace on the floor. Throwing it onto the bed, I start to unpack some of my weapons. "Wanna get out of here?" I ask. "Go kill some demons outside? I just… want to destroy things. I don't want to be here."

"Grace…" Faolan's tone takes on a slight warning edge.

"We should go," I insist, trying to keep the emotion out of my voice.

"No."

"Faolan."

"We could lose our place here. Xavier told me this place moves around. The Coven could move to the other side of the realm. Someone could get hurt." It's clear that he means me. *I could get hurt.*

And he's not wrong. It would be stupid to leave the oasis while it's still here. We're mostly protected here, one of the few places that we are. Cursing loudly, I throw my knives back onto the pillow and sit on the edge of the bed, staring at the ground.

Faolan sighs. "He's important to you, isn't he?"

"I don't know what to do, Faolan," I answer simply. "Maybe this is it. Maybe this is the sacrifice of the Bringer of Light. Maybe he's supposed to die tonight."

Faolan shakes his head and moves closer. "I'm asking how you feel about him, Grace. Not how important he is in this world for the prophecy."

"Yes," I force out between my teeth. The lights flicker around in the cave. "He matters to me. Is that what you want to hear? Do you want to hear that I'm terrified to watch him battle a demon that's attached itself to his soul?" I breathe in short puffs of air. "I'm so tired… of death." Faolan nods calmly and begins to head for the cave's entrance again. "Wait!" I jump to my feet.

"Yes, Grace?" He looks at me with those stupid guarded eyes again. I search them for something, anything that tells me that he still wants to be here and he's trying to leave this cave for self-preservation or something like that.

"It… it doesn't mean that you're second. I love him, but… Faolan, I don't know if I'm in love with him anymore. But he still loves me, and he's in pain. I don't know what to do here."

"I didn't say it did, Grace. I asked a simple question. You gave me a simple answer. That's all I wanted. I know he's still very much in love with you." He chuckles shortly. "This whole thing is going to heavily test the both of you. He needs you. As much as I hate it."

"Oh…" I resist the urge to stomp my feet and instead, storm across the bedroom. "You sound like that damned Enchantress. Test here and test there. I'm tired of being tested!"

"That's not for you to decide."

"No, it's for the Lady to decide, right? That's whose mercy I'm at?" I laugh wryly with a hint of hysteria. "My father is dead, my brother is dead, my mother has gone mad, my kingdom is falling, and I'm just leading a band of haphazard prophecy victims into hell trying to cure demonic magic. I was a musician, Faolan. *A musician.*"

"And I was a lot of things before my father started this war. But at the forefront, I am who I have to be for the sake of this realm."

"Don't you just… want to leave?" Words are coming out faster than I can think if I want to reveal them or not. "Let them take what they're already going to take and run away? With your connections, we could hide forever…" It takes me way too long to realize that I said 'we'.

"Of course, I do, Grace. But we can't live that way. We weren't born into those kinds of lives."

"I didn't ask for any of this responsibility. None of us did. We were chosen, but should we not get to decide"

"You did decide, didn't you Grace? When you decided not to go home and to join the Fae Court?"

"I didn't know what I was getting into; I was trying to protect my mother. And look how well that turned out."

"Are you prepared to abandon her and Aiden and the rest of the world to the House of Darkness? The demons?"

"*I don't want to answer this!*" I scream. The thin barrier keeping my magic restrained breaks, and every light in the room brightens to its maximum intensity before exploding. Glass flies everywhere and the room is plunged into darkness. My heart feels like it's trying to leap out of my chest. I can't get a handle on my emotions. Nothing feels safe right now. Duty over desire. Heritage over self. It's too much.

But suddenly, a small ball of light hangs over my head, and I look up to find Faolan's face close to mine. His eyes are softer, a little warmer than before as he looks at me. One of his hands raises up to grasp my cheek softly. He runs his thumb lightly across it. I want nothing more than to melt into him right now. "I'm tired, Faolan," I say quietly. "I'm bone tired… and Aiden is dying, and I want to fix it but I can't."

He shushes me lightly and leans in to kiss my forehead. "Come on." He helps me to my feet. "Come on, love." After my magic exploded, it's like all of the energy has drained out of me. I lean on Faolan heavily as he brings me down the couple of steps to the bath. As he takes down my hair and starts to pull at my clothes, I try to brush away his hands.

"Please," I beg quietly. "Not like this."

"I'm not even looking, Grace. Not this way." He cups my cheeks and forces me to look into his eyes. "Believe me, when I look at you, you won't be thinking about anything else but me." I nod slowly, feeling just a bit more reassured. With a nod, he turns me around and guides me into the bath. When my body is fully under the water, he begins to wash my hair. He untangles my curls lightly with his fingers and scratches at my scalp. He doesn't say a word; instead, he speaks to me through calming movements and soothing touch.

It's the most peaceful that I have felt in a long time.

When the water cools down, he grabs the towel from my bag and allows me to wrap myself up while he turns away. When I've dried off, he carries me over to the bed where he pulls a shirt over my head. I almost laugh when the smell hits me. It's his, something silk that feels cool over my skin. He lets me pull on some pants before waving me into bed

When Faolan draws the covers over me and tucks me in, I feel compelled to ask him, "Why won't you stay in the same bed as me?"

He chuckles lightly. "Grace, I don't have enough self control to sleep beside you again without you being *mine*." The hint of possession on the edge of his words makes me shiver. He notices, but only tucks me in tighter. "But I'll wait here until you fall asleep if it will make you feel better."

"Yes." I yawn. "You should stay."

"Alright," he answers softly as he rubs my back lightly in slow circles. "Close your eyes. And stop thinking, for the Lady's sake." With a light laugh, I comply. I don't know how quickly I fell asleep, but I know the methodical movement of his fingers through his shirt on me and a light hum sent me off to dreamland were enough to make me feel... not lonely. Not anymore.

Chapter Forty-Seven

Falling asleep in the Lower Realm, particularly in the oasis, is always a risk. I should have remembered that from my first time here. When I fall asleep, I instantly slip into a dream. The place is familiar, a tree swing at a small park where Leo and I used to spend time sitting together and chatting about our days. But the whole scene is slightly fuzzy around the edges. It's almost like I'm trying to remember something, but I can't quite place all of the details. Like many of my other dreams over the years, I feel very lucid. Every movement I make feels like I'm taking my own steps with agency, and when I pinch myself to see if I'll wake up, I feel pain.

I have no idea what I'm doing here. The first time I experienced a Lower Realm magic-enhanced dream, I had a vision of Leo's death. That was the past. But this doesn't remind me of any particular memory of mine. I rack my brain, trying to figure out if I should stay here and wait for the point to reveal itself or if I should try to walk in another direction and hope for the best.

Until I see my brother, Leo, sitting on a bench that suddenly reveals itself to me.

I gasp loudly and freeze in place as he flashes me a brilliant smile. "Hey, stranger," he says to me with a laugh. I can't even breathe. He looks exactly the same as when he left town for the Upper Realm all that time ago. His dark green military uniform fits snugly on his body, and the gold buttons shine in the sunlight. His hair is perfectly imperfect, softly curled with just a few strands out of place to give him just a hint of wildness. His eyes… oh, those eyes.

I can't take it anymore.

I sprint to him, hoping to reach him before he fades away completely and the dream gives way to a nightmare. But no nightmare comes. He catches me and wraps me up in the tightest bear hug. I take a deep breath in.. and it's *him. It's Leo.* My heart fractures, and suddenly, I'm sobbing uncontrollably. Tears stream down my face in rivers of despair and grief. Leo laughs softly and holds me tightly to his chest, smoothing down my hair like he used to do when we were younger.

"Hey, hey, hey, there's no need for that. It's alright," he insists. "It's alright." I don't listen, or more, I can't listen. I can't stop crying. To be able to touch and hold my brother even one last time takes every last bit of mental fortitude from me. Even if it's just a ghost. It gets so bad that I'm dry-heaving with the strain of my sobs. "Alright, Grace, calm down." Leo pulls back from me and holds my face. "Calm down. Look at me." He forces me to look up and directly into his eyes. He used to do this all the time when he wanted to tell me something very important. "We don't have much time, so I need you to take a breath for me. I'm not harmed. I died quickly. It wasn't painful, and I did it for the right reasons. I am not in any pain. I promise. I love you. Now please calm the hell down."

I laugh at his swearing, and then I'm laughing through the tears just as uncontrollable as the sobs. I double over, releasing all of my emotion in one fell swoop. It takes several more minutes for me to calm down enough to look back up at Leo. He smiles at me. "Better?" I nod silently. "Good. Let's sit down." He leads me to the swing where we both take a seat.

I take a deep breath. "Woo, this is…" I tilt my head and laugh nervously. "This is a lot to take in."

"I know, sis. But we don't have a lot of time to chat about what we need to. You need to tell me everything that has happened so far."

"Everything?"

"As much as you can. I know bits and pieces, but I need to know everything you know so that I can give you the best information."

"The best information about what?" I'm still confused.

"What I learned from my time as a mercenary. It may help you."

"With... with the prophecy?"

"Grace." Leo's voice grows more impatient. "You need to start talking."

Recognizing the gravity in his voice, I spill my guts. I start at the very beginning to his death and my mission to figure out who killed him. I walk him from the Middle Realm to the Upper Realm where I started my journey. I tell him about Aiden and the crazy adventure that we took all over the realms. He does seem irritated when I tell him about the first expedition to the Lower Realm, but probably because of my stubbornness in the whole matter. He doesn't flinch when I tell him about the duel of the heirs and how I am a half-Fae heir to the House of the Evening. I walk him through the war thus far, dancing around my romantic interactions with Aiden and Faolan. I think that's a detail best left out. Finally, I make it through a brief overview of every battle up until this point and Aiden's possession.

When I'm finished, I'm out of breath once again and have to take a minute to gather myself. Leo rubs my back lightly. "You've had a hard time, sis. I'm sorry I wasn't there to guide you through it."

My eyes prickle with tears again. I barely keep them from spilling over. "Our mother... I'm so sorry. I didn't mean to—"

Leo grips my shoulders and turns me to face him firmly. His eyes bore into mine. "You listen to me, Grace Richardson. What happened to our mother is not your fault."

"But, Leo, I left."

"You're right. You left. Could you have been better about the way you left? Sure. But if you had been, our mother would have kept you locked up tight in that house. Even as she deteriorated in her grief."

"You saw her grief?"

Leo frowns sadly at me. "Yes. I saw her pain. But I also saw the way she ignored yours. You would have slowly died inside too if you had stayed there much longer. You have to understand this, Grace. You did not break her. You were not the catalyst. You were not the final crack. Her mind had been dwindling for a long time, Grace. Please do not let her be the one who stops you from moving forward and fulfilling your destiny."

I gulp quietly and nod. I can't promise him that I'll be able to get rid of the guilt, but I can promise to try. Unsure of how much time we have left, I prompt him, "What can you tell me about what I need to do?"

"I learned a lot about the House of Darkness's plans simply by observing the people who were constantly coming in and out of camp. The soldiers from their House always traveled in groups, never in pairs or alone. At first, I thought they just were tight knit groups of friends. But no. None of them trusted each other. They were bonded together by the strength and fear of their commander, the High Lord. They would never allow each other to be alone with another House's soldier and certainly not with the mortal mercenaries." Leo looks at me pointedly, like *this is the part where you're going to pay close attention.* "One night, I was able to overhear a conversation regarding the value of black obsidian."

"How did you manage that?"

"Was walking home late one night outside of the taverns. It was well past midnight, and the House of Darkness soldiers are the only ones who stay up that late when it's a work week. Either way, it doesn't matter how I heard it. Only what I heard."

CHAPTER FORTY-SEVEN

"What did you hear?"

"First, I learned the importance of black obsidian, the substance that was being mined for, its crucial component in reading and understanding prophecies."

"Understanding prophecies? There's a way to understand them?"

"Yes. They can be understood on a broader and more detailed level. It doesn't always have to be simple poetic platitudes. The Half-Fae Coven has not told you everything that they know."

I swear loudly. "I knew it."

"They are waiting for you to ask."

"How was I supposed to know what to ask?" I ask incredulously.

"Why do you think I'm here?"

"They sent you."

Leo shrugs. "In a manner of speaking."

"You do realize this makes no sense, right?"

Leo laughs. "Yes, I'm aware."

As I chuckle and roll my eyes at his antics, the scene shifts. The fuzzy edges grow even more blurry, and I feel my body starting to be pulled out of the experience. I concentrate hard, trying to keep everything in focus. "Tell me what I need to ask. I'm being pulled out of this." My heart rate begins to rise again. "I'm not ready to go."

Leo pulls me into a tight hug one more time. "I know. But you can do this. I've always been right here for you. That won't change. I promise."

"Tell me what I'm supposed to ask."

As the dream fades around me, the last thing I hear my brother say is this: "Ask them to give your Divination specialist the full picture."

Chapter Forty-Eight

When I wake up, I come to violently. My body launches itself forward out of bed as I gasp. Faolan flies over to me in an instant from the other bed and grips my arms. "Grace!" he shouts. "Are you okay?" I try to catch my breath enough to speak, but it takes longer than expected. All the while, Faolan is looking over me, feeling my limbs and my heartbeat through my throat as he tries to diagnose what's wrong. "Grace, you gotta talk to me, darling."

"I'm okay," I finally wheeze. "I'm fine. It was a dream."

"A dream did that to you?"

"It's complicated. Dreams in the oasis are more like visions. Visions of the past or of… oh, I don't know what else of, but I had one, and I learned some things."

"What did you see?"

I turn to look up at his concerned face. "I talked to my brother."

Faolan blinks. "You talked to your brother?" He feels my forehead gently with the back of his hand. "Are you feeling alright? You've had a really hard time with all of this, and I think it may be getting to you."

"Faolan." I pull his hand away from my head and grip it tightly. "Look, I know it was him. This isn't the first time I dreamed about him here, and that dream turned out to be true. You don't have to believe me if you think it sounds crazy because I know that it does. But please, before you start fretting over me, please come with me to speak to the Half-Fae Coven and the others. There's something that we all need to be there for."

Although he doesn't seem to completely believe me, he doesn't hesitate to throw the covers off of me and pull me to my feet. We both quickly get dressed and wake the others. Aiden is still down for the count, sequestered away in a healing chamber somewhere in the oasis. I see no reason to disturb him during his recovery, not when we can recount the information later. I make sure that Luna stands beside me as our group of four moves into the Coven's cave.

The Enchantress and the other seven are waiting for us. By her smug smile, it seems like she has been waiting for us, or perhaps for me specifically. "High Lady Grace, I trust you had a restful night."

"I wouldn't say restful," I say coolly. "More enlightening."

"Do tell," she replies smoothly.

"I have a question for you. I want you to give Luna the full picture."

The Enchantress's smile only grows. "Are you certain?"

"Yes."

"Luna, step forward," she says.

Luna follows the sound of her voice and walks almost directly to her. The Enchantress carefully places two hands on both of her shoulders. "Do you wish me to explain what Grace is referring to before I commence?"

"Yes, please," Luna says politely.

"What Grace has asked me to do is give you the tools to unlock the full potential of your Divination powers. Although your blinding in this most recent battle was unfortunate, it does present an optimal opportunity for you to see prophecies in their entirety with many of the pieces spelled out to you. It will be far better than any other magic in this area that you have explored before. But, with that power, comes great responsibility. You will be the next steward of prophecies, and you will have to carry yourself nobly with such power. Do you accept the challenge?"

"I do," Luna replies.

"Good." The Enchantress looks over her shoulder and beckons for the Soothsayer to come forward. The woman steps forward and bows her head to Luna. When she lifts it, I notice that she is blind as well. Although Luna can't see it, she curtsies in return. Aira and Faolan murmur to each other at the sight. The Soothsayer then places her hands on both of Luna's shoulders, pressing their foreheads together. She begins to mutter in an ancient language, one that sounds familiar but not enough common inflections for me to put together. Her smoky eyes glow a brilliant blue and grow brighter the longer she chants. Suddenly, Luna's blank eyes reflect that same blue brilliance, and she begins repeating the same chant like she had studied it to perfection. The group watches in a mixture of horror and awe as the two of them slowly rise a few inches off of the ground. The pair rotate in a steady rhythm, the chanting growing more intense. This continues until finally, the two freeze and slam back to the ground.

Luna's eyes fly open as she gasps loudly. "It's so bright," she breathes.

Aira rushes over to her before the rest of us can blink. "Luna? Luna, are you alright?"

"Everything is so much clearer now," she says softly, reverently. "All the pieces of the puzzle are here. I see a clear border and many of the major pictures. Only a few more middle pieces to find."

"You've fully realized your potential now as a student of divination," the Soothsayer declares. "Now all you need is a guide." Out of the folds of her dress, she pulls out a small shiny black rock with jagged edges. Instantly, I recognize it as black obsidian. For something so powerful, it looks fairly innocuous. The Soothsayer presses it into Luna's hand, and Luna turns it over slowly, feeling all around it.

"This is black obsidian," the Soothsayer says. "If you concentrate your divination magic, you will be able to hear and understand the full extent of the prophecy."

"All of it?" Luna asks.

"As much as the Lady will allow you to see."

Luna closes her eyes and holds on tightly to the stone. I watch her with bated breath, hoping she'll see something useful. Her eyes suddenly fly open. "There's so much more to the story than we realized."

"What?" I ask, rushing over to her and gripping her shoulders. "What do you see?"

"During his initial planning of the invasion, High Lord Carron caught word that a new mine had been discovered in the House of Day after a large landslide with a highly unique magical signature. He bought control of the mine from the locals and sent his own contractors to start work there. He eventually hired some miners from the House of the Day and allowed them to subcontract to others, including mortals."

"My brother," I breathe softly.

"Yes. High Lord Carron needed black obsidian to ensure his victory. He was looking for a sure thing to tell him that what he was doing would be successful. When Leo blew up the mine, it collapsed the mostly excavated section that would have led them to the resource. This led him to start making visits to the Lower Realm. He decided that if demonic magic was involved, it didn't matter what kind of prophecies were in play."

"So he makes a deal with demons," Faolan says.

"One demon. An Elder." Luna's eyes flick back and forth rapidly like she's reading a book. "They make a deal that High Lord Carron gets his demonic magic for use and he will give the demons territory in the Upper Realm specifically for them to run around and have free rein."

"He's going to give them land?" Aiden asks, shocked.

"Yes. But now the Elder Demon decided that the deal was no longer in his best interest. He was hypnotized by the prospects of taking over all three realms at will. That is when he began to possess High Lord Carron. He's been calling the shots for a while now," Luna concludes.

"How are we going to fight them?" Aira asks.

"We all lead," she says bizarrely.

"What?" I ask.

"We all lead our own regiments. All of us. We each must engage in the fight one way or another. There's a final spell that needs to be enacted. By you, Grace." She stares deeply into my eyes. "You cast the final spell that has the chance to take out the High Lord."

"All by myself?" I'm horrified.

"Not entirely. Everyone lends power to you. If you can hold onto all of it, then you're able to use it."

"I have to hold onto everyone's power? How am I supposed to do that? I'm just one body."

"Don't push her," the Soothsayer snaps at me. "You are asking her too many questions. Black obsidian doesn't give you the prophecy in simple terms. There are metaphors to be deciphered, signs to be understood, and events to be sorted through. She will not know all of what she has seen until later when her mind has a chance to sort it out. Do not pressure her."

"What do you want me to do then?" I reply boldly. "We have to know."

"Give it some time," the Enchantress interrupts. "Go home and give it some time, and she will have more information later."

"Home? I'm not ready to just go home. You haven't fixed Aiden yet."

"We have done all that we can do with Aiden. He is on his way here now."

I feel backed into a corner. We have no cure, bits and pieces of information, and I have an impossible task to hold onto the power of eight powerful Fae in my one body.

Yeah... this is going to work out great.

Chapter Forty-Nine

The Coven allows us to wait with them until Aiden joins us. It doesn't take long for him to arrive. He looks much more like his normal self. His eyes are lucid, and he smiles at me with that same bright smile that he had when I met him. He makes a beeline directly to me and hugs me tightly. "Hey, you," he says in my ear. I hug him briefly before stepping back. I don't even look at Faolan to see his reaction. Luckily, Aira and Luna come up to him to congratulate him. The group begins to make their way toward the border of the oasis. I, however, stay in place.

The Coven may be finished with us, but I'm certainly not finished with them.

"There is something more," I say firmly. The others stop in their tracks, surprised. I hadn't exactly told them this part of my thoughts.

"What would you like to say?" The Enchantress grants me one more moment. I do not want to waste it.

"We need more help than the prophecy has allowed us to obtain. There are more demons involved now, and High Lord Carron grows more and more dangerous. I have seen firsthand what you can do. You have slowed the effects of demonic magic in Aiden. You have spent a lifetime fighting off demons from your home. You have more experience in this than we do, and we desperately need your help above this realm. I ask that you and your Coven join us in the Upper

Realm to defeat our enemies."

The Enchantress doesn't even take a moment to consider my request. "No," she says firmly. "We will not be joining you."

"We need your help," I plead to her. "You have more power than all of us combined."

"Not quite true," she answers with a way-too-calm tone.

"Maybe not, but your power would be more than enough to help us topple some of the demons in our world. You've dealt with them way more. We could use that kind of expertise up there. Please. We need you."

"There's nothing I can do, Grace."

"Bullshit. There has to be something. You can't fix Aiden, sure, but you *can* fix this."

"No," the Enchantress repeats firmly. "I can't. When the Coven put their magic into creating the oasis, we tied our magic to it. If we leave this realm, then the oasis vanishes and we put everyone here in danger. We will not be putting the rest of our society in danger to save yours." My heart sinks into my stomach. There goes our last chance.

"You may not be able to leave," Faolan interjects calmly. "But will you deny your constituents the opportunity to try?"

The Enchantress tilts her head slightly. "I do not know what you are speaking of."

"If you cannot leave, allow us to ask the half-Fae descendants if they wish to join the fight."

"Why in the world would they want to join the fight?" she asks.

Faolan doesn't hesitate. "For their freedom. To be free of this world entirely and live out their lives in peace and sanctuary in the Upper Realm."

"Under whose protection?"

"Under mine." The five of us speak at the same time. I smile softly.

It's good to know that everyone here believes that my brethren deserve a chance in the sun.

"We will offer them protection," I reiterate, "as the House of the Evening, Moon, Sun, Wind, and the rebuilt House of Darkness. And I imagine I can convince the other prophecy members to open up their Houses as well."

"And I can work on the other members of the War Council," Aira adds. "By the time we're finished, half-Fae will be able to live wherever they choose."

"Free of worry over demon attacks," Aiden says.

"Happy," Luna chimes in.

"Happy," the Enchantress repeats slowly. She considers Faolan's request for a while. But finally, I feel a rush of triumph when she nods. "You may ask them. But only once and as a large group. I will not have you coercing them into coming with you against their best interests."

"We wouldn't dare try," Aira says.

"All the same, those are my terms. Will you accept them?"

"Yes," I answer confidently.

"Fine. Then if you can find a way to break their exile, they are free to come with you. But why do you think they would want to? Fae put them in exile, put their ancestors in exile. Don't think they are going to be so quick to rush to their aid." The Enchantress simply bows her head and waves her hand to dismiss us. This time, we leave.

"How do we want to do this?" Faolan asks me. "How should we gather people?"

"I'm not sure," I reply quietly. "Do we even have anything that would particularly persuade the people to come listen to us?"

"I don't think we're going to need it," Aiden interrupts us. "Look." As I look up, I find hundreds of young Half-Fae waiting for us, watching us. At the head of the group, I find the Soothsayer corralling people around the lake. When she sees us, she strides to meet me. I step forward and bow to her. Before I can speak, she lays her hand directly on my shoulder. "I have laid the foundation. It is your job to make it count. They're ready for you." She pats me once before walking away to join the Enchantress in the cave.

"Who should speak?" Aira asks.

"That's my job," I say gruffly, walking to the front of the crowd. "It's always my job."

As I make my way to the lake, I am brought back to the first day I arrived in the House of the Evening. The speech that I gave on that day was enough to let the Fae people begin to trust me. It wasn't a lot, but it was just enough. I relied on my heritage on both sides to convince them that I wasn't going to take everything to hell.

Now ultimately, it may have gone that way, but at least it wasn't entirely my fault.

I just have to pull that off again.

"My brethren," I start slowly. "You may not think of me as one of you. I didn't grow up the way you did. I stayed hidden in the mortal world, raised as a mortal, and was begrudgingly accepted as a Fae when it was revealed that I was an heir to a noble throne. I am fortunate. I imagine there were many people just like me with partial noble blood that were shamed and sent into exile. Your ancestors. Now I can't take any of that back. It is not in my power nor is it my place to do so. But what I can do is offer you a chance."

I straighten my shoulders. "The people traveling with me will offer you sanctuary in at least three currently operating Houses and two more once they are rehabilitated. We believe that we will be able to convince our remaining allies to offer you an additional six Houses. Your exile will end, and you will be able to live a normal life in the Upper Realm for the rest of your lives and your descendants' lives. I am willing to sign a contract to that effect."

Murmurs break out all around me, but I press on. "All that I ask… is that you fight with us. You help me protect my realms, both of them, Upper and Middle. I know I have no right to ask that of you. Those aren't your worlds. But you have more experience fighting demons than anyone in this universe, and we need that to survive. Help us, and I promise you, you will have the life you deserve."

"How do you expect to break us out?" a male voice shouts out to me.

I pause. I hadn't exactly thought out that far. I have no idea how to answer the man's question, and the longer I stand here not answering, the more the people will lose faith in what I said. But suddenly, Aiden steps forward. "I have demonic magic inside of me. The Half-Fae Coven was able to slow its progression and help me to control the power temporarily. If we work together, I have a theory that we can break down the barrier for you and your friends. There's no guarantee that it will work, but there's no reason not to try." Aiden looks to me for my subtle approval, and I smile at him.

Looking around, I see that the Half-Fae people are beginning to come around to the idea. One by one, I see more and more nods throughout the crowd. "If you want to get out of this place, meet us at the barrier in one hour," I declare. "And if you don't, no hard feelings. May the Lady protect you." With a small wave, the crowd disperses. People head in different directions, having indistinct conversations with their family and friends. I hope that enough decide to join us. It could really help.

"Grace?" I hear my name from across the lake. I look up to find the Enchantress beckoning me over with a hand. I walk over to join her, separating myself from my friends.

"You were calling for me?"

"Yes. I would like to speak to you in private before you leave."

"I only have a moment."

"That's all I need." We move over to the cave and stand in the entryway. "You need to hear this. Grace, you are the only one with the grit to do what needs to be done," she says to me with a piercing look in her eyes.

I laugh incredulously. "That's not even close to true. There are seven other perfectly capable people involved in this prophecy who could have stepped up and taken the lead at any time. In fact, I'd gladly welcome it at this point. Maybe I'll finally hand things over to Gideon when we return home."

The Enchantress continues like I had never spoken. "Gideon has too much strength and no finesse. Aiden and Faolan inevitably still do their duty to their Houses or their creations when they don't want to. Kiara and Aira don't have the stomach for the task, and Cary is an independent woman first, not to be guided by any one hand. And Luna? She still has idyllic views of the future. You, my dear, were born for this."

"How do you know all of that? You've never met most of these people. You haven't spoken to anyone but me longer than two seconds!"

"That is of no concern to you."

"I don't want to keep making the sacrifices," I practically growl at her. "I don't want the grit that comes from being broken."

"Such is the life of the hero."

"I don't want to be a hero!"

"Neither did I." Her admission stops me in my tracks. "I was born in this realm, but not with all of the power that I currently possess. I went through a journey, just like you. I was forced into a leadership role, and I flourished as you have. And now me and my companions lead these people. We protect them. Herodom finds you. You don't often get to choose."

"And if you want to choose something else?"

The Enchantress smiles at me sadly. "You can always try. Better women than you and me have failed doing so. Perhaps you can defy fate, my dear." She pats my shoulder once. "For your sake, I hope you manage to."

Chapter Fifty

Our prophecy group leads the half-Fae that have chosen to join us to the entrance of the oasis. My palms are sweating as I look over to Aiden. While he seems to be much more back to his normal self, there's something still not quite right. It's almost like he can turn a switch on and off. One moment, he's full Aiden, and the next, he's someone much more neutral. Maybe the Half-Fae Coven had to lock everything down in order for the demon not to take over too much. Maybe he'll flip back and forth like this forever until the demon finally takes him over. I feel like I should have asked more questions before we left.

"How do you want to do this?" I ask Aiden.

"The same way we cast the spell in the House of Water," he answers, offering me his hand.

"I don't know if I have the magic types for the spell we need."

"I don't know either. You try disintegration magic, but a slower disintegration. I'll try earth elemental magic. Let's see where we end up."

When the two of us get to work, hand in hand, everyone waits with bated breath. Even while my brain is trying to focus on the magic casting, I keep thinking about whether or not Faolan is bothered by our holding hands. Closing my eyes, I imagine the barrier to the oasis like a brick wall that I can slowly dismantle piece by piece, row by

"

row. When I feel the first piece begin to quiver, I focus in hard on it. Aiden loans me his power while simultaneously working on the lower edges of the barrier. He grows heavy vines straight out of the ground and send them to pry at the magical barrier.

It takes a lot of energy from me to move each row. I almost want to close my eyes and sleep by the time we're halfway through. But Aiden's and my magical strength fuel each other. Together, we create a hole just wide enough for people to rush through. "Hey!" I shout hoarsely. "Someone needs to try. And fast." There's so much hesitation. The half-Fae inch closer, but none of them attempt to cross. "Hey!" I shout again. "We can't hold this forever!"

One man decides to be the first to try to cross. Closing his eyes, he runs through. When he makes it through unharmed and unrejected, he turns around with the biggest grin on his face. The barrier is suddenly flooded with people escaping their beautiful prison. With each person that passes through, Aiden and I feel a heavy jolt against our magic. The barrier is fighting back by draining us instead. We manage to wave at the half-Fae to hurry up before we have to drop our efforts. We then make our way through the barrier and collapse to the ground.

The people around us cheer. I grin and sag against Aiden in exhaustion. He squeezes my hand in return. *We did it.* Faolan and Aira rush over to help us to our feet and support us while we head toward the border. Once we reach it, we usher everyone across. It takes a while, but we all manage to reach the Middle Realm side. Once we're there, I turn to the leaders of our little group. "How do you feel about a train ride?"

* * *

Although there are very few trains leaving to Lisden with the chaos entering the city, I manage to persuade a conductor to bring us there. I tell him we're joining the war effort there. Technically the truth. We take up almost four cars by ourselves. Trains are past their ancestor's time, so the half-Fae are fascinated for the entire ride. I smile as I watch them whisper and chat with each other as they stare out the window at the world that has opened up to them. I am glad that this half of the Middle Realm still looks pretty. It's a good view before we get to the chaos.

When we reach the train station, the scene is incredibly dire. The conductor seems very nervous, and he ushers us off of the train rapidly. There's almost no one waiting here. Part of me wonders whether that is because all of the people who wanted to leave got out faster or because the refugees can't get to the train station to leave. I don't know what environment we are entering into, but hopefully we should have intel very soon.

Sure enough, several of Faolan's men meet with us at the exit of the train station to the city. Apparently, Faolan had sent them here to keep an eye on things just before we left for the Lower Realm. Faolan speaks with them in a hushed voice before returning to me. "The House of Darkness hasn't pushed into the eastern half of the city yet. No one is sure why. They appear to be preparing to take the center city area. We need to go meet them now."

"You mean it's starting right now?" I say.

We arm the half-Fae with what little supplies are available to us. Not enough of them have any kind of backup weapon other than their magic. But it seems like most of them don't really need it. There's a fire in their eyes that I haven't seen from even my own people in a while. These people are fresh and hungry. I can't believe that, given how often they have had to fight off demons.

It doesn't take us long to find the battle. It looks almost exactly like the previous battle in Lisden. Buildings falling down, mortals screaming and running for their lives, people lying dead in the street. It's giving me horrific flashbacks. I don't want to fail my people again. Instead of charging in, I wait to organize the group. I send out half-Fae in every direction, led by one of the prophecy group members or Faolan's guys. I imagine at least a few of them were leaders back in the oasis, but I don't want to take any chances. Once they disperse, I launch myself into the fight.

My focus is on protecting the mortals around me. Wherever I see a group having an issue by Fae or by demon, I move in, hands blazing. I fight with everything I have in me. Magic flies around us at rapid speed, but every life that I protect is one more person who will live another day. The mortals realize that I am trying to help, and they begin to stick close to me.

The Half-Fae Society are a well-oiled machine fighting like waves against the Fae and demon armies. They swarm around a small group of soldiers and practically consume them in their ranks. Colorful magic streams fly in and out of the tight group before the half-Fae emerge victorious. When they recede, nearly every soldier is knocked out or dead. It's beautifully horrifying to see.

This is not to say that we are winning by a landslide. Quite the opposite, actually. Whenever we take one Fae regiment down, another pops up to take their place. If we had our armies, maybe we could have made this more of a fair fight. But we are completely outnumbered, no matter how you look at it. The demons keep coming, and we struggle to hold our ground.

I keep trying to focus on the fight, but I can't help but keep my eye on Aiden and his magic. His spells seem relatively stable so far, albeit a little stronger than usual. But anything could happen when demonic magic is involved. Luckily, a group of the half-Fae seem to have chosen to bring him under their wing, and they stay close, fighting with him and preparing to temper his magic whenever necessary.

The battle ends unceremoniously with a quick retreat by the demons. They destroy what they can on their way back to the opposite side of the city to regroup. I don't know how much time we have. All I know is that we managed to hold the city for one more day together. Mortals, half-Fae, and Fae working together. Who would have thought?

Chapter Fifty-One

The crisis has been averted temporarily. We never would have made it without the half-Fae Coven involved. They fought like hell, and I'm impressed by that. Backed by some of the best black market weapons we could provide, they managed to hold their own against Fae they have never fought before. And the mortals too, I couldn't believe how much they were able to push back. The level of sacrifice for their home is equal to that of the Fae. I don't even want to think about how many perished under demon magic though. I'll need to send someone around to collect that information.

My thoughts then jump to my family on the other side of town. I have no idea whether or not the fighting got over to them. I call for Faolan, and he materializes beside me. "Faolan, please. I need to go check on my family. I need someone to go."

"I'll send someone over immediately," he replies before rushing off to grab someone he knows off to the side. I survey the damage around me. The city is in shambles. I used to come over to this side of town often for violin gigs, but I wouldn't recognize it today. I think I see a piece of a former patron's house lying in the street, but that house was at least two blocks over only days ago. I wonder what happened to the family. Despite that, the atmosphere is starting to perk up. Around me, the mortals have begun to address the half-Fae and thank them for their assistance. The two groups interact with each other like they've known each other for years. It makes me really happy to see that.

"*Grace?*" A familiar voice shouts from behind me, and it stops me in my tracks. "Grace Richardson!" *By the Lady, no one has called me that name in so long.* I spin around and immediately choke up when I see David, *David*, charging toward me. His hair has gotten so long, it flops over his shoulders and in his eyes as he runs. I rush back toward him at top speed. I throw my arms around his neck and just burst into tears. I'm not even sure why I feel that strongly to see him alive, but everything has been so intense for days and to see a familiar mortal face who doesn't hate me is astounding. Burying my head in his neck, I hold on tight, and David grips me back just as tight. I feel his tears falling on my head, and I am shocked. I haven't seen David cry before, not even at Leo's funeral. He's never been one to show that kind of emotion.

When I pull back to look at him, he barely lets me move. "David…" I finally say, my voice sounding much smaller than it has in a long time. "I…" I start to talk, but I realize I don't know what to say. We left things so horribly last time with Aiden and all.

"I saw you," he speaks to me instead. "I saw you in battle." My heart is wracked with fear of his reaction. I can't lose another friend. Not now. "Do you have magic?"

"Yes," I answer tentatively.

"How the hell do you have magic, Grace?"

"I… I'm half-Fae."

David looks at me, dumbfounded. "Are you serious?"

"Yes…"

"Was Leo Fae?"

"No, we had different fathers. My father is… was a High Lord in the House of the Evening."

"Wait, wait, wait." David is struggling to process this. "Are you a

Fae Lady?"

"A High Lady, now, yes." David's look of shock makes me feel incredibly uncomfortable. "I understand that you may have reservations about—"

To my surprise, the man laughs and spins me around again. My jaw practically drops down to my chest. "Look at you. Infiltrated the Fae ranks right at the very top. That's my girl."

"You… what?" I can't even form a coherent thought. "You were so pissed off when I showed up with Aiden!"

"You appear out of nowhere back from the Upper Realm, and I'm rushing to the gym to find you, and I walk in on you on top of another man. A Fae man! Given your experience and mine, I was a little shell shocked." David holds up a hand to stop me from arguing. "And I know… I know what I said was wrong. I regretted it the moment I sent you across the border again without saying goodbye. I regretted it even more when you didn't come back. I had no idea how to get information to you or hear from you without blowing your cover in the Upper Realm. All I could do was watch and wait and pray to the Lady that you weren't dead."

"I'm so sorry," I apologize as I hug him tighter. "I tried to send word to you through the black market, but I couldn't. The man I spoke to wouldn't take the message, and… well, as you can imagine, things got pretty complicated from there."

"I did get a message though," David insists.

"You did?"

"Yeah. Some single line parchment arrived under my door one day. All it said was "she is alive". I assumed you sent it."

"No…" I trail off. "I had no idea." My mind is racing. Is it possible that Faolan had allowed my message to be sent all those months ago? Or perhaps did he send it after he learned who I really was and what I had been trying to do? For the first time in ages, I feel my heart start to warm through.

"I'm so happy to see you. What have you been doing? How did you end up back here? It's been months."

"Oh, David, it's about the longest story ever." I squeeze both of his arms. "We need to find time to talk, but I have to check on things. I don't have time to explain."

"Hey, hey," he soothes. "What if I meet you back here in an hour?"

"What if you don't come back?"

"I will come back," he insists. "I promise."

"I'll explain everything then. I have to find someone." I squeeze David as tightly as I can, trying to soak up his memory just in case we can't find each other again. I rush off toward where the Fae have gathered to reconvene and share information. I spot Faolan right away, and I head right to him.

"There you are," he says. "Your family is fine. The fighting didn't make it over there this time. I'm working on setting up protection for them."

"Thank you so much."

"Of course."

"Faolan," I ask carefully. "Did you send my message to David all those months ago like I asked Mahlin?"

"Yes," he answers simply.

"Why? You didn't even know who I was at the time."

"Something about you captured my attention. I figured if you were willing to reach out to the black market publicly in House of Darkness territory, then your message must have been important. So I made sure it got sent."

"Thank you."

"It's nothing."

I lay my hand on his arm. "No... it's not nothing."

Faolan nods to me. "What are we gonna do next?"

"I need to speak to David and fill him in on everything that has been happening. We need to regroup and speak with the half-Fae. Their help has been invaluable."

"Yeah. Turns out they're just what we needed. The mortals fought like all hell too. Never seen anything like it. Wish they could join us."

A spark of an idea lands in my head. I turn to Faolan and throw my arms around him quickly. He catches me in surprise. "Wow, what did I say?"

"You've just given me the perfect idea. We need to call the War Council."

Chapter Fifty-Two

When I call the emergency War Council, I am skeptical on whether or not this is the best way to accomplish my plan. Transporting everyone to the House of the Day to meet us at the border is risky. Any of the convoys could be ambushed, and lives could be lost. Lady forbid someone kidnap one of the Council members. We'd have a whole mess on our hands. But I do think it is worth the risk if I can persuade them to agree to what I've got planned.

That's going to be a tall order.

Each of the convoys are sent through a different safe route down to the Middle Realm border. I try to make sure that each of the routes doesn't go through too heavily contested territory. Eventually, all of the Council members make it. With great effort, we cross back over into the Upper Realm via midnight train and meet them at their arrival. We usher them immediately into the House of the Day's palace. Faolan takes a moment to make sure that every soldier available is surrounding the city and the local borders. I don't want to take any chances if there is an attack. Wasting no time, I don't give the nobles any time to settle in, instead ushering them into a conference room.

"What in the world was so urgent that you decided to bring us all the way down here?" Tristan asks first. "That was the most shifty transport I've ever taken part in."

"I apologize for summoning you with such urgency," I attempt to soothe. "But trust me, what I have to say is worthwhile and needs to be said down here as close to the border as possible."

"Why?" Alena asks.

"Please take a seat," Faolan says. "Everything will be clear in a moment." At my nod, he opens the conference room doors once more to let in several mortal political leaders from the major cities, including Lisden. I can't help but smile smugly. It took a hell of a lot of convincing, but after the prophecy group and the half-Fae fought so hard to hold onto Lisden, they could see that we were willing to go the distance to make a deal. Upon seeing the mortal leaders, Jason immediately gets to his feet. "Grace, what is the meaning of this? What is going on?"

"I'll explain," I answer quickly, holding my hands up. "Please sit down, Lord Jason." I wave the mortal leaders forward. "Please join us." The men and women take seats at the far end of the table, sitting in a small 'U'. I figured seating them close together would make them feel more comfortable. I then stand at the head of the table. "As you all may have guessed, I have brought you together, Fae noble heirs and mortal government leaders, to discuss the wartime that we are currently under."

"Grace," one of the older mortal leaders from the city of Clinton says carefully. "High Lady Grace," he quickly corrects, "I'm afraid I don't know what we are doing here. I have interacted with many Fae over my time in the government, but I have never been invited to a conference like this. I am wary because I don't know if you're here to aid us or broker a deal by sacrificing us."

"How dare you speak to her in that manner," Jason snaps. "You have no right to—"

I whip around and get in his face. "If you do not shut your mouth, Jason, I will shut it for you." He has at least enough sense to close his mouth and stare at the wall. I turn back to the other man. "I apologize for my colleague's outburst. Rest assured, I will meet any others with the same harshness. We are not planning on sacrificing you to reach a deal with the House of Darkness. On the contrary, we'd like to work together."

"I'm sorry, what are you talking about?" Alena asks incredulously.

"Fae and mortals have been adversaries for centuries. The Fae have been interfering in mortal life since the beginning. You have always had a presence in this realm whether it was a direct plant in the government or regulating trade or taking a percentage of the agricultural output of every city. But like it or not, you rely on their presence for salt, grain, technology, and all kinds of little things that you don't think about on a daily basis. In return, you've provided funds, though at a highly reduced rate. Maybe some protection. Out of all of you, Lord Faolan has done the most to support the Middle Realm with the economic backbone of the black market."

The mortal leaders murmur to each other, glancing over at Faolan. He keeps his expression neutral. I suppose I should have considered making sure the mortals were aware of Faolan's position. He's both a hero and a villain in the Middle Realm's story. I also probably should have asked if it was okay to say such things. I inwardly cringe. *Whoops.* All I can really do is continue my speech and hope it doesn't come back to bite me later.

"What is your point?" Gideon asks.

"Let's cut to the chase. My proposal is that the Middle Realm provides us with the manpower that we need to overtake the House of Darkness's army. We provide them with magical weapons and training, and they put themselves on the battlefield for their realm and ours. In exchange, when we win, we give them back full control of their realm. No government oversight, no Fae installments. Give it back, free and clear."

There's a very… very long minute of silence. Everyone is staring at me like I've lost my mind. Well, maybe not everyone. Faolan looks pretty calm by comparison, and Luna seems very happy about the idea. But everyone else looks at me like I've grown three heads, including the mortals. At least they seem to have a bit of hope in their eyes.

But then the nobles erupt.

"Are you crazy?" Tristan shouts.

"You've gone completely nutty." Gideon chuckles.

"Grace, you've lost your fucking mind." Jason scoffs and shakes his head. "You really think any of our parents are going to agree to get rid of this practice that has been around for our entire lives, their entire lives, and their ancestor's entire lives?"

"They are not the ones that need to agree. When you joined this War Council, every High Lord gave decision making power over to us, over to you."

"You know that this is outside the scope of the war."

"Actually, it's not. It's not outside the scope at all. *This* is what it is going to take to win this war. You know as well as I do that we need to end this thing before the House of Darkness and the demons sweep the entire Middle Realm. Whether you like it or not, everyone's fate here is intertwined. If we fall, they fall. If they fall, we fall. We can't liberate ourselves until we liberate *them*. This is a good plan whether you like it or not. And if you can't stomach that, maybe think about if being slaves or worse to the demons of the Lower Realm is a better alternative than this."

The naysayers in the room fall silent at that. I smirk lightly. No one has a comeback. I feel fired up. They're going to have to take this deal if they want to survive. And if it gets my family and friends back home out from under the Upper Realm's thumb once and for all, being a hard-ass will have been worth it. I can't even imagine what kind of a difference it would make for everyone. Just to be able to regulate our own trade and set our own prices for things that the Upper Realm needs from us… maybe we wouldn't need the black market all of the time. Faolan might not be happy about that, but he's not showing it. I imagine he'll find some way to cope.

"There's more," I press on. "You can forget every story you've been led to believe regarding the ancient banishment of the half-Fae to the Lower Realm. They didn't die down there."

"*I'm sorry?*" Tristan practically shouts. "They would have to be thousands of years old at this point."

I resist the urge to roll my eyes. "They didn't survive this long. But they didn't die immediately either. They were able to form a community and build a safe haven where they could continue fighting off the demons, but live a full life. They had kids, and their kids had kids, and generation upon generation was created." The silence following my words is deafening. Everyone's eyes are trained on me. I motion for Faolan to open the doors. Six of the half-Fae join us in the conference room. I tried to pick people who I saw take the lead in the battle of Lisden.

"These are the people that helped us turn the tide in the Middle Realm. We broke them out of their safe haven, broke their exile, and promised them sanctuary in the Upper Realm if they agreed to help us. Now it's not everyone. Many weren't ready or willing to come assist. But these people were. Now, the nobles I took to the Middle Realm and I have agreed to give them safe haven in our Houses if they so choose. I believe we will be able to create a three-way treaty here that will benefit all of us and solidify protection for every walk of life here."

No one speaks. Many people stare at me openly. I know I've dropped a lot of new information on them. All I can do is sigh. "Look… this is one of the most complicated treaties that would ever have been attempted in the last several centuries. And I've given you a lot to think about. All I want to know… is do you think we can make a deal at all?"

"Where would we even start putting something like that together?" Gideon finally says.

"We would start right here," I reply. "With these people in this room. We put together a treaty that will last for the next thousand years. This is the best plan. Are you all at least willing to try?" I see a few nods, particularly from Aira, Luna, and Aurora. "Can we get a vote please?"

And with a slow, begrudging, but eventually unanimous vote, we enter a new chapter of realm history.

Chapter Fifty-Three

Treaty negotiations take over a week to finalize. Every policy, every idea gets debated back and forth for hours a day. And it isn't always civil. Jason and Gideon particularly clash with the mortal leaders over trade. In some ways, this makes perfect sense. Those two Houses are the most prominent avenues for Middle Realm products moving into the Upper Realm. It's ultimately their economies that are being the most affected. I have to step in multiple times to keep things from coming to blows. At the end of the day, though, everyone's reaction feels justified. We're trying to build something no one has ever tried. Emotions are running high. Anything could happen.

We finally reach a treaty with stipulations that all sides can agree on. The Middle Realm provides as many men and women as they can possibly spare, and we arm them appropriately, as equally as we would arm our own people. When we win this war, the Middle Realm will be granted their freedom from Fae control within the first season post-war. The nobles from each family will then establish new, fair trading agreements and make their own rules about mortals moving in and around the Upper Realm. The half-Fae will have sanctuary in any House that they want to and a spot in the Middle Realm if they agree to limit their magic usage around mortals. There's a lot of bureaucracy to be taken care of, but we've built a foundation for it. And I couldn't be more proud of that.

We return home immediately after the treaty is signed and kick things in high gear. To prepare for the final battle, we have to take swift decisive action. Nothing less will do. With the support of the War Council, the plans for the final battle are transferred fully over to the prophecy group. For the first time since this war began, I feel a deep-seated belief that we are going to pull this off. Gideon sends his second in command with the House of War army, along with the Houses of Wind and Moon and a large group of half-Fae, to clean house in the Houses of Sun and Fire. Now it's just a matter of sitting here and waiting to see what happens.

As if I already didn't have enough to think about, several days into the waiting period, Aiden knocks incessantly on my bedroom door until I open it. "What do you want, Aiden?" I say quietly.

"Go out with me," he says simply.

I want to be frustrated, but I'm trying to be gentle. He's been struggling so much recently with keeping the demon magic under control. "We've been over this, Aiden. I just… we're in the middle of a war, and I don't know what I'm doing right now."

"Well, I don't have a lot of time, Grace. You know that there's no guarantee I'm going to survive this war. You know what the prophecy says."

"Aiden, we're going to find a way to save you. If we've supposedly got all of this all-powerful magic, then it has to mean something. We're going to cure you. You don't need to worry about that."

"Stop lying to yourself, Grace." Aiden raises his voice at me. "It's a long shot."

"Well, I'm pretty good at beating the odds. I've been doing it since the moment I step foot in this realm. Do you not believe I can save you?" I snap.

Aiden sighs. "Grace, you know that's not at all what I meant."

The regret washes over me like a cold shower. I sigh to myself. "If you want to go out, we'll go out."

Aiden smiles. "Really?"

"Yes. What do you want to do?"

"I'll get everything arranged. Meet me at the front door in two hours."

"Today?"

"Yes, today. I'm not giving you another chance to change your mind!" With that, he rushes off down the hall. I chuckle softly. *That's the fastest I've seen him move in weeks.*

* * *

In the aforementioned two hours, I make my way down to the front hall. I decided to put on something light, a nice billowy shirt and tight pants. I don't really know what Aiden has planned for the day, but an outfit like this ought to cut it. It felt a little strange getting dressed up for a date with doom and gloom hanging over our heads at every turn. And the fact that I don't really want to go on a date with him. Or with anyone.

I didn't say anything to Faolan. Damn it all to hell, what is he going to say when he finds out?

Uh... why are you thinking about that right now? You haven't chosen. What could you possibly be worried about?

"Grace!" My thoughts are interrupted by Aiden's excited voice coming from the front door. "You're here."

"Of course I'm here. Where else would I be?"

He laughs and reaches for my hand. "Will you please come with me?"

I cautiously take his hand. "Where are we going?"

"Just out on the grounds. You'll see when we get there."

Aiden then jogs outside, and I'm forced to keep pace. It is so surprising how one afternoon with me is suddenly enough to make him his old self again. He leads me out to the palace gardens over by the large fountain. As we come up the path, I see what Aiden has been coordinating all afternoon. A large picnic blanket lays in the grass filled with an amazing lunch spread. There's sandwiches, salads, little cups of fruit, vegetable dips, and cookies. My stomach growls. I haven't eaten a full meal in multiple days.

The man lets go of my hand and chuckles. "I heard that. When was the last time you ate?"

"I had breakfast!" I protest.

"How much did you have?"

"I had an apple."

"A whole apple?"

I hesitate. "A part of an apple."

"More than a bite?"

"Mmm."

Aiden laughs out loud. "I knew it. Come on, sit down and dig in. Take a load off. Don't worry about things for a bit." He plops himself down on the picnic blanket and starts to load up a plate. I ease myself down next to him and grab my own plate. I load up with a little bit of everything. Okay, maybe a lot of everything.

I dig in and soak up a little sun. It's a really nice day out, the kind that makes you forget what's going on in the world. Aiden doesn't talk a lot at first, which I kind of appreciate. He lets me enjoy the food and the sunlight without it being overtaken by conversation. As I'm digging into my second cookie, he finally talks to me. "Are you enjoying yourself?"

"Yeah," I answer. "This is definitely the nicest break I've had in a while. Are you enjoying yourself?"

"Of course."

"Are you sure? You haven't said much."

"I don't need to. Sitting here next to you is exactly what I need right now. And your smile, seeing you happy… that's all I was looking for."

I roll my eyes, but smile softly at him. "You are way too cheesy."

"You love it."

"Maybe."

Aiden grins. "Who knew it would take me dying to admit that you like my sappiness."

"Oh, hush." My mood sours almost immediately when he brings up his impending death again. *Can't the man just keep his mouth shut about heavy things for two minutes? We were having such a nice time.*

"We could have been great together, you know," he says as he turns his head to me. His eyes have an odd sadness in them. "If we had had more time… if I hadn't been such an idiot… we could have been very… very good together."

"Don't say it," I hiss at Aiden through gritted teeth. "Don't say another word."

"I need you to hear this, Grace."

"We are going to make it out. Both of us. There's still time to find a solution."

Aiden lays a hand on my arm. "Grace." His eyes watch me so intently that I have to look away.

"Don't talk to me like it's the last time we're going to see each other." My voice comes out all choked up. "It's not."

"I want you to move on."

"Aiden…"

"I want you to move on past me. When it's all over and you've had a moment to breathe, I want you to find someone who makes you happy and go fall in love."

"I can't…"

"You can."

"How dare you say that to me!" I'm filled with a mix of rage and sadness. "Why would you bring me out here? I thought you wanted this to be a nice little date where you and I would reconnect before everything changes forever. But here you are to tell me to just give up on everything and pick someone else because you will just be disappearing anyway?"

"Grace… I love you. I don't want to cause you any more pain. I thought you wanted to be told it's okay to move on. If I had thought—"

"But that's the thing. You didn't think. You haven't been thinking this whole time. You've… you've been…" I can't even get the words out of my mouth. I push myself to my knees and then to my feet. "The meal was lovely. Thank you." Before Aiden can say another word, I run off, headed back toward the palace.

When he's out of sight, I storm up the stairs toward my bedroom. I slam the door hard behind me as my heart pounds in my chest. *It's not fair. It's just not fair.* Every fiber in my being is screaming to run away from this, to take the people I care about and flee. I don't even know where to, just anywhere. I feel an overwhelming need to shatter everything around me. My eyes land on my violin, and something in me snaps.

Gripping the neck of the instrument, I rip it violently off of the instrument rack, throwing the stand to the ground. I pull the bow from its place on the table and slam my foot into the balcony doors. They fly open, slamming into the walls on either side. I'm surprised I didn't shatter the glass. *I'll kick harder next time.* Swinging the violin to my shoulder, I yank the bow across the string in a hard slash. I launch into a fast, high melody. The bow moves fast, my fingers fly, and I let the emotions build up inside of me and release through intense music.

Similar to the night of Founder's Day and my attempted assassination, long purple strands begin to form around me. Instead of radiating out, however, they wrap tightly in rings and webs around me. The more I play, the tighter the knots become. By the time I finish my rage-filled song, I am surrounded by a swirling cloud of magic. I have to wait for it to die down before I can make it back to my bedroom, which takes quite a while with the height of my emotions tied to it. By the time I actually make it out, it's almost sunset. I give up on any kind of dinner or work getting accomplished and collapse in my bed.

Why does leading have to be so hard?

Chapter Fifty-Four

I don't see Aiden much before the final battle. I go out of my way to avoid him. Part of me is crushed doing so. I should want to spend as much time as possible with him in case things go south. But the other part of me can't get over how selfish he is acting in his final days. Why stab me in the heart like that? What was even the best outcome for him? Did he want me to be in love with him again, be with him for perhaps his final days, and then be devastated when he perished? Or was I supposed to pretend? It wouldn't really have taken that much out of me to have given him the love he needed to pass on. But what if he doesn't? Will he be chasing after me forever?

And I still haven't said yes to Faolan. What is holding me back? Is it Aiden? Is there still just a tiny part of me that loves him?

I am so confused.

But alas, the war goes on. With depleted forces and a mass redistribution of soldiers to the Middle Realm, it only takes a few weeks for sieges to overtake everyone except for the House of Darkness. We are isolating them on their home turf and in the Middle Realm, and it is working.

The night before we are scheduled to depart for the Middle Realm for the final battle, I call one last prophecy meeting. We all need to make sure we understand our roles here fully before we head out into battle with the others. I don't want what needs to happen here to interfere with what we'll each be leading on the ground. We are three concentric circles that will turn together to make this grand event turn out exactly how we want. Or at least that's the hope.

That's the strange thing about prophecies: they tell you how things need to come together in order to succeed, but don't give you any indication of whether you truly will succeed.

It's irritating.

I open the conference room up to the eight of us and lock the door behind us. When I take my seat at the head of the table, I feel like I'm speaking at a funeral. I wish it didn't feel like our funeral. We should feel confident, assured of ourselves. Instead, not a single person has a strong look on their face. We all look a little dead on our feet, like a gust of wind may knock us over. I hope we look much stronger come daylight.

"Tomorrow," I start quietly. "Tomorrow, we will be leaving for the Middle Realm. The House of Darkness has chosen to make their final stand there, and we will need to meet them there in order to end this thing once and for all."

"Don't you think they'll be expecting us?" Aira asks.

"They will be," Gideon answers. "But they know the war will be won or lost there regardless. It does them more good than harm to let us approach."

"So we engage. How does that go?" Cary asks.

"Each of us will be leading different forces," Luna answers. Everyone turns to watch her smoky eyes. Whenever she speaks now, everyone pays great attention to it. "We'll attack in balance: north, south, east, and west."

"And Luna will let me know when the time is right to begin the final spell sequence," I add. "So keep your attention split; make sure you keep checking in with me. It is going to be crucial that we are all prepared when the moment comes. So keep your wits about you."

"Do you think we're going to be able to pull that off?" Aiden asks.

"We have to," Faolan says.

"Our survival depends on it. All of ours," Gideon adds, trailing off at the end.

The conversation doesn't need to go any further. There's nothing more to say. Instead, we decide to just sit together as a group in silence. Eventually, Faolan gets up from the table and pulls a stray bottle of wine stashed in a cabinet where the House usually keeps desk supplies for the conference room. When I raise an eyebrow, he shrugs. "Thought it might come in handy at some point." Instead of getting glasses, Faolan simply takes a swig and hands it over to Gideon.

With a shake of his head, he tips the bottle back. "Ah, what the hell?" He takes a drink.

The bottle makes its way around the table steadily. Gideon passes it over to Cary, who doesn't hesitate in taking more than a few sips. She slides it over to Luna, and it makes its way around from person to person. There's something powerful to me about sitting around a table, sharing a drink with the people that you're prepared to die with. Nobody knows what's gonna happen tomorrow. Just because we have a plan doesn't mean it's going to work. Sometimes you can't save everyone no matter how hard you try.

Aiden takes a long slow drink before passing the remainder to me. I look down at the bottle and the last long sip left inside. When I glance back up, I see that the entire table is watching me. Everyone has a very calm stoic look on their faces. We have in fact resigned ourselves to our duty to the realm. And somehow, everyone looks to me as their leader. Not because of some prophecy, but because I managed to prove myself over many, many months. Closing my eyes, I tip my head back and down the last of the bottle of wine. I set it on the table with a soft clink.

"Hey," I say quietly. Everyone turns to look at me. "Tell me what you want."

Faolan's forehead wrinkles. "What do you mean, Grace?"

I look around the table and feel a swell of emotion in my chest. These people have been fighting for this for so long, but collectively we haven't taken a moment to think about what comes after. To have something to live for. "Tell me what you all want when this is over. I want to hear something that you want when we survive the war." I look pointedly at Aiden. "All of us."

It takes a moment, but Luna is the first to speak. "Happiness."

Aira nods slowly. "Returning home."

"Returning home and being with my family," Kiara echoes her desire.

Cary laughs to herself. "Y'all are way too sappy. I just want to get out of here and start causing reasonable chaos again."

I let myself laugh a little at her antics. Faolan chuckles too and turns to look at me as he answers my question, "I want to get back to doing what I want, when I want, and with whom I want." His eyes looking into mine make me soften just a bit to see that I was clearly one of the people he wanted to spend time with.

Gideon brings it back to a little more somber tone. "I'm trying to make it out alive and go home with as many of my men as I can."

His words linger in the air before everyone slowly turns to Aiden, who is staring down at the table with his hands crossed. My head tells me that I am a fool for asking this question in front of him knowing that he probably won't make it home. But my heart tells me that it's important to have hope and we can't give up on Aiden yet, no matter how terrible the odds are. When he raises his head, he looks up at me. "I want to live long enough to fall in love all over again."

I feel his words pierce me inside like a knife. He's so clear with his dream. He hopes to be able to convince me to love him again, to try things over again even though we have already said our last goodbyes. I can't bear to look at him, so I just look down instead.

"What's yours, Grace?" Gideon asks.

I curse his timing in my head. Now I have to come up with something. *What do I want after this? Can I even think of anything after this?* "I want a year," I finally start. "I want a year where nothing else happens. I just want to breathe normally for a year."

"By the Lady, wouldn't that be nice?" Cary laughs. The rest of the room gives a little chuckle.

"Luna," Gideon asks, "is there any more information you can give us about the prophecy? Any… any last minute something?"

The table turns to look at the girl as she smiles softly. "I can try." She closes her eyes, and her breathing nearly goes completely silent. The rest of us wait with bated breath to hear what she has to say. She opens her eyes slowly, and for the first time, her face falls. My heart sinks along with it. "Everything will turn out as it is supposed to. The prophecy will be fulfilled completely."

"And?" I ask.

Luna looks up directly at me. "And when it plays out, we all will end up where we are supposed to be. All of us."

We really don't know how to respond to that. It's not really news. Everything working out the way it is supposed to could be good or bad. But the prophecy will be enacted as it is intended to. We have all the pieces. All we can do is… wait and exist. Simply wait and exist.

Silently, I raise my glass, holding it out high in front of me. The others notice in waves, and one by one they raise their glasses to join mine. I don't speak this time, allowing for a purely silent toast. Instead, I internally ask for the Lady to spare us all come prophecy time. I imagine the others are doing the same. Then we all take a slow long sip, drinking to our health and our uncertain futures.

Chapter Fifty-Five

The march to the final battle isn't as busy and chaotic as I thought it would be. Instead, it's quiet. Not many people talk to each other. There's some quiet planning here and there, but no real casual conversation. Everyone is focused on what has to be done now. Everyone around here knows that this is likely to be the battle to end all battles. A lot of lives will be lost today. But if everything goes according to plan, we're going to win this one. Kiara takes time when we're nearly to the Middle Realm to distribute the blood magic potions to the prophecy group. Each one glows a different color, characteristic of our magic. We tuck them away and hope that they will work out.

Close to the end of the journey, I end up in a carriage with Aiden and Faolan. The two of them watch me in the same way, with concern and maybe even a little fear about what is to happen to me today. Faolan pretends not to be worried about it, but when I look in his eyes, there is an intensity that I haven't seen in a while from him. And Aiden? Aiden looks prepared to die. He seems like he's accepted his fate. The worry in his eyes is making sure that I am protected, that I am safe. My heart can't take it. I throw my hands forward and grasp both of theirs. They both look back at me in surprise. I say nothing, but squeeze both hands very tightly. Eventually, I receive squeezes in response.

In that moment, I feel strength.

When we reach the Middle Realm and the final battle commences, there is no ambush. One side doesn't even attack the other outright. It happens so formally. We meet sides across the battlefield and hold there. Waiting. As I look around, I see all of my friends, the other prophecy members, leading their own individual regiments or forces. After running through the details of Luna's new visions over and over again, we were able to put together exactly where everyone needed to be. While the battle will be chaotic, if we stay on task, the final moment should come together swiftly when the time is right. Cary, Aiden, and Gideon and I lead fighting regiments from the north, south, east, and west. According to Luna, the House of Darkness will exist as one large mass hoping to consume everything. If we approach from all sides, we can press inward and take them. Faolan is leading the supply line through our ranks, facilitating more weapons, potions, and other magical resources to reach those who need them. Kiara and Aira are both leading healer teams throughout our ranks. And Luna? Luna will be staying to the edges as much as possible, staying close to me. She'll fight, but not lead. I need her to be near me. She's the only one who knows when the final strike has to start. I need to know the second she knows.

The atmosphere is tense as we approach. As we come up over the ridge, we see the enemy. Something I notice right away is how similarly everyone looks. Our army looks almost exactly like theirs, minus the outfits. Our faces look the same, our features look the same. If someone had no idea which army was which, they wouldn't be able to tell us apart. It feels very sad to know that. It's brother fighting brother. I don't think I ever really realized it. Aiden's been fighting against his brother the whole time. Faolan and Cary, against their father. I wonder how many other families have been split up.

I wonder how many will be split up when it's all over.

I hold my breath as I lock eyes with the opposing House of Darkness general. He sneers at me, but there's the tiniest hint of fear behind his eyes that I pick up on. Nobody wants to die today. So we had better give this everything we've got. His lip quirks up every so slightly before he utters a war cry. Before I can react, I hear Gideon's booming yell and the House of War soldiers taking up the battle call. We charge together, toward whatever fate brings us.

Here we are, trying to keep the Fae realm alive, pitting brother against brother and hoping that it works out. Once again, I give it absolutely everything I've got. I let the mental control over my magic decrease just slightly, enough to give my spells the full unbridled power they deserve but not so much that I can't control at least the direction. Flames burn through the enemy's rank as swiftly as a wildfire, and I attempt to work through who it hits and who it won't. I keep my wings prepped and take off away from an attack whenever I need to. From the sky, I let it rain fire down on the cluster of people. I pray to the Lady that my own people aren't too badly injured by that.

In the air, I can see the entire scene. Faolan looks furious in his war-like headspace. He blasts through regiments left and right and snatches the light from their eyes. Whenever he is met with an attack, he meets it with a violence I have been on the other side of and barely lived to tell the tale. I'm glad he's fighting for us. Cary is the same way, but she has very little regard for her own defense. Her speed magic allows her to move through the crowd with dexterity, and she uses that to focus all of the rest of her power on attacks. She's a force to be reckoned with for sure. Her role to serve the realm is fulfilled by the fierce leadership she brings to the table. She protects her regiment as best she can. I'm proud of her.

Aiden is the wild card here with the demonic magic itching under his skin even more urgently now than before. He and Gideon focus their attention on the onslaught of the House of Darkness's demons. The demon possessing Aiden cries out for its brethren, but Aiden with the help of a little blood magic manages to keep enough control to summon his and the demon's powers to direct them at the enemy. Gideon clears the way for him by stabbing and slashing at every Fae surrounding the demons. The House of War's army follows his lead diligently and fights and falls for our cause.

Over the hill, I see the building of the second wave press at the edges. They're waiting for me to give the signal. The House of Darkness has no idea what's coming. I shoot off a firework of flame. Many of the opposing soldiers look up in confusion, but not my army. They know what's coming.

I laugh out loud as hundreds and hundreds of mortals and half-Fae suddenly pour down from the hills into the valley. The shouts of confusion from the opposition are drowned out by the war cries of those they hoped to oppress. Armed with magical weaponry and the will to survive, they join the fight. Interspersed between them are the half-Fae from the Lower Realm, those who decided to stay on after the battle of Lisden. They protect those without magic against the Fae and keep the demons at bay. I rush down to join them. Side by side with David, we push back. Soldiers fall left and right, magical blood soaking into the ground.

The carnage, although devastating, swings in our favor. The Half-Fae presence may have tipped us over the edge. The demons are being pushed back. The armies are being pushed back. We are winning.

Until the High Lord of Darkness finally enters the battlefield.

Now we're in trouble.

Chapter Fifty-Six

The High Lord of Darkness stalks through the battlefield with a calculated aura, leaving devastation with each step. The dark magic around him emanates in a black mist that covers the air around him. Every living thing that it touches falls to its power. The grass under his feet turns gray and brittle as he walks, and without a single spell being cast, the mist brings strong Fae to their knees, writhing and choking. The malicious intent practically oozes out of the man as he fights his way toward me.

I wave my hands to motion to my troops not to prevent him from reaching me. They all would willingly fight valiantly to the death to delay him, but there's no reason for them to sacrifice themselves. He's coming for me one way or another; might as well not block his path. As he stalks closer, I find that the demon is more present in High Lord Carron than it has ever been. Their features have blended together into a haunting portrait of what happens when you want too much power too fast. His face is harsher, meaner, and more angled. And his eyes are jet black, so black that there is no white left.

When he reaches me, he stops dead in his tracks and smiles broadly. "Grace Faelie," he says. "We meet again."

"Yes," I say. "I have to say, you've looked better."

The demon-Fae hybrid laughs loudly and harshly, forcing out every sound from his lips. "Is that how you address a man of my caliber?

Your opponent?"

"But you're not a man," I say simply. "You're much, much more."

The demon smiles creepily. "So you've figured it out, have you? Did you have a little help?"

"Perhaps."

"That meddling Coven never knows when to leave well enough alone."

"You mean, leave you and your kind to their desires."

"Perhaps you should be the one running things down there. Your kind all live down there, of course."

"Not anymore."

"Oh yes, you've brought them up here to see what sunlight looks like."

"Just keep going. You'll see how far your words take you when I send you back to the hell you came from."

"You think you can match me?" the demon-Carron asks. "There's nothing that you have that I have not conceived of. I know the counter to every spell you could possibly cast. With the power in my pinky, I could knock you and everyone in this town flat."

"Why haven't you then?" I spit back.

"Because I like watching you squirm. I like watching the light fade from your eyes when you realize that you failed. Your friends are gonna die around you, screaming and writhing in agony. And when they're all gone, Grace, I'm gonna take the breath from your body slowly. You'll die in just as much pain, your magic stripped from you. The last thing you will feel is pain."

I laugh in his face. I didn't listen to his mini speech intending on it, but it's like all of the fear and anxiety and determination bubbled up inside of me and just escaped through my chest as a laugh. He seems taken aback by it, and that's exactly where I want him. "How dare you laugh at me!" he shouts at me.

"Which you?" I ask. "The High Lord or the demon lord? I just want to be very clear about which one you believe I'm insulting."

As I predicted, the entity charges me in a flurry of dark magic. I have mere seconds to prepare myself before I throw up what is the most important shield of my life. I let my hands light ablaze, and I meet him. Darkness to fire. Darkness to light. For the first time, I am toe to toe with the most powerful demon in the realm. All I have to do is not die.

It's not an easy task. I am no match for his power. What I can do, however, is keep dodging, keep from heavy injury, and keep throwing spells. So that's what I do. I move around as quickly as possible, taking flight. I roll out of the way, duck under spells, let my wings stall and plummet me toward the ground to escape. All the while, I have not stopped sending spell after spell his way. Most of them roll off like raindrops, but a few land and cause some damage. That's all I need.

Faolan calls out to me, but I don't turn around to try to hear. Instead, I see what he is calling to me about as shadow soldiers surround me and shield me for a period of time. I feel the sheer magnitude of passion and power coming off of them as they deflect spell after spell that the demon-High Lord sends my way. Because of their strength and protection, I am able to push through much longer than I thought I would be able to.

I fight and I watch and I wait for Luna to give me the signal.

Come on, Luna.

Almost there.

"Grace!" Luna shouts from behind me. "It's time."

Finally.

Out of my pocket, I whip a potion vial out of my pocket, pop the cork, and immediately down the vial. The blood magic Kiara whipped up is bitter, but the possibility of winning dulls the taste. Out of the corner of my eye, I see Aira rushing toward me. With a massive push of wind, she sends a stream of power toward me. When it rushes into me, I feel the strength of her magic join mine. Hers is just the first, a large dose of healing magic to prepare me to absorb the rest of what is coming my way.

On the other side, I see Faolan standing with Cary. The two of them look at each other before extending their arms, sending streams of magic my way. As soon as they move, Gideon and Aira from their places in the ranks send their own magic toward me as well. With each new added strand of magic, I feel my whole being begin to shift underneath my skin. The demon-High Lord hybrid watches me in a fascinated horror.

Finally, I turn to find Aiden's determined face staring directly back at me. Most of his skin is now marred by the fluctuating demon magic underneath, and my own heart pounds in my chest when I realize that that magic will soon be inside me. Hopefully, he has enough strength to give it one last boost. The strain on his face is incredibly apparent as his magic begins to emanate from him intertwined with the demon magic pulling at his chest. He looks at me, body trembling with his focus, and mouths *I love you* to me. I mouth it back to him, unsure of whether I'm doing it to ease his soul or mine.

When he fires his magic straight at me, he screams in agony.

It's the most horrifying sound I have ever heard, one that is part him and part some dying piece of demon soul inside of him.

The magic slams into me and fills me up to the brim and spills over, shaking my entire body with its intensity. The demon magic inside of me feeds on the power, growing stronger and stronger. My head aches with the building pressure inside of it, my mind focused on trying to keep myself in charge. I thank the Lady silently for Kiara's blood magic potion, which has kept me from completely imploding.

This power is out of control. It tries to leave my body as soon as it has entered it. My magic wraps around it and latches on, yanking it toward me to keep it close. It fights hard to escape my grasp and keep from entering my body, but I give it everything I've got to force its hand. When the magic finally combines and enters me, every single sense of mine is heightened. I can hear every wisp of hair moving around me and the High Lord, and I can almost see his spells before he casts them.

I tip my head back and breathe it all in as the magic thrums in my body. Then I whip forward and train my eyes on the High Lord. My shield goes up with a flick of my hand, blocking his first dark cast. Then I attack, flying spirals of disintegration magic and fire. The wind around me intensifies as my strength increases. We go spell for spell, flame for flame.

"You think that amassing power is enough to overtake an Elder Demon?" the High Lord-demon hybrid growls at me. "You're a fool."

"This is not your realm," I shout. Some part of my consciousness observes that my voice sounds booming and echoey, so much so that it barely sounds like my own. "Go back to your home."

The demon laughs hysterically. "I'm not going anywhere. Me and my kin will take over this realm and your own and devour every single Fae until there is no one left to carry on the magical bloodline. There will be only darkness and demonic magic for all eternity."

"You are not welcome here," I speak much more calmly than the turmoil inside of my soul. "You have one more chance to leave."

"You do not command me! Even the Lady herself could not command me to return."

"This High Lady does." At that moment, without thinking about the move I'm about to make, I slam my hand directly into the demon's chest.

The darkness in the High Lord's body runs deep. I feel the core thrumming in my hands, pulling me in and threatening to consume me. The demon draws me in and promises me beautiful things: the return of my family, the life of Aiden, the stability of the realm under darkness. It whispers to me, beckons to me, pleads with me to take the darkness into myself. It calls out to the darkness currently residing within me.

With every ounce of power I can summon, I close my eyes… and light the world on fire.

The highest pitch scream I have ever heard rings in my ears.

Then… the world turns black.

Chapter Fifty-Seven

The world comes back slowly in individual senses. First, it's taste. All I can think of is copper. Then my sense of smell returns. There's a soft citrusy smell of lilies and a deeper warm scent that I can't quite recognize. I make a small sound as I start to feel the pressure of heavy fabric on top of my body. "Grace." A faint voice calls my name from far away. "Grace, love, can you hear me?" *Faolan. Only one person calls me love like that.* I try to open my mouth to reply, but my lips barely move. All I can manage is a hum.

When my eyes open for the first time, the scene around me is hazy. I'm in my own bed in my room. The sheets are cool and gentle against my skin. The balcony doors are open, bringing in light and fresh air. There's a subtle outline of Faolan's shape beside me. I hum once again, struggling to say something. Faolan takes my hand and grips it tightly. "Hey, hey, Grace, I'm here." My lips finally open, but no words come out. It's extremely disconcerting to be so helpless: no movement, no sound.

"Alright, take a deep breath, Grace." Faolan's voice lowers down to my ear. "Just breathe. I know that look; I know you're scared. Don't get yourself all worked up. You used up so much magic in that final blast that your core was severely depleted. Your range of motion should come back shortly now that you're awake, as will your voice." His other hand brushes over my head. "Just relax."

It takes many minutes for my muscles to loosen up just enough to make small movements. I start by trying to roll onto my side. Faolan helps me over, and when he gets down to the level of my face to look at me, I tear up. "Hello, beautiful." He grins at me.

"Shut up," I mumble.

He laughs, and it's the most beautiful sound that I've heard in weeks. "Thank the Lady. I've been waiting for you to wake up for days."

"How many days have I been out?" My voice is a little louder now, but infinitely hoarse.

"Six."

"Six?" I'm having a hard time wrapping my head around that. "Who's been running the House?"

"Neil stepped up. He's done just enough to keep things stabilized, no big changes. Gideon's been running point in the Middle Realm making repairs with David."

"How did we get home?"

"That part, admittedly, is a bit of a blur."

"Tell me what you can, then?"

He nods and squeezes my hand a little tighter. "When you cast that final spell, the battlefield lit up brighter than the brightest flame I've ever seen. It knocked out anyone within a mile radius. I came to in a hospital in the Middle Realm surrounded by mortal and Fae healers. I tried to look for you, but they wouldn't let me leave until they cleared me."

"You didn't manage to fight your way out?"

He laughs once. "Believe me, I tried. They actually had to restrain me, I was fighting so hard. Eventually, I healed up and found you in an isolated room. You were still radiating so much power; it was almost impossible to reach you."

"Almost?" I smile softly.

He smiles back. "Almost. I got to you eventually. You stayed unconscious the entire time, for six days like I said. You barely moved. It's like you were in some sort of suspended animation state. Do you remember anything?"

I shake my head. "No. The last thing I remember was the explosion. And the white light." I shift my elbow further up the bed. "Can you help me sit up?"

"Of course." Faolan rushes to his feet and puts one arm around my back and another under my legs to shift me up against the headboard. I groan in pain as my muscles protest. "Are you okay? Did I hurt you?" he asks as he kneels back down beside me.

"Yes, I'm fine. You didn't do anything. Just… my body getting used to movement again."

"Don't strain yourself," he instructs gently.

"I won't."

Faolan slowly gets off of his knees and rises up to his full height. "I should probably go tell someone you're awake now. We've been waiting a long time for you." His hand slips from mine slowly.

"We?" I ask hoarsely. "Is… is Aiden…"

Faolan shakes his head slowly. "I'm sorry, Grace. He's gone."

Something inside of me fractures just that little bit further. I knew deep down as soon as I opened my eyes that he could be dead, but it's always harder hearing it for the first time. The tears don't come yet. I'm not surprised by that. I can barely summon the energy to breathe, let alone cry.

With a soft pat on my head, Faolan turns to the door. "I'll give you some space."

With what strength I have, I practically lunge sideways to grab his hand. "Not yet," I plead. "Don't go yet. I don't want all those people in here right now. I need… can you please stay?"

"Yeah," he agrees as he moves to the other side of the bed and climbs in, sitting next to me. "I can stay." With a gentle arm, he pulls my body into his shoulders. I relax into the warmth. He waits with me for over an hour before reluctantly pulling away and going to bring me some food and something to drink. When he's gone, I sink back down into the pillows, my strength practically gone. I need to find more if I'm going to take care of business now that I am awake.

It takes almost two days for me to be able to sit up long enough to start taking more formal meetings. There are way too many. Faolan helps to regulate them as best he can. He practically growls at anyone who tries to stay too long. If I didn't keep waving him off, it's highly likely he would have started throwing people off the balcony. Half of the nobles in the palace want to know how I managed to survive the final battle. Apparently, the prophecy group hasn't been telling them shit. Which is honestly how it should be. I don't have many more answers than they do, and the ones that I do aren't for sale. Not after everything we went through. They can either accept me or try to take me down.

No one seems up for the latter, so I think I'll be okay.

Then it's time to assess the damage. Generals and diplomats bring me charts, lists, inventories of everything that's been lost. I offer the treasury to help build some of that back. I persuade others to do the same. Those that can, do. The others offer people to travel and help with construction, feeding, and healing.

Finally, and definitely most importantly, I have to plan Aiden's funeral. With his father and brother apparently apprehended and in our dungeon and his mother in custody, it falls to me. Some of his soldier friends offered to carry the load since I was so drained, but I refused. I want to do my best. The funeral for Aiden has to be a beautiful, intimate affair. The people of the House of the Sun may want to mourn him. I don't know. But I'm not going to have his body sitting in a room for any more days. I plan the entire event from my bed with a rotating cast of Council members, soldiers, and servants.

We have an evening funeral for him away from the chaos of the day. I don't know if that's what he would have wanted, but I think he would have been okay with it. Also, right after dinner is where I get a second wind, enough to get up and go somewhere. Because I'll go into another coma before I miss this event.

Faolan carries me from my bed down to the river. My attendants have dressed me in a lace black dress that sits lightly on my skin and doesn't aggravate the majority of my injuries. For the majority of the War Council, it is the first time they have seen me since the final battle. They all look at me with a mixture of joy that I'm alive and fear of the power that they witnessed. I don't blame them. I would be looking at me that way too.

When he sets me on my feet, Faolan stands behind me so that I can lean on him. I'm sure it looks strange to people for me to be so blatantly supported by the man I've been sneaking kisses with while attending the funeral of my ex. Or… sort of ex. I hate that they might be thinking that. If I could stand on my own right now, I would. I feel terrible being weak at the funeral of the man who ultimately saved us all.

People who knew him as a young man like Master Xavier and Aiden's commander speak first. They share stories about his magical and military escapades. They remember him as a strong, brave man who was a quick learner, a loyal friend, and one who served his House well even when his House was headed in the wrong direction. Once they finish their speeches, the small gathering of people looks to me. I take a step away from Faolan and curse when I wobble on my feet. He reaches out to grab me, but I wave him off.

If I'm going to speak, I'm going to speak on my own.

Very slowly, I make my way to face the group in front of the river. "Aiden Çaelic never hesitated when it came to serving his House or helping his friends. He took pity on a mortal girl looking for her brother's killer and saw that mission through to the end, even when it took him into dangerous territory. He was a good son. He fought for his family's redemption right until the very end when it was clear that they could not be persuaded. He fought for the House of the Sun's livelihood and morality and convinced hundreds of other soldiers to join him in the fight. And at the end of it all…" I choke up and have to stop to bend my head down and wait to compose myself. "At the end of it all, he made the ultimate sacrifice so that *we* could make it out of there alive. He won this war for us." With a weak strain of magic, I pull my strength together and shoot a soft purple strand toward the sky. "To Aiden."

The other Fae around me follow suit, shooting strands of color into the air. "To Aiden," they echo my cry. The magic drains what strength that I have left, and my legs buckle underneath me. Within seconds, Faolan is by my side, holding me up. He doesn't pick me up, just put my arm around his shoulders to stay upright. *Thank the Lady.*

Aiden's body in a mahogany coffin is carried down by his soldier friends from his regiment and laid into a canoe. With a wave of multiple hands, the candles surrounding the coffin light up. Everyone else brings candles down to float in the water around the boat. With a soft shove, the canoe is sent down into the water. We all stand in solidarity as we watch Aiden slowly float away down the river. All around the riverbank, more candles and lights join him from our people lining the shores.

It's beautiful.

Sometime while watching it, I started crying. It's one of those soft slow cries that creeps up on you before the floodgates open. I sob as silently as I can so as not to draw attention away from anyone else's grief, but some noises escape my mouth. Faolan wraps both arms around me firmly and squeezes. He's careful not to cover my face so that I can keep my eyes pinned on that boat until it floats out of sight.

The pain overwhelms me, so much so that it blocks out everything I feel until long after I have been brought upstairs to sleep. When I am left alone, all I can do is cry.

Aiden is gone.

Chapter Fifty-Eight

When I regain the majority of my strength, there are two major orders of business to deal with. The first is to see that the half-Fae and mortals who participated in the final battle are attended to. With the treaties now in play, the Middle Realm and the Upper Realm are now officially on equal footing when it comes to trade. I send them home with supplies and rebuilding materials for every governor's town. I can't offer too much as we have to rebuild our own realm, but together with my fellow allies, we give them a proper sendoff. We never would have broken the demon line without their overwhelming force.

As for the half-Fae, many of them leave the palace right away and make journeys to every corner of the realm. We also try to send them on their way with a little extra to start off their new lives. Although I get a few specific goodbyes, most of the group leave without a trace. I imagine it's better that way. I don't think they ever want to see me again. And I don't blame them one bit. They've been burdened with so much responsibility, particularly in the Lower Realm, for crimes they never committed. For crimes their ancestors never committed. I am happy to see them go.

The second task is to deal with the prisoners of war. And no trial was greater awaited than those of the High Lords. While I was unconscious, once High Lord Carron was down, morale dropped quickly. High Lord Halden of the House of Fire was caught trying to flee toward the border. The High Lord of the House of Sun and his son actually surrendered to the nearest military official they could find. They probably thought they could get off easier if they turned themselves in.

But I don't plan on it. Ultimately, they are responsible for Aiden's death.

On the day of the trial, we open up the grand ballroom to every ruler, diplomat, and important figure in the realm. The War Council sits on the raised platform with twelve thrones, a tight fit. The room is packed from wall to wall. It reminds me of the first War Council meeting in the House of Peace so long ago where Aiden, Neil, and I had to stand against the wall in order to hear. Except now I'm at the head of the nobles instead of my father. I feel a pang of sadness in my chest when I think about it. There's been so much death.

Once everyone has filed in, I raise my hand to settle the room. It grows quiet almost instantly. "Bring them in," I order. The doors to the ballroom open, and a series of armed guards bring in all three high-profile prisoners. I expected some sort of reaction from the crowd, but it is dead silent. The only sounds that can be heard is the movement of shuffling feet against the parquet floor. The High Lords and Lord Nicholas are forced to their knees in front of our platform. The House of the Sun nobles choose to keep their heads down to show a semblance of respect. The House of Fire High Lord, however, keeps his eyes trained on mine. He looks so smug, even now at his lowest. It disgusts me.

"High Lord Thomas Orion Halden." My voice booms over the crowded room. "Nicholas Adrian Çaelic, Senior, and Nicholas Adrian Çaelic, Junior. You have been accused of high treason to the House of Fire and to the Upper Realm itself. You have allied yourself with demonic magic, conquered territory that was not yours to conquer, cost the Realm thousands of lives, and contributed to a genocide in the Middle Realm. How do you plead to these charges?"

"Guilty." The House of the Sun nobles answer in unison. High Lord Halden does not answer.

"High Lord Halden, we are waiting on you," I repeat.

"I do not plead," he answers steadily.

"High Lord Halden, you will enter a plea to this Council," Cary orders sternly.

"I will not," he hisses stubbornly. "It doesn't matter what I plead. This Council will find me guilty anyway."

"So you believe that you are guilty," Cary states harshly.

The High Lord only chuckles. "I know my actions look guilty. I only did what I thought was just."

"Just?" I can't believe he has the balls to kneel here and spout off how he felt justified to kill all of these people.

"Just. For my people. For High Lord Carron's and mine. For centuries, our Houses have traded with all of you, given you aid, offered more of our fair share. And everyone else abandoned us when we were down on our luck, when our economy needed stimulating. Our people were starving to death while you had more than enough land to sustain all of us. So what you wouldn't give, we took."

"And you feel justified to take it? What about the Middle Realm?"

High Lord Thomas laughs darkly and looks up into my eyes. "Outside of you, High Lady, no one cares about mortal lives. They're a dime a dozen. They had land, and they couldn't fight back. Since you and everyone else chose to fight us rather than concede their losses, High Lord Carron and I knew that they wouldn't. We could have taken their land and left you all alone. But you, High Lady, just had to get involved."

"Of course, I had to—" I practically leap out of my throne, but Faolan throws an arm out to stop me. When I snap my head to glare at him, he shoots me a warning look. *Don't.* Deep down, I know he's right. The High Lord knows he's getting a rise out of me. He wants to see me break.

Well, I won't give him the satisfaction.

"Do you have any regrets, High Lord Halden?" I ask firmly.

"No. I would do it all again. And this time, I'd win."

"Very well. The Council will deliberate." Alena of the House of Light waves her hand and casts a silencing spell around us so that we can debate the subject in private. To be fair, however, the discussion doesn't last very long. We know he's guilty; it's just a matter of what to do with him. To my surprise though, the entire group is in relative agreement of the scale of the punishment needed. When I call for a vote, it is unanimous. When the wall of silence is removed, I get to my feet and stare down at the prisoners.

"High Lord Thomas Halden, you have been found guilty by this Council on the charges of high treason," I declare.

The subject in question rolls his eyes. "Figures."

"As such, you will be afforded the highest punishment of the realm, execution by beheading."

His eyes lose their humor. "No."

I continue as if I didn't hear him. "Your sentence will be carried out tomorrow morning at dawn. Your family will be stripped of their titles and exiled to the House of War where they will be kept under house arrest."

"Don't touch my family, you half-Fae whore!"

Faolan stiffens beside me, but I lay a hand on his to stop him from moving. "Calling me names, Thomas, doesn't change the facts. Your reign here is done. You have failed, and you will pay for your actions." I wave to the guards standing behind the High Lord. "Take him away." The two men grip Thomas under his arms and begin to move him toward the door. He bucks violently against their hold, swearing and cursing me, my House, my future family, anything he could think of, it seems. I don't even give him a courtesy glance. Eventually, the guards have no choice but to drag him out the door.

When the room is silent again, Gideon speaks. "What do we do with them?" he indicates the High Lord of the Sun and his eldest son. My blood boils as I look at them. The father's head hangs down in despair while the brother stares straight ahead at the wall behind the throne with dead eyes. It is so clear they expected this to work out for them, that somehow they were going to be able to keep their power and Aiden at the same time. Even though Aiden was clearly on our side the entire time.

"What's the protocol?" I manage to get out through gritted teeth. "For pleading guilty to treason to the realm."

"There hasn't been an incident in centuries," Aira says flatly. "Most of the treason to the realm examples are legends. Most of them die in battle. A few get exiled."

"We could exile them," I consider carefully.

"Please." A quiet voice comes from the High Lord.

My head whips around to look at him. "Please what?" I snap.

He gulps. "Please have mercy."

"Mercy." I consider the word. "Were you considering mercy while the Houses of Darkness and Fire destroyed innocent lives all over the Upper and Middle Realms?"

"High Lady Grace, Aiden would—"

"*Do not say his name!*" I shout and leap to my feet. Everyone in the room takes a few steps back, a few startling at the force of my voice. "How dare you bring his name into this room and expect me to fall all over myself to help you just because you said it? You're not even good enough to say his name."

"He was my son."

"And he was a hero," I whisper harshly. "He did everything he could to save his House from destruction at the hands of his own father and brother. He stole an army, fought off demons left and right, including one inside of his very soul, and sacrificed himself and his magic to save us all."

"Would he not have asked for mercy on our behalf?" the younger Nicholas has the nerve to speak.

"He may have asked, but he would have understood that you needed to be punished for what you have done. You aren't unwilling participants in all of this. I saw your signatures on those alliance agreement pages. You knew what you were getting into. The unintended consequences weren't what you were expecting? That is no one's fault but yours." Spinning around, I move back toward the group of Council members. "It's time to deliberate."

The discussion for the leaders of the House of the Sun goes on longer than for the House of Fire. There are more questions to be asked. Several of the Council members speak on how good they were prior to their alliance, asking for a more lenient punishment. Others, including myself, push for a harsher one. Maybe not as harsh, but harsh nonetheless. In my opinion, it doesn't really matter what happened before the war. What matters are the actions during, the ones that were taken and the ones that weren't. It is not a unanimous vote, but a begrudging consensus was drawn.

When I approach High Lord Nicholas and the older son, they look at me fearfully. I don't show a shred of emotion. I want them to worry right up until the moment that I speak. "High Lord Nicholas Çaelic and Lord Nicholas Çaelic, Jr., you have been convicted of treason to the Upper Realm in the highest degree. While you may not have directly caused as much damage as your allies, you contributed to mass casualties, catastrophic damage, and the collapse of the economic structure of all Twelve Houses. The Council has determined that you and your entire family will be stripped of your titles, and a new family will be installed on the throne. You will also be exiled from the House of the Sun effective immediately until three generations of your family have lived and died. You will take up residence in the House of the Day where the realm will be keeping an eye on you for a very long time."

The son doesn't look up at all, but the former High Lord meets my eyes. "I never thought it would go this far," he pleads lightly before trailing off, seemingly knowing that he is sunk. I don't acknowledge his words, only wave to the guards to take both men away. The entire throne room stands around, looking to me to see what to do next. But I don't know what else they could want for me. I fixed their war, sentenced the traitors, planned to rebuild the realm. I can't be expected to make every little speech for every House.

"You're all dismissed," I decide on saying before exiting quickly out the side door before anyone can question me.

Chapter Fifty-Nine

The worst part of the post-final-battle affairs is the hosting of the victory ball. I was very insistent to the rest of the War Council that I did not want to host it after we had lost so much. I wasn't ready to. But the majority of the members assured me that it was customary to do so. Despite there having not been a war in ages, most diplomatic resolutions result in some sort of grand event. And this one, having involved so many houses, will be the grandest event of them all.

I stand in the mirror in a deep red ballgown, contemplating locking the door and hiding in my room for the rest of the night. I feel such a heaviness in my chest at the losses we have suffered over the last few months. Why in the world would people want to celebrate a victory when we lost so many lives along the way? And with the House of the Sun nobles stripped of their power and carted off to their new dwelling only hours ago, my mind has been on Aiden all night.

My very first ball was with Aiden. While he didn't escort me, he did keep me entertained for the majority of the night. Dancing around with him at balls was one of my favorite things to do with him. He was always so goofy about it. He would do formal dances, but he would also launch into silly spins and prances that would make me crack up and have to hide my laughs behind my hand. When I was with him, things seemed to just fade to the background. I could let loose and have a little fun.

It's going to be so strange without him tonight.

A soft knock pulls a resigned sigh from my mouth as I get up to answer the door. Neil stands waiting for me in the doorway. He looks at me solemnly. "Hey, Grace."

"Hello. I'm surprised to see you."

"I'm your heir. I thought it only proper for me to escort you downstairs myself."

"Well… thank you. I appreciate it."

"Hey," he says. "It's gonna be alright."

"I don't want to go," I tell him honestly.

"I don't either. This was always one of my least favorite parts of the job. The events. Everyone looking to you. You can't step out of line without someone watching you and commenting on your appearance or your poise."

"I like the parties. Just not this one."

Neil nods. "I understand." He gulps. "You know, you put together a good funeral for Aiden. I didn't know him as well as I should have. I mostly spent time with his brother; we were both the oldest. But he was a good man, a good soldier."

"The most honorable of all of us," I say quietly.

Neil offers me his arm. "Are you ready to face the crowd?"

"As ready as I'm going to be." I close the bedroom door behind me and take my stepbrother's arm. He leads me down the hallway to the staircase, and we wind all the way down to the first floor.

Time to face the music.

When we enter the ballroom, it's like the memory of the war has been lifted from the entire place. Every inch of the room shines. The windows have all been replaced, and the chandelier twinkles down on us all like before the war. Everyone is dressed in their finest, and tonight, it's not just the nobility. Soldiers, townspeople, integral connections to navigating the war-torn realm: they're all here. I pushed for that. If we had to have a victory ball, it was going to be a victory for all of us. Smaller parties will be happening all over town, courtesy of the House of the Evening. I don't think there's ever been more Fae from all different Houses in the same place at once. At least I could do that. When Neil and I cross the floor, the conversation in the room simmers down to a silence. I suppose they are expecting me to make some kind of speech.

Well, maybe I'm not in the mood for a good speech.

"Welcome," I finally settle on. "It has been a long fought war. We have lost many, many soldiers and civilians, and I would like to start this evening off by taking a moment of silence." I watch the room slowly bow their heads and grant me the silence and peace that I need to come up with something better.

"Thank you all for joining me in that. Tonight, we honor the sacrifices that we all have made and that others have made during this fight. We take the time to celebrate our freedom from warfare with each other, noble and citizen, rich and poor. Everyone had a role in this fight, and you all performed it well. To those of you who lost loved ones, we extend our condolences. To those who lost land or property, we hope to help rebuild you over the next several years. But tonight, we leave all of that for another day, and we celebrate with each other that we made it."

I signal for a glass of wine, and an attendant hands me one. "I propose a toast..." The people around me raise their glasses. "To peace."

"To peace," the crowd repeats.

"Please enjoy the ball." With that, the band strikes up a tune, and people begin to talk and laugh again. Many move together to dance. I slip out toward the wall and stand there, leaning against it and taking in the moment. For the first time in a long time, I hear joyous laughter and conversations in the moment or of the future. Part of me is still slightly tense, looking toward the windows like there's going to be another attack. But nothing comes. The people wanting to take over everything are locked up or dead.

Dead. Aiden is dead.

"You don't have to stand here all by yourself." Faolan's voice comes from behind me.

I chuckle lightly. "Maybe I want to stand over here by myself."

"It's a party. You know you can relax a little bit."

"I just keep waiting for something to go wrong."

"Nothing's gonna go wrong tonight," he reassures me. "I posted some people outside just in case. You don't need to keep watching the windows."

I feel oddly happy that he thought to do this. I'd like to think that maybe he did it for me. I start to reach a hand over to touch him in thanks, but my sadness for Aiden stops me. I lower my hand awkwardly back down to my side and turn away again to scan the room.

"May I have the dance, High Lady?" Faolan asks me as he extends forward a hand. His eyes look into mine, searching to see if there is any desire left behind my sadness. I try to find a shred of it myself so that I can confidently take his hand. Instead, I find a resignation and a tiny smile to fake happiness enough to allow him to take mine. He pulls me slowly onto the floor. Instead of the center of the room, we keep to the edges of the room. He even steers me behind a column to get a little bit of privacy from prying eyes. If I felt happier, I would be grateful for that.

The band plays a slow song, and Faolan gently moves me to his chest. I allow myself a moment to rest my forehead against him. The song is over half over before he finally speaks to me. "How are you holding up?"

"Not well," I whisper back.

"I'm sorry." He cups my cheek and tilts my head to look up at him. "I am sorry, Grace, about Aiden."

"I don't want to talk about Aiden," I say as I shake my head.

"You should talk about him. It might make you feel better."

"You of all people should know that talking about things doesn't always make it better."

Faolan sighs. "I just don't want you closing yourself off. Trust me, it doesn't end well for anyone."

"Do you know what he said to me… in one of our final meetings before he died?" He shakes his head. "He asked me to move on for him. To find love again. To be in love again. The selfish bastard," I swear under my breath.

"He wanted you to be happy. That's the one thing we have always agreed on."

"Faolan…"

"I'm serious. I just want you to be happy. Whatever that is."

"And you want that to be with you."

"If it comes up."

"Faolan, I… I don't want you to feel like my consolation prize."

"Stop lying to yourself, Grace." He shakes his head with a bit of a scoff. "I was never a consolation prize. I was your first choice. I am your first choice. Aiden being gone doesn't change that."

As he spins me around the floor, we watch each other with the same carefully guarded eyes that we did on our first dance together at the Spring Solstice. The movements between us feel fateful, but also rehearsed. The flow that was there before isn't quite right. We step in time, round and round each other until the music ends. Instead of moving into the next dance, we stand together awkwardly trying to decide whether to dance again or move separate directions. It certainly feels like a metaphor for our lives right now.

"Lady Grace," Faolan finally speaks. "What you're feeling? It isn't about me. It's about you." After dropping that bomb on me, Faolan chooses simply to kiss my forehead and pull back. I almost go after him. But instead, I let him disappear back into the crowd. Now, I stand awkwardly in the middle of all of this joy, wondering why I can't bring myself to just... *try* to be happy. All this beauty around me, and all I feel is sorrow.

Perhaps I need a little more time.

I just want a little more time.

Chapter Sixty

In the days after the ball, things truly start to feel as though they will settle down. Over the first couple of nights, those Houses who were liberated by the group exit first with their lines of dignitaries and nobles. It takes a lot longer for those who fought alongside us to finally exit. Soldiers eventually leave with enough horsepower to get home. I tried to send them with enough supplies to aid their Houses, but many turned them down. People are ready to not rely on each other for once. To rebuild from what they have.

When the prophecy members leave, I feel like I'm saying goodbye to friends. That's not something I've really ever had before. Kiara is the first to leave with her family. Hers is a quick goodbye. I knew she meant to be more sentimental, but she was eager to get home with her family. It has been to long. It has been too long for all of us. Aira goes next. She promises to visit as soon as she can. Luna embraces me like a sister. I hold onto her as well tightly. I didn't know that I would regret the whole journey ending. Even Gideon, the bastard, I see him getting a little teary-eyed when he says goodbye to me.

Then it's just down to me, Faolan, and Cary. And to be honest, I have no idea where they're going. Faolan goes missing for a couple days after the ball. Cary too. I imagine they are working things out in their own way, privately, by themselves. Faolan's probably got some hidden space in the palace where full blown meetings are happening over the future of the House of Darkness. I almost seek him out to ask. But after the ball, after… everything, I can't bring myself to. So I wait for him to come to me.

And when everyone else is gone, when the palace is all but empty, there is a soft knock on my bedroom door. With only a moment's hesitation, I open it to find Faolan. His expression is so different from what I have seen in him before. It's softer. A partial smile instead of a smirk, hopeful even instead of sure. "Hey," he says.

"Hey," I respond back as he walks into the room.

"So… the world has finally left your home."

I chuckle lightly. "It would seem that way. I notice that you have been… somewhat absent from the whole ordeal."

"I'm not one for lengthy goodbyes. Besides, I had to figure my own things out."

"What kind of things?" I ask. "Where do you go after this? Back to the House of Darkness?"

Faolan chuckles lightly. "No."

"No?"

"The House of Darkness is in shambles. The people who wanted something better for themselves through this war find themselves worse off. They need a leader who is going to be able to take them into the future and heal the mental wounds as well as the physical landscape. And me? I look too much like my father. I will be a constant reminder of what they lost."

"That's not true. They will accept you."

Faolan shakes his head firmly. "You don't know them like I do."

"What happens now then?"

To my surprise, he smiles. "I ceded the throne to Cary."

"You put Cary in charge?" I raise an eyebrow.

He laughs. "Yes, and she accepted. She's gonna take the House in a new direction. And the other Houses trust her. She'll be able to rebuild relationships and trade."

"Where will you go?"

"Anywhere I want. I'll be running the black market full-time from now on."

"And that's what you want?"

Faolan smiles lightly. "Honestly? Yeah. The political scene is fun to manipulate, but not much fun to do all the formal work and interactions. You know that I work best from the shadows." When he smirks at me, I just roll my eyes. "You should come with me."

The request makes me freeze. "Come with you?"

"Yeah." To my growing shock, he kneels down in front of me on both legs, taking my hands. "I want you to come with me. We can run the black market together. See the realm in a much more pleasant setting. Visit your hometown. We can go anywhere we want to go. All you have to do is say yes."

My heart is pounding in my chest. He's looking up at me with more hope and genuine desire in his eyes than I have ever seen in him before. My palms start to sweat. "You want me to run away with you?"

"Don't think of it as running away," he says. "You never really felt at home here. You've been playing this game for years. So have I. I've been so focused on trying to be perfect for my father that I was never able to throw everything I had at something that actually made things feel worthwhile. Come with me, and we can build something together. The realms are still gonna need a black market to keep things moving, especially in the first few years."

"Do I have any time to think about this?" I stall.

Faolan's eyes fall slightly. "Do you need time?"

"I mean, of course I do. That's such a big question to ask me."

"I didn't realize there was a possibility of you staying at the palace."

"Of course, there is. I'm the High Lady. What am I supposed to do, spend all this time saving this stupid realm and then leave the position I had to fight to keep?"

"But you don't actually want the job, do you?"

"I don't know! What if I did? What if I did want to stay? What if I had plans for this place?"

Faolan smiles with a hint of sadness in his eyes. "Then you should stay."

"Really?" I furrow my brows. "You… you want me to stay?"

"No. No, I don't want you to stay. I want you to come with me. But if you want to stay, I want what you want. Whatever's best for you, you're not gonna hear a complaint from me."

"Why can't you stay?" I find myself asking. Something in me moves me closer to him, and I run my hands lightly over his arms. "Why don't you stay here? You can be a part of this court, or you could do your own thing. I don't care what you do. Just… stay here."

Faolan shakes his head. "Grace, you know I can't do that."

"Why do I know that? Why does it have to be that way?"

He runs his hands gently over my hair, lingering on my cheeks, before taking both of my hands off of his arms and holding them. "Because you are a High Lady. You're the hero of this story. And the hero doesn't end up with the villain's son."

"Maybe this one does," I say desperately.

"They won't accept me. I may have helped win the war, but nobody outside these walls knows anything about who you and I were together. You will be run out of here, or you will die, and I am not willing to let that happen just to love you."

"Faolan," I breathe.

"It's all or nothing, Grace. And it's not your fault that it is. But I can see now that I shouldn't be making you choose. So I won't."

"But—"

"Shh." He lays a finger over my lips. "Don't try to convince me otherwise. Because you will, and I can't take that risk."

"Don't go," I whisper almost silently.

"I don't want to, Grace."

"Then just stay for the night. Don't leave yet. Just for the night. Please."

"Come with me," he asks again, as if he almost can't help himself. He stands awkwardly near me with his head tilted down, searching for a different answer in my eyes. But I don't have one for him. All I have is this pressing need inside of me, a need to show him that I'm still deeply in love with him, it's just the state of the world right now that I can't deal with, not him. He blinks one more time, and I catch a glimpse of those beautiful amber eyes. And I just can't take it anymore.

I lean forward and kiss him deeply and suddenly. He reacts with surprise and takes a moment before pushing his hands into my hair and holding on tightly. He kisses me like he needs me in order to keep breathing, and I don't think I could draw another breath either. My hands grip at his back desperately, like I could press him into me and absorb him to keep him around forever.

When I try to step back to catch my breath, he doesn't let me. He steps forward with me and kisses me again. That's the moment where it all comes together and falls apart at the same time. I feel something in me crack, and I can't get close enough to him. I tear off his shirt roughly, ripping it from his body and tossing it aside, not bothering to see whether I actually damaged it or not. Faolan seems to have the same idea as he tugs at my clothes.

We are not slow and steady. We tear into each other like we're hungry to touch, to taste. His lips on my skin feel like kisses of fire, everywhere. I can barely breathe the way he builds me up and sends me soaring over the edge. There's not a single Fae in this fucking realm who can match the passion and the feeling of us. Not a single fucking one. Nobody can come close to this. I will never come close to this again.

When he kisses me tenderly, I break apart in his arms. I grip onto his body so fucking tight that he can barely roll us to our sides. He whispers hushed promises and hushed apologies into my ear as I struggle not to cry. He tells me that he loves me, and for the first time, I whisper it back to him. Then he cradles me close to his chest silently, and we both wait, praying to the Lady that sleep never comes and the dawn never rises. But eventually, we both drift off.

Chapter Sixty-One

When Faolan leaves the following morning, it takes absolutely everything in me not to run after him. He leaves me with a simple forehead kiss and a soft smile before riding away on the back of his horse. I stand in the palace doorway and watch him leave until he disappears completely from view. It takes another half hour of me hoping he'll turn around and come back for me to pull myself away from the outdoors,

The next few weeks are busy. There's barely any time for a break. We are navigating the restoration of our cities and towns, authorizing more money to restore trading routes and economic markets, and hosting all sorts of diplomatic officials to discuss the new state of alliances around the realm. I take the throne in the morning, and I don't give it up until the late evening. Neil sits on my left, answering questions that I don't have all the answers to and strengthening my position if it is repeatedly questioned. I do appreciate his presence, but it's not quite the same as Aiden or Faolan. He's much more businesslike than either of them. Help for the logistics, but not much else.

Finally, one morning, I just can't take it anymore and cancel absolutely every meeting or interaction on my list. I tell everyone not to disturb me while I sit in the throne room. To be honest, I should pick a different room that isn't the source of all of my stress. But I can't think of anywhere else to be. So instead I just sit there, slumped in my throne, staring off into space. I don't know how long I was there before Neil came into the room.

"Did you really cancel every meeting we had this morning?" Neil asks incredulously.

"Yes," I respond quietly.

"Why?"

"I did not want to deal with people today. But I had to at some point, so I decided to clear the morning instead."

Neil stares at me for a moment. "Can I speak frankly?"

"Yes."

"Look." He sighs and sits down next to me on his throne. "We've been through a lot together at this point, right?"

I chuckle dryly. "That's an understatement."

"We set aside the majority of our differences and worked together to take back the realm, correct?"

"Correct." I raise an eyebrow. "Where is this going?"

"Can I be frank with you?"

"Please do."

"I have no idea what you're still doing here."

His statement catches me off guard. "I… what are you talking about? I'm supposed to be here. This isn't about the heirship again, is it?" I throw my hands up. "I thought we had worked through that by now."

"Hear me out, Grace. It's not about the heirship. But at the same time, I guess it is. Do you actually want this job?"

"Of course I want the job! I chose the job. I've been doing the job for months now."

"Grace, every time I see you, it's like you're going through the motions. Don't get me wrong," he says quickly when he sees me narrow my eyes, "you're doing a good job. You've introduced strong policies, you've facilitated the reconstruction of the House, and you built bridges with the Middle Realm that are really gonna change things around here. But… you don't look like you enjoy it."

"I enjoy it enough. I'm just tired." I wave him off with a hand.

"But you're not just tired. Grace, be honest with yourself. Why are you still here?"

"Our father believed that I had what it took to lead. I'm leading."

"Oh, come off it, Grace." Neil laughs and looks me directly in the eye. "Father may have come around to the idea of you leading, but you know in your heart he brought you here at least partially because of the heirship laws." I don't want to admit that he's probably right, so I say nothing at all. The quirk of his lips indicates he's clearly noticed. "Would you want the job if Dad hadn't installed you here?"

"Will you quit beating around the bush and just say what you mean, for the Lady's sake?" I finally snap. All of these questions that he's asking me are making me uncomfortable.

Neil looks slightly taken aback by my frustration, but presses on. "There are rumors… that Faolan asked you to join him in running the black market. And you turned him down."

"Where are you hearing rumors?" I ask, looking at the far wall to avoid his eyes.

"Are they true?"

I sigh. "Yes, he did ask me. I told him that I couldn't abandon my House. He understood."

"Have you ever thought about the fact that you keep choosing duty over what you want?"

I laugh. "I'm sorry, what do you know about what I want?"

"I know you took on an entire realm as a mortal to find out what happened to your brother. I know that when you got here, you decided to protect your mother and come stay here even though you wanted to go home with the answers you had found. I know you took on the prophecy in stride and led our alliance to victory against the House of Darkness. You lost Aiden, our father, and still you pressed on. Aren't you finished? Aren't you just… done?"

"I don't want to talk about Aiden."

"Well, you're going to have to! You're letting your loss cloud everything that could be good in your life."

"Stop it, Neil."

"I will not stop, Grace." He comes over to me and takes my hands for the first time. "You cared about Aiden. You loved him once. It was obvious to everyone here. But the way you looked at Faolan after he left… it was different. And the way he looked at you was the same. Thought it was sickening, actually." I can't help but let out a tiny chuckle. Neil smiles lightly. "You have been choosing other people your entire life. At least as long as I've known you. You're not happy here. Why not go?"

I consider his words carefully. As much as I don't want to admit it, Neil does have a point. Putting things back together is great and all, but it doesn't make me happy. I don't think I've felt anything remotely close to happiness since I sent Faolan away. "What about the House?"

"I'm prepared to take over and continue the work that you were doing. I'm not looking to overhaul anything in your original plan or do anything drastically fucked up. The people may have a hard time getting over the change at first, but they'll bounce back. The sooner we do it, the better."

"Woah, I haven't even thought about—"

"Grace."

"Don't pressure me here. Don't push me."

"If someone doesn't push you, Grace, you will throw away your life."

"How do I know you're not saying this just to take my throne?" I try to joke.

Neil shakes his head. "Come on. We've made it farther than that by now."

I sigh and nod lightly in agreement. "Yes, we have… Do you think he'd be open to it? I… rejected him pretty hard."

"There's only one way to find out," he prods gently.

As I turn the idea over in my head, sitting on that throne, I'm slowly realizing that if I stay, this is my entire life right here. I'll live and die in this room, surrounded by hordes and hordes of people needing things and wanting things and needing me to make big decisions forever. I think back to when I spoke to the Enchantress in the Lower Realm about not wanting to be the leader for the rest of my life. And yet here I am, putting myself in this position for what? For duty to a father that no longer exists? To protect a mother who doesn't even remember me? Why shouldn't I have something that I want for once? Why don't I stop running away from what I want and start facing it, daring to… to just try to have something that is mine?

"I guess I could send out a message," I say softly before smiling.

In a rare moment of affection, Neil walks over and gives me a brief hug. "Good for you, sis." Hearing 'sis' makes my heart feel full, and I stand up and hug him back. Although brief, the embrace seems to end something that had been hard fought for so long. While I am afraid, there's a part of me that finally relaxes without the weight of the realm, or in this case, the House of the Evening on my shoulders.

Chapter Sixty-Two

Once I make the decision to go after Faolan, there is a lot to be done. I have to bring Neil up to speed on all of the little projects and legislation that I put in place over the last few months. I want to make sure he is set up for success. I need to speak to a couple of key officials so that they know that the House of the Evening have not abandoned them and their needs. Neil and I ultimately decide not to tell everyone, only who needs to know. At the end of the day, it will be better if as few people as possible know where I'm headed. There's always a chance that someone may seek Faolan out to kill him because of his father's legacy.

Then comes the message sending. One way or another, I need to make Faolan aware that I am on my way to him. I pinpoint one of the servants in the palace that I know is on the black market payroll and ask him to send a message through the grapevine. *Ana requests a meeting with the master.* Vague enough that not everyone would know, but specific to Faolan's and my experiences together. By the Lady, I hope he remembers our first encounter.

The waiting is the hardest. I wish I could have just left right away and been off to find him the same night I made the choice. But I did make a commitment to this House, and I want to see it through to a point where it is stable and on its way back up. It's only fair. Waiting, though, aches like nothing I've ever felt before. It's not like grieving pain; it's like a yearning instead.

One afternoon, I decide to escape to the music room to find some quiet. I don't feel the need to play today, so instead I trail my fingers lightly over the fine instruments. I linger on the violin. I wonder if I'll have the chance to play wherever I stay with Faolan. I don't know if there's some sort of home base of the black market or whether we will travel from place to place without a firm place. But I imagine he'd find a way for me to play.

A sound startles me from behind. I spin around to find the High Lady entering the room. One look at her eyes and I can tell that Neil has informed her of my departure. I suppose I should have thought of this."I hear you're on your way out of the palace." Elise keeps her voice even, but it's hard not to hear the absolute glee in her tone.

"Yes," I reply simply. "That is the plan."

"Well, I wish you luck in your future endeavors."

I laugh. "Don't say things that you don't mean."

"Why do you assume that I don't mean them?"

"With all due respect, Lady Elise." I turn to look at her. "You have hated me from the moment I walked into this palace. Well wishes from you mean very little. Possibly even less because I know you are only so happy to have me leaving for good."

"Perhaps," she admits. "But at the end of the day, you did save the realm from destruction and House of Darkness domination. So perhaps there's more to be said for someone like you."

I chuckle. "Perhaps, Lady Elise. Perhaps."

"Where are you headed?"

"Neil didn't tell you?" I raise an eyebrow.

"No. He wanted to respect your privacy."

"Then you'll have to respect that." I turn back to my violin.

"Is it Lord Faolan?" The question comes as a surprise to me. I'm surprised that she noticed under all that hatred for me.

I tilt my head lightly with a wry smile. "He's not a Lord anymore. He renounced his throne."

"I would have never given up a crown for a man."

"Not even my father?"

My question quiets her. I turn around and watch her think for a while. "I may have… for your father. But I didn't say that as an insult. I never would have because I am too drawn to it. You… you have something that even I myself lack."

That just may be the kindest thing that woman has ever said to me. I respond in kind by curtsying low to her. "May the Lady protect you, Lady Elise."

To my surprise, she bows to me. When she lifts her head, she nods once. "And you as well, Lady Grace." Before I can contemplate that this is the first time she has used a title with me, she has turned and left. I leave the music room and return toward my wing of the palace.

Walking into my bedroom, I shut the door carefully with both hands. I stand there looking at the wood before closing my eyes. There's only a couple more days that I am willing to wait before going out and searching for Faolan myself. Why hasn't he written back? Or at least sent a message through someone else to let me know he was on his way or that he didn't want to see me. I suppose he could not want to see me. I rejected his offer of running away together for no good reason, really. Maybe he's not coming.

"Are you ever going to turn around and look at me?" A familiar voice carries over from the balcony.

I spin around fast, my heart catching in my throat. Faolan leans against the balcony door frame, watching me with that familiar broad smirk on his face. He looks just the same, and yet so different. His hair is more wild, softer, and he's dressed in a looser form of his typical all black look. His eyes sparkle with an invitation that I am so happy is still there.

In three bounds, I am across the room and in his arms, kissing him like I need him in order to breathe. And I just might. He cradles my face in his hands, kissing me back with the same amount of passion. *This is right. This feels... complete.*

"You came," I breathe against his lips when I finally tear myself away.

"I'll always come back from you, Grace," he whispers back as his lips brush against mine again. The next kiss is tender, gentle, and yet so powerful. "Are you ready?" he asks me quietly with a huge grin.

"Ready? I still have to pack my stuff," I laugh.

"Pack? What do you need to pack? Grab your violin and your necklace, and I'll bring you anything you'd like. There's nothing here that I will not provide for you. Come with me, love. Come away with me now."

It only takes me a few seconds to realize he's right. I've said my goodbyes. There's no reason for me to stay longer just to gather things that I don't really need. I pull away from his hands and quickly load my most sentimental objects into a bag. Faolan stops me from putting the bag on my back and slings it over his own shoulder instead. "Shall we?" he says.

"Yes." I smile back at him. Hand in hand, we head toward the balcony, leaving the doors thrown open. When Faolan looks at me with a question in his eyes, I nod to him reassuringly. We jump off the balcony, free falling and catching the wind on two pairs of wings.

And it's off to my next adventure.

Acknowledgments

Above all, I want to thank my amazing production team for helping me get this book completed and published. As always, thanks to Milan Krstevski who has rounded out a truly spectacular set of covers for this trilogy. This book is no exception. Also, thank you to my editor, Beth Hale. This was the first book of mine that she has edited even though it is at the very end of the series. But her notes and editorial suggestions matched exactly the voice I was trying to capture.

This book would not have come to fruition without the support of those who contributed to my presale campaign:

My family, Julie Hammer, Morgan Hammer, Todd Hammer, Joan Ohlweiler, Jack Ohlweiler, Jane Gargett, Matt Gargett, and Brennan Gargett.

My partner, Daniel Sage.

My partner's family, Amy Sage Boyd and Cindy and Rick Lewis.

Fantastic family friends, Jane Philion, Michelle Lynn, Emma Corriveau, and Casey Cloud.

My mentor, C.W. Stacks.

My friends, Liberty Bassett and Jessika Rucker.

Finally, I want to thank all of the readers who have been with me from the beginning of the series. I couldn't have done it without all of you behind me. Thank you for all your interactions with me over the last several years. Keep 'em coming. I'll always do my best to respond.

I hope to see you continue to stick by me as I write my next books and series. I love you all dearly.

About the Author

Cady Hammer has been a writer for most of her life. From the time she was eleven years old writing her first novel between classes, she always looked to the world to bring inspiration. She was often teased for being in her own world, but never hesitated to invite others along on the adventure. She graduated from the College of William and Mary with a Bachelor of Arts in History and is now pursuing a Master of Arts in Public History.

Cady is the author of the Chasing Fae Trilogy and loves to create stories that take people away from the world for a while. She creates her universes with inspiration from her studies, trying to create a place that feels so real that readers have to explore it. These stories explore the complexities of relationships crafted around the idea that love, friendship, and grief are all interwoven. She hopes to one day become a bestselling author alongside her desired career in museum work.

You can connect with me on:

🌐 https://cadyhammer.com
🐦 https://twitter.com/CadyHammer
📘 https://facebook.com/cadyhammerauthor
🔗 https://instagram.com/cadyhammerauthor
🔗 https://pinterest.com/cadyahammer
🔗 https://www.tiktok.com/@cadyhammerauthor

Subscribe to my newsletter:

✉ https://dl.bookfunnel.com/bo920xlof6

Also by Cady Hammer

Don't miss these other works!

Chasing The Past: A Chasing Fae Collection
From the universe of *Chasing Fae,* this short story collection highlights three characters from the House of the Evening, a lorddom of the nightlife, music, and art. Each of these characters represents an important part in Grace Richardson's past and future.

A Chance Meeting: When Amelia, Grace's future mother, meets Alexander for the first time, she is intrigued by his mysterious appearance and his disdain for the art she loves so much. She works to teach him the joy of creating and ends up learning a little bit about seizing life herself.

Taking My Place: Elise may not be as high ranking of a girl as the other daughters of the men her father works with, but she plans to find and take her place in the House of the Evening no matter who gets in her way.

Coming To Terms: Grace's half-brother, Neil, has never had to compete for anything. As the heir to the House of the Evening, he will inherit everything to make his own. But when his father brings home a bastard daughter, his world gets thrown into a tailspin.

The Ivy Labyrinth: Volume 1

Kristy Fitzpatrick just can't catch a break.

As a mortal in a magical world, she often feels disconnected from the rest of her mystical, more exciting classmates. The only thing that she has to compete with in the classroom is her mind.

But even for a magical being like her impulsive naiad best friend, Brianna, life is far from stable. Centuries ago, when a fully formed labyrinth sprang from the ocean, the magic emanating from its ivy walls caused all kinds of devastating magical consequences that affect the planet every year from magical instability in beings all over the world to chaotic natural disasters.

Every year, four high school students are chosen to enter the labyrinth and try to break its hold on the world by solving a series of complex riddles and challenges. Most never come out.

But when Kristy's school is selected as the home of the next four students, despite her lack of choice in the matter, she sees an opportunity to do something that no other student has managed to do so far: survive the labyrinth.

In Volume 1 of this Hunger Games-meets-Maze Runner high fantasy story, Kristy is about to learn whether her mind and body are up to the task. Because somehow, as she tests her own limitations, the Labyrinth is learning how to best her and her companions. There is no telling what kind of obstacles could come next.

www.ingramcontent.com/pod-product-compliance
Lightning Source LLC
Chambersburg PA
CBHW072042190726

48294CB00005B/1370